I am a romantic in the wrong century, she thought. I live in the 1990s. I should be in the 1890s. I bet I could have found true love a hundred years ago. Look at Sean. All I'm going to find around here is true grease.

Annie stood straddling the bike, and leaned against a stone pillar to catch her breath.

The first falling happened.

from *Both Sides of Time*

Also by Caroline B. Cooney

PRISONER OF TIME
FOR ALL TIME

THE FACE ON THE MILK CARTON
WHATEVER HAPPENED TO JANIE?
THE VOICE ON THE RADIO
WHAT JANIE FOUND

THE RANSOM OF MERCY CARTER
BURNING UP
WHAT CHILD IS THIS?
DRIVER'S ED
TWENTY PAGEANTS LATER
AMONG FRIENDS
CAMP GIRL-MEETS-BOY
CAMP REUNION
FAMILY REUNION
OPERATION: HOMEFRONT

Caroline B. Cooney

THE TIME TRAVELERS

Volume One

TWO NOVELS

Published by Laurel-Leaf
an imprint of Random House Children's Books
a division of Random House, Inc.
New York

This is a work of fiction. Names, characters, places, and incidents
either are the product of the author's imagination or are used
fictitiously. Any resemblance to actual persons, living or dead,
events, or locales is entirely coincidental.

This edition contains the complete and unabridged texts of the
original editions. This omnibus was originally published in
separate volumes under the titles:
Both Sides of Time, copyright © 1995 by Caroline B. Cooney
Out of Time, copyright © 1996 by Caroline B. Cooney

www.randomhouse.com/teens

Educators and librarians, for a variety of teaching tools, visit us at
www.randomhouse.com/teachers

RL: 5.7

Reprinted by arrangement with Delacorte Press
ISBN: 0-553-49480-5
January 2006
Printed in the United States of America
10 9 8 7 6 5 4 3 2 1

Contents

BOTH SIDES
OF TIME

FOR DORIE

CHAPTER 1

It was Annie's agenda that summer to convert her boyfriend, Sean, into a romantic man. It would not be easy, everyone agreed on that. Sean was far more likely to be holding metric wrenches than a bouquet of roses for Annie.

Annie did not know why she went out with Sean. (Not that you could call it "going out." It was "going to.")

Sean's spare time involved the repair of mechanical objects, or preventive maintenance on mechanical objects. There was always a lawn mower whose engine must be rebuilt, or an '83 pickup truck acquired in a trade whose every part must be replaced.

Annie would arrive at the spot where Sean was currently restoring a vehicle. She would watch. She would buy Cokes. Eventually Sean would say he had to do something else now, so good-bye.

Nevertheless, on this, the last half day of school, Annie had planned to hold hands for cameras, immortalized as boyfriend and girlfriend. But Sean—the least-romantic handsome boy in America—had skipped.

The girls met in front of the mirrors, of course, to compare white dresses and fix each other's hair. Usually everybody dressed sloppily. It was almost embarrassing to look good for a change. Annie Lockwood had gotten her white dress when she was bridesmaid in a garden wedding last year. Embroidered with a thousand starry white flowers, the skirt had a great deal of cloth in it, swirling when she walked. At least the dress was perfect for romance.

Everybody was exuberant and giddy. The moment school was exchanged for summer, they'd converge on the beach for a party that would last all afternoon and evening.

Annie brushed her thick dark hair into a ponytail and spread a white lace scrunchy in her right hand to hold it.

"So where is the Romance Champion?" asked her best friend, Heather.

"He's at the Mansion," Annie explained, "getting his cars ready to drive away."

Sean would be at the old Stratton Mansion, getting his stuff off the grounds before demolition.

Sean loved destruction. Even though it was his own home being torn down, Sean didn't care. He couldn't wait to see the wrecking balls in action. It was Annie who wept for the Mansion.

2

The town had decided to rip it down. They were right, of course. Nobody had maintained the Mansion. Kids had been rollerskating in the ballroom for decades. Roof leaks from the soaring towers had traveled down three floors and ruined every inch of plaster. To the town, it was just a looming, dangerous hulk.

But oh, Annie Lockwood loved the Mansion.

The girls hurried out of the bathroom at the same second, not fitting, so they had to gather their skirts and giggle and launch themselves through the door again The whole half day was silly and frivolous. Annie decided she was good at silly and frivolous, and it was a shame they didn't get to behave that way more often. School ended with hugs, and seniors got weepy and the freshmen vanished, which was the only decent thing for ninth graders to do, and everybody shouted back and forth about the afternoon plans.

"See you at the beach," called Heather.

Annie nodded. "First I have to collect Sean."

"Good luck."

That Sean would agree to play beach volleyball when he had a car repair deadline was highly unlikely. But Annie would certainly try.

When the school bus dropped her off, she didn't even go into the house to change her clothes, but retrieved her bike from the garage and started pedaling. The frothy white dress billowed out behind her in fat white balloons. It was a ridiculous thing to bicycle in. She pulled off the scrunchy and let her hair fly too. Her hair was dark and romantic against the white of her dress.

3

I'm going to ruin the dress, she thought. I should have changed into jeans, especially when I know perfectly well Sean is just changing the oil on some car and he'll want me to help.

I'll help you, she promised the absent Sean. I will repair your entire personality, you lucky guy. By the end of summer, you will have worth.

Lately, Annie had been reading every advice column in existence: Ann Landers, Dear Abby, Miss Manners. She'd become unusually hooked on radio and television talk shows. She knew two things now:

A. You weren't supposed to try to change other people. It didn't work and afterward they hated you.
B. Mind Your Own Business.

Of course nobody ever obeyed those two rules; it would take all the fun out of life. Annie had no intention whatsoever of following either A or B.

She pedaled through the village toward Stratton Point. The land was solid with houses. Hardly a village now that eighty thousand people lived here, but the residents, most of whom had moved from New York City, liked to pretend they were rural.

It was very warm, but the breeze was not friendly. The sky darkened. They were in for a good storm. (Her father always called a storm "good.") Annie thought about the impending thunderstorm at home, and then decided not to think about it.

Passing the last house, she crossed the narrow spit

4

of land, two cars wide, that led to Stratton Point. Sometime in the 1880s, a railroad baron had built his summer "cottage" on an island a few hundred yards from shore. He created a yacht basin, so he could commute to New York City, and then built a causeway, so his family could ride in their splendid monogrammed carriage to the village ice cream parlor. He added a magnificent turreted bathhouse down by a stretch of soft white sand, and a carriage house, stables, an echo house, and even a decorative lighthouse with a bell tower instead of warnings.

Decades after the parties ceased and nobody was there to have afternoon tea or play croquet, the Mansion was divided into nine apartments and the six hundred acres of Stratton Point became a town park. The bathhouse was used by the public now. The Garden Club reclaimed the walled gardens, and where Mr. Stratton's single yacht had once been docked, hundreds of tiny boats cluttered the placid water. Day campers detoured by the echo house to scream forbidden words and listen to them come back. *I* didn't say it, they would protest happily.

The nine apartments were occupied by town crew, including Sean's father, whose job it was to keep up roads and parks and storm drains. Nobody kept the Mansion up.

Annie pedaled past parking lots, picnic areas and tennis courts, past Sunfishes and Bluejays waiting to be popped into the water, past the beach where the graduating class was gathering in spite of the look of the sky. She passed the holly gardens and the nature paths, more parking lots, woods, sand, meadow, and finally, the bottom of the Great Hill. The huge brown-shingled mansion cast its three-towered shadow over the Hill.

Pity the horses that had had to drag heavy carriages up this steep curve. Biking up was very difficult. There were days when Annie could do it, and days she couldn't.

This was a day she could.

Stretching up into the hot angry clouds, the Mansion's copper trimmed towers glimmered angrily, as if they knew they were shortly to die. Annie shivered in the heat, vaguely afraid of the shadows, steering around them to stay in the sun.

Sean would be parked on the turnaround, getting his nonworking vehicles working enough to be driven away before the demolition crew blocked access to the Mansion.

At the crest of the Great Hill, the old drive circled a vast garden occupied by nonworking fountains and still valiant peonies and roses. There was Sean, flawless in white T-shirt and indigo jeans, unaware that his girlfriend had arrived. Derelict vehicles were so much more interesting than girls.

It won't work, she thought dismally. I can't change Sean. Either I take him the way he is, or I don't take him.

Annie wanted the kind of romance that must have happened in the Mansion back when Hiram Stratton made millions in railroads, and fought unions, and married four times, and gave parties so grand even the newspapers in London, England, wrote about them.

She imagined Sean in starched white collar, gold cuff links and black tails, dancing in a glittering ballroom, gallant to every beautiful woman over whose hand he bowed.

No.

Never happen.

I am a romantic in the wrong century, she thought. I live in the 1990s. I should be in the 1890s. I bet I could have found true love a hundred years ago. Look at Sean. All I'm going to find around here is true grease.

Annie stood straddling the bike, and leaned against a stone pillar to catch her breath.

The first falling happened.

It was a terrible black sensation: that hideous feeling she had when she was almost asleep but her body snapped away from sleep, as if falling asleep really did involve a fall, and some nights her body didn't want to go. It was always scary to fall when you were flat on the mattress. It was far, far scarier to fall here on the grass, staring at Sean.

Her fingertips scraped the harsh stones of the wall. She couldn't grab hold of them—they raced by her, going up as she went down. She fell so hard, so deeply, she expected to find herself at the bottom of some cliff, dashed upon the rocks. She arched her body, trying to protect herself, trying to tuck in, trying to cry out—

—and it stopped.

Stopped completely.

7

Nothing had fallen. Not Annie, not her bike, not the sky.

She was fine.

Sean was still kneeling beside his engine block, having heard no cry and worried no worries.

Did my heart work too hard coming up the drive? thought Annie. Did I half faint? I didn't even skip breakfast.

The hot wind picked up Annie's hair in its sweaty fingers. Yanking her hair, the wind circled to get a tighter grip. She grabbed her hair back, making a ponytail in her fist and holding it.

Just a breeze, she said to herself. Her heart was racing.

There was something wrong with the day, or something wrong with her.

"Hey, ASL!" yelled Sean, spotting her at last. Sean referred to everything by letter. He drove an MG, listened to CDs, watched MTV, did his A-II homework.

Annie's real name, depressingly, was Anna Sophia. Every September, she asked herself if this school year she wanted to be called Anna Sophia, and every September it seemed more appealing to go to court and get a legal name change to Annie.

Sean had adopted her initials and called her ASL. Everybody thought it was romantic. Only Annie knew that Sean's romance was with the alphabet.

When she let go of her hair, the wind recaptured it.

The leaves on the old oak trees did not move, but her hair swirled horizontally as if she were still biking.

For a strange sliding moment, she saw no decrepit

old cars under the porte cochere, but matched chestnut horses with black manes and tails. They were alive, those horses, flicking their tails and stamping heavily. She could smell the distinctive stable perfume of sweating animals.

What is going on here? she thought.

"They've sold the marble floors, the fireplace mantels and the carvings on the staircase, ASL," said Sean happily. "Antique lovers love this place. Town's probably going to get enough money from the fixtures to pay for demolishing it."

It was so like Sean not to notice her dress, not to comment on the last day of school, and not to care that good things were ending forever.

She climbed the high steps onto the covered porch. The immense double oak doors were so heavy she always felt there should be a manservant to hold them for her. Of course, the doors were padlocked now, the windows boarded up, and—

The doors were not padlocked. The handles turned. What a gift! Annie slid inside.

The front hall still had its marble floors, giant black and white squares like a huge cruel chess game. Antique dealers had taken the gryphons from the staircase—little walnut madmen foaming at the mouth—but nobody had yet touched the mirrors. The house was heavily mirrored, each mirror a jagged collection of triangles, like the facets of diamonds. Fragments of mirror dismembered Annie. Her hands, her face, her dress were reflected a thousand times a thousand.

It was not as dark inside as she'd expected it to be. Light from stairwells and light wells filled the house.

This is the last time I'll ever be inside, she thought, going overboard emotionally, as if this were also her Last Visit to the Lockwood Family As It Ought to Be.

Don't think about home, she ordered herself. Don't dwell on it, because what can you do? Mind Your Own Business. That's the rule, everybody agrees.

Outdoors the rain arrived, huge and heavy. Not water falling from the sky, but thrown from the sky, angry gods taking aim. She expected Sean to come inside with her, but of course he didn't. He angled his body beneath the porte cochere and went on doing whatever mechanical thing he was doing.

Annie resolved to find a boyfriend with interests other than cars and sound systems. He'd be incredibly gorgeous and romantic, plus entranced by Annie.

The stairs loomed darkly.

These were stairs for trailing ballgowns and elbow length white gloves, the sweet scent of lilac perfume wafting as you rested your fragile hand on the arm of your betrothed.

It was difficult to think of Sean ever becoming a girl's betrothed. Sean had a hard time taking Annie to the movies, never mind getting engaged. He was the sort who would stay in love with cars and trucks, and end up married quite accidentally, without noticing.

Annie walked into the ballroom. Circular, with wooden floors, it had been destroyed by decades of tenants' children's birthday parties. The upholstery on

10

its many window seats was long gone. Only the tack holes remained.

I wish I could see the Mansion the way it was. I wish I could be here a hundred years ago and have what they had, dress as they dressed, live as they lived.

Oh, she knew what they had had: smallpox and tuberculosis and no anesthesia for childbirth. No contact lenses, no movies, no shopping malls, no hamburgers. Still, how nice to have both centuries . . . the way her father was having both women.

I try not to hate him, or Miss Bartten either, she thought, but how do I do that? My mother is this wonderful woman, who loves her family, loves her job, loves her house—and Daddy forgets her? Falls in love with the new gym teacher at the high school where he teaches music?

The musical Daddy had put on last year was *West Side Story,* which he'd postponed for years because you had to have boys who were excellent dancers. There was no such thing.

But when Miss Bartten joined the faculty, she convinced the football coach that the boys needed to study dance for agility and coordination, and now had in the palm of her hand a dozen big terrific boys who could dance. This was a woman who knew how to get what she wanted.

Daddy and Miss Bartten choreographed *West Side Story* . . . and on the side, they choreographed each other.

Mom suspected nothing, partly because Daddy was knocking himself out trying to be Super Husband. He bought Mom dazzling earrings and took her to restaurants, and told her he didn't mind at all when she had to work late . . . especially because Wall Street was forty-five minutes by train and another thirty minutes by subway, and that meant that Mom's day was twelve hours long. Dad and Miss Bartten knew exactly what to do with those long absences.

Annie sat on a window seat. How odd, thought Annie. I was sure the windows were boarded up. But none of them are.

From here, she could not see the wreckage that tenants had made of the gardens and fountains. In fact, the slashing rain had the effect of a working fountain, as if the stone nymph still threw water from her arched fingers. Rain stitched the horizon to the sea. Sean of course noticed nothing: he was a boy upon whom the world had little effect.

I want romance! she thought. But I want mine with somebody wonderful and I want Daddy's to be with Mom.

Fragmented sections of Annie glittered in the old ballroom.

Violins, decided Annie, putting the present out of her mind. And certainly a harp. A square Victorian piano. Crimson velvet on every window seat, and heavy brocade curtains with beaded fringe. I have a dance card, of course. Full, because all the young men adore me.

Annie left the window seat and danced as slowly and gracefully as she knew how. Surely in the 1890s

12

they had done nothing but waltz, so she slid around in three-beat triangles. Her reflections danced with her.

My chaperon is sipping her punch. One of my young men is saying something naughty. I of course am blushing and looking shocked, but I say something naughty right back, and giggle behind my ivory fan.

The second falling came.

It was strong as gravity. It had a grip, and seized her ankles. She tried to kick, but it had her hands too. It had a voice, full of cruel laughter, and it had color, a bloodstained dark red.

What is happening? she thought, terrorized, but the thought was only air, and the wind that had held her hair in its fingers now possessed her thinking too. She was being turned inside out.

It was beneath her—the power was from below—taking her down. Not through the floor, but through—*through what?*

The wind screamed in circles and the mirrors split up and her grip on the world ended.

Or the world ended.

"Hey! ASL!" bellowed Sean. "Get me my metric wrenches."

But ASL did not appear.

Sean went inside. How shadowy the Mansion was, with so many windows boarded up. The place had a sick damp scent now that the tenant families had been moved out. It did not seem familiar to Sean, even though he had lived there all his life till last month. He had a weird sense that if he walked down the halls, he would not know where they went.

"Annie?" He had to swallow to get the word out.

Sean, who did not have enough imagination to be afraid of anything, and could watch any movie without being afraid, was afraid.

"Annie?" he whispered.

Nobody answered.

He went back outdoors, his hands trembling. He had to jam them into his pockets. She'd gone off without him noticing, that was all.

He couldn't concentrate on the cars. Couldn't get comfortable with his bare back exposed to the sightless, dying Mansion.

He threw his tools in the back of his MG and took off.

Annie's bike lay in the grass, wet and gleaming from the storm.

CHAPTER 2

Strat had been thinking of lemonade. He ambled toward the pullcord to summon a kitchen maid and looked through a ghost.

His dry throat grew a little drier.

Of course the heir to the Stratton fortune was also heir to a practical streak, and did not believe in ghosts. So it wasn't one.

Still, the sweat from the baseball game turned as cold as if he'd sat in the ice wagon. The white cotton shirt stuck to his chest, and Strat was sorry he'd tossed the baseball bat into the sports box in the cloakroom. He wouldn't have minded having something to swing.

Not only did the ghost approach Strat, it actually passed through him. He held very still, wanting to know how ghosts felt. Were they mist or flesh? Dampness or cloud?

Real hair, long shivery satin hair, slid over his fin-

15

gers. His shudder penetrated the ghost, which reached with half-present hands to feel him. Its touch missed, reaching instead an old Greek statue in the wall niche. It stroked the fine white marble and then fingered the fresh flowers wreathed around it.

Strat decided against blinking. A blink was time enough for a ghost to vanish. He tried to breathe without sound and walk without vibration. The ghost moved slowly, fondling every surface. In fact, it acted like a plain, garden-variety thief, which just happened not to have all its body along. A ghost looking for something to steal.

Don't evaporate, thought Strat, following the shape.

It lingered over a huge cut glass bowl, whose sharp facets were prisms in the sunshaft, casting a hundred tiny rainbows on a white wall. It paused in front of a mirror panel, studying itself.

The ghost, and the ghost's reflections, became more solid. More vivid. And more female.

Strat was present at her birth.

The fall ended as swiftly and completely as had the first.

Out of breath and shaky, Annie struggled for balance. The wind was gone, but her heart still raced. The ballroom was strangely bright and shiny.

And full.

She was in an empty room, she could see how empty it was, and yet it was full. She had to take care not to bump into people. Even the air was different: it was like breathing in flowers, so heavy was the scent.

And then—clearly—sweetly—

—she heard a harp. A violin. And a piano.

I did fall, thought Annie. Over the edge into insanity. Quick, walk outdoors. Check the oil stains on Sean's fingers. See how he steps right in the puddles without noticing his feet are wet. Listen to him tell me to fetch and carry.

But she did not go outdoors.

She went deeper and deeper into the condemned and collapsing rooms of the Mansion. As the sky turned violet from the passing storm, so did the Mansion turn violet, and then crimson, and gold. It filled with velvet and silk. It filled with sound and music. It filled with years gone by.

Annie Lockwood had fallen indeed.

She tried to think clearly, but nothing had clarity. Some strange difference in the world filled her eyes like snow and her ears like water. She couldn't see where she was putting her feet; couldn't see even the things she knew she saw.

The Mansion was changing beneath her feet, shifting under her fingertips. The world's molecules had separated. She was seeing fractions. Had she fallen into prehistory? Before the shape of things?

She had never known fear. She knew it now.

And then, beneath her own fingers, shape began.

The old walls, where paint had been layered on paint in a dozen ugly shades, turned into rich wallpaper that felt like velvet. Floors lost their splinters and grew fabulous carpets of indigo blue and Pompeii red. Ceilings lost their sag and were covered with gold leaf Greek-key designs.

She began seeing people. Half people. Not ghosts; just people who had not entirely arrived. Unless, of course, it was she, Annie, who had not entirely arrived.

I'm not real, she thought. The Mansion became real, while I, Annie Lockwood, no longer exist.

In the great front hall whose chessboard floor had always seemed such a reflection of cruelty, she looked up through banisters heavy with monsters. Etched glass, like lace printed on the windows, dripped with sungold. Twelve-foot-high armloads of heavy suffocating fabric fell from the sides of each window and crept across the floor. The staircase was both beauty and threat.

Whatever she was, she still possessed sight. She had to turn her eyes away from the glare. She could half focus now, and in the shadows beneath the great stair was something dark and narrow. Half seen, or perhaps only half there, were half people. But they were full of emotion, and the emotion was Fury.

Fury like a painting. There was fighting. Hissing and clenched fists and fierce words. How black it was, compared to the glittering sunshaft! Black that slithered with its own sound. Smoke like apples and autumn filled the air.

And then somebody fell. It was like her own fall getting here: steep and jagged and forever. The sound of breaking bones was new to Annie's ears, but there was no doubt what had happened. A skull had cracked like glass in that dark space.

Annie whirled to get out of there. Around her, the walls became heavier and more real.

I'm in the Mansion, she thought, but it feels like a tomb. Am I locked in here like a pharaoh's bride with all my furniture and servants?

She patted surfaces, trying to find the way out, as if there were some little door somewhere, some tiny staircase up to . . .

To what?

What was happening?

A dining room now. Real cherry wood. Real damask. Real pale pink roses in a real china vase.

The fury and the blackness and the smoke froze halfway into her mind, like history half studied.

What had she seen on the stairs? A real murder?

I don't need a real murder, thought Annie Lockwood. I need a real way out.

She waded through half-there rooms, reaching, touching, making wishes—and bumped into somebody.

Strat followed her, hypnotized. She wore a white dress, rather short, several inches above her ankles. She wore no gloves. She had no hat. Although it was midafternoon, her hair was down.

In the evening, when his mother back in Brooklyn Heights was preparing for bed, she would take down her hair. When he was a little boy, Strat had loved

19

that, how the long U-shaped pins released that knot and turned Mama into a completely different, much softer person.

His ghost was continuously becoming a different softer person. Strat gasped. *The girl's legs were bare.*

But she was almost his own height! This was no eight-year-old. Bare legs! Perhaps it's a new sort of tennis costume, he thought, hoping that indeed tennis costumes were going to feature bare-legged girls from now on.

They had installed a tennis court on the estate, and Strat was quite taken by the game. When he began Yale next year he intended to go out for baseball and crew and tennis. Strat did not see how he was going to do all the necessary sports and still attend class.

Harriett and Devonny adored tennis and played it often, but Strat could not imagine either girl without white stockings to cover her limbs.

His sister, Devonny, had no chaperon to chastise her for unbecoming behavior. Father, Mother and even Florinda thought anything Devonny did was becoming. Devonny might actually take up the bare-legged style.

Harriett, however, had a so-called aunt, a second cousin who'd never married, poor worthless creature, and Aunt Ada was now Harriett's chaperon, eternally present to stop Harriett from enjoying anything ever.

Strat understood why Harriett wanted to marry young and get away from Aunt Ada, but Strat, although he loved Harriett, was not willing to marry young or even ever, as it did not seem to be a very desirable position.

Certainly neither his father nor his mother nor any of his three stepmothers had found marriage pleasant.

Devonny argued that all these women had been married to Father, and who could ever be happy under those circumstances? Whereas Harriett would be married to Strat, and therefore live happily ever after.

Strat was about as certain of happily ever after as he was of ghosts.

The ghost ahead of him touched everything. She ran her fingers over banisters and newel posts, over statuary and brass knobs and the long gold-fringed knots that cascaded from the rims of the wine-dark draperies.

Strat didn't risk speech. He simply followed her. In spite of the fact that the house was occupied by a large staff, plenty of family and several houseguests, the ghost seemed to feel comfortably alone.

She passed through the library, the morning room and the orangerie where Florinda's plants gasped for breath in the summer heat. Then she turned and headed straight for him. Strat stood very still, looking right through her, which was so strange, so impossible, and once more she bumped into him.

She didn't quite see him, and yet she said, *Oh, I'm so sorry.* Her voice was not quite there. Her lips moved, but the sound was far away, like bells on a distant island.

Even though he couldn't quite see her, he could judge that she was beautiful—and puzzled. There was

21

a faint frown on her lovely face, as though she, too, was trying to figure out why she was here, and what she was after.

She climbed the stairs.

Strat followed.

She touched the velvet cushions stacked on the landing's window seat. Strat's mother, who had had the house designed back before Father disposed of her, adored window seats. The house was tipsy with them. Nobody ever sat in one. They weren't the slightest bit comfortable.

The ghost girl touched the paintings on the wall. Mama adored Paris even more than window seats and had visited often, buying anything on a canvas. Father had not permitted Mama to keep a single French oil.

Now the ghost girl touched the Greek statues in the deep niches that lined the second landing. It was very fashionable, acquiring marbles from ancient civilizations. They had more back in Manhattan in the town house.

The girl proceeded to go through every bedroom.

She went into Father's bedroom, where luckily there was no Father present; Father lived in his study or on his golf course. He'd had his own nine hole course landscaped in a few years ago. It was too placid a sport for Strat, but it kept Father busy and away from his two children, and this was good.

Now she went into his stepmother Florinda's bedroom, and even into Florinda's bath. Strat stayed in the hall. Strat happened to know that Florinda was there, preparing for tonight's party, but no scream came from

22

Florinda, although she was a woman much given to screaming and fainting and whimpering and simpering.

Florinda didn't see her, thought Strat. I'm the only one who sees her. She's mine.

Strat loved that. He loved owning things. He loved knowing that every dog, horse, servant, bush, building and acre of this estate were—or would be—his. Now he had his own ghost.

All of her flawless. And so skimpily dressed! No corset, no camisole, no bloomers, no petticoats, no stockings, no hat. Strat yearned to imagine her without even the thin white dress, but it would not be honorable, so he prevented himself from having such a fantasy.

The girl walked into *his* bedroom.

This time Strat went along. Straight to the window she went, and that was sensible, for Strat's tower had a view all the way down the coastline to the city of New York. Strat liked to pretend he could pick out the steeples of Trinity Church, or the new thirteen story Tower Building on Broadway, but of course he really couldn't. What he could see was miles of congested water traffic on Long Island Sound: barges and steamers, scows and sailboats.

Strat's ghost gasped, stifling a cry with her hand, clenching frightened fingers on top of her mouth. She whirled, seeing the room and the furnishings, but not Strat. There were tears in her eyes. Her chin was quivering.

Strat was not fanciful. He disliked fiction, reading

23

only what he had been forced to read in boarding school. He'd dragged himself through *The Scarlet Letter* and *A Tale of Two Cities* and the latest nightmare, *Moby Dick*. Books that long should be outlawed. Strat preferred to read newspapers or science books. Actually, Strat preferred sports.

His stepmother, Florinda, and his sister, Devonny, were addicted to bad cheap novels full of hysterical females who fell in love without parental permission or saw ghosts or both. He'd never waste time on that balderdash. So it was amazing that he was imagining a half-there, beautiful girl. Strat hardly ever imagined anything.

What would it be like to kiss a girl like that? Strat had done little kissing in his life.

His experiences with girls were either in public, like the ever popular ice cream parlor, or chaperoned. Harriett, for example, was never available without Aunt Ada. This winter, Aunt Ada had come when Strat took Harriett ice skating; Aunt Ada had come when he took Harriett on a sleigh ride; Aunt Ada had come to the theater with them, and the opera.

Strat was pretty sick of Aunt Ada.

If Aunt Ada were to fall down the stairs and break her hip, Strat would eagerly find nurses to care for her, hoping Aunt Ada would spend many months, or maybe her lifetime, as an invalid.

If there was one thing that his ghost girl was not, it was chaperoned.

The girl slipped by him. He tried to catch her arm, but she ran too quickly for him, rushing down the stairs so fast and lightly she hardly touched them. Her little white shoes clicked on each gleaming tread. Mama, of course, had had carpet commissioned to cover the stairs; Florinda, of course, had had it torn up. Each stepmother seemed to feel that a gesture of ownership was required.

The girl ran out the front door, unmanned at the moment by a servant, since the staff was so busy putting together the party. Strat tore after her. His own bike was tilted up against the big stone pillars of the porte cochere, and there, astonishingly, lying on the grass, was a second bike.

Her bike.

She got on, and Strat, laughing out loud this time, got on his. She half heard him laugh, turned, and half saw him. The fear that had been half there was now complete, and had her in its grip. "It's all right," called Strat. "You're all right, don't be afraid, it's only me, I won't hurt you. Wait for me!"

She took off with amazing speed. Definitely not a girl who waited for anybody.

"Stop!" he yelled. "You're going too fast!" She was safe at that speed as long as she didn't meet horses coming up, but once she reached the bottom of the Great Hill, she'd be on gravel and the wheels would fly out from under her. He wondered if ghosts could break bones.

Strat pedaled furiously to catch up. The two of them flew down the curve and out onto the lane. Neither fell, but she had to stick both feet out to steady herself. Her skirt flared up wonderfully and he was shocked but happy.

He caught up.

They pedaled next to each other for a full minute, and then she stopped dead, so fast he nearly went over his handlebars. She balanced on her toes like a ballerina and they stared at each other.

Strat was entranced. She was his possession; his mirage; his very own beautiful half-ghost. "Good afternoon," said Strat.

"Who are *you?"* she said, as if greeting an exotic Red Indian.

"Hiram Stratton, Junior," he said cheerfully.

"I'm Annie Lockwood. What's going on? Everything is really strange. Like, where are the picnic grounds? Where are the parking lots? What happened to the traffic? And what on earth are you wearing?"

Strat felt that since it was his estate, he should be the one to ask questions. Irritated but courteous (a boy on stepmother number three and boarding school roommate number eleven knew how to be polite even when extremely irritated), Strat said, "I'm not sure to what you are referring, Miss Lockwood. But you just walked right through my home, room by room, when my own personal plan called for having iced lemonade."

She rewarded him with a wonderful smile, infectious and friendly. He had to smile back. Poor Harriett's teeth stuck out and overlapped. Miss Lockwood's smile was white and perfect and full of delight. *She* would never have to keep her lips closed when the photographer came. "Iced lemonade sounds wonderful," she told him. "I have had a super weird day. And I am so sweaty," she confided.

Strat was appalled. What lady would say that word? Horses might sweat, but ladies were dewy.

"What are you wearing?" she asked again, looking down at his trousers as if he were as undressed as she.

He was wearing perfectly ordinary knee-length breeches. A perfectly ordinary white shirt, with lots of room in it, was neatly tucked in in spite of the chase she had just led.

Strat considered his lemonade offer. He was not willing to take Miss Lockwood back to the house. Share her with his sister, or Harriett, or Florinda, or his father, or Aunt Ada or the staff? Never. There was no way he could possibly explain what he had just seen. The birth of a ghost? Besides, she was his. He wanted to find out who she was, and how she got here, and he wanted her to be his own personal possession.

"Let's cycle into the village," he said. "I'll take you to the ice cream parlor. We'll have a soda."

"Deal," she said unfathomably. "Do I call you Hiram? You must have a nickname. I mean, they couldn't have saddled you with the name Hiram and then called you that."

"The boys call me Strat," he said uncertainly. Girls, of course, called him Mr. Stratton. Even Harriett, whom he had known forever, and who was now his own father's ward, called him Strat only in small gatherings, and never when there were strangers around.

But the girl had no qualms about getting familiar.

"Strat," she repeated, smiling again, giving him the strangest shiver of desire. "Let's race. I'll win." She took off.

Strat could not believe this. Let's race? I'll win? Girls weren't allowed to do either one!

To his shame, it was immediately clear that Miss Lockwood might just do both. Strat took off after her and the contest was fierce. Gravel spurted from their tires. Wind picked up her long unbound hair so it flowed out behind her like some wonderful drawing. Strat stood up on the pedals and churned hard. There was no way he would tolerate a beating by a girl who hadn't even existed ten minutes ago!

But the race ended long before they reached the village, for Miss Lockwood stopped short, staring at the gatehouse.

Brown-shingled, intricately turreted, it was a miniature of the Mansion. Its long arm crossed the lane to prevent unwanted carriages from entering. The gatekeeper smiled from the watch window. "Good afternoon, sir."

Strat waved.

"What is this?" said Miss Lockwood. She was so frightened she was angry.

"The gatehouse," he said soothingly. "You must have passed it on your way in." But she didn't come by bike, he thought, nor by carriage, nor by boat. I saw her. She came by . . .

Strat had no idea how she had come, only that he had been there when it happened. Where had her bike come from? He had witnessed her arrival and there

28

had been no bike. He did not exactly feel fear, but rather a confusion so deep he didn't want to get near the edge of it.

"There is no building like this," she said, her voice getting high. "And that field. And that meadow. *Where are the houses?*"

"The land's been sold for building," agreed Strat. He tried to keep his voice level and comforting, the way he did with Florinda during fainting fits. "It's become fashionable to build by the water. Two or three years, and we'll have neighbors here."

She really stared at him now. It was unladylike, her degree of concentration on him. "Strat, who are you?" Her voice wasn't ladylike either; it demanded an answer.

It unsettled him to be called Strat by a person who had known him only moments. "I think a more interesting point is who you are, Miss Lockwood. And where you came from. When I followed you, as you trespassed in my house, you were—" He couldn't say it. Half there? Nonsense. It was too foolish. Too female.

"When I felt the cushions and the drapes, I couldn't believe it," she said. "They were real and I was there. Velvet and silk."

Strat wanted to touch her velvet cheek, and stroke her silken hair. He had never wanted to touch anything so much.

Am I just curious to see if she's real, he thought, or is this love?

He desperately wanted to find out what love was.

29

Things with Harriett were so settled and ordinary. Strat wanted something breathless and wonderful.

Perhaps I shall fall in love with Miss Lockwood, he thought. True love, not just being attentive to Harriett.

His sister, Devonny, was an expert in affairs of the heart, but Devonny said Strat did not get to participate, as he simply belonged to Harriett and that was his only heart possibility.

One more look at Miss Lockwood and Strat wanted her as his heart possibility. "Let's leave the bikes here, Miss Lockwood," he said, fighting for breath as if she had pulled him underwater. "Let's walk on the sand."

And she said "Yes," taking his hand as if they had known each other for years.

Harriett and Devonny went through the sheet music, planning what each girl would play on the piano for the singing that night. Harriett and Devonny had very different tastes. Harriett liked sad ballads where everybody died by verse six and on verse seven you wept for them. Devonny liked madcap dances where you couldn't get the words out fast enough to match the chords she played.

Harriett did not tell Devonny how upset she was. It was very important, when you were a lady, to hide emotions and maintain a calm and dignified face. If you were to frown and glare and grimace, your complexion would be ruined and you would get wrinkles early.

But Strat, she had clearly seen from the window,

had gone cycling with some girl in a white sports costume. How much easier tennis would be in an outfit that short. But it was unthinkable to display your limbs like that. Harriett could not imagine who the girl might be.

It couldn't be a servant; Harriett knew all of them; and they would be let go immediately were they to dress so improperly or even for a moment to entertain a thought of romance with young Mr. Stratton.

Of course you read novels in which the Irish serving girl fell in love with the millionaire's son and they ran off together, and Harriett loved that sort of book, but in real life it was not acceptable. Especially *her* real life. And the Irish serving girl they had, Bridget, was even now holding the parasol for Florinda's stroll through the garden, so it was not Bridget out there with Strat.

Harriett did not usually like to face the beveled mirrors that were omnipresent in the ballroom, but she forced herself. Harriett was plain and her teeth stuck out. She was two years older than Strat. She did not have a wasp waist like Devonny. No matter how tightly Bridget yanked the corset, Harriett remained solid. Her hair was on the thin side, and did not take well to the new fashions. She had always expected to pin false ringlets into her hair where necessary. But of course she had to reach womanhood when the style became simpler, and women fluffed their hair on top of their heads, plumping it out like Gibson girls. Harriett's hair neither plumped nor fluffed.

Sweet Strat always complimented her anyway.

31

How lovely you look, he would say. How glad I am to see you, Harriett.

And he was glad to see her, and he did spend many hours with her, and he even put up with Aunt Ada.

But underneath, Harriett was always afraid. What if she did not get married? Of course, with her wealth, she would find some husband, somewhere. But she did not want some husband somewhere. She wanted Strat, here.

The mirrors cut her into fragments and multiplied her throughout the ballroom. Wherever she turned, she saw how plain and dull she was. Don't cry, she reminded herself. Don't slouch.

These were the rules Aunt Ada gave Harriett, when what Harriett yearned for was love.

Devonny would have reported in to Harriett if Strat had ever said he was thinking of another girl. The family assumed that Strat and Harriett would wed, but the fact remained that Strat had never, by the slightest syllable, suggested such a thing.

And he was eighteen now, and she twenty.

He should, by now, have suggested such a thing.

She did not want him going to Yale. All those other young men would have sisters. Beautiful sisters, no doubt. And each needing a railroad baron's son in wedlock. Strat would go to parties without Harriett, and be dazzled by beauties especially prepared to snag him. And one of them might—for the rich and beautiful chose each other, and Harriett, although richest of all, was plain.

She wished they didn't use that word wedlock. It sounded very locked up and very locked in.

Unless you were Strat's father, of course, who unlocked every marriage as soon as he arrived in it. He was the only man Harriett had ever met who had actually had a divorce, and he had had three of them. Would son be like father? Would she be sorry, wedlocked to Strat?

Pretending an errand, Harriett left Devonny at the piano and ran up the great staircase and down the guest wing, praying no houseguest would hear her footsteps and join her. The highest tower had its own narrow twist of steps, and the fullness of her skirts made climbing it difficult. The tower had two window seats (the influence of the first Mrs. Stratton reached everywhere) and also a tiny desk, a telescope for viewing ships and birds and stars, and beautifully bound blank journals for making entries about those birds and stars. Apparently nobody was all that fascinated by natural history because the journals remained blank.

At the top she could turn in a circle and see the entire island.

Mr. Stratton senior, of course, had built a causeway linking the island to the village, but Harriett still thought of it as an island, because when she was a little girl, it could be reached only at low tide, ladies lifting their skirts in a most unseemly way, and children darting among the horseshoe crabs.

There, on the long white stretch of sand, where fragrant beach grass stopped and tidal debris began, walked Strat and the unknown girl . . . arm in arm.

33

Be ladylike, Harriett said to herself. Do not spy on your dearest friend. Take this calmly and return to the piano.

She focused the telescope. It displayed Strat and his beautiful stranger sitting together in the sand. After a bit they crawled forward to where the sand was still wet from the tide, to build a castle. The girl kicked off her shoes and was barefoot in the sand.

I will not cry, said Harriett to herself. I will not let him know that I saw. I will not ask. I will mind my manners.

She burst into tears anyway. I will so ask! Who does he think he is! He can't—

But he could, of course.

It was his estate, and the barefoot girl was his guest, and he was not affianced to Harriett, and he had all the rights, and Harriett had none.

"What are you doing up here?" said Devonny. "Goodness, Harriett, you're all puffy-eyed! What's the matter?" Devonny searched the view and immediately saw what was the matter.

"Harriett!" she shrieked. "Who is that girl? Look what they're doing! Harriett, what *are* they doing? I've never seen anybody do that! Harriett, who is she?"

She is, thought Harriett, the end of my hopes.

CHAPTER 3

Annie had no pockets, but Strat's were deep and saggy, so she filled them with beach treasure—mermaids' tears. Sand-smoothed broken glass brought in by the tide. When she slipped her hand into his pocket, Strat tensed as if she were doing something daring, and then let out his breath as if she were the treat of a lifetime. He looked at her the way Annie had always dreamed a boy would look at her: as if she were a work of art, the best one in the world.

Strat's hair was blunt cut in an unfamiliar way. Longish, somehow, even though lots of boys Annie knew wore their hair much longer. His shirt collar was open, the collar itself larger than collars should be. His pants were high-waisted, instead of slung down toward the hips, and his suspenders were real, actually holding the pants up, instead of decorating his shirt.

Annie concentrated on details, because the large

event was beyond thought. If she began adding things up, she would get a very strange number, a number she did not want to have. Yet she certainly wanted to have Strat. "Strat," she repeated. It suited him. He was both jock and preppie, both formal and informal.

He arranged her hand lightly on his forearm, joining himself to her in a distant, well-mannered way. Down the sand they walked.

The beach wasn't right. There were dunes. The beach Annie knew had been flattened by a million bare feet. Here, the tide line was littered with driftwood from shipwrecks and mounds of oyster shells, as if no beach crew raked and no day campers collected treasure.

Nobody was there except Annie and the boy from the Mansion.

Nobody.

Even on the most frigid bleak day in January, Stratton Point wouldn't be empty. You'd have your photography nut, your birding group, your idiot who plunged into the water all twelve months of the year, your joggers and miscellaneous appreciators of nature.

Absolutely nobody else was on the half mile of white sand. In spite of the heat, Annie trembled.

"Miss Lockwood," Strat began.

She loved the Miss Lockwood stuff. It took away the shivers and made her giggle.

There was a courtliness to Strat that she'd never seen in a man or a boy. He was treating her like a fragile dried rose. A contrast to Sean, who often told (not asked) her to throw his toolbox in the back of the truck for him.

The sun caught her eyes, blinding her for a moment, and she pulled back her hair to see him better. His features were heavier than Sean's, firmer, somehow more demanding.

"Please forgive me any rudeness, Miss Lockwood, but I am unsure . . ." His voice trailed off, his mouth slightly open, waiting for a really good phrase. His nose was sunburned.

He is so handsome, thought Annie. If I'd ever seen him before in my life, I would certainly remember. And I would remember the gatehouse, if it existed. What happened here? Who is he? And who am I?

"I was there when you arrived," he said finally. "And I am unsure about what I saw."

The only possibility was too ridiculous to say out loud. *I fell down, Strat, and I think the fall was not between standing and sitting. I think it was between centuries.*

Right.

"I'm pretty unsure myself, Strat," she said. "What is going on? Do *you* know? I've lost track of some time here. Maybe a whole lot of time. Don't laugh at me."

"I would not dream of laughing, Miss Lockwood," he promised, and now his features were earnest, worried and respectful.

Annie tried to imagine any boy on the football team or in the cafeteria talking as courteously as Strat. They'd be more apt to swear as they demanded information.

Far to the east, the thunderstorm quickstepped out to the ocean, black clouds roiling over black clouds. Above Strat and Annie, the sky turned lavender blue, not a single remaining wisp of cloud.

It's a dream, she thought. I'm having an electric storm of the mind, just as the sky had its electrical storm. Little flashes of story are sparking through. Nothing makes sense in dreams, so I don't have to worry about sense.

But she had senses, the other kind, in this dream: touch and feel, smell and taste. The smell, especially, of a beach at low tide. Hot summery salt and seaweed. You did not carry smell into your dreams. "I know we're at Stratton Point," she said carefully.

He raised his eyebrows. He looked wicked for a moment, capable of anything, and then he grinned again and looked capable mainly of being adorable. "I'm a Stratton," he said, "but we call the estate Llanmarwick."

"I've lived in the village all my life, and I've never heard anybody use that word."

"Well, we certainly get our supplies delivered. Llanmarwick with two l's," said Strat cheerfully. "Mama got it from a novel about Wales. I do believe it's a fake word. Of course Florinda would like to change it. She wants to call it Sea Mere, but Devonny and I are fighting to keep Llanmarwick."

Annie felt no shyness, the way she normally would with a strange boy, or even a very well-known boy, because so little was normal here. "Let's sit," she whispered, pulling him down beside her in the hot com-

38

forting sand. Were his cute little knickers really corduroy? Could she feel him? Or like the half-there furnishings of the Mansion, was he insubstantial? She explored him with an interest she had never felt for Sean, and Strat turned out to be substantial indeed.

His skin was real. His sunburn, tan and freckles were real. His eyebrows barely separated and she threaded a finger down his nose and back up between his brows. He seemed to feel he had been given permission by her touch to do the same, and her movements were mirrored. Whatever she did, he reflected back.

Mirrors, she thought, caught on a sharp fragment of knowledge. What is it about mirrors that I should remember?

"Shouldn't you be wearing your hat?" he said abruptly. It was one of those sentences to fill space, when you don't want to talk at all, but you don't know what else to do.

You are so lovable, she thought, you're like a teddy bear dressed in sweet old-fashioned clothes. "I would never wear a hat. Maybe if I took up skiing, I'd jam some knitted thing over my ears, but that's just a good reason not to ski. I hate flattening my hair."

"You never wear a hat?" He was unable to believe this.

Their eyes met on the subject of hats, of all things. Well, she had wanted a conversation that went beyond machines and cars, and she had it.

He was wearing a hat: a flat, beretlike cap with a little brim, the sort men wore in movies about early

39

cars with running boards. It was gray plaid and cute. She took his hat off, taking time to run her fingers through his heavy hair, as if she, having met Strat, now owned him. She put his cap on her own head and gave him a teasing half-smile. "There. Fully hatted," she said. "Better?"

Then there were no facts and no time span, only sense. Touch and feel and smell and sight: these four as perfect as dreams. It is a dream, she thought. Real life isn't this wonderful.

So if it's a dream, there is nothing to do but sleep it out, enjoy whatever comes, because when I awaken—

A sound Annie had never heard in real life, only on television, filled her ears. A heavy metal striking; a thudding clippy-clop, clippy-clop.

Annie leaped to her feet. There, beyond the bayberry bushes and the sea grass and the dunes, were four beautiful horses, rich ruddy brown with braided manes, grandly pulling a carriage decorated like a Christmas tree, with golden scrollwork: the Stratton initials. The guard in the little gatehouse had lifted the gate, and the carriage passed onto Stratton Point without missing a beat.

Annie filled with time.

Filled with fear.

No.

There is no such thing as falling through time.

Without her permission, the facts added themselves up. The view from the bedroom tower, from which there had been no interstate bridge across the river. The wild empty beach. This boy, with his oddly cut hair, manners, clothing. That carriage.

No.

They're filming an historical movie, she informed herself. Somebody paid a trillion dollars to take down the phone poles and lay turf over the parking lots and close off the beach. Somehow on the last day of school, nobody talked about this, although obviously the entire village is cooperating to the fullest.

The horses snorted, and stamped, the rich aroma of their sweat masking the scent of the sea. Annie forced herself to look way up the beach and over the clear meadow to the old stables. *They were not old.* They were new. The doors had not been taken off so that tractors and trucks could fit through. Horses lived in that stable.

"Strat?" she whispered. The ocean roared in her ears, although there were no waves to speak of; the day was calm. It's fear roaring in my ears, she thought. "What year is this, Strat?"

"Miss Lockwood, it is 1895."

She felt as if she would fall again, and she clung to him. It was a circumstance with which he was familiar—fainting women—and he responded much more comfortably than to the bike race. The carriage moved on, while Annie remained within his arms. "This really is 1895?" said Annie.

"It really is."

She had half fallen to the ground. He'd knelt to catch her, and now she was sitting on his bent knee,

Strat staring at her like a man about to propose. "We have a problem," said Annie. "I live in 1995."

"I'm good at guessing games," he said. "I'll have this in a moment. Is that a clue to your street address?"

But Annie Lockwood had finished her own guessing game and was pretty sure of the truth. She tucked his arm tighter around herself, as if she were an infant to be comforted by wrapped blankets. Eighteen ninety-five. Not only is this boy really a Stratton, she thought, my parents aren't even born yet—my grandparents aren't born yet! "I'm sorry I dizzied out on you, Strat. I just caught on, that's all. I really am in 1895. I've fallen backward a century. Which can't happen. I have to figure out what has gone wrong, Strat."

"Sun," said Strat with certainty. "Young ladies are never allowed out in the sun without hats, and this is why. Your constitution isn't strong enough. Young ladies are too frail for the heat. We'll go home and you'll rest on Florinda's fainting couch."

She saw that he did not want to accept the century change at all, and would far rather have some unchaperoned girl who needed to rest on a fainting couch. Who was Florinda, and why did she faint so often that she needed a special couch on which to do it?

"No, Strat, you were there. You're the one I bumped into, aren't you? You saw half of me when I saw half of you. It isn't too much sun, Strat."

Fragments like triangular photographs, caught in the mirrors of the Mansion, flickered in Annie's mem-

42

ory. She saw again the blackness shifting, smelled the apples and autumn, heard the crack of bone.

What did I see? she thought. Did I see it in this time, or as I fell through? I remember the blackness had its own sound. But that is as impossible as changing centuries.

Strat's face shifted too, becoming young and upset. "I was there," he admitted. "And you're right, it wasn't sun. We were indoors, you and I, and most of the drapes were pulled to keep out the sun. I don't know why I said that. I'm sorry."

They touched but not as they had before: they touched to see if the other was real, if the skin was alive and the cheek was warm.

"I've fallen through time. I'm from a hundred years later, Strat." She had no watch. The sky was a late-afternoon sky. A four or five o'clock sky.

"Was it frightening?" said Strat.

"Yes. It was really a fall. I could feel the time rushing past my face. There were other people in there with me. Half people." I'm not the only one changing centuries, thought Annie. Other bodies and souls flew past me. Or with me. Or through me.

"Are you frightened now?" said Strat, discarding the scary parts and eager to move on into the adventure. "Don't be. I'll take care of you. You'll stay with us. We'll have to come up with a story, though. We can't use time travel. It's too bad Devonny isn't here, she's wonderful at fibs."

Stay with him? thought Annie, touching the idea the way she had touched Strat's face. Stay in the Mansion, he means! I'd have my wish. I'd see how they live, and wear their dresses, and dance their dances! I'd have both lives. Both centuries.

The last time she'd had that thought, she had also thought of Daddy having both women. Now the knowledge of Daddy's affair traveled with her over the century and ruined the adventure. She shook her head. "I have to get home, Strat. How will I get home? I don't know how I got here, never mind how to go in the other direction. I should go right now, before they worry. Mom will have left a message on the machine asking about the last half day."

Strat had no idea what that meant.

"Of course, Mom isn't home from work yet," added Annie, "which means that so far nobody's worried."

"Your mother works?" said Strat, horrified.

"Well, she doesn't swab prison toilets," said Annie, laughing at him. "She works on Wall Street."

"Your mother?"

"She's a very successful account executive."

Annie envisioned her mother, with that distinguished wardrobe, black or gray or ivory or olive, always formal, always businesslike. That briefcase, bulging, and that Powerbook, charged, as indeed Mom was charged every day, eager to get to New York and get to work. Annie thought her mother very beautiful, but Daddy had changed his mind on the definition of beauty.

What if I can't get back to her? thought Annie. She'll need me and I won't be there! How could the universe let me fall through like that? Why didn't I go

44

through the first time I fell? What made it happen the second time? How can I find the way back out? Is it a door? A wish? A magic stone?

Strat led her up the sloping sand to the causeway as gently as if he were comforting a grieving widow. Now he was actually lifting her bike for her, quite obviously preparing to help her get on. Could any girl on earth require help to get on her bike? He was being so gentle with her she felt like a newborn kitten, or a woman who used fainting couches. How maddening.

"My constitution," said Annie Lockwood, "just happens to be superlative. Especially in the sun. I can whip you at beach volleyball any day of the week, fella. As for tennis, you'll be begging for mercy. Bet I can swim farther than you too."

"What is volleyball?" he asked. "I do play tennis, though, and I'm perfectly willing to beg for mercy. But if you are so hale and hearty that you can whip me, then let us forget fainting couches. May I have the honor of escorting you to the village to the ice cream parlor, Miss Lockwood?"

He was not being sarcastic. He was not being silly. He was actually hoping for the honor.

Nobody says things like that, thought Annie. Not out loud. You'd be laughed out of school. Laughed off the team.

"Before you change centuries again, of course," added Strat.

It didn't matter what century you saw that grin in. He had a world-class grin. Annie decided to worry about changing centuries after ice cream.

They mounted their bikes.

He stared at how much of her leg was revealed until she adjusted the white skirt to cover her thigh. All this attention was delightful. Sean wouldn't have noticed if she'd danced on the ceiling.

"Let's not race," said Strat. "Let's pedal slowly."

Let's keep that skirt in place, translated Annie. "Okay," she said.

"If we run into my friends," said Strat, as they moved down a road that was not paved, but graded and oiled, "I'll introduce you, of course. May I know your real name? Annie must be what your family calls you."

I do have a real name, thought Annie. And what's more, a *perfect* real name. Perhaps I was meant to fall through. Perhaps it was intended that I should visit another era, and my parents had no choice but to give me the name of another era. "Anna Sophia," she said. It was supposed to happen. I must stop worrying about getting back. Everything will happen at the right time, just as I must have fallen through at the right time.

She was wildly exhilarated now, unworried, ready to have a huge crush on this sweet boy.

He claimed to love Anna Sophia as a name, but continued to call her Miss Lockwood.

They pedaled a quarter mile.

Miss Lockwood held her hand out to Mr. Stratton, and he took it in his, and they pedaled hand in hand, and did not worry about traffic, because there was no such thing.

*   *   *

Bridget, the little Irish maid, loved parties as much as Miss Devonny and Miss Harriett. Of course, she didn't get to dance, but she got to look. She would help the ladies dress, and help with the ladies' hair, and for a moment or two could actually hold the diamond brooch or the strings of pearls.

She'd been up since before the sun, and would not be permitted rest until the party ended and the ladies were abed. She wasn't tired. Bridget was used to work.

She'd left her family in Ireland only three years ago, when she was thirteen years old, walking country lanes until she reached the Atlantic, and crossing that terrible ocean in the bottom of an even more terrible boat, and she had been hungry all those thirteen years but she was not hungry now.

She'd done the right thing, coming to America. It tickled Bridget that she was taking care of a fourteen-year-old, Miss Devonny, who was not even allowed to cross a street by herself, while she, Bridget, had crossed an ocean. Bridget enjoyed life, and she certainly enjoyed the Mansion. The party tonight would be magnificent, things undreamed of in all Ireland. And although she couldn't dance at the dance, she nevertheless had a dance partner.

She was stepping out with the grocery delivery boy. Of course Jeb's parents, staunch Congregationalists, were horrified that their son was in love with a Catholic. They were going to send him out West, or enlist him in the army—anything to get him out of the vile clutches of Bridget Shanrahan. So her romance with Jeb was more romantic than anything Miss Devonny or Miss Harriett would ever have—clandestine meetings, dark corners, plotting against parents, and the true and valid fear that they would never be permitted to marry.

Bridget polished. She polished silver, she polished brass, she polished copper, she polished wood. The Mansion gleamed wherever Bridget had been, and in the beautiful wood of the piano Bridget looked at her reflection and hoped that her clutches were not vile, but also hoped they were strong enough to work.

I have gotten what I wanted so far. The thing is not to give up. My sisters and brothers gave up, and they're still back there, starving and hopeless.

Tears fell onto the perfect piano and she swiftly soaked up the evidence. Weakness was very pretty in a lady like Miss Florinda. But Bridget had not had the luck to be born a lady. Weakness would destroy her. She prayed to Our Lady for help. *Please let Jeb stand up to his family and love me most!*

Harriett could tell by the way Strat tossed back his head and faced the girl sitting on his knee that he was having a wonderful time. I have never sat on his knee, she thought. I have never sat on any man's knee. No man has held my face in his hands like that.

Her heart blistered. Her hands turned thick and heavy like rubber, while the hands of that girl on the beach were touching Strat in ways Harriett had never thought of, never mind dared.

"Well!" said Devonny. "We have to nip this in the bud! You and I have planned the most magnificent wedding in America for you and Strat. Photographers will come from Europe. We'll all go on the honeymoon with you. It won't be any fun if Strat marries somebody else, Harriett."

"I don't know that he's proposing marriage to her," said Harriett, as mildly as she knew how. Her heart was not feeling mild. She was using up all the control she possessed at this moment, and when Strat came back—with this girl?—she would have no self-control left. She would be stripped down to the heart and do something crazed and stupid.

"He'll have to marry her if he keeps that up," said Devonny.

Harriett knew slightly more about the facts of life than Devonny. Strat was not compromising the unknown girl's future. Not yet.

"I still say I want your honeymoon in the Wild West," said Devonny, as if Harriett had been protesting.

Devonny never planned her own wedding and honeymoon, only her brother's to Harriett. It was the thing now to take your entire wedding party to Yellowstone. There was a fine new lodge, built by Union Pacific Railroad. The party would frolic for a few weeks at those geysers, and see a grizzly bear, and then go on to the Pacific Ocean. Perhaps a few weeks in that little town of San Francisco would be pleasant. They would wander in the hills and find gold.

Strat was gold enough. If only Harriett could have Strat—if only she could become his wife! The horror of being a spinster gripped Harriett by the spine, as if not being married could paralyze her.

When Strat came back for the party this evening, would he bring this girl? Would he introduce her? Would he say, This is Miss Somebody, with whom I have fallen in love? Would he expect Harriett to be friendly to her?

Of course he would. He always expected the best of Harriett.

"Strat wandered," said Devonny, using the verb to mean unfaithful. "He's going to do that, you know. He will be like Father. You must put up with it, Harriett, even after you're married."

They were very sheltered young ladies, but they knew the truth about fathers. Harriet's father had had mistresses, strings of them, and her mother had not been allowed to mind. Of course, Mother had died young of tuberculosis, sparing Harriett's father the trouble of worrying about his wife's feelings. Harriett's father then died, thrown from his horse in a silly pointless race. Harriett missed her father dreadfully. She knew, in a distant sort of way, that she wanted Strat to be her father as well as her husband, and she knew, less distantly, that there was something wrong with that. But if only she could be married to him, then everything would be all right, and the gaping holes where she was not loved would be filled.

Devonny's father was also a gaping hole of loveless-
ness. He would certainly not be missed were he to
meet with an accident. He was completely sinful, di-
vorcing his wives and getting new ones. Divorce was
unthinkable, except in Devonny's family, where it was
thought of quite routinely. Strat and Devonny's mother
had been placed in a town house in Brooklyn, and
hadn't been given enough money to leave.

Harriet hoped Strat had more of his mother in him
than his father. Mr. Stratton senior was a rude cruel
man who drove himself through life like a splinter
through a palm. But Strat was sweet and kind. On
Strat, beautiful manners sat easily, and Harriet had
never known him to be anything but nice.

Be nice to me, Strat, she prayed. Let me have what
I want. You.

Her eyes forced her to look down the white line of
sand to where it narrowed at the causeway.

The girl climbed on her cycle, and Strat mounted
his, and they cycled away, laughing and talking, and
the girl's hair and skirt flew out behind her like a
child's, yet romantic as a woman's.

Aunt Ada had worn nothing but black for decades.
In the evening, her black dress was silk, dripping with
jet beads, and cascading with tied fringe. Even the
shawls that kept her narrow shoulders warm were
black. It was a true reflection of her life. Not one ray of
light existed for her. She'd been scowling for so many

years that even her smiles were downward, though very little made Ada smile.

The woman who did not marry ceased to have value, and Ada's value had ended long, long ago. The woman who did not marry had to beg, and Ada had begged from Hiram Stratton a place in his home, and been assigned the task of chaperoning Harriett.

He paid Ada nothing.

She had a room with a bath; she had clothing suitable for her station; she had a place in the family railcar and on the family yacht and at the family table. Last place.

But Ada had no money. Quite literally, Ada had not one penny. Not one silver dollar. Even the Irish maid earned money. Not once in her adult life—which was a long one—had Ada been able to make a purchase without groveling and begging for permission.

A few months ago, Ada had overheard a conversation between Devonny and Harriett. "The minute you're wed to my brother," said Devonny, "you must get rid of Aunt Ada."

"Oh, of course," said Harriett. "Can you imagine spending my entire life with that old hag marching at my heels?"

Ada was a hag, and she knew it. She was forced to know it by the mirrors that covered the walls as sheets cover beds. Wife number one had put up those mirrors, and wives two through four were so vain and so fond of their reflections that they had not taken them down. Little triangular sections of primping females—

or females too ugly to bother, like Ada—reflected a thousand times in each great room.

Get rid of me? thought Ada. And where would I go then?

The village had a poorhouse, of course. A farm to which the failures of society were sent, Ada supposed, to plant and dig turnips.

I may have become an old hag, Harriett Ranleigh, but I am not a fool, and if you are going to get rid of me when you marry young Mr. Stratton, then the first thing I will do is prevent the marriage. The second thing I will do is acquire enough money to be safe without you, Harriett Ranleigh.

Ada rubbed her hands together. They were cold dry hands.

She was a cold dry woman. In her youth, she had tried to be warm and affectionate, like other girls. But it had not worked for her, and no man had asked for such a hand in marriage. In middle age, Ada tried to make friends of neighbors and relatives. This failed. When Mr. Stratton had asked her to supervise his motherless ward, Harriett, Ada had thought she might love this little girl. But she had not grown to love Harriett, and as the years went by, Ada realized that she did not know how to love anybody.

This knowledge no longer caused her grief. She no longer wept at night. She simply became more angry, more dry, and more cold.

She usually wore gloves, as much to keep her hands warm as to be fashionable. The fingernails were yellow and ridged and looked like weapons.

Today, thinking of Harriett, whom she hated and feared, Ada raked them suddenly through the air, as if ripping the skin off Harriett's face. Across the room Ada saw shock on the face of the little Irish maid.

"Get out," said Ada, glaring. Ada despised the Irish. The country should never have let them in. It was disgusting, the way immigrants from all those worthless countries were just sailing up and strolling onto dry land. They were even commemorating immigrants now, as if it were a good thing! That ridiculous new Statue of Liberty the young people insisted they had to see! Disgraceful.

She tucked her shawl tightly against the high-collared moiré dress, and the fabrics rasped like her thoughts. You cannot waste time being fearful, Ada ordered herself. You must channel your energy into being strong and hard. There is nobody who cares about you. Nobody. You must do all the caring yourself. And if damage is done while you are taking care, remember that men do damage all the time, and never even notice.

Ada smiled suddenly, and it was good that little Bridget was not there to see the smile. The lowering ends of Ada's thin lips were full of fear and rage.

And full of plans for Harriett.

CHAPTER 4

Walker Walkley liked the finer things in life. He did not have enough of them, but if he planned right, he could acquire enough. Throughout boarding school Walk had cultivated Strat. Strat liked company, and did not understand what this friendship cost him, either in money or in pretense.

Walk had managed to live like Strat, and off Strat, for four wonderful years, and now he was going on to Yale with Strat, but it might not be that easy to sponge at college. Walk needed certainty, and he had pretty well decided on Strat's sister, Devonny.

Strat would be delighted. And Devonny, handily, was much too young for marriage, so Walk would become affianced to Devonny, and have all the family privileges, but he could postpone actually bothering with Devonny for years.

Strat would be spending July at Walk's lodge in the

Adirondacks. It was run-down and primitive now, the twelve bedrooms in desperate need of refurbishing, the immense screened veranda over the lake in worse need of repair and paint, but Strat never noticed these things, and if he did, would assume that hunting lodges were supposed to look like that. Musty old stuffed moose heads on the wall and rotting timber in the floor.

Walk worried about discussing the finances with Mr. Stratton senior, who was a tough and hostile man under the best of circumstances. He might not look kindly upon a youth whose purse was empty. He might feel Devonny should marry up, rather than down. Therefore Walk must dedicate himself this summer to being sure that Devonny fell in love with him.

Of course, Harriett Ranleigh had the most money of all. Plain women were easy. A few flattering lies and you owned them. But Strat had Harriett by her corset ties. The rich always figured out a way to get richer.

Walk controlled his jealousy, as he had controlled it for so many years, and planned his flirtation with Devonny Stratton.

In the kitchen, the maids washed a cut glass punch bowl so big that two girls had to support it while the third bathed it in soapy water. The raised pineapple designs were cut so sharply they hurt the maids' hands.

The gardener's boys had brought armloads of flowers into the house, and for a moment or two, Florinda

56

supervised the arranging of flowers. But when her friend Genevieve appeared, ready to take a turn around the garden, Florinda called Bridget. "Get my parasol, Bridget. You hold it for me." Florinda's wrists tired easily.

Bridget had not finished polishing. She would get in trouble for not completing the job, but she would get in trouble for not obeying Miss Florinda too. In neither case were excuses permitted. Bridget fetched the parasol, and walked behind the ladies, her arm uncomfortably outstretched to protect Miss Florinda from the sun.

The sun bore down on Bridget's face, however, and multiplied her freckles. Jeb loved her freckles. He had kissed them all, individually. Now there would just be more to kiss.

Bridget permitted herself a huge, cheek-splitting grin of joy when Miss Florinda and Miss Genevieve were not looking. Servants were not permitted emotion.

Harriett and Devonny set up the croquet game, for the grass had dried quickly in the ocean breeze. Strat failed to return, and even Walk wasn't around. The great Mansion felt oddly deserted, and the air felt strangely thin, as though something were about to happen.

"Ladies," said a booming voice.

Harriett steeled herself to be courteous. She knew the voice well. It was Mr. Rowwells, who had some sort of business connection with Strat's father. Naturally the details were never discussed in front of the ladies.

Mr. Rowwells was perhaps ten years older than Harriett, maybe even fifteen. Nobody liked him. Especially Harriett.

Devonny therefore spent lots of time trying to make Mr. Rowwells think Harriett adored him. Harriett had considered throwing Devonny off the tower roof if she did it again, but Devonny just giggled and whispered to Mr. Rowwells that Harriett would probably love to go for a carriage ride with him that evening. It had seemed just a joke between the girls, but now, threatened by Strat's half-dressed young woman, she saw Mr. Rowwells more clearly as a man who wanted a wife.

"Why don't we start our game of croquet," suggested Mr. Rowwells, "since the young gentlemen appear to have started their own game without us."

How fraught with meaning the sentence was. Harriett quivered. Was Mr. Rowwells hinting that Strat's game included a different young lady? Had Mr. Rowwells also seen the bare-legged girl kissing Strat?

Harriett lifted her chin very high. It was a habit that helped keep emotion off her face, providing a slope down which pain and worry would run, like rainwater. "Why, Mr. Rowwells, what a good idea. Devonny, you and Mr. Rowwells be partners. I shall run inside and see who else is available to—"

But they never found a fourth for croquet.

One of the maids began screaming, and from the

58

windows opened wide for the sea breeze, they heard her curdling shrieks for help.

Mr. Rowwells of course got there first, because Devonny and Harriett were hampered by long skirts and by the corsets that kept them vertical. Mr. Rowwells didn't want the young ladies to see what had happened, and cried that they were to keep their distance. Harriett would have obeyed, but Devonny believed that a thing grown-ups told you to keep a distance from would prove a thing worth seeing, and so she elbowed through the servants, and Harriett followed.

It was one of the servants.

Dead.

He had fallen on the steep dark back stairs that led to the kitchen in the cellar, and he had cracked his skull.

His eyes were open to the ceiling, and spilled on his chest were the sweet cakes and sherry he'd been carrying. The silver tray was half on top of him, like armor.

"Matthew!" cried Devonny, horrified. She tried to go to him, but it was impossible, for he was lying awkwardly upside down on steps too narrow for her to kneel beside him.

Matthew had been with them for years. Every spring when they opened up the Mansion, she was always glad to see Matthew, and see how his children had grown, and give them her old dresses. What a terrible thing! Matthew had five children, only three old enough for grammar school. What would become of them?

Devonny was her father's daughter. Before she was anything else, she was practical. She stared at the glittering silver tray. To whom had Matthew been carrying that?

Certainly not Father. He detested sherry.

Florinda, who adored sherry, was strolling with Genevieve, who had come hoping to get a donation for the Episcopal church. Aunt Ada, had she wanted sherry, would have had to wait for Florinda and Genevieve to return. Would Walker Walkley have dared order sherry? Would Mr. Rowwells?

The stairs were covered with ridged rubber, to prevent slipping. The ceiling was very low, so that the servants had to stoop. The treads of the Great Hall stair formed the ceiling of the kitchen stairs. One tread was rimmed in blood.

"Get up, young lady," snapped Aunt Ada. She took Devonny's arm in pincers like a lobster's, roughly propelling her away from the body. Swiftly Aunt Ada bundled Devonny and Harriett into the library, whose thick doors and solid walls would prevent the girls from learning a single thing.

"The poor babies," whispered Harriett, who had played with them many times, chalking out hopscotch, and twirling jump ropes and sharing cookies. "No father."

No father meant no home. Without Matthew's work here in the Mansion, Devonny's father would not permit that big family to take up space above the stable.

"Do you think Father will provide for the babies, Harry?" Devonny cried, using the old nursery nickname. Harriett was touched, but she knew well, as did Devonny, that Mr. Stratton was not a charitable man.

"It is hardly his responsibility," said Aunt Ada coldly. "These immigrants have far too many children. Your father cannot be expected to concern himself."

Devonny suddenly realized that she hated Aunt Ada. And she was not going to call her "Aunt" anymore. And if Father chose not to be charitable, that didn't mean Devonny had to make the same choice. Well, actually it did, because Devonny could do nothing without her father's permission, but she pretended otherwise. "It is *my* responsibility, then," said Devonny sharply, "and I shall execute it."

Harriett smiled.

Ada's wrinkle-wrapped eyes vanished in a long blink.

The word execute shivered in Devonny's mind like the silver tray. If Matthew had slipped, would he have fallen in that direction? Could the tray have ended up where it did? How did he so totally crush his skull? He had not fallen down the entire flight of stairs. He had evidently been on the top step and simply gone backward. And there was blood on a tread above him—as if his head had been shoved into the upper stair and he had fallen afterward.

Had he been murdered?

Devonny did not repeat this idea to Harriett, who

61

would only scold her once more about the novels she read. (Harriett read theology and philosophy; Harriett was brilliant; it was a shame she was not a boy, for brains were useless in a lady.)

Devonny certainly could not mention her suspicion to Second Cousin of Somebody Else Ada.

Father?

Father, unfortunately, was the kind of man who believed women had the vapors. Of course, he kept marrying that kind of woman, so he had proof. He would simply tell Devonny to lie down until the sensation passed. He would tell her not to worry her sweet head about such things. He would not be interested in how Matthew died, he would be concerned only that the party and the running of his household not be adversely affected.

She would have to talk to Strat.

Which led Devonny again to the girl on the sand. Devonny knew every houseguest. The girl was not one. So who was she? And where was Strat? And when had Matthew died?

Had the girl on the sand been there?

Had she done it?

Jeb's father did not bother with discussions. Jeb's father was a man of few words, and he had said them once: "Do not step out with the Irish Catholic again." Jeb had not listened. Therefore his father moved from talk to flogging. Jeb hung onto the fence post and set his teeth tightly to keep the pain inside while his father's leather belt dug into his bare back.

Jeb loved Bridget. She was sweet and hardworking and her funny Irish accent sang to him, comforting and bawdy both. He yearned for her.

But she was Catholic. It was a sin against God for her even to think of becoming Protestant. He would have to become Catholic. "Why can't we be nothing?" Jeb had said. Bridget thought less of him after that.

His father stopped. He didn't even wipe the blood off his belt, just slid it into the pant loops. "Well?"

"I won't see her again," said Jeb.

His father knocked Jeb's jaw upward with a gnarled fist to see in his son's eyes whether Jeb was lying. But even Jeb did not know whether he was lying.

She was tired of him calling her Miss Lockwood. Strat, however, could not manage anything as familiar as Annie. So he called her Anna Sophia. "Anna Sophia," he sang, opera style, "Sophia Anna." His deep bass voice rang out over the road.

Her hair was making him crazy. When they paused at the corner of Beach and Elm, he could not resist her hair. He picked it up, making a silken horsetail between his hands, which he twisted on top of her head the way fashion dictated this year. When he let go, the hair settled itself. There was not the slightest curl to the hair; it might have been ironed. He threaded his fingers through the hair like ribbons. He could not imagine ever touching Harriett's hair like this.

"Where do you live?" he said, because he had to say something, or he would go even farther beyond the rules of behavior.

"Cherry Lane."

He loved her voice. Aunt Ada saw to it that Harriett's voice was carefully modulated. Anna Sophia did not sound like a girl required to modulate anything.

"I don't suppose Cherry Lane is even here," she went on. "It can't be, because our houses were built in the fifties."

Strat was about to argue that plenty of houses had been built in the fifties, until he realized she meant the *nineteen* fifties, which didn't exist.

"The road isn't even paved," she cried. "Not even here in the village."

"Nothing in the country is paved," he said.

"No sidewalks!"

"This is hardly Manhattan."

"What kind of tree is this?"

"It's an elm," he said, "and this is Elm Street."

"Oh, what a shame they all get Dutch elm disease and die," said Miss Lockwood. "They really are beautiful, aren't they?"

Trees? She knew the future of trees? Strat believed neither in time travel nor ghosts, but Anna Sophia was making him think of witches. What power did she have, to know the death of things?

What power did she have to make him shiver every time he looked at her, and never want to do another thing in his life except look at her?

Forget Yale, forget parties, the Mansion, New York.

Strat was out of breath with all the things he no longer cared about.

"There is no Cherry Lane, I was right. But look, Strat. There are cherry trees! It's an orchard. I never knew that. I thought it was just a pretty name, maybe out of Mary Poppins. Our house would be right about there, Strat, where the fence ends."

"Miss Lockwood, you're making me so uncomfortable. I feel as if you really might have come from some other time. Don't talk of death and change."

Don't talk of death and change. Anna Sophia turned back into Annie, whose parents most certainly did not want to talk of death and change. Although in their case, it would be divorce and change. She knew suddenly that Mom knew all about Miss Bartten. Mom knew and had chosen to pretend she didn't, praying praying praying it would go away and they would never have to talk of change or enter a courtroom to accomplish it.

Above them the elms created a beautiful canopy of symmetry and green. Strat eyed them anxiously, after what she had said.

I know the end of the story, she thought. I know the elms will die, but maples will take their place. It's my own story that scares me. I don't know the end of it.

He touched her hair again, drawn like a gold miner to a California stream.

65

She half recognized where they were. A few buildings were exactly the same as they would be a hundred years later. The ice cream parlor was in a building that no longer existed—the bank parking lot, actually. She did not tell Strat this because he was so proud of the ice cream parlor.

It had no counter, and nobody had cones. It had darling round white tables with tiny delicate chairs. Light and slim as she was, Annie sat carefully, lest the frail white legs of her chair buckle beneath her. Ice cream was served in footed glass compotes sitting on china saucers. Their napkins were cloth, and their spoons silver with souvenir patterns.

Strat could hardly take his eyes off her.

He was forced to do so, however, because his best friend, Walk, as shocked as Strat had been by the girl's clothing and hair and bare legs, came over to be introduced. "Hullo, Walk," said Strat uneasily, getting to his feet. "Miss Lockwood, may I present my school friend, Walker Walkley."

She got up, smiling. "Hey, Walk. Nice to meet you."

Walk practically fell over. He had certainly expected her to call him Mr. Walkley. Strat flushed with embarrassment in spite of ordering himself not to. He half wanted to give Anna Sophia instruction and half wanted her to be just what she was. He fully did not want to be embarrassed in public. Nobody was pretending any longer not to see how unusual this girl was. (Strat preferred the word unusual to words like indecent or unladylike.)

Walk knew perfectly well the last thing Strat wanted was company, so of course he said, "May I join you?"

Why couldn't Walk have stayed at the estate, napping after their baseball game? Why had he come into town for ice cream too? "What a pleasure," said Strat helplessly. Miss Lockwood had already sat down, forgetting the second half of the introductions. "This is Miss Anna Sophia Lockwood, Walk."

"Miss Lockwood," said Walk, bowing slightly before seating himself. "One of the Henry Lockwoods?"

"I think he was a great-grandfather," she agreed.

Strat flinched, but Walk simply assumed he was being given genealogy. Luckily Walk had superior manners. Strat did not want Walk asking how they had met. Walk would never initiate such a topic. Miss Lockwood of course might initiate anything. Strat did not want to share her, and above all, he did not want to share her time travel theory.

He kicked her lightly under the table.

She smiled at him sweetly, a companion in lies. Neatly she settled his own cap back on his head and right there in front of the world—*in the middle of a public ice cream parlor!*—kissed him on the forehead.

It was the kiss of a fallen woman, who would do anything anywhere, and Walker Walkley gasped.

Strat heard nothing. He had never known such a creature existed on this earth, *and she was his.* Strat, too, fell with as much force as if he'd fallen a century.

He fell completely and irrevocably in love with Anna Sophia Lockwood.

*   *   *

The sun set.

Sailboats returned.

The final marshmallows were toasted. Picnic baskets were closed. Tired families trooped over sandy paths to swelteringly hot cars.

The last day of school. And Annie Lockwood had never come home.

Her family tried not to panic. They made the usual phone calls: boyfriend, girlfriend, other girlfriends. The clock moved slowly into the evening, and they began to think of calling the police.

Was it too early to call for help . . . or too late?

CHAPTER 5

"This," said Strat, his voice full, "is my friend, Miss Lockwood."

Harriett, Devonny, Florinda and Genevieve, accustomed to thinking mainly of men, knew immediately what Strat's voice was full of: adoration.

It was worse than Harriett could have dreamed. The girl displayed *bare* legs, *tangled* hair, *no* hat, *tanned* nose and *paint* on her eyelids. There was a gulping silence in which good manners fought with horror. Strat was in love with *this*? This hussy?

Florinda fluttered dangerously. Devonny never allowed Florinda to think she was in charge. The latest stepmother was too feathery in brain, body and clothing to be permitted any leeway. "Florinda, darling," said Devonny, "our poor friend Miss Lockwood has ruined her clothing. I shall just rush her upstairs to borrow some of mine."

Harriett was filled with admiration. Devonny was so quick. And of course fashion was always a good thing, and there was no time when Devonny and Harriett, though six years apart, were not eager to think of clothes. Harriett never visited with fewer than two Saratoga trunks full of costumes, prepared for any possible fashion occasion, and she was even prepared for this one.

"Or my wardrobe," said Harriett. "I think Miss Lockwood is too tall for yours, Dev."

And what a smile Harriett received from Strat. "Oh, would you, Harry? That would be so wonderful! I thank you," he said.

It warmed her that Strat would bring out that little term of endearment. She waited for explanations—who Miss Lockwood was, where she had come from, and why, but Florinda interfered. "Strat, the most dreadful thing has happened. Utterly impossible. I am feeling quite undone."

This was always the case. Harriett was not surprised when Strat didn't bother to ask what dreadful thing. Florinda might not even be thinking of Matthew's death, because she was apt to be overwhelmed if the roses had black spot. Aunt Ada of course had placed herself in charge of the disposal of Matthew's body. This was probably just as well for Strat. He could get Miss Lockwood by Florinda, and Genevieve was a mere beggar passing through, but Aunt Ada would have posed considerable difficulties.

Strat will have to take over the Matthew situation, Harriett said to herself, and perhaps he will forget about Miss Lockwood. I can shut her in a tower and throw away the key.

This sounded wonderful. Harriett didn't even feel guilty. At least Miss Lockwood would have a smashing gown to wear during her imprisonment.

It was of no interest to Walker Walkley that a servant had fallen on the stairs. Walk's mind was seething with new plans. What great good fortune that after baseball he'd cycled straight down to the village. Strat had actually taken the little hussy home with him. Astounding how stupid men would become when their minds were overtaken by physical desire.

Walk understood the fun that lay ahead for Strat. Walk had worked through his own household maids, having gotten two with child. Those babies were disposed of through the orphanages and the girls themselves sent on to other households. Walk's father was proud of him.

There was to be a huge party tonight. Strat never even glanced at Harriett, not even when he thanked her for offering her own wardrobe. Walk studied Harriett. The lovesick expression in Strat's eyes was very hurtful to her.

Perhaps, thought Walker Walkley, a little consolation is in order for Harriett. Me.

Forget Devonny. Anyway, Devonny had a rebellious streak, the kind that must be thoroughly crushed in females. Mr. Stratton senior, who had spent his life crushing everyone in sight, indulged Devonny. Devonny would prove a difficult wife. Harriett, plain and desperate, was obedient . . . and much, much richer.

He exulted, thinking of her money, her land, her houses, her corporations, her stocks and bonds and gold and silver. Mine, thought Walker Walkley. Mine!

Harriett would bear the children Walk required, and be an effective mother. Meanwhile, he would also have all the fun he required. That's what women were for.

The key was to help Strat with his little hoyden. Walk must make it easy for Strat. Then Walk would dance with Harriett. Walk understood homely ladies. Offer them a ring and a rose and mention marriage and they were yours.

Keep it up, Miss Lockwood! thought Walker Walkley, retiring to his room to prepare for the evening. He closed the door behind himself, and leaned against it, laughing with glee.

Annie, too, believed that fashion was always a good thing. She had been awestruck by what the other girls at that ice cream parlor had had on, and could hardly wait to have clothes like that herself.

Somehow Strat had gotten her into the Mansion without explanations. In 1995, these two girls, Harriett and Devonny, would have peppered her with questions; it would have been like *Oprah* or *Donahue*. *Yeah, so waddaya think you're doin' here, Annie?*

But in 1895, they simply stared with falling-open mouths at the sight of Annie's bra. It was her prettiest.

Pale lavender with hot pink splashes of color, like a museum painting of flowers.

Devonny gasped. "Where—what—I mean—I haven't—"

Harriett said quickly, "We can lace her into something decent."

And they did.

Annie would never have submitted to it, except that Harriett and Devonny showed her they were wearing the same thing. It was, thought Annie, a wire cage you could keep canaries in. The cage was flexible, and by hauling on cords fastened to each rib of the cage, they tightened it on her. It completely changed the shape of her body. Her waist grew smaller and smaller, and where it had all been crammed, Annie was not sure until she could no longer breathe. "You squished my lungs together," she protested. "What's happening to my kidneys and my heart? I can't breathe!"

"Of course you can," said Harriett. "Just carefully."

"Why are we doing this?"

"Fashion," said Harriett.

"Don't you faint all the time from lack of oxygen?"

"Of course," said Devonny. "It's very feminine."

"Does Strat approve?"

"Strat?" repeated Devonny. "My goodness. How long have you known my brother?"

Annie had forgotten they called each other Miss and Mister. I'm missing my cue lines, she thought. I must work harder to fit into the century. How long *have* I known Strat? I didn't bring a watch into this century. "Two or three hours, I think," she said.

Considering the circumstances, the girls chattered quite easily. Devonny and Harriett had apparently decided she was from some low part of town. A branch of the Lockwood family that had intermarried and grown extra fingers and forgotten how to wear corsets, probably licked their dinner plates instead of washing them. It was clear that anything Hiram Stratton, Jr., wanted, he got. Even a half-naked townie.

The door opened.

There was no knock first. In came a girl in a brown-checked ankle-length dress covered by an enormous white apron. The apron was starched so much it could have stood alone. It was hard to guess the girl's age. Her hands were raw like old women who scrubbed all day and never used lotion. Her face, though, was very pretty, remarkably fair complexioned. She had black hair, black eyes and a sparkly, excited look to her.

Devonny and Harriett did not say hello, nor even look over. She might have been a houseplant.

"Miss Devonny," scolded the girl in a melodious voice, half singing, "how could you start dressing without me?" Not a houseplant. A housemaid.

Annie was awestruck. Devonny's own maid there to dress her! Clicking her tongue, the maid relaced Annie tight enough to crack ribs. Then she quickly and expertly lowered a pale yellow underdress over Annie's head. She had never worn anything so soft and satiny against her skin.

Devonny and Harriet sorted through Harriett's gowns.

"Here." Harriett produced a daffodil-yellow dress festooned like a Christmas tree, sleeves billowing out like helium balloons around her shoulders, and looping white lace like popcorn strings. Annie felt like an illustration of Cinderella.

Ooooh, this is so neat! she thought. And I get to dance at the ball too! I wonder what happens at midnight.

"Bridget, what shall we do with her hair?" said Devonny.

The maid brushed Annie's hair hard, holding it in her hands as Strat had done. Annie adored having somebody play with her hair. Bridget looped it, pinned it, fluffed it, until it piled like a dark, cloudy ruffle. Bridget released tiny wisps, which she wet and curled against Annie's cheeks.

She stared at herself in the looking glass. A romantic, old-fashioned beauty stared back.

Annie Lockwood decided right then and there to stay in this century. A belle of the ball, where men bow and ladies wear gloves. Of course, without oxygen, she was not sure how long she'd survive. If only somebody could take a photograph for her to carry home and show off.

Annie stole a look at Harriett's dressing table. Creams to soften the skin and perfumes from France, weaponlike hat pins and hair combs encrusted with jewels, but no eye shadow, no mascara and no lipstick. She had so much clothing on, layer after layer, and yet her face felt naked. Nobody suggested makeup. They don't wear makeup, thought Annie. What else don't they do?

It occurred to her, creepily, that perhaps the photo of her had already been taken and she herself, a hundred years from now, would find it in some historical society file.

Music had begun: the very harp she had heard falling through. From downstairs came the clamor and laughter of guests. Annie could smell cigars and pipes, hear the clatter of horses' hooves and wooden wheels and the laughter of flirting women.

Every wish had arrived, exactly the way Annie had daydreamed. She would dance with Strat, so unlikely and so handsome and gallant. She would pin a yellow rose on this dress fit for an inaugural ball, flirt with men in frock coats, drink from crystal goblets and laugh behind a feathered fan.

"I will be introducing you, I expect," said Harriett. "I fear I'm not quite sure what to say, Miss Lockwood."

"Anna Sophia Lockwood," Annie told her. The name she had despised all her life sounded elegant and formal, like the dress.

"Yes, but people will want to know—well—"

"I'm just here briefly," said Annie. She wanted these girls to share the mystery and astonishment. "Tell your guests that I'm passing through on a longer journey. A journey through time."

Harriett stared.

Devonny interlocked her fingers within long white gloves.

Bridget shivered and stepped back. "Are you," whispered Bridget, "some sort of witch?"

How ancient was Bridget's accent. How foreign. Annie lost track of the century. Had she fallen deeper than she'd thought? Was she caught in a place where witches were burned or hung? Where was Strat?

Maybe I am a witch, thought Annie, because what power could let me, and no other, travel through time?

Fear trapped the girls.

She had been a fool to hint at the time travel.

The best defense is a good offense, she reminded herself. If it's good enough for a field hockey locker room, it's good enough for a Victorian dressing room. "I'm just a Lockwood," she said lightly. "And you, Bridget?"

"I'm a Shanrahan, miss," said Bridget.

"She's Irish," said Harriett, as if saying, She's sub-human.

Bridget flushed and began to dress Miss Harriett. The petticoat of silk draped over Harriett's cage was a treasure, vivid pink, ribboned and ruffled. Next Bridget lowered a gown of hotter pink over it. Harriett's gown was fit for a princess. It was awesome.

And Harriett, poor Harriett, was not. She just wasn't pretty.

Annie's heart broke for all plain girls in all centuries. In the looking glass, as huge and beveled as every other mirror in this great house, she saw the terrible contrast between herself and Harriett. "You're very kind to help me like this," Annie told her.

Harriett seemed out of breath. The corset, Annie

thought. We women are crazy. Imagine agreeing to strap yourself into a canary cage before you appear in public.

"I saw you, Miss Lockwood!" cried Harriett. "From the tower. You and Strat."

A century might have fallen away, but Annie knew everything now: Harriett was in love with Strat and terrified of losing him. Annie wanted to console Harriett, who was being so kind to her, saying, Oh, it was nothing, just plain old garden-variety friendship.

But they had not been plain.

I almost possess Strat, thought Annie. Harriett knows that. His sister, Devonny, knows that. Perhaps the maid Bridget knows too. He is almost mine. If I stay . . . Strat . . . the Mansion . . . the roses and the gowns and the servants . . . they would be mine too.

She had a curious triangular thought, like the mirrors, that she must look at this only from her own point of view. If she let herself think of Harriett . . . But this is only a game, she thought, a dream or an electrical storm. No need to think of anybody else.

Bridget dabbed perfume on Annie's throat and wrists and produced the gloves with which her hands would stay covered all evening. The scent of lilacs filled Annie's thoughts and she was seized by terror.

What if she *was* on a longer journey?

What if—when she was ready to leave—*she left in the wrong direction?* What if she fell backward another hundred years? Or another thousand? *What if she could not get home?*

She looked out a window to remind herself of the constancy of sky and sun, but the window was stained glass: a cathedral of roses and ivy; you could not look through it, only at it.

A clock chimed nine times and Annie thought: *I'm not home.*

Mom is home now, and Tod and Daddy, supper is over, and I'm not there. They've called Heather, and they've called Kelly, and I'm not there. They've called Sean and he'll say, Well, she was at the beach for a while but I don't know what happened to her next. They'll get scared around the edges. At the edges will be the horrible things: drowning, kidnapping, runaways, murder, rape. Nobody will say those words out loud.

But it's getting dark. And it will get darker, and so will my mother's fears.

Harriett put both arms around Annie. "Are you all right, Miss Lockwood? You looked terrified. Please don't be afraid. You're among friends."

"Oh, Harriett," said Annie Lockwood, "you're such a nice person." She was overcome with guilt. I can't do this to Harriett, she thought. But I want Strat, too. And I must have fallen through time for a reason. It must be Strat.

Walker Walkley caught the little Irish maid in the hallway and swung her into his room. "Mr. Walkley," she protested, "I have work to do."

"Spend a little time with me first," said Walk, putting his hands where Bridget did not even let Jeb put hands.

Bridget removed his hands and glared at him.

How pretty she was, fired up like that. Walk grinned. He put his hands right back where he wanted them to be.

"Please, Mr. Walkley." The maid struggled to be courteous. She could not lose her position.

Walk laughed and continued. She'd enjoy it once they got started.

Bridget had few weapons, but she used one of them. She spit on him. Her saliva ran down his face.

Oh! it made Bridget so angry! America was perfect, but Americans weren't. These men who thought she was property!

"Touch me, Mr. Walkley," said Bridget Shanrahan, "and I will shove you down the stairs and you'll die like Matthew."

Walker Walkley wiped his cheek with his white handkerchief, nauseated and furious. She had made an enemy.

And said a very dumb thing.

"And are we prepared?" said Aunt Ada.

"We are prepared."

"The little Lockwood creature is the answer to my prayers," said Aunt Ada. "I needed a solution, and moments later, it occurred."

Ada prayed often, and read her Bible thoroughly. It was a rare occasion on which she felt that even God

80

cared whether she had what she needed. Now, so late in life that she had reached the rim of despair, had a guardian angel finally appeared for her too?

It was a nice thought. Ada studied her hands as if they were wands that accomplished things against nature. "Lust has power," she said. "We'll encourage the boy to enjoy himself. We need only an evening or two."

Their smiles slanted with the need for money.

Miss Lockwood had been beautiful on the beach, the wind curving her hair against his face, but here in the ballroom Strat thought she was the loveliest female he had ever seen. The men were envious of him, and lined up for the chance to partner with her.

She had not known any of the dances, but she'd proved a quick learner, willing to laugh at herself. Right there in the ballroom, without a blush, she let each partner teach her another step. She was so light on her feet. She and Strat had spun around the room like autumn leaves falling from trees: at one with the wind and the melody. Now she was dancing with Walk, and Strat was so jealous he could hardly breathe.

"Strat, I have to talk to you," said Devonny in his ear.

Strat didn't want to talk. He wanted to dance with Miss Lockwood now and forever. He didn't want his little sister placing demands and awaiting explanations. He could not explain Miss Lockwood, he just couldn't. It would sound as if he had had too much to drink or started on opium. Time travel, indeed; 1995, indeed.

"Look at me, Strat, so I'll know you're on this planet. We have three subjects we have to cover."

Sisters were such a pain.

"First, you have to be nice to Harriett. Don't you see you're destroying her?"

He had not thought once of Harriett since he had met Miss Lockwood. He did not want to think of her now. If he looked Harriett's way, he'd get back some reproachful expression. I haven't made any promises. I haven't even made any suggestions. I have nothing to feel guilty about, Strat told himself.

Guilt swarmed up and heated his face.

"Second, who is she, this Miss Lockwood?" Devonny tapped a silk-shod foot on the floor for emphasis.

"She's a friend, Dev," he said, "and that's all I'm going to say for now."

His sister looked at him long and hard.

"What's three?" he said quickly.

"Matthew was murdered."

"Devonny, you mustn't bother your little head about it," said her brother. "It's bad for you." He smiled that infuriating male smile, telling her she was a girl and had to obey. Nothing got Devonny madder faster. This was when she knew she was going to wear trousers after all, and be fast, and bad, and scandalous. Show Father and Strat a thing or two.

Which made her madder? Saying her head was little, or that Matthew's death didn't matter enough to bother?

Men! They—

But it was a new world, with new tools, and it occurred to Devonny she could go around her father and brother.

Other hearts in that ballroom beat with love and hope, jealousy and pain. Devonny's beat with terror and excitement. What would Father do to her? It would be worth it just to see!

Devonny slipped out of the ballroom and crossed the Great Hall to the cloakroom. Here she approached the machine nervously. She did not often have the opportunity to touch the telephone. Young ladies wrote notes. Servants responded when the telephone rang, and servants took and delivered messages.

Devonny gathered her courage.

Harriett was left stranded. She had no partner. It was unthinkable. Strat was blind tonight, and Harriett was both furious and deeply humiliated. How they all looked at her, the other ladies; each of them prettier; and how they looked at Miss Lockwood, the prettiest of all.

She saw Walker Walkley feeling sorry for her. Any moment now Walk would rescue her, and she hated it, that she was plain and needed rescue. How could Strat put her in this position! Why did there have to be Miss Lockwoods? Harriett hoped Miss Lockwood rolled down the hill and drowned in the ocean.

Walk moved toward her from his side of the ballroom, and Mr. Rowwells approached from the opposite side. I don't want to be pitied, thought Harriett, I want to be loved. I don't want anybody to be kind to me. I'd rather be a spinster. An old maid.

But then she would be like Aunt Ada. Mean to people because life had been mean to her.

Oh, Strat, thought Harriett, fighting off tears she

could not bear to have anybody see. Please remember me. Please love me.

"My dear Miss Harriett," said Mr. Rowwells, "might I have the pleasure of a stroll with you? Perhaps a turn on the veranda? The evening air is delightful."

Well, she would rather be rescued by Mr. Rowwells, who meant and who knew nothing, than by Walk, who knew everything. Harriett bowed slightly and rested her glove on his arm. Her guardian, Mr. Stratton senior, said that Mr. Rowwells was a fine schemer, an excellent capitalist. Mr. Rowwells had made a fortune in lumber, but one doubted he could make a fortune in his new venture. He actually thought mayonnaise could be put in jars and sold.

Mr. Rowwells was trying to get investors, but men with money burst out laughing. Women needed things to do, so even if you could put mayonnaise in a jar, you'd just be taking away their chores. A woman with time on her hands was a dangerous thing. (Except of course women like Florinda, who could not be given chores in the first place, because of delicacy.)

Mr. Rowwells chatted about small things and Harriett tried to be interested, but wasn't.

In June the garden air was so heavy with rose perfume that ladies were claiming to be faint from it. Harriett felt faint too, but not from perfume.

Perhaps it is a good thing that I love books and knowledge, thought Harriett. I will go to college, since I cannot have Strat.

She had never met a female who had attended such an institution. The mere thought of going away from home was so frightening that she felt faint all over again.

I would be twenty-four when I emerge, and might as well be dead. Nobody will marry me if I'm that old.

Harriett had been taught to hide her intelligence. She could of course imitate the first Mrs. Stratton, reading at home, becoming an expert on Homer and the Bible, able to recite Shakespeare and Milton and Wordsworth. But in exchange for being better educated than Mr. Stratton, Strat and Devonny's mother found herself divorced and replaced.

A very very bad part of Harriett had a solution to the problem of Miss Lockwood. She would introduce Miss Lockwood to Mr. Stratton senior. Even for him it would be quite an age difference—he was *fifty* now! But rapidly tiring of Florinda. Yes. Harriett would seize that flirty little Miss Anna Sophia and wrap her little hand inside Mr. Stratton's great cruel fingers and—

No. It was too nauseating. Harriett didn't wish on anybody the prison of being wife number five for Mr. Stratton.

I just want to be wife number one for Strat, she thought.

Mr. Rowwells soldiered on, trying to find topics. Since Harriett was considering only the possible death or dismemberment of Miss Lockwood, Mr. Rowwells wasn't getting anywhere.

"What does interest you, my dear? Surely you and I have something in common!" Mr. Rowwells patted her hand. In situations like this, Harriett was always glad to have gloves on.

"I am interested in scholarship, Mr. Rowwells. I wish to continue my education. I have thought of requesting Mr. Stratton to permit me to attend a women's college."

"College?" repeated Mr. Rowwells. She had stunned him, and she liked that.

"I would be well chaperoned," explained Harriett, lest Mr. Rowwells think she was a guttersnipe like Miss Lockwood.

"Capital idea!" he said. "I will encourage your guardian. And of course, Miss Ada would accompany you. You have a great mind, Miss Harriett."

What was wrong with God, to let a girl be born with brains instead of beauty?

"I'm sure you are well acquainted with the classics," said Mr. Rowwells. "Perhaps you could instruct me."

"Why, Mr. Rowwells, I would love to share my favorite books with you," she said, and she almost meant it; she almost wanted to sit with him and discuss books, which were safe, instead of love, which was not. Harriett blushed, imagining what Strat and Miss Lockwood would talk of.

"The color in your cheeks becomes you," Mr. Rowwells complimented. "The color of the roses by the fountain."

Oh, how she wanted to look becoming.

They walked to the far edge of the garden where no gaslights illuminated the darkness. "The moon is rising over the ocean, Harriett. It's shining in your hair."

"It is?" said Harriett eagerly.

*　　*　　*

On the back stairs, Bridget was forced to step over and over on the bloodstains where Matthew had died. She could hardly put her foot there. Miss Ada had slapped her for showing tears in front of the guests. She had a handprint on her cheek now.

I must think of nothing but service, Bridget told herself, nothing but doing my work, finishing the tasks, not looking where I put my shoe.

But the cook had news.

"What?" gasped Bridget. "Already? Matthew's not cold yet, and Mr. Stratton's told the family to leave?"

"It's true," said the cook, who'd been crying, like all the staff.

Mr. Stratton had to know that Matthew's wife had nowhere to go. And no money to pay for it.

"What a wicked man," said Bridget. "They're all wicked. Mr. Walkley is wicked."

"He try to yank you into his room?" said the cook knowingly.

"I spit on him," said Bridget.

"You should have laughed and slipped off with a smile. He'll get you for it."

Bridget had been sick with fear imagining herself out on the street. But if she had five babies, what would she do? She must think about them, not herself. "Young Mr. Stratton isn't cruel," said Bridget. "I'll tell him about Matthew's family. He won't let them be put out."

"Glued to that girl, he is. Can't hear a word being

said. Poor Miss Harriett. She's about to die herself. The only one in this family who could help is Miss Devonny. She has spunk."

Bridget went upstairs to refill the punch bowl. Beautifully gowned women and handsomely dressed men flirted and schemed and danced. Nobody saw Bridget because servants were invisible. The problem of Matthew had been made invisible, and soon the problem of Matthew's family would be made invisible.

Jeb, marry me, prayed Bridget. Mother of God, tell Jeb to marry me and take me away from these awful people.

The man with the greatest temper also had the greatest bulk. Mr. Stratton senior had spent much of his fifty years consuming fine food and wine. He was so angry he could hardly see his son. "Stop prancing around with that girl, Strat. You know quite well, young man, what is expected of you."

"Father, please. She's a wonderful person, she—"

"The personality, or lack of it, in your little tramp doesn't matter. You march back in there and spend the evening with Harriett."

Strat could not ignore Miss Lockwood. He had told her he would take care of her and he had meant it. He had never meant anything more. It terrified Strat to talk back to his father. How did Devonny do it so easily? "She isn't a tramp, Father."

Hiram Stratton's flat eyes drilled into his son's.

"Oh? Who are her parents? Where did she come from? Why is she unchaperoned?"

Strat never considered mentioning another century to his father. He'd been beaten several times in childhood and had no desire to repeat the experience. Young men headed to Yale and expecting to control enormous fortunes could not run around babbling that they were in love with creatures from the next century. Forget whipping; he might find himself in an asylum chained to a wall.

"Father, she was down on the beach. I realize I shouldn't have befriended a stranger. But I was drawn to her. She's a wonderful, interesting, beautiful—"

His father gestured irritably. "Maids like Bridget exist for a man's entertainment, Strat. No doubt that's what your Miss Lockwood is, somebody's maid sneaking around our beach on her day off. But a man enjoys himself quietly. He certainly does not offend a wealthy young woman who hopes to marry him."

Strat could not think.

Thinking, actually, did not interest him in the slightest right now. His thoughts were so physical he was shocked by them. He could never have expressed them to his father. He did not know how he was going to express them to Miss Lockwood. And there was no way he could make a detour and put Harriett Ranleigh first.

The lines in his father's face grew deeper and harsher, as if his father were turning into a monster before his eyes. "Here are your instructions," said his father in a very soft, very controlled voice. He leaned down, beard first, thrusting gray and black wire into Strat's face. "Wipe that dream off your face and out of your heart. You go out there now, and ask Harriett to dance, and spend the remainder of this evening dancing with her and be sure that the two of you have made plans for tomorrow before you say good night. And your good night to Harriett Ranleigh is to be affectionate and meaningful. Do you understand me?"

If he did not hold on to Miss Lockwood, she would fall back through. Like Cinderella, she would vanish at midnight, but she would leave no glass slipper, and he could never find her again. "Father," he began.

His father spoke so softly it was like hearing from God. "You will obey me."

I can't! I love her too much. I would give up anything for her.

"Answer me," said his father.

"Sir," said Hiram Stratton, Jr., bowing slightly to his father, and escaping from the library, without adding either a yes or a no.

The walls of the ballroom were lined not only with splintered mirrors, but with old women. Terrifying old. Annie did not think people got that old in 1995; or perhaps they got that old, but continued to look young. These women looked like a coven of witches: women with sagging cheeks, ditch-deep wrinkles, thin graying hair and angry eyes.

They were the chaperons.

Each was an escort to a beautiful young girl, and jealousy radiated from their unlovely bodies.

The one who chaperoned Harriett had locked eyes with Annie. Behind her missing teeth and folded lips, the old woman was gleeful with knowledge Annie did not possess.

The sexes were separated and stylized like drawings come to life. Yet in spite of how formal these people were, in spite of their manners and mannerisms, the room reeked emotion, swirling beneath feet and through hearts.

Strat led her through another dance, and she followed, and the room felt as thick as her brain. Thick velvet, thick damask, thick scent of flowers, thick fringe dripping from every drape.

Strat himself seemed desperate, engulfed in some drama of his own, hiding it with manners. Slowly, he danced her out the glass doors and onto the veranda. Far off, where the village must be, not a single light twinkled.

No electricity, thought Annie, waking from the trance of the ballroom.

Strat had enough electricity for two. His eyes stroked her as his hands could not. "Let's walk down the holly lane," he said. "We have to talk about—"

"Capital idea," said Walk, suddenly appearing next to them, his smile as sly and gleeful as the chaperon's. "Midnight! And a stroll. James! Miss Van Vleet! Miss Stratton! Richard! Strat here wants a midnight ramble under the stars."

"How delightful!" cried Miss Van Vleet.

"Might I take your arm?" offered James to Miss Van Vleet.

"Where is Harriett?" said Walk. His eyes were hot and full of meaning when he looked at Strat. "We mustn't go without Harriett."

Strat flinched.

"Miss Ranleigh is in the library with Mr. Rowwells," said Aunt Ada. Her face was wrinkled like linen waiting for the iron. "Do go without her. She won't mind at all."

The young people paired up. Nobody walked alone. It was unthinkable that a girl should be without a boy's arm. How sweet they looked in the soft yellowy gaslight, like a sepia photograph on a relative's wall.

Walker Walkley took Devonny's arm after all. His smile, like the crone's, seemed to have more knowledge than a smile should.

He's sly, thought Annie. I don't trust him.

The weird enclosure of the stays kept her posture extremely vertical. Since she couldn't bend at the waist, it was necessary to hang onto Strat when the party descended the steep hill.

Perhaps I'm in both places at one time, thought Annie. Perhaps my 1995 self is turning off the television and getting ready for bed.

The topic was whether young ladies should be educated.

"I am going to college," said Devonny.

"Nonsense," said Walk. "Too much knowledge is

not good for the health. A woman's place is in the home, obedient to her husband or father. You wouldn't let Devonny go, would you, Strat?"

Strat seemed to reach the topic from afar. Eventually he said, "I believe they're quite strict at a female college. Chapel every day, of course. Chaperons. Harriett has also talked about it. She yearns to learn more."

"Harriett has learned too much already," said James grumpily.

Miss Van Vleet mentioned the newly formed Red Cross. She expressed a shy interest in helping the downtrodden.

"Oh, Gertrude!" cried Devonny, forgetting education. "That's so wonderful, I would love to do that! I am so impressed. I would—"

"No," said Strat sharply. "Neither Father nor I would permit such a thing."

How astonishing that Strat thought it was his business. Even more astonishing that pretty Miss Van Vleet was actually Gertrude. These people did not know how to pick names.

The gentlemen discussed how much control brothers should exert over their sisters.

Should her brother, Tod, ever dream of taking charge of Annie, he would end up in the emergency room, she decided. And then, less proudly, realized that Sean controlled her as fully as the Stratton men controlled Devonny. And I let him, she thought.

The others romped on ahead.

She was blessedly alone with Strat.

How dark it was. The moon was a delicate crescent, the way everything here seemed so delicate, so polite.

Strat was like a perfect toy. A birthday gift. How delightful that Time had given him to her!

She flung her arms around this wonderful boy, and Strat became real: the whole thing became real; he was not a toy, but a frantic young man who simply adored her.

Strat stopped himself from kissing her and stepped back. "We cannot," he said, all self-control. "People would say things, Miss Lockwood. I cannot allow them to say things about you."

The way he said that pronoun, you, took Annie Lockwood over the edge. When she had fallen through time, she had felt a roaring in her ears, but now the roaring was within. Heart and mind collapsed. The falling, this time, was into love.

If she had had a fainting couch, she would have used it, and pulled Strat down on top of her. "Who cares about people's opinions?" She began laughing with the joy of it. "I love you, Strat."

He touched her cheeks with shy fingers. Then he took her hand, the glove between them delicate cottony lace that was barely there, and yet completely there.

I, too, thought Annie, am barely here. Don't let midnight come! Don't let this be a magic spell that ends. *I love him.* Love is for always. Please.

Strat, who wore no canary cage, was having as much trouble finding enough oxygen as Annie. They gasped alternately, like conversation.

"I care about their opinions," said Strat finally. "And I care about you. There are rules. You must obey the rules."

Strat's rules made him keep walking to join the rest of the party; it would damage Annie's reputation, perhaps, to be alone with him in the night even for a minute.

"Do you have a choice?" said Strat suddenly. "Coming and going? If you have to return, and return quickly, can you choose to? How did it come, the time traveling? Please tell me about yourself." His voice ached like a lover's. He needed details.

"Oh, Strat, I have a wonderful family but they're not doing very well right now. My father loves somebody else and I don't know what to do."

Strat nodded. "My father nearly always loves somebody else, and his wives never know what to do either. Then he tells them they're being divorced and that settles that."

"Will you be that kind of husband?"

He shook his head. He mumbled things, words of love and marriage, rules and promises.

He wants to marry me, thought Annie Lockwood, dumbfounded. I am actually standing with a man who is thinking of marriage. To me.

For Strat, a promise was made of steel, and a rule of iron. How beautiful. He had virtue. He followed the rules in order to be right. To be righteous. Men and rules. If Daddy had obeyed the rules, if he had restricted himself the way these people do, my family would be all right.

The clippy-cloppy of horses' hooves and the metallic clunking of high thin-spoked wheels interrupted the night.

"It's the police cab!" shouted Walk joyfully, running back toward the Mansion. He whopped Strat on the back as he loped past. Some things didn't change over the century. Boys showed their friendship by hitting each other. Annie was never going to understand that one. "They think Matthew was pushed, you know. Utter tripe, of course, that sort of thing would never happen here, but some immigrant with a hot temper might have done it. They're letting anybody into the country now."

Strat said they couldn't go back if the police were there, they had the ladies to think of.

If he knew the cop shows I watch on TV, thought Annie, what would he think? I who probably know a thousand times more about violence than he does.

"The ladies, thank you," said Devonny, "are just as interested, and this lady happens to be the one who telephoned the police. So there."

"You used the telephone?" said her brother, equally impressed and furious. "You spoke to the police? Did you have Father's permission?"

"Of course not. He wasn't interested. He said it was an unfortunate accident and even if it *wasn't* an unfortunate accident it was *going* to be an unfortunate accident."

Annie grinned, liking Devonny, thinking what friends they could be.

"What are we talking about?" demanded Miss Van Vleet. "Who is Matthew? Why was it not an unfortunate accident?"

"Matthew," said Devonny, "is a servant. His little girls get my old dresses. Matthew died on the stairs. I felt, from the force and violence of the wounds to his skull, and the fact that there was blood above the body, that it was not caused by gravity. Matthew was murdered."

"Oooooh!" said Miss Van Vleet, thrilled. "I'm sure you've been reading too many novels, Devonny. But let's hurry."

They hurried, while Strat and Annie hurried a little less, and were momentarily in their own dark world again.

"I love you, Miss Lockwood."

"Annie," she corrected him.

"Annie," he repeated softly, the intimacy of that name a privilege to him. "I'll take care of you, Annie. I won't let anybody hurt you. I won't let anything happen. I promise."

He kissed her cheek. It was not the kiss of a brother or friend. It was definitely not the kiss of movies or backseats. It was not conversation, and yet it stated such intent, such purpose.

If anything had ever been "sealed with a kiss," it

was this moment between this boy and this girl on that lane by the sea.

I won't be going back, thought Annie.

I'm here.

And I'm his.

CHAPTER 7

He had disobeyed. Sons had been disinherited for less. How was he going to make up to Harriett for this, and still have Miss Lockwood, and not get in trouble with his father?

Anna Sophia danced her way up the Great Hill. Strat had told her not to worry, everything would be all right, and she had believed him. If I can get her by Father and Ada, thought Strat, then in the morning . . . In the morning, what?

No solutions came to mind.

When the young people reached the porte cochere, the police cabriolet still there, tired horses quiet and motionless, the police themselves were not in evidence. Mr. Hiram Stratton, Sr., was not about to allow his houseguests to be concerned with a nasty and trivial affair. The police had been sent to the basement and kitchens, which, after all, were Matthew's domain. And

Hiram Stratton, Sr., thank the dear Lord, was also in the basement, telling the police what to do and when to do it.

Strat's stepmother fluttered and dipped in front of him like a chicken losing feathers. Her corsage drooped and her hair was falling out of its pins.

"Hullo, Florinda," said Strat. "Which room have you given to Miss Lockwood?"

Florinda swooped and worried. "Which room?" she repeated nervously.

"The French Room, of course," said Devonny, glaring at her brother. "Come, Miss Lockwood. I'll show you the way. Florinda, you needn't think about it again."

Florinda was relieved. So were Devonny and Strat, because Father wouldn't know. "Until morning, anyway," Devonny muttered to her brother.

"Did Father tell you what my orders were?" whispered Strat.

"Of course not. But I live here, Strat. I know what your orders were, and I agree with them. You should have escorted Harriett. But I don't want Miss Lockwood sleeping on the sand, so I'll put her in the French Room, and in any event, I expect when I confess that mine was the unidentified female voice telephoning the police, Father will be too angry with me to remember you. It'll pass by as long as you send Miss Lockwood home in the morning."

Things always look better in the morning. Father can't do anything to or about Anna Sophia now. I don't have to worry till morning.

101

He wanted a good night kiss, the kind lovers give each other behind closed doors, but he was in the Great Hall, and Walker Walkley was watching, and Florinda was fluttering, and James was curious, so Strat merely smiled in a detached way and Devonny whisked Miss Lockwood up the great stairs.

Miss Lockwood's fingers grazed the bulging eyes of the walnut gargoyles, and Strat shivered, for his father could just as easily graze her life, and change it. For the worse.

The second floor was dark and wondrous. Chandeliers of yellow gaslight illuminated walls papered in gold. Niches were filled with feather bouquets and stuffed birds and marble statuettes. The pretty little maid reappeared. Her apron was stained now, the starch out of it. Bridget looked exhausted.

"Miss Lockwood," said Devonny crisply, "will need the loan of my nightclothes. She will use the French Room. You may retire when Miss Lockwood and I are abed. And you are not again to wear a soiled uniform in my presence, Bridget."

"Yes, miss. I'm sorry, miss." Her voice sounded as whipped as her body looked. Bridget escorted Annie into a huge and utterly fabulous bedroom, fit for a princess. Bridget shut the door neatly behind them and matter of factly began to undress Annie.

The clothing Harriet had loaned her was not one-person clothing. You could not undo fifty tiny buttons down your back. You could not untie your own laces.

You could not lift your gown over your head by yourself. It was like a wedding gown; you needed bridesmaids to deal with the very dress.

Bridget now lowered a nightgown over Annie, soft ivory with tucks and ruches and pleats. It was fit for a trousseau, but then, so was everything Annie had seen.

The private bathroom was surprisingly similar to her own at home, but immensely larger, with fixtures of gold. The tub could have held an entire family. The marble sink did have hot water, and the toilet, bless its heart, flushed.

Bridget brushed Annie's hair over and over: a massage of the scalp and the soul. Everybody should be pampered like this, thought Annie. Of course, nobody will do it for Bridget, and that's where it all breaks down, but I might as well enjoy it anyway.

Every stroke of the brush moved her closer and closer to sleep. Bridget tucked her in as if she were two instead of sixteen. The bed was so thickly soft she expected to suffocate when she reached bottom. What if I fall back home again while I'm asleep? she thought dimly. What if I don't wake up at the Mansion, but a century later?

What if—

But sleep claimed her, and she knew nothing of the night at all.

She did not hear the police leave.

She did not hear Bridget staggering up to the attic after an eighteen-hour day.

And nobody heard Harriett weep, for she smothered her tears in her pillow.

Devonny had a morning gown sent to her room. Annie loved that. You had your evening gowns, so of course you had to have your morning gowns. Why hadn't she ever had a morning gown before?

Her morning gown was simply cut, waist higher and sleeves less puffy. She coaxed Bridget not to lace her up so tightly. Breathing was good and Victorian women did not do enough of it. Florinda did practically none at all, which was doubtless why she kept fainting.

Breakfast was quite wonderful.

This, thought Annie, is the way to live. Everyone should have a screened veranda high on a hill, with views of the ocean and a lovely soft breeze. Everyone should have servants too. You snap your fingers and they bring anything you want. I approve of this world.

It seemed odd to have no radio: no morning talk show, no traffic report, no news of the world.

There was a newspaper, but only for the men. The gentlemen had chosen to have breakfast indoors, in the formal dining room. Annie caught a glimpse of them, but they had not bothered to catch a glimpse of her. Women had their moments of importance, but not now.

How little Strat resembled his father—thank goodness. His father was corpulent, big rolls of him sagging beneath his great black jacket and white pleated shirt, with a mustache that crawled into his mouth and eyebrows that crawled on his forehead. Annie tried to imagine the pretty little cloud wisp that was Florinda actually choosing to marry this gross man. How very badly Florinda must have needed the shelter and money that Hiram Stratton provided.

Miss Van Vleet, Mr. Innings, Mr. Walkley, Florinda and Genevieve were not up yet. The four of them, Harriett, Devonny, Strat and Annie, were dining together as if they always did.

Harriett was having coffee and a single waffle. She had poured maple syrup on her waffle. Annie was absolutely sure the coffee was Maxwell House. She had not expected them to have brand names a hundred years ago.

Strat was having coffee and waffles and bacon and potatoes and biscuits, which seemed like enough.

Devonny was having oatmeal.

Annie had asked for cereal, meaning Rice Krispies or Cheerios, and had received the sturdiest oatmeal in America. Devonny had added brown sugar and raisins and milk to hers, but even when Annie copied her, it was pretty revolting.

Bridget was right there. She looked thinner this morning, and very tired. Annie felt guilty because Bridget was working so hard while Annie was doing absolutely nothing to help, a situation Annie's mother would not have tolerated for one split second, but a houseguest named Anna Sophia Lockwood of course did nothing.

"Would you prefer something other than oatmeal, Miss Lockwood?"

"May I have a piece of toast?" Nobody was having

toast, and perhaps they hadn't gone around singeing their bread in 1895.

But Bridget vanished, down into the bottom of the Mansion where the kitchen was, and came back quickly with thick-cut toast slathered with butter, and adorable little jars of jam to choose from.

Annie was happy. What would they do today? She could hardly wait. She and Strat were communicating by eyelash, by chin tilt and by coffee cup. She memorized him across the table. All this and love too. She could not believe her luck.

Strat kissed the air lightly when nobody else was looking and she kissed back, but her timing was off. Harriett had been looking.

Harriett poked her waffle with her silver fork and seemed to come to a decision.

"I have some news," said Harriett. "I should like to convey this while just the four of us are dining." She took a deep and shaky breath. "Mr. Rowwells proposed marriage to me last night."

Harriett's heart hurt.

It was as if she had laced her stays inside her chest, crushing her very own heart. Please jump up, Strat. Please cry, *No, No, No!* Tell me you love me and you don't want me to do this.

For Harriett did not want to do it.

Mr. Rowwells had turned out to be twelve years older than she. Harriett was unsure of the mechanics of marriage, and would like very much to know how children were produced, but nobody seemed to know that if they weren't married, and if they were married, they seemed determined to keep it a secret.

Whatever it was, you did it in the same bed.

Harriett was pretty sure you did not wear all of your clothing.

She did not want to imagine Mr. Rowwells without all of his clothing. She certainly did not want to imagine herself without all of her clothing while Mr. Rowwells was standing there.

Bridget hurried in with more hot coffee. This was usually Matthew's job. Harriett was terribly sorry for the little babies who had lost their father and chastised herself. She should be thinking of charitable things to do for the widow instead of whimpering because Hiram Stratton, Jr., had a fickle heart.

Harriett had always hoped that her friendship with Strat, their history together, their easy comfort with each other, would override the beauty of houseguests who came and went.

Well, she'd been wrong.

Strat cared only for looks, and he was sitting here throwing kisses to Miss Lockwood as if she, Harriett, did not exist.

She had existed for Mr. Rowwells.

Mr. Rowwells, when they sat together in the library, did not want to hear about books, or college, or education, or even about the games and activities planned for summer.

He wanted to marry her. Now. He was deeply deeply charmed by her, he said. She was perfection.

Harriett tried not to remember that she was also wealth. Immense wealth. Which her husband, when she had one, would control.

But without a husband, was anything worth the bother? You had to be married. And she had been asked, and might not be asked again.

Strat was stunned. Mr. Rowwells! Marry Harriett? It was indecent. Strat had assumed that Aunt Ada had assigned Mr. Rowwells to be kind to Harriett last night. A proposal of marriage went beyond kindness.

He tried to read Harriett's expression. Was she in love with Mr. Rowwells? Did she want this to occur?

Everybody had thought he would eventually marry Harriett. It had sort of been there, expected and ordinary. Not marry Harriett? It was terrible and lonely to think that he would not always have her in his life.

And yet—not marry Harriett? It meant he could think about other girls. About Anna Sophia Lockwood. *Annie.* Strat's heart nearly flew out of his chest.

He was swamped by the scent and touch of her: her hair and lips, her hands and throat. He was possessed by a physical misery he had never dreamed of. It was not joyous to be in love, it was aching and desperate.

I'll ache when Father finds out, he thought. After he whips me for not getting hold of Harriett's money, he'll send me to a factory to work fourteen hours a day. He'll tell people I'm learning the business. He won't mention that he won't be giving me the business after all.

Strat tried to think, but like last night, thinking was a difficult activity.

Suppose he offered Harriett a counter proposal. Suppose he cried out: *No, No, No, No*, Harriet, you and I are destined for each other, I love you dearly, I cannot let you go to another! He would be making his father happy. He might or might not be making Harriett happy.

But he definitely would not be making himself happy.

He knew what his father would say about happiness. It had nothing to do with anything. Money and promises were what counted, and Harriett had the first and Strat should have given the second.

He had to collect himself, behave properly. He could not ignore Harriett to look longingly back at Annie, nor rip Annie's clothing off, which was the utterly indecent thought that kept coming into his mind and which he kept having to tromp down.

He floundered, wanting to do the right thing for Harriett, of whom he was very fond, and the right thing for himself, but it was too quick. Harriett had shown poor manners in springing this. People needed to be prepared, and she should have had Aunt Ada tell them privately so they could think of the proper things to say.

Should he offer congratulations? But who could be happy about the prospect of a life with Mr. Rowwells? Besides, the event that was going to happen along with

Harriett's marriage to Mr. Rowwells was his own execution.

Devonny said, "That's disgusting, Harriett. He's disgusting. He's old and disgusting."

They all giggled hysterically, but Harriett's giggles turned to tears and she excused herself, holding her big white linen napkin to her face, and ran back into the house and up the great stairs to her room.

"Strat, you pitiful excuse for a man," said his sister. "You should have told her you love her and you don't want her to marry Mr. Rowwells. What if she says *yes?* Then where will you be?"

Strat knew where he would be.

With Annie.

Surely, love this strong was meant to be. Surely no parent would stand in the way. Surely even Strat's father would understand that this was not ordinary, his love for Miss Lockwood, and it was providence that Mr. Rowwells had stepped in to take care of Harriett.

Oh, the brutal necessity of marriage. Poor poor Harriett! Poor Florinda. Poor those other three wives. Poor Ada, who'd had no marriage. And maybe, just maybe, poor Miss Bartten, who wanted it so badly she was willing to destroy a marriage to get her own.

And me, thought Annie Lockwood, straddling time. What am I destroying? Will I end up with a marriage? All I wanted was a summer romance.

She did not want to think about any of this. For none of this was love and romance: it was power. I have the most power, she thought. It makes me the father, the man in the story.

She refused to have heavy thoughts. It was a perfect morning with a perfect boy. She studied the perfect embroidery on the glossily starched linen napkins.

A servant approached uneasily. "Sir?" he said to Strat.

Annie loved how they called each other Sir and Mister and Miss.

Strat raised his eyebrows.

"The police are here once more, sir, and wish to converse with the young people about last night. Matthew's unfortunate accident, sir."

Prickliness settled over Annie, as if in her own time she had read about this, and knew the ending, and the ending was terrible and wrong. She forgot the melodrama of Harriett's flight.

Was I sent here to change the ending? But if that's the case, I should remember more clearly, I should know what to do next.

She was afraid of Time now, and what it could do and where it could take you, and the lies it could tell. It was time to face something. Police. Death. Murder. Stairs. Time.

Strat escorted them into the library, Devonny on one arm and Annie on the other.

The library was Victorian decorating at its darkest and most frightening. The high ceilings were crossed by blackly carved beams. The walls were covered with books, the sort whose leather bindings match. The books sagged and were dusty and the room stank of

111

cigars and pipes. Dried flowers dropped little gray leaves beneath them. Drapes obliterated the windows, and huge paintings with gold frames as swollen as disease hung too high to see. Carpets were piled on carpets, and the pillars that divided the shelves were carved with mouths: open jaws, the jaws of monsters and trolls.

Mr. Stratton's immense bulk was tightly wrapped in yet another dark suit, with vest and jacket and silk scarf. Mr. Rowwells was his likeness: younger, not so corpulent, but creepily similar. The hag chaperon stood in a corner, as if made for corners.

She was the one Annie most didn't want to think about. Aunt Ada was wreckage, and yet also power.

The police were apologetic and unsure. Next to Mr. Rowwells and Mr. Stratton, they were thin and pale and badly dressed. Mr. Stratton had done everything in his power to intimidate them, and he had done well, but he had not entirely succeeded. They had returned.

Mr. Rowwells tamped his pipe. A faint scent of apples and autumn came from the tobacco. His face was overweight: drooping jowls and heavy hanging eyelids. How could Harriett want to get near him, let alone get married?

I'm playing games, thought Annie, but this is Harriett's life.

She tried to figure out how much of this was a game, and how much was real. Swiftly and sickeningly, it went all too real.

"That's her!" Mr. Rowwells jabbed a thick fat finger

at Annie. His fleshy lips pulled back from his teeth and his nicotine-stained fingers spread to grab her. The heavy lids peeled back from bulging eyes. "She's the one who pushed Matthew!" he shouted. "I saw her!" His eyes were like the stair gargoyles, bloodstained.

The room tilted and fell beneath Annie's feet.

Elegantly costumed people rotated like dressed mannequins, and the faces locked eyes on her.

What do they see? Do they see the witch that Bridget saw? Will they hang me? How do I explain traveling through time?

"Get her!" shouted Mr. Rowwells.

They advanced like a lynch mob.

Her own long skirt was eager to trip her. It grabbed her ankles so they didn't have to. She seized the cloth in her hands and whipped around to race out of the library, but Strat hung onto her. She ripped herself free of him. *I wasn't sent to make things right, I was sent to take the blame. I fell through time in order to be punished for a murder I didn't commit.*

Annie flew through the Great Hall, slipping on the black and white squares. Her frenzy was carrying her faster than theirs, or perhaps they did not dream that a lady could conduct herself like this. They were shouting, but not running. Strat was close behind but she made it out the door.

She took a desperate look toward the village, to see if 1995 lay there, with its bridges and turnpikes and cars.

It didn't.

Being outside won't save me, she thought. Only

113

time will save me. But I don't know how I got here, so I don't know how to go back.

She ran.

Strat ran after her.

"Annie! Miss Lockwood! Stop!"

She ducked through an opening in the stone walls surrounding the garden. If she remembered it right from childhood picnics, there should be a path to the stables.

Strat caught up. He wrapped both arms around her, like a prison.

But it was not simply a path to the stables. It was a path through time. She had been running the right way.

She could hear the noise of Strat's century, the cries of the household, the whinny of a horse, but she could also hear her own. Radios and the honk of a horn and the grinding of combustion engines.

Although it had never happened to her before, and possibly never happened to anyone else before, she knew that one step forward and she would be gone.

Strat's embrace softened. He too wore morning dress, as if for a senior prom: black suit, white shirt, the cut of his trousers and the fall of his hair from his century and not hers. Oh, how she adored him!

I love him. How could I have thought he was a toy? He's so wonderfully real. I'm the one who isn't real!

"I love you," said Strat.

Words half formed and were half there, just as she was now half formed and half there. *I want to stay,* she tried to tell him, *I love you, but I don't want to be hung for somebody's murder! Last night, Strat, you even asked if I could get out if I had to. I have to, Strat.*

She tried to kiss him, but she possessed no muscles. She was on both sides of time, and on neither.

"Please," whispered Strat. "Choose me."

Was that true? Was it her choice? Had she chosen to travel? Or had it been chosen for her?

I will always choose you! she cried.

But choice was not hers after all. He was going, or she was going, whichever way time spun.

The tunnel of time swallowed her.

"It wasn't you he was pointing at!" yelled Strat. His words blew from his mouth like wind. "It was the maid! It was Bridget! Just a fight between servants!"

I love you, Strat, she cried, but there was no sound, for she wasn't there anymore.

Strat threw all her names after her, as if one would surely catch and hold. "Stay, Annie! Anna Sophia! Miss Lockwood!"

A nightmare of history flew through her head and shot past her eyes.

Strat cried out once more, but she could not quite hear him, and the sound turned into quarreling seagulls and there she was, on a bright and beautiful morning, alone on the shabby grounds of a teetering old building soon to be torn down.

CHAPTER 8

Bodies surrounded Bridget, each tightly cased in heavy waistcoats or rigid corsets. Each chest filled with air and fury and took up more space and pressed harder against her. Beyond the flesh and cloth, the jaws of leering gargoyles gaped back. The bodies closed in on her like a living noose. She clung to her apron as if it could protect her life the way it protected her dress. "No," sobbed Bridget. "I never. It isn't true! May Jesus, Mary and Joseph—"

"Don't start with your Catholic noises, miss," said Mr. Stratton senior. He loomed over her, his great girth in its satiny waistcoat brushing against her white apron.

Bridget's head pounded. She could not even begin to think about Miss Lockwood and young Mr. Stratton racing out of the house like hound dogs. "But, sir, Mr. Rowwells is not telling the truth. He could not have seen me push Matthew. I did no such thing! Why would I ever?"

"Ah, but I think you would, Bridget," said Walker Walkley, with his fine mouth and sweet eyes. He had not joined the living noose, but stood like a portrait of himself, casually displayed against the scarlet leather bindings of a long row of books. "When you followed me into my room last night, Bridget, and tried to force your affections upon me, and when I, a gentleman, refused you, did you not spit upon me? Did you not threaten me? Did you not say that if you had a chance, *you would shove me down the stairs like Matthew*?"

Everybody in the room gasped, a chorus of horror.

"I spit on you," said Bridget, "because *you*—"

"A threat, I may point out," said Walker Walkley smoothly, talking now to the police, so that nobody listened to the end of Bridget's sentence, "only hours after Matthew was found dead on the stairs."

Aunt Ada smiled inside her toothless mouth. Her lips folded down like pillowcases. "Wicked, shameless, lying creature," said Ada. "You killed Matthew!" Ada stepped away from Bridget. As if it were a dance step— perhaps the dance to a hanging—all the ladies and gentlemen stepped back. "To think, Hiram," said Ada, "that after she killed Matthew, she attended to Miss Devonny!"

"I trusted my daughter in her sleep to a murderer," said Hiram Stratton. He turned to the police. "Thank you for coming. I was incorrect to try to dissuade you from your duty. I am most grateful for your persistence. Had you not returned for more questions, I

117

should never have realized what kind of person I was harboring on my staff."

An officer on each side of her gripped her arms above the elbow, tightly, as if she were some sort of animal about to be branded.

"Miss Devonny," whispered Bridget. "Please. You know I didn't." Had not Bridget waited on Miss Devonny all these months? Brushed her hair, tended her in her bath, told her stories of Ireland, listened to Devonny's stories of stepmothers?

But Miss Devonny did not answer. In fact, she turned her face from Bridget's, believing that what she did not see, she need not think about. Devonny would take the word of a gentleman before she ever considered the word of a serving girl.

I have no friends, thought Bridget. And Jeb . . . will he come to the aid of an Irish Catholic accused of murder?

"Take her away," said Mr. Stratton to the police.

"No!" shrieked Bridget. "Miss Devonny! You know I wouldn't do any such thing! Don't let them say things like this about me! It was Mr. Walkley who tried to yank my dress right off!"

"It just goes to show," said Mr. Stratton, mildly, for Bridget was no longer of consequence, "that no immigrant can be trusted. We shouldn't have accepted that Statue of Liberty, with that sentimental poem about taking in the huddled masses. They're nothing but murderers carrying disease."

Walker Walkley put his arms around Devonny,

118

turning her head gently against his chest, to protect her from the sight.

"Thank goodness my fiancée is not here," said Mr. Rowwells. "I demand that there be no discussion of this in front of Miss Harriett. She is too delicate to be apprised of the fact that the very maid who attended her is a murderess."

The police removed Bridget as they might remove a roadblock; she was a thing. No one in the library thought of her again. The question now was far greater than Bridget or Matthew. The question now was money. Harriett's money.

"Fiancée?" said Mr. Stratton dangerously. "What are you talking about, Rowwells? Where is my son? Ada, pry him away from that crazy girl and get him in here. You are not, Mr. Rowwells, affianced to Harriett Ranleigh."

Mortar had fallen from the stone pillar that once supported the porte cochere. Rotted shingles had peeled away and paint was long gone from the trim. Every window was boarded and a thick chain sealed the great doors.

The air felt empty, as if Annie were alone in the world. Sounds were faint, as if they had happened earlier, and were only echoes.

She shivered in the damp crawling shade of the Mansion. In the turnaround lay hamburger wrappers, soda cans and an old bent beach chair, its vinyl straps torn and flapping. Annie's century at its ugliest.

How could a thing so vivid have been only in her mind, nothing but electrical charges gone wild? Could Strat have been just a twitch of her eyelid in sleep?

No, she thought, he was Strat, my Strat, and I have lost him. Forever. If it is 1995, then he is dead. To me and to the world.

She fell kneeling onto the grass and the one syllable of his name seemed to tear out of her throat with enough force to cross time. *Strat!*

Perhaps the syllable did, but Annie didn't.

And love. Love couldn't cross time either. Love was gone. Only loss remained.

She sobbed, but tears have never changed history.

Annie Lockwood got on her bike.

It had not gone a hundred years with her. Nothing had gone a hundred years with her. Because she hadn't gone a hundred years. Of course it had been a dream; what else could time travel be but a dream?

She felt thick and heavy and stupid.

It was hard to sit on the bike, hard to find the pedals. At the top of the steep drive, she waited for the horses, but of course there was neither horse nor carriage. Against the old stone walls, leaves were mounded in rotting piles, for the gardeners who had swept were long gone.

She tightened her hands on the brakes and went slowly down the Great Hill. No golf course at the bottom, but picnic grounds: a hundred wooden tables spread unevenly over high meadowy grass.

Annie pushed her feet down alternately. It seemed like a very foreign skill, one that she had seen, but never done herself. The same, but oh, so different road she and Strat had followed. When? A hundred years ago? Hours ago? Or not at all?

She rode away from the silence and death of the old Mansion, into the racket and life of the public beach.

Hundreds—perhaps thousands—of people were enjoying the Stratton estate on this hot and sunny day in June. Bathing suits and Bermuda shorts, beach towels and suntan lotion, Cokes and bologna sandwiches. Lifeguards and tennis courts and hot dog concessions. Station wagons and BMWs and Jeeps and convertibles.

Her ears were filled by rushing noise, waterfalls in her head, as if she had swum too long underwater.

Where did time go, when you traveled down it?

Was it today or tomorrow? Should she ask? *Excuse me, is this the day school ended, or the day after? I need to know if time went on without me or just sat here waiting for me to get back.*

Annie Lockwood pedaled on, as exhausted as if she had traveled a hundred years.

"And did you," said Mr. Stratton, "plight your troth to Mr. Rowwells?"

How yellow he seemed, his teeth tobacco-stained and his face jaundiced. His beard bristled at Harriett, and the tips of his huge mustache sagged into the words he spat at her. He was her guardian, the one who protected her from life, but it was not Harriett's welfare he cared about; it was his.

121

Harriett could not bear to look at Mr. Rowwells, who was less heavy and hairy only because he was younger than Mr. Stratton, and hadn't had time to acquire as much belly and beard. But he would, and Harriett would be his wife while he did it. Mr. Rowwells' ugly bristly face would brush up against·hers and she could never turn away.

She had said yes when he asked for her hand, and had let her hand rest in his, sealing the agreement.

A short word. An easy word.

A dangerous, complete word. *Yes.*

No! shrieked Harriett's heart. No, no, no, no, no, no, no! I cannot marry this man. I cannot do with him whatever it is that married people do.

But she had said that word, that little word yes, and it was a promise, and promises could not be broken. Oh, if she actually stood in the aisle in front of the altar and said, "No," the rector at the Episcopal church would not force her to go through with the ceremony. But the shame and the scandal would be worse than the marriage.

Nobody would associate with her. She would have no friends.

She tried to imagine being friends with Mr. Rowwells the way she was friends with Strat. Oh, Strat, Strat, I love you so! Where did Miss Lockwood come from and why did you fall in love with her?

Mr. Stratton moved closer. She felt burned by the smoking anger of her guardian. His waistcoat slithered against the silk jacket lining, and the chain of his pocket watch bounced against the rolls of his flesh. I will be chained by marriage, thought Harriett, just as Bridget is now chained in jail. Perhaps they are the same thing: jail and marriage to someone you don't like.

"Did you," said Mr. Stratton once more, his fury darkening the room, "accept the marriage proposal of Clarence Rowwells?"

I could lie, thought Harriett. I could say I listened to Mr. Rowwells' proposal and didn't respond. But I did respond. I said yes.

I am a lady, and ladies give their word, and never break it.

"I said yes," said Harriet. Something in her died, seeing her future. College? What was that? She would never know. What about the lovely wedding Devonny had planned? What about the laughing honeymoon?

Mr. Stratton's fist slammed down with the force of a steam piston. He did not hit her. He hit the back of the leather chair, and then he hit it a second time, and a third. His cigar-thick fingers stayed in a yellow fist that he swung toward Aunt Ada. "Where were you when this was taking place?" he hissed, his boiler steam building to explosion. "Why do you think I have housed you all these years? For my entertainment, Ada?"

Ada did not flinch. Mr. Rowwells did not tremble. They seemed almost a pair, and Harriett suddenly knew that not only would she be married to Mr. Rowwells, she would never be free of Ada; they would jointly own her.

"I was attempting to corral young Mr. Stratton,"

said Ada venomously. "He went flying after his little tramp, Hiram." Ada did not, as she usually did, put a hand up to hide her toothless condition. Her smile was hideous and wet. "Like father, like son, Hiram. Young Mr. Stratton thinks only of the flesh of beautiful girls."

I am not beautiful, thought Harriett. All my life I will look into mirrors and see a plain woman. I don't love Strat any less. I'm not even mad at him. I am the fool who said yes. I could have said no, and I didn't, because at the moment I thought any marriage was better than no marriage.

I love everything about Strat. I will always love everything about him. "You may place no blame on Strat," said Harriett quietly. "I am a woman of twenty who knows her own mind. I did consent to the proposal of marriage from Mr. Rowwells."

There could be no more argument.

She could never retrieve those words.

Even if Strat were to forget Miss Lockwood, and repent of his ways, and want Harriett back, it could never happen now.

For Harriett Ranleigh had given her word.

Bridget stood very still in the middle of the cell. Perhaps if she did not move, not ever again in this life, the filth and horror would not touch her. The cell was in a windowless cellar, and even though it was noon, no light entered the hole into which she had been shoved.

The scrabbling noises were rats. When she was too

tired to stand she would have to lie down among them.

She thought of the little room she shared with two kitchen maids, the thin mattress on the iron cot, the freshly ironed heavy white sheets, cotton blankets, and breeze off the ocean. She thought of the breakfast she had not yet had, for the family must be served first. She thought of the money wrapped in a handkerchief and saved so carefully for her future.

Bridget was not romantic. She knew better. Life was harsh, and she'd been foolish to think that would change. Jeb would be humiliated that he'd ever been seen in her presence. He'd believe the stories about her because they were told by gentlemen. Would Mr. Walkley and Mr. Rowwells lie?

No, and how did they make fortunes? Being kind? No. By putting people like me in places like this.

I will not cry, Bridget said to herself.

But she cried, and it was not over Jeb, or the lost hopes for her life, or even the rats, but because Miss Devonny had not said a word in her defense.

"Well, Walker Walkley," she said to the rats, "you are a rat if there ever was one. You seized your chance for revenge. And now I surely would shove you down the stairs if I could ever get you to the top of one. As for Miss Devonny, she'll probably marry you. And if that's the case, she'll get what she deserves. A rat."

So much traffic!
Everybody who owned a car had decided to circle

the old Stratton roads, make sure the ocean was still there, get a glimpse of summer to come.

Annie biked on the shoulder to avoid being hit. Just because they were sight-seeing did not mean anybody drove slowly or carefully. The road wound around two huge horse chestnut trees on which kids had been carving initials for generations. From this distance, the Mansion had kept its aura. The towers still glistened in the sun. The great veranda, with its views of shore and beach, still looked down on her.

She was blinded by tears, a rush of emotion so strong she could not believe it came from dreams on the sand. Oh, Strat! You were real, I know you were! I loved you, I know I did!

A horn blared so hard and close that Annie all but rode her bike right into a battered, rusted-out old van, every window open, dripping with the faces of teenagers she didn't know. They were laughing and pointing at her, their fingers too sharp and their mouths too wide. "Nice dress!" they yelled sarcastically. "Where's the party? What's your problem, girl?"

She was wearing the morning gown. A simple dress by the standards of Harriett and Devonny, but in 1995—!

She jerked the bike off the road and down a dirt footpath into the holly gardens, where green-spiked walls hid her. The van honked several more times but moved on without pursuing her. People didn't like to get out of their cars, even at the beach.

Long rows of tiny hand-sewn pleats. Long bands of

delicate gauzy lace. Beneath them, the ribs of her corset.

I was there. It happened. This is the dress that Bridget put me into! This is the—

Bridget!

A century too late, a full hundred years too late, she heard Strat's voice, and understood. It was Bridget that Mr. Rowwells had accused, not Miss Lockwood.

"Oh, no!" she cried out loud, as if the Strattons were there to hear her. "But I know what happened. I have to go back!"

I wasn't listening to Strat. Why don't I ever listen? What's the matter with me? I thought only of myself. I panicked. I was afraid of 1895. Afraid of what they could do to me, without my family, without my own world. I found an opening and I fled.

They will do it to Bridget.

Even the nicest people had spoken cruelly of the Irish. They would believe anything of an Irish maid. Bridget as murderer was easier than the truth, so they would let it stand.

How vividly now Annie remembered the fury with which Matthew's life had been taken; *had* to be taken; for Matthew was the one who could not tell what he had learned.

Annie could not hurry in the ridiculous morning gown. She peeled it off and stood in the underdress. Annie was still overdressed for the beach, though Harriett and Devonny would have fainted before appearing in public in an undergarment.

Her bookbag was still strapped to the bike. She

wadded up the morning gown, shoved it in with the gum wrappers and broken pencils and extra nickels, and leaped back on. "I'm coming, Bridget!" she yelled.

But how will I do it? What wand or witch took me through when I fell? What magic stone or cry of the heart? Where exactly was I standing, and what exactly was I thinking and touching?

I got in, she said to herself, and I came out, so I can go back. I have to.

But it was no magic stone or glass that appeared in front of Annie.

It was a police car, very 1995, its driver very angry, and its purpose very clear.

They had finished the short subject of where Miss Lockwood had gone. Harriett and Devonny were unwilling to accept Strat's idea that she had gone to another century.

The young people were back on the veranda, as if nothing had happened. As if no lives had been changed. Mr. Rowwells had cornered Mr. Stratton in his library, and forced a discussion of Harriett's property. Without her present, of course. Any hope that Mr. Rowwells was actually fond of her was gone.

Harriett secured her morning hat to her hair with her favorite hat pin, which was six inches long with a pearl tip. She need not worry that Strat would see she was close to tears. Strat was close to tears himself.

For a while, nothing was heard but the stirring of coffee.

When Aunt Ada joined them, it seemed unlikely that the subject of century changes would come up again.

Besides, Devonny was more interested in Matthew and Bridget than in broken hearts. "Do you really think Bridget approached Walk like that?" said Devonny. "Bridget was shy with Jeb. She wanted to be a lady. She was always copying my behavior."

"Do not contradict Mr. Walkley's statement," said Aunt Ada sharply. "He has explained what Bridget did and that is that. Where are your manners?"

"I'm worried about Bridget," said Devonny. "What will happen to her?"

"There are prisons for women," said Aunt Ada. "I expect she'll be locked up forever. Or hanged. It's better to hang them. Otherwise they have to be fed for decades."

"I should have spoken up," said Devonny, knotting her skirt between her fingers. Aunt Ada yanked Devonny's fingers up and glared at her for fidgeting. "I should have insisted on more proof," said Devonny.

"Mind your posture," snapped Ada, smartly whacking the center of Devonny's back.

Devonny straightened. I hate you, she thought, and I like Bridget. I've heard rumors about Walker Walkley. He's supposed to be very loose and free with the maids in his household. If Bridget came to his room and offered herself, would he say no?

Devonny wondered what it meant, for a girl to offer herself. What exactly did they do next? Was it something she wanted to know? Yes. Desperately.

I believe, Devonny said to herself, that Walker Walkley knows, and likes it, and he would laugh and say yes.

So Walk is lying that Bridget tried to force herself on him. It was probably the other way around. Therefore Walker is also lying that she threatened him.

And if I don't believe that Bridget accosted Walk, I also don't believe Bridget accosted Matthew. And I still don't know to whom Matthew was bringing the sherry.

Devonny was angry with herself for thinking too slowly. Why had she not brought this up when Bridget and the police were there? Why must she think things out hours later, possibly too many hours later to fix the situation?

But even if I don't believe Walk, she remembered, there is Mr. Rowwells. He saw Bridget push Matthew. *He* wouldn't lie. You couldn't have *two* gentlemen lying!

Devonny thought of Harriett marrying Mr. Rowwells instead of Strat. It was disgusting. Devonny didn't even want to be in the wedding party now. How would they have a good time? What difference would the world's loveliest dress make, if you were marrying Clarence Rowwells? As for Strat, mooning over some creature he claimed lived in another world—he was worthless!

Why had Miss Lockwood run away? When that finger had pointed, why had she thought it pointed at her?

But Mr. Rowwells could not have confused Miss Lockwood, who would have been bare-legged and hatless at the time of Matthew's murder, with Bridget in her big white starched apron.

"She says people have orange juice every morning," Strat offered.

Devonny got oranges in her Christmas stockings, because they were so unusual and special. "Strat," said his sister, "unless you want my coffee in your face, tell the truth."

"That's what she said."

"Nobody cares what she said," Devonny told him. "We care where she went, and where *you* were back when we needed you in the library, and who she is, anyhow."

"I was looking for her," he said miserably. "I looked everywhere."

When he'd caught her, hidden in the shade of dancing trees, she'd turned with strange, slowed-down gestures, as if she had miles to go. Her hair had been piled so enticingly, her eyes so large and warm, her pretty lips half open.

And then, he'd lost sight of her. She wavered, becoming a reflection of herself. She literally slipped between his fingers. He was holding her gown, and then he wasn't. He'd had a strand of her hair, and then he didn't.

And then nothing of her had been present.

Just Strat and the soft morning air.

When he stopped shouting, he tried whispering, as if her vanishing were a secret, and he could pull her out. "Annie! Anna Sophia! Miss Lockwood." And then, louder, achingly, "Annie! Annie!"

She had not come. She was not there.

The lump in his throat persisted. Perhaps he was getting diphtheria. He would rather have a fatal disease than a fatal love. At least people would be on his side. If he died of not having Miss Lockwood, his family would simply be scornful.

He tried to laugh at himself, in love with a person who did not exist, but nothing was funny. His chest ached along with his throat, and his eyes blistered.

He looked up and saw his sister's disgust and Harriett's sorrow. Her eyes too were blistered with pain. Strat wanted to hold Harriett's hands, tell her he was sorry that he had failed her, that he was worthless, that he—

But Mr. Rowwells arrived, and claimed his property, and Harriett Ranleigh rose obediently in the presence of her future husband and left.

CHAPTER 9

Policemen a hundred years ago had come in a high black carriage, worn no weapons, been nervous and unsure. The officer who got out of this gray Crown Victoria with its whirling blue lights was a man in charge. He was middle-aged, overweight and very angry. "Annie Lockwood?" he said grimly.

She didn't need to ask if time had gone on without her. It definitely had.

"Just where have you been, young lady? There has been a search organized for you since late last night."

"Please," said Annie, trying desperately to span her two centuries and her two problems. "I can't talk to you now. I have to get back to—well, you see, a hundred years ago—"

He popped the trunk and stuck her bike in with his rescue kit and blanket. "The beach closed last night at ten o'clock. We combed the sand, we searched the breakwaters. We had the Mansion opened up, we walked through every room, including the most dangerous, to see if you'd fallen through a floor. We've questioned each and every car to enter Stratton Point this morning, in case they were here yesterday and saw something."

Annie swallowed.

"How much cop time do you think you wasted, young lady?"

"I'm sorry."

"How much sleep do you think your mom or dad got last night?"

She began to cry.

"Your mother brought your school pictures for us to show around. But we were right. You just went off, without letting anybody know where or why, the way stupid thoughtless teenagers do." He opened the front door roughly, as if he would like to treat her that roughly, but he didn't, and Annie got in.

"So you were here all the time," he said. "Ignored the sirens? Ignored everybody calling your name? Ignored the flashlights and the searchers? Would you like to know what I think of kids like you?"

She knew already. And he was right. Kids like that were worthless.

Her mind framed answers she didn't dare say aloud: I wasn't worthless! I fell through time. I really wasn't here. I didn't hide from you. I didn't mean for you to waste all those cop hours.

At the very same moment that a search party had been flashing its beams into the dark and moldering

134

corners of an unoccupied ballroom, she had been dancing with Strat on its beautifully polished floor.

"Who was with you?" said the cop. "Is he still here?"

He was right about the pronoun: it had certainly been a boy. But explain Strat? When even Annie did not know whether he was still here? Or always here? Or never here?

And what about Bridget? Time went on. The policeman had just made that clear. So time was also going on a hundred years ago, and whatever was happening to Bridget was happening now.

"I'm sorry," she said, trying not to sob out loud. "I'm sorry you had to waste time. I guess I—um—fell asleep on the sand."

Like he believed that.

He not only took her home, he held her arm going up to the front door, as if she were a prisoner. She was afraid of him, and yet she was only going home. What was Bridget feeling, who might be hung? Did they have fair trials back then? Who would speak for Bridget?

"Where have you been?" screamed her father, jerking her into the house. He was shaking. He tried to thank the policeman, but he was so collapsed with exhaustion and relief and fury that he couldn't pull it off.

"We've called every friend you ever had looking for you!" shrieked her mother. She was trembling.

"I'm sorry," said Annie lamely. Around her were the television and stereo, stacks of tapes for the VCR, ice maker clunking out cubes, dishwasher whining, her brother, Tod, sipping a Coke, wearing a rock star T-shirt . . . How was Annie supposed to tell where she had been?

I changed centuries, I witnessed a murder, I fell in love. Right.

"You better have a good excuse for this," said her mother, voice raw.

"There is no excuse good enough for this," said her father.

Annie shivered in the white undergown and her mother's eyes suddenly focused on its hand-sewn pleats and lace. Mom knew Annie's wardrobe, knew the dress she'd set out in yesterday morning, knew that not only did Annie not own a dress like this, but nobody anywhere owned a dress like this.

But her mother did not comment on the dress.

"I just fell asleep on the sand," said Annie finally. "I'm sorry. I'm so sorry. It was so hot out, and I was exhausted from the end of school, and I went down to the far end of the beach where all the rocks are and you can't swim, and nobody even picnics, so I could be alone, and I fell asleep. I'm really really sorry. I just didn't wake up. It's been a very stressful year and I guess I slept it off."

The cop shook his head, then shook hands with her father and left.

"I'm so sorry," Annie said once more. And she *was* sorry; sorry they'd been scared, sorry she wasn't still with Strat, sorry she couldn't save Bridget, sorry, sorry, sorry.

She burst into tears, Mom burst into tears, and

they hugged each other. Mom was going to accept this excuse. Perhaps Mom had had so much practice accepting Dad's thin excuses that thin was good now; she was used to thin. Even when Mom's fingernails, bitten and broken from the shock of a lost daughter, touched the work-of-art gown, Mom asked no questions.

Dad, however, was too much of an expert at thin excuses. He recognized thin when he saw it.

Tod, of course, being her brother, knew perfectly well she was lying like a rug. These, in fact, were the words he mouthed from behind Mom and Dad. *Lying like a rug,* he shaped.

"I feel like thrashing you," yelled her father, circling the furniture to prevent himself from doing just that. "Putting us through last night. Scaring your mother and me like this."

"I'm sorry," she said again.

"You are grounded! No boyfriend, no beach, no bike, no car, no nothing. You'll have a great summer, the way you've started off."

If there was one thing Annie hadn't been, it was "grounded." She'd been airborne. Century-borne. Time-borne.

And now she was stuck in a conversation they might repeat forever, Dad shrieking, Annie being sorry.

"Let it go, David," said Mom finally. "She's fine. Nothing really happened. Let's not ruin the weekend."

It isn't so much that she accepts thin excuses, thought Annie. Mom just plain doesn't want to know the truth. Because what if the truth is ugly? Or immoral? Mom prefers ignorance.

"I want to know what really happened," said Dad fiercely. He brushed his wife aside as if she were clothes in a closet.

It was that brush that did it for Annie. That physical sweep of the arm, getting rid of the annoying female opinion. She could see a whole long century of men brushing their wives aside.

Annie had never thought of telling her father off. She and Tod, without ever talking about it, had known that they would maintain silence, even between themselves, on the subject of Dad and Miss Bartten.

But the flight between centuries upset her master plan. The loss of Strat and the failure to save Bridget loosened her defenses. A year of pretending exploded in the Lockwoods' faces.

Annie said from between gritted teeth, "You do, huh? You want to tell Mom what really happens when *you're* not where you're supposed to be? You want to tell Mom about Miss Bartten? You want to tell Mom who's with *you* when *you* fall asleep on the sand?"

Her father's face drained of color. He ceased to breathe.

Her brother Tod froze, cake halfway to his mouth.

Annie was holding her breath, too, from rage and fright.

But somebody was breathing, loud, rasping, desperate breathing.

Mom.

Mom, who had never wanted to know, never

wanted to acknowledge what was happening to her life—Mom knew now.

For better or for worse, in her wisdom, or in her total lack of wisdom, Annie had made her see.

Fat white pillars stood beneath a sky-blue ceiling. Trellises supported morning glories bluer than the sky. The remaining houseguests strolled the grounds, eager for a most difficult weekend to close. The boys could not put together a ball game, there were too few of them, and they were worried about Strat. His father had once, at immense cost to himself, shut down a railroad spur forever rather than have union workers tell him what to do. What would Mr. Stratton do to his son?

Strat had disobeyed, and hardly even knew it. Mind and body clouded by his missing Anna Sophia, he was wandering around the estate stroking things and muttering to himself. Strat was saying even now that he wished he'd thought to bring out the camera. "I have a new tripod," he said miserably. "I should have taken her photograph." He frowned a little. "Do you suppose she would have photographed? Would her picture have come out?"

"Strat!" yelled Devonny. "She was there! She was real! She wore Harriett's clothes, Bridget brushed her hair, she ate her toast, she existed! Of course she would photograph!"

Strat sighed hugely.

"She's here somewhere," said Devonny. "She can't

get off the estate without going by the gatehouse. Of course, the woods are deep, and perhaps she crept in there, but I refuse to believe she's living off berries. She'll be back, but this time she'll claim to be a desperate orphan."

Harriett wore a hat with heavy veiling, not to ward off the sun but to hide her red eyes and trembling mouth. She slipped away from the topics of murder and missing girls, and walked down the hill and across the golf course to the sand.

Once Harriett had loved collecting sand jewels. Dry starfish and gold shells and sand-washed mermaids' tears.

Behind the veil, real tears washed her face. The mermaids' tears rested soft and warm in her palm, as if tears, like marriage, lasted forever.

"You had to say something, didn't you?" shouted Tod. "You couldn't just wait for it to end by itself, could you? You had to start things!"

"I didn't start anything! Dad started it."

"It was going to work out, Annie," said Tod, "it was going to end, and they would've stayed married."

Tod and Annie spent a hideous afternoon hiding in the hall, trying to overhear Mom and Dad. The word divorce was not used. Tod was hanging on to that. He wanted his family so much he could have killed his sister for starting this, and had to remind himself that a boy who wanted his family intact could not begin by killing his sister.

Mom used few words. She used tissues, and kept walking between window and computer, as if a view or a keyboard would supply answers.

Dad told the truth. He told more of it than even Tod or Annie had dreamed of. But he didn't want a divorce either. He wanted it all. He wanted them both.

What is this? thought Tod. A hundred years ago when men had mistresses? It doesn't work in 1995, Dad. Grow up.

Eventually their mother invited the children to be part of the discussion. Tod said he was fine, thanks, he didn't really—

"Come here," said Mom, her voice as heavy as Stonehenge.

They went there.

"Sit," said Mom, like a dog trainer.

They sat.

"You knew?" she said.

They nodded.

"How long?" she said.

They shrugged.

"A long time then," she said. She looked for another long time at her husband and then she got up and went to her room.

Dad looked mutinously at his daughter, as if he intended to blame her for this, and Annie said, "Dad. Don't even think for one minute about blaming me."

Dad fished in his pocket for his car keys. He would just get into his car and drive away. That was the good thing about 1995: you could always drive away. What would Harriett's life, or Bridget's, be like if either girl could just get in her car and drive away?

I do deserve blame, thought Annie. When in doubt, shut up. That's the rule. I smashed it. Maybe I smashed the whole family.

She saw her two worlds at once, then, like transparencies for an overhead projector lying on top of each other.

She had smashed another family too.

She had smashed Harriett. Damaged Strat. Interfered with lives that had been fine without her.

The convenient knock on the door was Sean, interrupting them.

Dad escaped. "Don't forget you're grounded," he threw over his shoulder. "And you'd better have something nice to say to Sean too. He's been as worried about you as we were."

"Sean? Worried about *me*?" she said in disbelief, and opened the door.

Sean stormed in as if he owned Annie Lockwood. "Well?" he yelled. "You better have one good excuse, ASL. Just where were you last night?"

CHAPTER 10

"What is the matter with you?" bellowed Mr. Stratton. "I said that the topic of Matthew was closed!" How well he resembled the dark and horrid carvings in his own library.

"Bridget did not push Matthew, Hiram," said Florinda. "She was with me in the garden. She was holding my parasol. I am on my way to the village to get her out of that jail."

If the trees had walked over to join the conversation, Hiram Stratton could not have been more amazed. Florinda talking back? To him?

"Oh, Florinda, I'm so glad!" cried Devonny. "I'll go with you. I should have spoken up for her. I knew it at the time, and I failed her in her hour of need."

"No daughter and no wife of mine will approach a jail," said Mr. Stratton. He positioned himself in front of Devonny and Florinda, but they were outdoors, with room to maneuver, and Florinda simply walked around him to the carriage.

"We must," said Florinda. "We have a responsibility to Bridget. I cannot imagine what Mr. Rowwells saw, but it was not Bridget."

"Florinda, you know how confused you become in too much sun. You have the time amiss," said Aunt Ada.

Way down on the beach, Mr. Rowwells caught up to Harriett. It seemed to Devonny that if Harriett ever needed Ada as a chaperon it was now.

"Ada, this is my household," said Florinda. "I do not have the time amiss, and Bridget could not have pushed Matthew."

"Do not contradict me," said Ada.

Hiram Stratton, Sr., stared back and forth between the two women as if learning tennis by watching the ball. What had happened to his neatly ordered household?

"It is you, Ada," said Florinda, "who is daring to contradict me. Whose home is this?"

Devonny was delighted. Florinda might have a use after all. Mean and nasty Ada would be removed, while Florinda would save people, and even take care of Matthew's babies.

Mr. Stratton's anger smoked once more, and Strat tensed. His father had never struck Devonny or Florinda that Strat knew of, but this was striking posture. A blow from such a man could loosen teeth or break a jaw.

144

Strat moved casually between his father and the ladies.

"We wouldn't be faced with anything, Devonny," Mr. Stratton spat out, "except that you interfered where you have no right even to have thoughts."

His father brushed Strat aside, and advanced on Devonny.

"Father, I do have the right to have thoughts," she said nervously. She did not move back.

Florinda removed a hat pin from the veiling of her immense hat, and admired the glitter of the diamond tip. Or perhaps the stabbing quality of the steel.

Both Stratton men were stunned. Was she actually repositioning her hat? Or was she making, so to speak, a veiled threat?

"Young ladies," said Mr. Stratton senior, refusing to focus on the gleaming hat pin, "do not talk back to their fathers."

Strat forced himself to put Miss Lockwood out of his thoughts. He had to end this scene, whatever it was. Folding his arms over his chest, trying to take up more space against the great space his father's chest consumed, he said, "Father, perhaps you and I should be the ones to go to the village and discuss Florinda's evidence with the police."

"Florinda's *evidence*? You have never cared a whit for Florinda's word or opinion until now. And you've been correct. Florinda rarely gets anything right. She didn't get this right either."

"Why are you so eager to have Bridget be responsible?" cried Devonny.

"Because nobody else could be! Do you think one of *us* pushed Matthew?"

Devonny believed Florinda. Which meant Mr. Rowwells had lied, and since Devonny also believed Bridget, so had Walk lied. Why lie? Did they have two different reasons, or one shared reason? "If Florinda is right—"

"Devonny," said her father, pulling his lips back from his teeth like a rabid dog, "go to your room. Florinda, wait for me in my library. The topic of servants is closed."

I'll go into town to collect Bridget, thought Strat. Then what will I do with her? I can't have her around Devonny. Think how Bridget behaved with Walk! I'll have to give her money, I guess, to make up for this, and put her on a train, or—

But Florinda had not moved. "Hiram, I will not have Bridget punished for something she did not do."

The sunny day seemed to condense and darken around them. For a moment Strat thought it was time falling; that Annie would come back in such a darkness; but it was his father's fury that darkened the world.

"And I will not have a wife who disobeys," said Hiram Stratton, Sr. "You may do as you were told, Florinda, or you may prepare yourself not to be my wife."

"What do you mean, where was I? None of your business, Sean!" shouted Annie. Any ladylike behavior

146

she might have picked up in 1895 was quickly discarded. Ladylike meant people ran over you. Forget that. Annie was in the mood to run over others, not to be run over herself.

She would have guessed Sean's reaction and she would have been wrong. Big, tough, old Sean wilted. "I'm sorry, Annie," he said humbly. "I was so worried. You just disappeared. One minute you were there and the next minute you weren't. There was no trace of you." Sean looked at her nervously. "Who were you with?"

Why was everybody so sure she'd been with somebody? If a person chose to vanish, she could do it all by herself. "I fell asleep on the sand," she said sharply. This was beginning to sound quite possible, even reasonable. Annie could almost picture the cozy little sun-drenched beach where it had happened.

"Come on, ASL. Since Friday afternoon? When half the town was looking for you?"

"Half the town did not look for me," she said, trying to distract him.

"The half that knows you went looking," he said. "Your friends. Your family. Your neighbors. The cops. People on the beach who were sick of getting tans. We were afraid you'd fallen through a floor in the Mansion or gone swimming in a riptide. You scared people." Sean kicked the carpet with his huge dirty sneaker toe. "You owe me an explanation."

I am a century changer, she thought. I have visited both sides of time. People think they own time. They have watches and clocks and digital pulses. But they are wrong. *Time owns them.* I am the property of Time, just as Harriett will be the property of her husband.

"Your face changed," said Sean. "Tell me, Annie. Tell me who you were with and what you were doing."

I was with Strat. What if I never see him again, never touch him, never kiss, never have a photograph?

She was swept up by physical remembrance: the set of his chin, the sparkle in his eyes, the antiqueness of his haircut. Oh Strat! her heart cried.

How dare Sean exist when Strat did not? But then, how was Sean supposed to know that he didn't measure up to somebody a hundred years ago?

I failed Time, which brought me through. I didn't do my assignment. How easily Time can punish me! All it has to do is not give me Strat again. What if I pull it off, and change centuries once more, and Time punishes me by sending me to Tutankhamen? Or Marie Antoinette? Or even an empty Stratton Beach before settlement: just me and the seagulls and the piles of oyster shells?

"I'll forgive you," said Sean. "I can get past it."

"Pond scum!" shouted Annie. She looked around for something to throw at him. "Forgive me for what? Get past what? You do not own me, Sean, and wherever I was is none of your business. So there. I'm breaking up with you anyway. It's over. Go home."

I am a mean, bad, rotten person, she thought. How could Sean have any idea what I'm talking about? I'm doing this too roughly, too fast. But I have places to go!

I have to get back, I cannot give Strat up. A minute

ago I thought I had to, but I don't. I can have it all, I'm sure of that. Somehow I can go back, but not upset Mom and Dad. Somehow with or without me around, they'll keep the marriage alive so that when I do get back . . .

I cannot have it all.

If Mom can't have it all—career, family, husband, success, happiness, fidelity—how could I possibly think I could have it all? In two separate centuries yet? I can have one or the other, but I cannot have both.

Sean was trying to argue, but she had lost interest in Sean, exactly as Strat had lost interest in Harriett.

Oh, Harriett! You were kind to me, and loaned me your gowns, and did what you knew Strat wanted you to do, and where did you end up? Alone. Abandoned. And hurt so badly that you accepted a marriage proposal from a man nobody could like.

Life interfered yet again. Heather and Kelly stormed in. They were just as mad at Annie as everybody else. Maybe it was true that half the town had been searching for her.

Heather and Kelly didn't believe a single syllable of the sleeping-on-the-sand nonsense. "You better tell us what really happened," said Heather, "or our friendship is sleeping on the sand, too."

"I was time traveling," said Annie, to see how they reacted. "I fell back a hundred years to find out what the Mansion was really like." A huge lump filled her throat. She could at least have left Harriett and Strat to live happily ever after. But no, Bridget would be hung and Harriett would marry that Rowwells creep.

And if I *could* go back, she thought, I'm so selfish that I'd keep Strat. Harriett would still have to marry her creep.

"Annie, this is when people hire firing squads to do away with a person," explained Kelly. "People who say they were time traveling get executed by their best friends. Sean, get lost. She'll tell us if you're not here."

They were right. Annie would tell everything. Girls did.

The problem, however, thought Annie, is that I can tell you everything, but you cannot possibly believe everything.

"I'll wait in my car," said Sean. "I'll wait fifteen minutes, and then ASL and I are going for a drive."

"Don't make it sound so threatening," said Annie.

"I'll take you to Mickey D's," said Sean. "I'll buy you a hamburger."

Annie was not thrilled. Sean's offer did not compare to the offers made in other centuries.

"And fries," Sean said. "And a vanilla milkshake."

Annie remained unthrilled.

"Okay, okay. You can have a Big Mac."

Romance in my century, she thought, is pitiful. "Fine. Sit in the car," said Annie.

The instant the door shut behind Sean, Kelly said, "I demand to know the boy you were with, and exactly, anatomically, what you were doing all night long."

How shocked Harriett and Devonny would have been. The idea that a lady might have "done" something would be unthinkable. Strat, too, would be appalled. Ladies weren't even supposed to know what "something" was, let alone do it. They'd *really* be shocked if Kelly hadn't used careful polite phrasing just in case Annie's parents were around to overhear.

I did something, thought Annie, starting to cry. I hurt people on both sides of time.

Devonny went into the library with Florinda.

I hate men, she thought. I hate marriage. I hate what happened to Mother and to Florinda and next to Harriett and soon to me. Men ruling.

Suddenly her silly stepmother seemed very precious, the one that Devonny had always wanted to keep. Mean and harsh as Father was, to be without him would be starvation and social suicide for Florinda. "Florinda, was Bridget really with you?"

"Of course she was really with me. Why would I lie?"

"If you aren't lying, Mr. Rowwells is."

"Gentlemen never lie," said Florinda, with a desperate sarcasm.

"Father lies to you all the time and you spend half your life having vapors because of it."

"You mustn't speak that way of your father," said Florinda, with no spirit. No hope.

"Florinda, we must get Bridget out of jail."

"I have been told not to bring up the subject again."

"You must call the police and tell them that Bridget was with you and they will release her."

"I can't use the telephone without permission," said Florinda.

"I did."

"You're a child, you can get away with things. Your father adores you, but he doesn't adore me, I haven't given him a son, in fact his last two wives haven't given him sons either, and he's tired of me and I cannot argue anymore. Devonny, I have nowhere else to go."

Father had to provide for Mama because Strat and I would not have tolerated anything else, thought Devonny. But he doesn't have to provide for Florinda because she produced no children.

Florinda's small elegant hand tucked around Devonny's. They were both crying. "Bridget turned Walk down, Devonny, anybody could see that. Bridget's mistake was not letting him have his way. That's the rule, Devonny. They must have their way."

Why can't we ever have our way? thought Devonny Stratton. Why must Harriett be Mr. Rowwells' property? Why must I be Father's?

She looked at her stepmother, frail and lovely, like a torn butterfly wing, and thought how Father would love an oil portrait of Florinda as she was now: pale and submissive and trembling.

CHAPTER 11

The second week after school ended, fewer teenagers congregated at the beach. Many had started their summer jobs. They were selling ice cream and hamburgers, mowing lawns and repairing gutters, sweating in assembly lines and teaching swimming. They were visiting cousins and going to Disney World and babysitting for neighbors.

Annie's job was at Ice Kreem King, a beach concession that sold soft ice cream treats, candy bars and saltwater taffy. It was sticky work. Nobody wanted a plain vanilla cone. They wanted a sundae with strawberries and walnuts and whipped cream, or a double-decker peanut butter parfait. Annie wore white Bermuda shorts, a white shirt with a little green Ice Kreem King logo and a white baseball cap, backwards. Over this she wore a huge white apron now sloshed with dip: lime, strawberry, cherry, chocolate and banana frosted her front.

It was hard to believe in the lives of Florinda, Devonny and Harriett at a time like this.

It was all too possible to believe in her own life.

Her desperate mother was even more torn between reality and dream than Annie. Mom loved work, even loved her commute to New York, because she read her precious newspapers on the train: *The Wall Street Journal* and *The New York Times*. Mom didn't even buy them now. Her hands shook when she tried to fold the paper the way train readers do to avoid hitting fellow passengers. Her eyes blurred when she tried to read the tiny print of the financial pages. She couldn't concentrate.

It was easy to know what Mom wanted. She wanted her marriage back. She wanted her happiness and safety back.

It was even easier to know what Dad wanted: he wanted it all.

Miss Bartten had gotten very bold, and even phoned him at home.

Tod, who loved the telephone, and maintained friendships across the country with people he didn't care about so he could call long distance at night, would no longer answer the phone. The answering machine was like a crude, loudmouthed servant. Miss Bartten's bright voice kept getting preserved there, demanding Dad call her back.

And he did.

Nobody was taking steps to resolve anything.

They seemed to be hoping Time would do that for them.

For Annie Lockwood, Time achieved a power and dimension that made clocks and calendars silly.

By day, Annie was a servant to the ice cream whims of a vast beachgoing public. Each evening, she and whatever family members were there for dinner ate separately, trying not to touch bodies or thoughts or pain. Annie had no idea how to help her mother and no interest in helping her father. And yet she, too, wanted their marriage back and their love back.

Since she'd broken up with Sean, girls kept asking who would replace him.

In her heart, Annie had Strat, who was no replacement for anybody; he was first and only. Beneath her pillow lay a neatly folded white gown with hand-sewn pleats. She wept into it, soaking it with pointless tears, as if those century-old stitches could telegraph to Strat that she was still here, still in love with him.

She felt at night like a plane flying in the misty clouds: no horizon, no landmarks, no nothing. Oh, Strat, if I had you I would be all right. And what about you? Are you all right? Are there landmarks and horizons for you? Do you remember me?

Devonny was boosted up into the carriage by servants, while Florinda helped lift the skirt of Devonny's traveling gown. Strat and Devonny were being shipped back to New York City. Walk was to go along, so Strat would have normal masculine company and not mope

155

around stroking doorknobs and mirrors as if Miss Lockwood might suddenly pop out.

The first time Father overheard Strat actually calling out loud to a girl he then explained had been missing a hundred years, Father thrashed him. Took his riding boots off and whaled Strat with them. Strat hardly noticed, but returned to the Great Hall, where, he claimed, he had witnessed Anna Sophia's birth. This time Father chose a whip, the one Robert, the coachman, used on the horses, Strat noticed. He didn't call Anna Sophia again. But he looked for her. His eyes would travel strangely, as if trying to peer beyond things, or through them, or into their history.

Father was fearful that Strat was losing his sanity and had even communicated with Mother on the subject. The final decision was in favor of a change of air. Fresh air was an excellent solution to so many health problems.

Most houseguests were long gone, but Harriett would of course remain at the Mansion while Father and Mr. Rowwells continued to work on the marriage arrangements.

Florinda had refused to let go of the topic of Bridget and the parasol. Finally Father had gone down to the police, and Bridget had been set free. How Devonny wanted to see Bridget again! She yearned to apologize for what Bridget had endured, see if Jeb had visited and give Bridget some of her old dresses to make up for it, but of course Father would not have Bridget brought back into the household after her loose behavior with Walk.

Florinda could not persuade Father that Walk might have lied, or been the one who was in the wrong. When girls like Bridget did not cooperate, they must be dismissed. But she had won Bridget's freedom, and that success gave Florinda pride.

Summertime had failed Devonny. It was not the slow warm yellow time she looked forward to. Not the salty soft airy time it had been every other summer. It was full of fear and anger and worry.

Now they were losing their usual months at the beach, losing the Mansion and tennis and golf and sand. They were losing Harriett; and Strat of course had lost Miss Lockwood. Devonny's lips rested on Florinda's cool paper-white skin, skin never ever exposed to sun, and whispered, "Will you be all right?"

They both knew that if Father got rid of her, she would never be all right, and if Father kept her, he might be so rough and mean that she would never be all right either.

Visions of her father's rage kept returning to Devonny. Who else but Father himself could get angry enough to push—

No. Even inside her head, in the deepest, most distant corners of her mind, Devonny could not have such a traitorous thought.

"I will be fine," said Florinda, kissing her back. "Say hello to your dear mother for me, and visit the Statue of Liberty, and send me postcards."

Postcards were the rage. Florinda sent dozens every week. They had had their own postcards made up for the Mansion, its views and ornate buildings. "I'll write," promised Devonny.

Trunks, hatboxes and valises were strapped on top and stacked inside the carriage. It was four miles to the railroad station, where their private railroad car would be waiting for them. Devonny knew where Jeb's family lived. She was hoping that when the carriage went by, she'd see Bridget, leaning on Jeb's strong arm, or sweeping Jeb's porch, and she would know that Bridget was all right.

"Here, sit by me," said Walker Walkley, smiling wonderfully.

It certainly went to show that you could not judge a person by his smile. Devonny said, "Thank you, Walk, but I like to ride facing forward. I'll sit next to Strat." She kissed Florinda one last time, wondering if it really was the last time.

Walk made Strat change sides of the carriage so that he was sitting next to Devonny after all.

Heather and Kelly, part of the not-working group, picked their way past a thousand beach blankets and towels, looking for their own crowd's space on the sand. Nobody actually went into the ocean and got wet. If you wanted to swim, you went to somebody's house with a pool. The beach was for tans and company and most of all for showing off one's physique.

Sean had a spectacular physique. He was showing off most of it. There was not a girl on the beach who

158

could figure out why Annie Lockwood had dumped him. Was she insane?

"Annie's afternoon break is at three," said Kelly. "I'll go get her and she can hang out with us for fifteen minutes."

Sean shrugged as if he didn't care, and then said, "I always thought we'd get married or something." He kicked sand.

"Married?" Heather laughed. "Sean, you two never even went to the movies together!"

"I know, but I sort of figured that's how it would go. ASL can't break up with me." Sean shoveled the sand with his big feet. In moments he had a major ditch.

"What's the trench for?" asked a boy named Cody. "You starting a war here, Sean?"

"He's trying to make peace," said Kelly, hoping Cody would notice her. Kelly had always wanted to go out with Cody.

"Annie Lockwood is only a girl, Sean," Cody said. "She's nothing. Forget her. The beach is full of girls. Just pick one. They're all alike and who cares?"

Cody was not her dream man after all. Kelly crossed the hot sand to get Annie from the concession booth. She wasn't friends with Annie this summer the way she'd expected to be. Annie felt like two different people. As if she'd left some of herself someplace. It was creepy.

* * *

"Do you think Harriett will be all right?" said Devonny.

"She'll be fine," said Strat.

"Do you think Father will still let her go to college?"

"I would hope not," said Walk. "Live by herself in some wicked godless institution? The sooner they wed, the better."

"You're going to college," Devonny pointed out.

"We're men. Young ladies are ruined by such things."

Young ladies are ruined by things like you, thought Devonny. She flounced on the seat and moved the draperies away from the window, staring out at the empty dunes and the shrieking terns.

Strat was overcome with guilt about Harriett. His good friend, and he had abandoned her to a winter marriage. A marriage with no summer in it. No laughter, no warmth, no dancing, no joy. Just money and suitability.

He had caused this and he knew it, but every time he tried to wish it undone, he thought of Miss Lockwood. It was more than thinking of her: it was drowning in her.

The carriage moved slowly around the curving lanes, through the golf course, past the ledge where you could see distant islands, and down again where you could see only the lily pond and the back of the Mansion.

Cherry Lane, he thought. Annie's house was built in the cherry orchard. If I went there, and called her

160

name . . . I could tell Robert to halt the carriage by the cherry orchard. I could run through the grass and the trees calling her name, and maybe . . .

Walk would report to Father, Father would decide Strat had gone insane, and would choose an asylum on a lake where Strat would be strapped to an iron bed and given cold water and brown bread.

He tried to school Annie out of his mind. Tried to carve her memory out of his heart.

But he too moved the draperies aside to stare out the window.

"What do you want to break up for?" said Sean.

That Sean would be shattered was the last thing Annie had expected. She hadn't thought Sean even liked her very much. She certainly hadn't thought his eyes could produce tears. Every time the two of them talked, he'd rub the back of his hand hard against his eyes, which grew redder and wetter. Annie felt nothing.

"You don't even care, do you?" whispered Sean.

Why didn't people take things the way you planned for them to? She wanted to be nice to Sean. She wanted to break up easily. He wasn't cooperating. "I'm sorry, Sean, but we never did much of anything, and the only time you ever spoke to me was to ask me to get you a wrench or something. You never said—" She didn't want to use the word love; the timing was impossible; if she said love, it would give a second-rate high school relationship something it had never had. "You never said you cared much, Sean."

She was afraid she might actually try to define love for Sean: she might actually tell him about Strat.

Sean was dragging out a cotton handkerchief now and mopping up his face. The beach crowd thinned out. People like Cody decided that even swimming was better than seeing a boy crack up in public over a girl. "ASL, we have the whole summer in front of us," said Sean. "I want to spend the summer together."

Doing what? Rebuilding the transmission on your car? "Sean, I'm really, really sorry, but I think it's time for us to break up."

"It isn't time! I love you!"

Wonderful. Now he had to love her. Now when she—

When I what? thought Annie. When I have Strat? I don't have Strat. I don't even know where Strat is, or if he ever was.

She rallied. "And stop calling me ASL. It's dumb and I'm through with it."

"The way you're through with me? You're going to throw me out like a lousy nickname?" Sean muttered on and on, like a toddler who was sure that if he just whined long enough his mother would break down and buy him the sugar cereal with the purple prize.

Summer time is actually a different sort of time, thought Annie. It lasts longer and has more repeats, more sun, and more heat. We'll have these same conversations day after day, stuck in time. Now, when I want to travel in time.

Time did not stand still. Somehow you could go back and possess time gone by, but your own natural time continued.

Summer when her parents would decide what to do with their failing marriage. Summer when their daughter would vanish forever, without a trace? How could she do that to them? It would be pure self-indulgence to dip back into the past century. Dad was self-indulgent. He should have stopped himself.

Annie must stop herself. These were real lives, all around her, both sides of time. Real people were really hurt. If she went back, it would be pure self-indulgence. Exactly the same as Dad going back to Miss Bartten.

I can't go back just because I was pampered and coddled and dressed so beautifully. I can't go back just to find out what happens to them. I can't go back just to see if Florinda is still arranging flowers and Gene-vieve is still asking for a donation and Devonny gets to go to college and Gertrude volunteers for the Red Cross.

I must stop myself and not go back. Look what I did to Harriett's life by entering it. And Bridget. It's been ten days for me, so it's been ten for Bridget.

Clearer than any of them, clearer even than Strat, she saw Aunt Ada: toothless mouth and envelope lips, eyes glittering with secrets. She could actually feel, like velvet or silk, the emotions that had roiled through that elegant ballroom, jealousy and greed filtering through the lace of hope and love.

"Oh, Annie! Pay attention for once! You're so annoying," said Heather. She pointed down the beach, where Sean had joined Cody in the water. "He's better than nothing! What are you going to replace him with?"

"Sean isn't a mug. He didn't fall off the shelf and break, so I don't need to replace him."

But could I go back for love? I love Strat. Strat loves me. Is that a good enough reason to hurt two families? It's good enough for Miss Bartten.

Heather, who didn't have a boyfriend, was very into other girls' boyfriends. "Summertime, and you throw away a handsome popular interesting guy?"

Annie pointed out an unfortunate fact. "Sean is only handsome and popular. He isn't interesting."

"So who were you with all night at the beach?" said Kelly softly, coaxingly.

A odd distant boom sounded. Kettle drums, maybe? The beginning of a symphony? But also like a car crash, miles away.

Hundreds of beachgoers turned, bodies tilted to listen. Cody and Sean and the rest took a single step back to dry sand.

The boom repeated: this time with vibration, as if some giant possessed a boom box loud enough to fibrillate hearts. They felt the boom through the bottoms of their bare feet.

"The Mansion!" yelled Sean, first to figure it out. "They're ahead of schedule! They've started knocking it down." Girls moved to the back of his priorities, the way girls should. "Come on," he yelled. "Let's go watch the demolition."

* * *

Annie Lockwood screamed his name once, the single syllable streaking through the air like the cry of a white tern protecting its nest. *"Strat!"* And then she was running. She fought the sand, which sucked up her flimsy little sneakers, and she made it to the pavement, and ran faster than she had ever run anyplace. Against her white shorts and shirt, her bare legs and arms looked truly gold.

If the Mansion came down . . . if there was nothing left . . . *how would she ever get back?*

"Strat!"

The wrecking ball, a ton of swinging iron, was indifferent to the shrieks of a teenage girl on a distant path. Massive chains attached it to a great crane. It hit the far turret, from which Harriett had once looked out across the sand and watched Strat fall in love. The tower splintered in half but did not fall, and the wrecking ball swung backward, preparing for its next pass.

Annie felt as if it hit her own stomach. *How will I get back if there is nothing left but splinters?*

Blinking lights and sawhorses stood in her path. Signs proclaimed danger. "You can't go no further today," said a burly man in a yellow hard hat. He was chewing tobacco and spitting. "It's dangerous. No souvenirs."

I don't want a souvenir. I want Strat.

She had never wanted anything so much in her life, or dreamed of wanting anything so much. She could have turned herself inside out, peeled herself

165

away from the year, thrown herself like a ton of swinging iron a hundred years away.

"Strat!" she screamed.

Strat ripped open the carriage door and leaped out while the four horses were still clippy-clopping along. Robert, the driver, yanked them to a stop. Strat was yelling incoherently, dancing like a maniac in the middle of the road.

Walker Walkley was pleased. If Strat were to go insane, he, Walk, could not only marry Devonny, but he could become the replacement son. They were barely a few hundred yards from the Mansion. Robert was a solid witness and would testify to young Mr. Stratton's seizure. This was good.

Devonny was frantic. If Strat were to go insane, she, Devonny, would have to protect him. And how was she going to do that, when she had failed to protect either Bridget or Florinda?

Through the open swinging carriage door, Walker Walkley saw it happen. Anna Sophia Lockwood. Transparent. And then translucent. And then solid.

His hair crawled. His spine turned to ice and his tongue tasted like rust. *There are ghosts.*

"Annie!" said Strat, laughing and laughing and laughing. He swung her in a circle, while he kissed her flying hair. "Robert!" he yelled, remembering the trouble he was in. He almost threw Annie into the carriage with Devonny and Walk. "Hurry on, Robert, forget this, you didn't see a thing."

Robert, probably knowing what a large tip he would get, obeyed.

Devonny shrieked, "Strat! She's naked. And she may be a murderer. Don't you put her in here with me. Where did she come from? Where are her clothes?"

"She isn't a murderer, Dev. I don't know who did it, but it wasn't Annie, she wasn't here yet, I saw her coming the last time and I know."

"Saw her coming?" repeated Devonny.

Walk, who had just seen what Strat meant, scrunched into his corner, unwilling to be touched by the flesh of a ghost.

"She did travel over the century?" whispered Devonny.

"Of course," said her brother.

They're all insane, thought Walker. Do I really want to marry Devonny and have that insanity pass to my children?

"Well!" said Devonny, gathering herself together. "She can't sit here with nothing on. Walk, close your eyes. Strat, turn your back. Thank goodness I have a valise in here." Devonny undid the straps of a huge leather satchel and pulled out a gown to cover the girl up.

Walk put his hands over his eyes, but naturally stared through his fingers anyway. Every inch of her was beautiful. All that skin! Husbands didn't see that much of their wives. Nevertheless, Walker did not envy Strat. Nothing would have made him touch a female who came and went by ghost.

Sean of course had taken his car.   •

He wouldn't waste time floundering over sand and grass when he could drive. He saw his girlfriend running and tried to clock her, because she was really moving. She should take up track. When ASL twisted through the woods, he could see her no longer. But he knew the name now. The guy she'd spent the night on the beach with. Scott or Skip or something. Whoever it was, Sean would beat him up. No Skippie or Scottie was fooling around with Sean's girl.

Sean felt great.

He'd show Skippie a thing or two.

His car came around the long curve from which the Mansion was most visible. He saw the wrecking ball hit the square turret and stopped his car in awe. There was nothing like destruction.

And he saw Annie Lockwood.

Her dark hair, half braided, and now half loose, was oddly cloudy. He meant to drive toward her, but he had the odd, and then terrifying, sense that the road was full. He could see nothing on the road. Only he, Sean, occupied that road, *and yet it was full.*

He half dreaded a collision, and yet there was nothing there with which to collide.

He half waited, and half saw Annie slip through time, and had half a story to tell when people demanded answers.

CHAPTER 12

It had been hard to believe when it happened before—
centuries grazing her cheeks and swirling through her
hair. But this time—as if a godmother waved a wand—
time simply shifted. There was no falling, no rush of
years roaring in her ears.

I didn't touch anything magic, thought Annie.
There was nothing to touch. So what does it? Is it true
love? Did he call me back, or did I call him back?

She was wild with joy, and did not want to let go
of him. His lovely neck, his perfect hair, his great
shoulders—but here was Devonny demanding to
know why she was naked. "I'm not naked. I'm wearing
plenty of clothes," she protested. "Shorts and shirt,
clean and white."

"You are disgusting," said Devonny. "But I suppose
murderers are." She pulled out an Empire-style dress
of pale blue, embroidered with darker blue flowers and

white leaves, a dress so decorative Annie felt she had turned into a painting to go over a mantel. It was very tight by Annie's standards, but these people wanted their clothes to be like capsules.

"I'm not a murderer, Devonny," said Annie. I'm so happy to see her! thought Annie. Has it been a hundred years or ten days since we talked last?

Devonny gave the boys permission to look again.

Strat and Annie looked at each other with smiles so wide they couldn't kiss, couldn't pull their lips together long enough to manage kisses. For once Devonny actually met Walk's eyes, and together they squinted with a complete lack of appreciation. Strat should not be in love with a possible murderess, lunatic or century changer.

"Strat and Devonny and I are quite frantic to see the Statue of Liberty, Miss Lockwood," said Walker Walkley, to interrupt this unseemly display, "and are going into the city for a change of air."

Devonny produced a large oval cardboard box, papered, ribboned and tied like a birthday present. From this she drew out a truly hideous straw contraption, with tilted double brims, decorated with wrens in nests that dripped with yellow berries.

"I have not been frantic to see the Statue of Liberty," Strat corrected. "I have been frantic to see Anna Sophia."

Roughly Devonny pinned up Annie's hair, stabbing her head several times, just the way Annie would have if she'd been as irritated with *her* brother's choice of girlfriend. Slanting the grotesque hat on Annie's head,

170

Devonny flourished a pin with a glittering evil point. Annie flinched.

"Don't worry. People hardly ever get killed with hat pins," said Strat, grinning. "It is essential to be in fashion."

"No wonder your courtship has to be so formal," said Annie. "We can't both get under the brim of the hat to kiss. I refuse to wear this." She was sure Strat would hurl the hideous thing out the carriage window, but instead he tied it beneath her chin and secured the veiling that hid her neck, throat and cheeks.

"No way!" cried Annie. Trying to see through the veil was like holding a thin envelope up to the sun to try to read the contents.

But Strat would not let her take the hat and veiling off. "I'm thinking as fast as I can," said Strat, his mood swerving from love to responsibility. "Father is in a terrible mood. Finding you will make things worse, so we won't let him know. You'll come into the city with us, that's how I'll protect you. You'll be a friend of Devonny's. We'll smuggle you into the railroad car, and—"

"She won't be a friend of mine," said Devonny. "She killed Matthew."

"Devonny, will you be quiet?" said her brother. "She did not kill Matthew."

"Then who did?" demanded Devonny. "Bridget was in the garden with Florinda when Matthew was pushed down the stairs. Mr. Rowwells saw some young girl do it, and it wasn't Bridget, so it had to be her."

Behind veils and ribbons and straw and birds' nests, Annie tried to think. But they planned their fashion well, these people who did not want women to think. The heavy gloves, the tightly buttoned dress bodice, the pins and ties and bows—they removed Annie from Strat, removed her from clear thought, made of her a true store-window mannequin. Merely an upright creature on which to hang clothing.

"They'll hang you," said Devonny to Annie, "but at least you'll have clothes on."

"They'll hang me?" For a moment Annie had no working parts. No lungs, no heart, no brain.

Strat flung himself around her. "I won't let them touch you. They have no proof, and I saw you come through, so I know you didn't do it. I will save you, Annie."

"Strat, this isn't a good idea," said Walker Walkley. "Your sister has undoubtedly guessed correctly. Your father forgave you for what happened with Harriett, but he won't forgive you for sheltering a murderess. Put this female out on the road and let the police find her."

The police? thought Annie. If they were that mad at me for wasting their time on a search, how mad will they be if they think I murdered somebody? Would they really hang me? What would I say at my trial? *No, at the time I was a hundred years later.* Not a great defense. *I sort of saw what happened, it was very dark, and the blackness rasped around me, and . . .* Oh, the jury would love it. All the way to the gallows.

Her mouth was terribly dry. She had no corset this

time, but even so, she could not get enough breath. She had thought only of love, not of consequence.

"We need to go into New York on schedule, Strat," said Walk, "and not refer to this again. Your father will lock you up too. You must think clearly. There is a lot at stake here."

"Annie's life and freedom are at stake," said Strat intensely. He moved her forward on the seat, putting his own arm and chest behind her, so he was protecting her back, even in the carriage.

He meant it. Her life and freedom. At stake.

Stake. Did they use stakes in 1895? Did they tie women to poles and burn them? Surely that was two centuries earlier.

Nothing felt real. Not her body, not her hands inside the heavy gloves, not Strat on the other side of the veil.

"Would they really hang me?" whispered Annie.

"I won't let them," said Strat.

Which meant they would . . . if they caught her.

Harriett was wearing a similar hat. By tying the veil completely over her face, claiming fear of sun, she could prevent Mr. Rowwells from touching her skin. It was very hot, yet not a single inch of Harriett's skin was exposed. She wore long sleeves, hat, veil, gloves and buttoned boots.

How could Devonny and Strat leave me here like this!

Tears slid down her face behind the veil.

173

But by accepting a marriage proposal, she had become a different person; property instead of a young girl. Until the agreements were settled, she could not be taking excursions. She must stay here with her guardian and her fiancé.

When Harriett had asked about college, Mr. Stratton simply looked at her. "You made a decision, Harriett, of which you knew I would disapprove. College is not a possibility."

She wanted to throw herself on his mercy, and say she was sorry, and she was afraid of Mr. Rowwells, and she loved Strat, and she would give all her money to the Strattons forever if she could just cancel this engagement, but something in Mr. Stratton's eyes filled Harriett with anger: that this should be her lot in life, to obey.

So she let it go on, when the only way it could go was worse.

"I wanted to do the right thing by you," said Jeb through the bars. "So I came to say good-bye."

"And how is that the right thing?" said Bridget, her temper flaring. She did not come close to him. She was too filthy now, and could not bear for Jeb to see her like this, especially when he was not coming from love, but duty.

"I was wrong to step out with you," said Jeb. She thought perhaps his cheeks colored, saying that, but there was so little light from the lantern the jailer held that she couldn't be sure. "My father and mother are giving me the money to head West. I'm going to try California. I have my train ticket." Jeb forgot he was a man leaving a woman, and said excitedly, "You can go all the way by train now. I'll see buffalo and Indians, Bridget. I'll see prairies and the Rocky Mountains and the Pacific Ocean."

"Yes, and I hope you'll see the devil too," snapped Bridget. She was crying. She wanted to stay strong, but he was leaving her and she did not have a friend in the world who could get her out of this. The other servants had crept by, one by one, bringing better food and trying to bring courage, but they could not bring hope.

After all, Bridget came close to the boy she had loved, overcome by terror and loneliness. "Jeb, please! Go to the Mansion and—"

"Bridget, I'm taking the next train. You attacked Matthew, and there was no reason but your Irish temper, and you have to pay now."

And he was gone.

And with him the jailer, and the lantern, and the last light she ever expected to see before her trial.

Florinda and Harriett circled the garden. Florinda was wearing less protection from the sun than Harriett, but they were both gasping for breath. "I have just learned something dreadful," said Florinda.

Everything was dreadful now, so Harriett did not bother to respond.

"He lied," said Florinda. "Hiram told us he went to the police and explained about Bridget, but Hiram didn't go at all. Bridget is still in jail and nobody in authority knows that she was with me when Matthew was murdered."

Harriett stared at Florinda. "He lied? But why, Florinda? Why would he lie to us?"

"I expect because it's easier. Bridget is just a servant and we are just women."

"I don't want to be *just* a woman!"

"You have money of your own," Florinda pointed out. "You could choose not to marry and never have that cigar-smoking lump touch you."

Harriett did not argue with this insulting description. "I gave my word."

"Yes, well, they break their word all the time, don't they?"

The gentlemen appeared on the veranda.

How frightening they were, in those buttoned waistcoats and high collars, with those black lines running down the fabric, as if attaching them to the earth they owned. Like judges at the end of the world, thought Harriett. If only I could be permitted to judge them instead!

Mr. Stratton actually snapped his fingers to call Florinda. He was having a brandy, and wished her company. Briefly. He just liked to look at her, and then would dismiss her. She was a property, a nice one, but on trial herself now, and might soon be replaced.

Florinda bowed her head and obeyed.

Harriett was getting a terrible headache. Far too much heat trapped in far too much clothing. Far too many terrible thoughts in far too short a time.

For who had the worst temper of anyone on the estate?

Mr. Stratton.

Who struck people who could not strike back?

Mr. Stratton.

Who had lied about rescuing Bridget, and was allowing a young girl to carry the blame for a murder?

Mr. Stratton.

Harriett followed Florinda slowly. Nobody would question her laggard pace. Ladies were expected to be leisurely. Once she went indoors, she would have to remove the hat and veil. It would take all her control to keep a calm face. She could not imagine ever looking at the face of Mr. Stratton again. Like Florinda, she would have to keep her head bowed and her eyes averted. There was no point in begging Mr. Stratton again to help Bridget.

In this heat, in this shock of knowledge, Harriett could see little point in anything.

"Sherry," Mr. Rowwells told the servant. "And what will you have, my dear?"

"Lemonade, please," said Harriett.

Aunt Ada did not join them. Mr. Stratton was as angry at Ada as he was at Strat over this fiasco. Yet Ada did not seem to mind, or to be afraid, in the way that Florinda minded and was afraid.

Ada was far more at risk than even Florinda, though. Ada had nothing, absolutely nothing, not a stick of furniture nor a penny in savings. Yet Ada was calm. Spinsters dependent on unpleasant relatives did not normally experience calm. What did that mean? Was Ada no longer dependent?

"Well, Rowwells," said Mr. Stratton. "Golf this afternoon?"

"I think I need to spend time with my fiancée instead," said Mr. Rowwells. He smiled at Harriet, who managed not to shudder.

He wants to be kind, she said to herself. He wants me to love him. He wants my money, but after all, we must get along as well. I must make an effort. The quicker I allow Mr. Rowwells to accomplish this marriage, the quicker I will get out of the house of a man who shoves servants down stairs instead of just firing them. How could a gentleman care enough about a servant to bother with killing one? What could Matthew have done or said to make Mr. Stratton so angry?

"What might you and I do this afternoon, Harriett?" said the man with whom she would spend her life.

I shall pretend to be Anna Sophia, thought Harriett. I shall pretend to be a beautiful creature with lovely hair and trembling mouth. I shall pretend that it is Strat who loves me, and Strat who holds my hand. I wonder if I can keep up such a pretense for an entire marriage. Perhaps I will die in childbirth and be saved from a long marriage.

"Mr. Rowwells," she said, "on such a day I would love to sit in the tower, and feel the ocean breeze. With you at my side."

Mr. Rowwells was delighted. At last this difficult fiancée was showing some proper affection.

Up the massive central stairs they went, Harriett first. Down the guest wing and up the narrower steps to the next floor. And then up the curving beauty of the tower stairs, like a Renaissance lighthouse, painted with a sky of cherubs, clouds and flowers.

The tower was furnished, of course, because the Mansion had no empty corners, jammed with seats and pillows and knickknacks and objects. A tiny desk on which to take notes about migrating birds or lunar eclipses balanced precariously. No one, in fact, had ever taken notes on anything.

But paper lay on the desk, ink filled the little glass well and a pen lay waiting on the polished surface.

It seemed to Harriett that her entire life lay waiting on a polished surface.

She looked out across the white empty sand where only a few days ago her life had fallen apart, when the boy she loved found another to love.

A private railroad car!

Annie had learned about these in American history, but she didn't know they were still around. Then she remembered that they weren't *still* around; she was back when they *were* around.

It was beyond twentieth-century belief.

Oriental carpet covered floors, walls, window brackets and ceiling. Every shade and flavor of cinnamon and wine and ruby filled the room. Fatly stuffed sofas and chairs were hung with swirling gold fringe.

Brass lights with glittering glass cups arched from the walls.

Wearing a veil indoors was rather like wearing very dark sunglasses. She adjusted the veil, feeling like an Arab woman peering out the slits of her robe.

"Hello, Stephens," said Devonny to a uniformed waiter. Or servant. Or railroad officer. He too dripped gold. "This is Miss Ethel St. John, who will be traveling with us. Miss St. John does not feel well and will use Miss Florinda's stateroom."

Ethel! thought Annie. Where do they dredge up these names? Hiram, Harriett, Clarence, Gertrude and now Ethel! At least it makes Anna Sophia sound pretty.

Strat led her to a bulging crimson sofa strewn with furniture scarves, and sat her down. He unfastened the ribbons that tied her hat beneath her chin and tucked back the veil like a groom finding his bride. "I love you, Annie," he whispered.

Her heart turned over. How physically, how completely, love came, like drowning or falling. He would take care of her, and how wonderful it would be. No cares.

We will go into Manhattan, and I will find out what a town house is, and see New York City a hundred years ago. I will become clever at the piano, and spend time on my correspondence. Devonny and Florinda and I will dress in fashions as beautiful as brides all day long. No more striving to be best, or even just to live through all those tests of school and life in the twentieth century. No more talents to display and polish, no more SATs, no more decisions about college or a major or a future career.

In Strat's world—now hers—this safe, enclosed, velvet world, there was only one decision. Marriage.

Her heart was so large, so aching, she needed to support it in her hands. Or Strat's. "I love you too," she told him. They were engulfed in tears: a glaze of happiness instead of sorrow.

"Why, there's Jeb!" cried Devonny, kneeling on the opposite sofa to see out the windows. "Excuse me, Stephens, I must speak to Jeb. Don't let the train leave yet."

Stephens had to lower special gleaming brass steps so that Devonny could get off. Leaning off the stairs himself, he thrust his hand high to signal the locomotive about the pause. "You look as if you're giving a benediction, Stephens," said Devonny, giggling. "Jeb! Come here! Talk to me!"

A startled Jeb turned from boarding a coach. "Miss Stratton," he said. He flushed and stumbled toward her, dragging a big shabby case held together with thin rope. He could not meet her eyes. "I have to leave, Miss Stratton. You have to understand. People are laughing at me for being such a fool, stepping out with some Irish girl that kills people."

"But Jeb—" said Devonny.

"I just said good-bye to her in the jail, that was the right thing to do, I've done right by her," he said defiantly, as if Devonny might argue, "and now I'm off to California."

"In jail?" repeated Devonny. "Bridget's in jail?"

"Of course she's in jail," said Jeb, thinking that rich women were invariably also stupid women.

"*Right now she's in jail?*" said Devonny.

Stephens said, "Miss Stratton. The train must leave. You must step back into the car. Now."

But Devonny Stratton jumped down onto the platform instead, yanking her voluminous skirt after her. "Strat!" she bellowed, like a farmhand. Jeb on the platform and Stephens in the private car doorway stared at her. "Strat!" shrieked Devonny. "Miss Lockwood! Walk! Get off the train! Now! We cannot leave! We are not going into New York. Father lied. Bridget is still in jail. We must rescue her forthwith!"

Mr. Rowwells set his sherry on the little writing table.

His mustache needed to be trimmed. Its little black hairs curled down over his upper lip and entered his mouth, as if they planned to grow over his teeth. I cannot kiss him, thought Harriett. I don't care if I am going to be a spinster. I don't care how great the scandal is. I shall break off my engagement to him. I will not be capital. I will marry for love or I will not marry.

Far below them spread the world of the Strattons: groomed, manicured, wrapped in blue water. She could see Mr. Stratton getting out of the carriage onto the first green. He never walked when he could ride, not even on the golf course.

Thank goodness for gloves. Harriett felt the need for layers between them.

They talked of Mr. Rowwells' world: groceries and money, new kinds of groceries, and increasing amounts of money. He talked of his hopes for mayonnaise in jars and perhaps pickles and tomato catsup as well. Harriett was not surprised that it would take a tremendous amount of capital to start such an enterprise.

That's what I am. I am only money. And even that is not good enough for Strat.

She could not be angry at Clarence Rowwells. There were limited ways in which to raise capital, and marrying a rich woman was one. He had seen his chance to slip into her favor while Strat was mooning over Miss Lockwood. One hint that he thought her pretty; one hint was all it took.

His big hairy hand removed her hat, feeling her hair and her earlobes and her throat. He nauseated her, and she said, "I wish you to do something for your bride."

"My dear. Anything."

"I wish you to save Bridget."

Mr. Rowwells stared at her. His hand ceased its movements, lying heavy and hot like a punishment.

"You are wrong that nobody cares about an Irish maid," said Harriet. "I care."

His big hairy hand came alive again, stroking her throat. It fingered the little hollow where her cameo lay on its thin gold chain, and she had the horrible thought that he might rip the cameo off her. A queer vibrating emotion seemed to come up from him, like vapor from a swamp. She fought off unreasonable fears.

"You can do it quite easily, Mr. Rowwells," she said, envying him so for being a man. "You know what happened, Mr. Rowwells."

His stare grew cold, like a winter wind. "I know what happened?" he repeated.

Inside her gloves, her hands too grew cold. They seemed to be on two sides of the same words, and she did not know why his side was so cold and frightening. "With Matthew," she said. She gathered her courage to say an insulting thing to her future husband. "Mr. Rowwells, I know why you lied."

He had lied, of course, because Mr. Stratton, the murderer, had told him to. That must have been part of the deal to get a favorable marriage settlement. Mr. Rowwells would accuse Bridget. Nobody would question the word of a gentleman, and nobody would question Mr. Stratton. Mr. Stratton was the murderer, so lying made Mr. Rowwells his accomplice. An unfortunate decision, but not irrevocable.

An extremely odd smile decorated Mr. Rowwells' face, as if painted there, as clouds were painted on the blue ceiling. She was afraid of the smile, afraid of the way he loomed over her. Afraid, even, cf the way he tipped the little glass of sherry past his hairy-rimmed lips.

"Sherry," she whispered. "Sherry! You were the one for whom the tray was carried. Matthew was taking *you* sherry. *You* are—*you* are—"

He was the murderer.

She had betrothed herself to a murderer.

Not Mr. Stratton, after all, but his houseguest, Mr. Rowwells.

Harriett's emotions came back. The sense of defeat vanished and the heat exhaustion dropped away like clothes to the floor.

"Well! That settles that!" She flounced her heavy skirts, each hand lifting the hems, preparing to descend the curling stairs. "You and I will have an excursion this afternoon after all!"

Harriett was filled with relief, and even joy. I don't have to marry him! she realized. What an excuse! Nobody has to marry a murderer!

"We shall go to the police station, Mr. Rowwells," she said triumphantly. I don't have to fantasize about dying in childbirth, I can go to college, and Florinda is right, I need not marry. "You, Mr. Rowwells, will be a gentleman and admit your activities! Whatever Matthew did to annoy you, and however much it was an accident that you struck him so hard, you have a civic duty to discharge. And apologies to make to Bridget! You—"

Mr. Rowwells' heavy hand remained on her throat. The fat, splayed fingers took a different, stronger position. "I think not," he said.

"A gentleman—" said Harriett.

"Do you truly believe that the rules of gentlemanly behavior apply when the gentleman is a killer?"

The sun glittered on the open tower windows. The breeze came warm and salty on her cheeks. The sound of splashing water and the cries of triumph on the golf course reached her ears.

"Harriett, my dear, if I have thrown one down the stairs, why would I pause at throwing another?"

CHAPTER 13

Annie loved that: *forthwith*. It sounded like troops coming to the rescue. Devonny was going to be a wonderful sister-in-law.

"Bridget is still in jail?" said Strat. "But Father said—"

"This is ridiculous," said Walker Walkley, shouldering Stephens out of his way. "Devonny, get back on the train this instant. We are not disrupting our schedules because of a serving girl."

"A serving girl you lied about, Walker Walkley!" yelled Devonny. "Hiram Stratton, Jr.! Get off the train with me!"

A hundred heads popped out a hundred open coach windows as ordinary passengers delighted in the scene.

"I suggest we continue into the city," said Walk, trying to convey this opinion in all directions.

If only we could, thought Strat. Annie will be in danger if I do what Devonny wants, and that is the last thing on earth I want. But we do have to get Bridget out of jail. I cannot let her languish there, nor go on trial, not when I believe Florinda's story. But what if they put Annie in jail instead of Bridget?

He looked desperately back at his century changer. She had taken off the hat and veil. Cascades of dark hair, romantic as silk, fell toward him, and her beautiful mouth trembled, the way a girl's should, needing him.

"Come, Strat," said Walker Walkley. "Get your sister to behave and let's get this train moving. We must not have a scene."

"Walk, did you know Father lied about getting Bridget out of jail?"

"Of course."

"Why didn't you tell me?"

"I thought you knew. All the gentlemen knew."

Strat was beginning to wonder about this word gentlemen. It was supposed to mean good manners, good birth and good upbringing. "You ꞁed too, then," he accused his friend.

"It wasn't really a lie," said Walk irritably. "It was a reasonable action. Your father didn't bother with Florinda's silliness because it meant nothing. Of course Bridget killed Matthew. If Bridget didn't, then who did?" demanded Walk.

"Mr. Rowwells killed him," said Miss Lockwood softly. "He and Ada together. They were both standing there. I was coming through time when the murder

188

happened. It's confused for me. I remember the scent of Mr. Rowwells' pipe: apples and autumn. I remember the rasping of blackness. Silk on silk, I realized later."

"Ada's shawl!" cried Devonny. "It always makes that sneaky sliding sound."

"They struck Matthew down gladly," said Anna Sophia.

"Mr. Stratton," said Stephens, "the train must leave the station. Now. You must sort out your difficulties on the platform, or in the car, sir, but not both."

"Right," said Strat. He lifted Anna Sophia to the ground.

Stephens shrugged, the brass steps were pulled up and the train pulled out of the station. Only Jeb left the village. Robert, who had not even had time to depart from the station, brought the carriage around.

Walker Walkley tried to think this through. Walk did not care for risk; the thing was to make others take the risks. The thing was to stay popular with those who had the power. At school, Strat had had the power; here, Mr. Stratton had it. How was Mr. Stratton going to react to all this coming through time nonsense? Whose side should Walk be on? Would he be better off trying to impress Devonny, Strat or Mr. Stratton? Whose friendship would prove more fruitful?

" 'Gladly,' Anna Sophia? Do you mean that?" Devonny was shocked. "They enjoyed killing him? But why? Why would they want him dead at all, let alone enjoy it?"

"This is utter nonsense," said Walk. "No gentleman would bother that much over a servant. I refuse to

189

believe Mr. Rowwells had anything to do with it. You females are always having the vapors."

"I," said Annie, "have never experienced a vapor in my life. And I never will."

As Annie, this was true: she had never had the vapors. But as Anna Sophia, it was a lie: she *had* had the vapors. When I came back through time, she thought, I should've stopped the carriage right there on the estate and told Strat everything I remembered and trusted him to follow through. But I got vapored, thinking about how I might be hung.

She tried to figure out the rules, if any, of time travel. But all her rules had been broken, even the basics, like gravity. She didn't know whether she could save herself, *and* have both sides of time, *and* keep everybody safe, *and* still end up happily ever after.

"And as for being a gentleman, Walker Walkley," said Devonny, "you lied about Bridget making advances to you. *You* tried to yank *her* clothes off, didn't you, and when she fought you off and escaped, you decided to take revenge, didn't you?"

"She's only a maid," said Walk testily. "Who cares?"

Strat was stunned. He and Walk had both been brought up to believe that honor mattered. Both had memorized that famous poem *I could not love you, dear, so much, loved I not honor more.* And Walk had dispensed with honor? Had lied to hurt an innocent girl? A girl who rightly tried to protect her virtue?

Hiram Stratton, Jr., came out of the trance that had held him in its grip. It was amazing, really, how clouded he'd been by the love and the loss of Anna

Sophia Lockwood. He had not been paying attention for ten days.

"Come," he said. "Devonny. Annie. Get in the carriage. We're going home. We have been thinking of Bridget and Anna Sophia, but first there is Harriett. Harriett is betrothed to a murderer. She might even be alone with him now. He wouldn't hurt her, since he needs her money. We'll extricate Harriett from whatever has been signed and deal with Clarence Rowwells. Father doesn't want Harriett wed to Rowwells. He'll be delighted to prove Rowwells a murderer."

Walk shifted opinions on everything and hurried to open the carriage door for the ladies as Robert mounted to the driver's seat. Now that Strat was talking so firmly, his was a better side to be on.

"You're not coming, Walk," said Strat. "You are no longer welcome in our house."

Walk stared at his friend. "You cannot think more of an Irish maid than of me!"

"I can."

"Strat, I'm your best friend! This will blow over. We'll forget about it."

"I won't forget about it. There has been too much lying. A servant in my house is helpless, and instead of protecting her in her helplessness, we use it against her. And call ourselves gentlemen."

You *are* a gentleman, thought Annie. How she loved him, ready to do the right thing for the right reasons!

"But Strat, I have no money," said Walk desperately. "I have no place to go."

But Strat did not believe him, because Strat did not know worlds without money, could not imagine worlds without money, and assumed Walker Walkley would simply blend into another mansion with another heir and never even miss an evening bath.

Strat got into the carriage with his sister and the girl he loved, and closed the door on the whining desperation of his best friend.

"Good riddance," said Devonny. She yanked the gold cords that closed the drapes, and the sight of Walker Walkley standing in the dust was hidden forever.

But horses are slow, and time, which has such power, went on without them.

"Harriett, my dear," said Clarence Rowwells, "the papers are signed. Your guardian signed them for you. Although you do not have a will, you are affianced to me. In the event of your sad demise, your money will come to me anyway." How he smiled. How his mustache crawled down into his mouth, as if it were growing longer this very minute, and taking root.

"This will actually work better, Harriett. I will have the fortune without the bother of marriage."

Harriett pressed her back against the glass window walls of the tower. "Why? I cannot understand. Why kill Matthew? Why kill me?"

"My dear Miss Ranleigh, I made a fortune in lumber, and I purchased a vast house and a fine yacht, and I lost the rest gambling. I cannot keep up pretenses much longer, especially not in front of a man so keen as Hiram Stratton. Ada and I agreed we would prevent your marriage to young Stratton so that I might have you instead. We, after all, would enjoy your money so much more than young Stratton would. I paid Ada, of course. Ada's task was simply not to chaperon you."

So Harriett had been right, down on the veranda asking for lemonade and wondering about the truth. Ada had become independent. *I could have given her money,* thought Harriett. *I could have paid her a salary. Why did I never think of such a thing?*

Harriett had detested having Ada around all the time, but it had not crossed her mind how much Ada must detest being around Harriett all the time.

Mr. Rowwells was afraid but proud of himself. There was a great deal at stake here; Harriett could see the gambler in him. Everything on one throw. But the throw was her own life.

"Ada and I planned that I would compromise your virtue, if necessary, so you would be forced to wed me. Oh, we had many plans. But none were needed. You poor, plain, bucktoothed, mousy-haired fool, you listened when I told you that the moonlight made you pretty."

Even through her terror, the description hurt. She guessed that he had told Ada she was attractive too, and such is the desire of women to be beautiful that toothless, wrinkled, despairing Ada had warmed to him also.

Tears spilled from Harriett's eyes. *I don't want to be*

plain! I didn't want to live out my life plain, and I don't want to die plain.

"And then Miss Lockwood fell from the sky, as it were. Where did she come from? It was most mysterious, her coming and her going. But so useful. She removed young Stratton from the scene in one evening and you were mine instead." He seemed regretful, all those fine plans for nothing.

"Did you kill Miss Lockwood too?" said Harriett. "Is that how she vanished so completely? Did you or Ada drown her in the pond?"

"You would have liked that, wouldn't you? Jealous, weren't you?" said Mr. Rowwells. "No, I don't know what happened to the beautiful little Lockwood. But I didn't mind that young Stratton went insane over her loss. Any Stratton loss is a gain of mine."

She had begun trembling, and he could certainly see it. Her body, face, mouth, all were shivering. She was ashamed of the extent of her fear. I cannot die a coward, she thought. I must think of a way to fight back.

She tried to stave him off. "But where does Matthew come into it?"

Rowwells shrugged. How massive his shoulders were. How fat, like sausages, were his fingers. The corset, tied so tightly by Ada herself this morning, hardly gave Harriett enough breath to cry out with, let alone hit and fight, and rush down the stairs, and not get caught.

"Prior to Miss Lockwood's arrival, prior to young Stratton's feverish excitement that blinded him to you,

194

Matthew overheard us planning what I would do to you in the carriage. The details would only distress you, and one scrap of me is a gentleman still, so I shall omit the details. Ada, however, felt it would be quite easy to make you believe you had to marry quickly, or else have a child out of wedlock."

She closed her eyes. What rage, what hate Ada must have felt in order to make such plans. Toward *me,* thought Harriett, unable to believe it. But I am a nice person!

"Matthew, unfortunately, was not willing to accept money." Clarence Rowwells was still incredulous. What human being would choose anything other than money? "Matthew," said Mr. Rowwells, as if it still angered him, as if he, Rowwells, had been in the right, "Matthew said he would go straight to Mr. Stratton with the conversation." Mr. Rowwells actually looked to Harriett for understanding. "What could I do?" he said, as if he, a rich, articulate man, had been helpless. "I had to stop Matthew. I chased after him, arguing, offering him more money, and there he was, stalking down the stairs as if *he* were the gentleman!"

Clarence Rowwells was outraged. Matthew had dared to act as if he knew best! "Matthew was taking the tray back to the kitchen," said Mr. Rowwells, "and he would not stop when I instructed him to. I grabbed him and slammed him against the stair tread and that was that." He dusted himself, as if Matthew had been lint on his jacket.

Well, thought Harriett, I know one thing. I would actually rather be dead than be married to Clarence

Rowwells. And I know, too, why Ada feels independent. What could Clarence Rowwells do now except pay her forever? All she need do is stay away from stairwells and towers.

The man's chest was rising and falling as he nervously sucked in air. He does not want to hurt me, she thought. How can I talk him out of this? How can I convince him to let me go? "Nobody will believe there could be two violent deaths in as many weeks," she said. "They will know I could not have fallen by accident."

"This is true," he agreed. His hands, like wood blocks, shifted from her throat to her waist, and placed her solidly on the rosebud carved stool in front of the tiny desk. "It was no accident, though," he said. "Poor Harriett. So in love with young Mr. Stratton, heartsick at finding herself about to wed a man she does not love. A fiancé," he said almost bitterly, "that she does not even like to look at."

So he too had feelings which had been hurt. He too had wanted to be told he was attractive. But that hardly gave him the right to do away with her.

With a giddy sarcasm, he went on. "This sweet young woman chooses to hurl herself off the tower instead. What a wrenching letter she leaves behind! How guilty young Strat feels. How people weep at the funeral." He dipped the pen in the inkwell and handed it to her.

"You cannot make me write!" cried Harriett.

He shrugged. "Then I will pen it myself. I write a

196

fine hand, Miss Ranleigh. Prepare to meet your Maker."

The glass broke.

A thousand shards leaped into the air, like rainbows splintering from the heat of the sun.

CHAPTER 14

The gun smoked.

"Really, I feel quite faint," said Florinda. "Harriett, you must never go unchaperoned. Look at the sort of things that happen. Men try to throw you out of towers." Florinda's lavender silk gown was hardly ruffled, and her hair was still coiled in perfect rolls. Her lace glove was covered with gunpowder. Florinda said, "Mr. Rowwells, I suggest you sit on the window seat before you bleed to death. Harriett, I suggest you descend the stairs. Mind your skirt as you pass me. Use the telephone. You have my permission. Summon the police."

"I miss all the good stuff!" moaned Devonny. "Florinda shoots a murderer and I'm not even here! Life is so unfair."

"I could shoot him again for you," said Florinda. "I didn't hit him in a fatal place the first time."

The young people collapsed laughing. Mr. Stratton did not. Discovering that he was married to a woman who shot people when they got in the way was quite appalling.

"He was about to throw me off the tower," said Harriett. "He thought I knew that he was the murderer. Of course I didn't know. I just thought his lies were because—" she caught herself in time. She didn't want Mr. Stratton to know she had thought *he* was the murderer.

"I," said Florinda, "had thought of nothing else since I realized it could not be Bridget. The only odd thing I could come up with was that Ada never chaperoned Harriett when she was with Mr. Rowwells. What a strange decision on her part. Then I noticed that Ada had new clothes. She hasn't worn them. They are maroon and wine silk instead of black. She was celebrating something. Going somewhere. I decided to sit on the stairs beneath the tower and be Harriett's chaperon. Luckily, Mr. Rowwells wasted time telling Harriett why he killed Matthew. Time enough for me to fly to the gun room and get the pistol."

Annie was awestruck. She herself would have used the telephone, summoning professional rescuers. She would have dialed 911, saying, Please! Come! Help! Save me!

"Call the newspapers!" said Devonny. "We want to brag about Florinda. Nobody else has a stepmother who gets rid of evil fiancés."

"We will not call the papers," said Mr. Stratton. What was the world coming to? His women were behaving like men. He chomped cigars and sipped brandy, but neither helped. "The doctor has removed the bullet and bandaged the arm. Mr. Rowwells will recover."

"What a shame," said Devonny, meaning it. "Florinda, we should take up target practice."

"Why? Who are *you* planning to shoot?" said Florinda.

"Stop this!" shouted Mr. Stratton. "I am beside myself!"

Beside myself, thought Annie. Now that I'm a century changer, I hear more. Is Mr. Stratton really beside himself? Is he a second person now, standing next to the flesh of the real person, but no longer living in it?

It is Ada who is beside herself, she thought. Poor, poor Ada. Living a dark and loveless life, swathed in black thoughts, willing to do anything to rescue herself. And now she has done anything, and life is even worse. She has Bridget's cell; she has inherited the rats and the filth.

She found herself aching for Ada. If time had trapped anybody, it was Ada. What might she have done, with a car and a college degree and a chance?

"We must try to lessen the scandal," said Mr. Stratton severely. "I require that joking about these matters cease."

But his requirements were not of interest to his son, daughter and wife, and after a few more minutes of confusion, he retreated to his library before the next round of giggles began.

Mr. Stratton would never understand females. He had generously had Robert collect Bridget and bring her back to the Mansion. But the maid was at this moment in her attic room packing. Now that he'd given her back her position, what was she doing? Going to Texas! On money Florinda had demanded he give the girl!

Why Texas? Devonny had asked.

Because Jeb's taken California, said the girl.

Whereupon Florinda commanded Hiram to allow Matthew's wife and five children to remain in the stable apartment! Hiram Stratton was very uncomfortable with the way Florinda was making things happen. It wasn't ladylike.

But the vision he would keep forever would be the sight of Ada, spitting, shrieking obscenities, kicking and biting. The lady he had kept in his home to teach Harriett and Devonny how to be ladies was a primitive animal.

I had no money, she kept screaming, what did you think I would do in old age? I had to have money!

In the quiet smoky dark of his library, Mr. Stratton thought that perhaps Harriett and Devonny should go to college after all. Perhaps women—and education—and money—

But it was too difficult a thought to get hold of, so Mr. Stratton had a brandy instead.

*   *   *

Time was also the subject elsewhere in the Mansion.

"Let's all hold hands and time travel together," said Devonny. "I want to visit the court of Queen Elizabeth the First."

"It doesn't work that way," said Annie. She did not want them joking about it. It was too intense, too terrifying, too private, for jokes.

"How does it work?" asked Harriett. She was astonished to find that Strat was holding her hand. She wore no gloves, nor did he, and the warmth and tightness of his grip was the most beautiful thing that had ever happened to her. Harriett knew he was just reassuring himself that she really was all right. She tried not to let herself slip into believing that he loved her after all. The worst punishment, she thought, will be leaving my heart in his hands, when his heart is elsewhere.

"I don't know how it works," said Annie.

"It must take a terrible toll on your body to fall a hundred years," said Devonny.

Miss Lockwood's body looked fine to Harriett.

"Did you touch something?" said Devonny. "Perhaps we should try to touch everything in the whole Mansion and make wishes at the same time."

Miss Lockwood shook her head. "No, because remember, the second time I traveled, we weren't in the Mansion, we were out on the road, you were in the carriage."

"Was it true love that brought you through?" cried Florinda, clasping her hands together romantically.

202

"Strat, was your heart crying out? Or Anna Sophia, was yours?"

My heart was the one crying out for true love, thought Harriett. It's *still* crying out. It will *always* cry out.

Harriett too saw Ada as she had been when the police took her away. In the midst of the obscenities and the drooling fury at being caught Ada had the very same heart that all women had. Ada had cried out for decades trying to get love. She had settled for money. She had had time to buy a few dresses and dream of a rail ticket. But it was Bridget, after all, who would take the journey.

"Mr. Rowwells told his attorney that he and Ada actually wondered if they had summoned you from another world, Miss Lockwood," said Florinda.

"I wondered that too. Did somebody summon me? Did somebody need me for something special? But if they did, I failed them and it," said Miss Lockwood.

Harriett could admire Miss Lockwood as simply a creature of beauty. She could see how much more easily all things would come to a girl who looked like that. Including love. How cruel, how viciously cruel, then, to let a woman be born plain.

"As for Ada," said Devonny, "I cannot believe Ada has special powers. If she did, she would have used them to get money years ago, or time travel herself to a better place, or fly away from the police when they took her this afternoon."

This afternoon.

It was still this same afternoon.

Truly, time was awesome. So much could be packed into such a tiny space! Lives could change forever in such short splinters of time.

Bridget came up timidly, her possessions packed in canvas drawstring, like the laundry bags in Strat's boarding school.

Florinda hugged her. "I apologize for the men in my household, Bridget."

"I accept your apology," said Bridget. She had lovely new clothes that had been Miss Devonny's, and the heavy weight of silver pulled her skirt pocket down. More than anything, she was glad to be clean, glad to have spent an hour in Miss Florinda's bath.

"Texas!" said Florinda. "I'm so excited for you."

Florinda is trapped, thought Bridget, by her husband and fashions and society. Florinda can only dream of the adventures that I will have.

"Go and be brave," whispered Florinda, and Bridget saw that behind the vapors and the fashion, the veils and perfumes, was a strong woman with no place in which to be strong.

But it was Harriett who muffled a sob. Florinda swept Harriett up, hiding the weeping face inside her own lacy sleeves.

What have I done! thought Annie Lockwood, so ashamed she wanted to hide her own face. I've waltzed into these people's lives, literally—I waltzed in the ruined ballroom, waltzed down the century, waltzed in Strat's arms—and I destroyed them. I took their lives and wrenched them apart. For the person who needs to go and be brave is Harriett, and I don't think she can. Not without Strat.

Bridget swung her canvas bag onto her shoulder. Poor Harriett. Bridget had never attended school, but she'd walked into the village school a few times, when there were special events. It looked like such fun. You and your friends, sitting in rows and learning and laughing, singing and spelling.

Bridget could spell nothing.

And what good had it done Harriett to be able to spell everything? To read everything and write everything? She was just another desperate woman weeping because she had no man's loving arms to hold her.

But Strat, being a man, was too thick to know that he was the cause of the tears. "You are exhausted, Harriett," he said immediately. "You must rest. There has been too much emotion in this day for you."

The ladies smiled gently, forgiving him for being a man and too dense to understand.

"Write to me, Bridget," whispered Florinda over Harriett's bowed head.

Bridget smiled. Of course she could not write to Florinda. She could not write.

"Good-bye," she said, and Bridget went, and was brave.

The setting sun fell, and a long thin line of gold lay quiet on the water. Dusk slipped in among them. The carriage taking Bridget back to the station clattered heavily down the lanes of the Stratton estate.

Strat bade Harriett and Devonny and Florinda good night, and took Miss Lockwood on his arm. They walked the long way through the gardens, out of view of the veranda. The moon rose, its delicate light a silver edge to every leaf.

"I love you," she said. "I will always love you." Her throat filled with a terrible final agony. *I could not love you, dear, so much, loved I not honor more.* Somehow I've got to love honor more than Strat. I have to be a better person than Miss Bartten.

Annie had tasted both sides of time, and each in its way was so cruel to women. But she must not be one of the women who caused cruelty; she must be one who eased it. "I can't stay, Strat," she whispered.

"Yes, you can!" He was shocked, stunned. "That's why you came back! You love me! That's how you traveled, I know it is, it was love! Anna Sophia, you—"

"Marry Harriett," she said.

He stood very still. Their hands were still entwined, but he was only partly with her now.

"I love *you,*" whispered Strat.

But she understood now that love was not always part of the marriages these people made. He was affectionate toward Harriett, and would be kind to her; Harriett needed Strat; that was enough.

And my mother and father? she thought. What will be enough for them?

She'd cast her parents aside without a moment's thought when she changed centuries. But they were still there, going on with their lives, aching and hurting because of each other, aching and hurting because of their daughter.

"I've been cruel," she said. "To you and to my parents, to Harriett and to Sean. And I'm going to be punished for it. Time is going to leave my heart here with you, while my body will go on. I was thinking what power I had, but really, the power belongs to Time." She touched his odd clothes, the funny big collar, the soft squashy tie, the heavy turned seams. Cloth—in this century, always cloth that you could touch. And only cloth that you could touch. "Oh, Strat, it's going to be the worst punishment! I'm going to leave my heart in your century and then have to go occupy my body in the next."

He looked glazed. He too clung, but for him the cloth was nothing; he neither saw it nor felt it. "Annie, I love you. If you stay with me," he promised, "I'll take care of you forever. You'll never have to make another decision. I'll protect you from everything."

He had made the finest offer he knew how to make.

And on his side of time, his side of the century, how could he know how unattractive the offer was? For Annie wanted to be like Bridget, and see the world, and make her own way and take her own risks. Every choice made for her? It was right for Harriett, but it would never be right for Annie.

"No, Strat. I love you. And I care about Harriett and Devonny and all that they are or could be. So I'm going."

Her tears slipped down her cheeks, and he kissed them, as if he could kiss away the desperation they shared. And then, hesitating still, he kissed her lips. She knew that she would never have such a kiss again,

207

in his world or in hers. It was a kiss of love, a kiss that tried to keep her, a kiss that tried so hard to seal a bargain she could not make.

A kiss in which she knew she would never meet a finer man.

Miss Bartten had this same moment, thought Annie, this fraction in Time where she could have said, No, we're stopping, I won't be the woman who hurts others.

Oh, Strat, you are a good man. And I know you will be good to Harriett, who needs you.

Annie, who had wanted that kiss the most, and dreamed of it most, was the one to stop the kiss.

"I need something of yours to take with me," she told him, sobbing. Her tears were unbearable to him, and he pulled out his handkerchief, a great linen square with his initials fatly embroidered in one corner. It was enough. She had this of Strat, and could leave.

"I'm going," she said to Strat, and knew that she did control at least some of Time. She was a Century Changer, and in her were powers given to very few. *I love you, Strat,* said her heart.

"No!" he cried.

The last sound she heard from Strat's side of Time was his howl of grief, and the last thing she felt were his strong fingers, not half so strong as Time.

Her heart fell first, going without her, stripped and in pain, the loss of Strat like the end of the world.

She was a leaf in a tornado, ripped so badly she could not believe she would emerge alive.

The spinning was deeper and more horrific than the other times. There were faces in it with her: terrible, unknown, screaming faces of others being wrenched through Time.

I am not the only changer of centuries. And they are all as terrified and powerless as I.

Her mind was blown away like the rest of her.

It learned only one thing, as it was thrown, and that was even more frightening than leaving her heart with Strat.

She was going *down*. Home was *up*. Home was future years, not past years! *Down through Time?* Was she going to some other century?

Home! *She had meant to go home.*

My family—my friends—my life—

The handkerchief was ripped from her hand. Wherever she went, whenever she landed, she would have nothing of Strat.

Strat! she screamed, but soundlessly, for the race of Time did not allow speech. Her tears were raked from her face as if by the tines of forks.

It ended.

The falling had completed itself.

She was still standing.

She was not even dizzy.

She stood very still, not ready to open her eyes, because once her eyes were open, the terrible unknown would be not *where* she was, but *when* she was.

Would it be the gift of adventure to do it again? To visit yet another century? Or would it be a terrible punishment?

Why was any of it happening, and why to Annie Lockwood?

When did she really want to find herself?

She thought of Strat and Harriett, of Devonny, Florinda, and Bridget . . . and again of Strat. Will I ever know what happened to them?

She thought of her mother and father, brother and boyfriend, school and girlfriends. I *have* to know what happens to them!

She opened her eyes to see when, and what, came next.

OUT OF TIME

CHAPTER 1

Annie Lockwood had not forgotten about Strat, of course. But she had forgotten about him this morning. She woke up fast, and was out of bed in seconds, standing in front of her closet and changing every fashion decision she had made yesterday.

Her American history class was off to New York City today. Forty minutes by train. Since they were going to the United Nations first, the teacher wanted them to look decent, by which he meant that the girls were not to follow the current fad of wearing men's boxer shorts on the outside of their ripped jeans and the boys were not to follow the current fad of wearing T-shirts so obscene that strangers would ask what town the class was from, so as to be sure they never accidentally went and lived there.

Actually, it was nice to have an excuse to look good.

Grunge had hit the school system hard, and those who preferred pretty, or even clean, were out of the loop.

Annie had a long, dark blue dress, a clinging knit bought for a special occasion. It didn't stand out from the crowd, but Annie did when she wore it. She put on the hat she'd found at the secondhand store. It was a flattened bulb of blue velvet. How jauntily it perched over her straight dark hair. Perfect. (Unless she lost her courage and decided the hat, any hat, especially this hat, was pathetic.)

She whipped downstairs to get her brother's opinion. Tod generally did not bother with words. If he despised her clothes, he would gag or pretend to pass out, or maybe even threaten her with butter throwing. (Butter left out on the counter made a wonderful weapon, especially if it got in your sister's hair.) If Tod liked her outfit, though, he would shrug with his eyebrows. This was a great accolade, and meant she looked okay, even if she was his sister.

She was kind of fond of Tod, which was a good thing, since they were the only people left in their family.

Annie and Tod hadn't bothered with breakfast since Mom had left. Breakfast was only worth having if somebody else made it for you.

The house was literally colder without Mom, because Mom had always gotten up way earlier and turned up the thermostat, so when Annie and Tod came down to the kitchen, it was toasty and welcoming. Even though Mom's commute to New York meant

2

she'd caught her train before Annie and Tod came down, they always used to feel Mom in the house. They could smell coffee she had perked and hot perfumed moisture from her shower. Orange juice was always poured, cereal and milk out, toast sitting in the slots waiting to be lowered. On the fridge was always a Post-it to each child:

ANNIE—ace that history test, love you, Mom.

TOD—don't forget your permission slip, love you, Mom.

But "always" was over.

In the kitchen (where the front of the refrigerator was bare) her brother was drinking orange juice straight from the carton. Since she was doing the same thing these days, Annie could hardly yell at him. She just waited her turn. He smiled, orange juice pouring into his mouth, which caused some to dribble onto the linoleum.

"Nice manners," said Annie, and the word *manners* triggered a rush of memories. There were too many, she didn't want this—

Her head split open. Time came in, with its black and shrieking wind.

There were others in the black wind with her. Half people. Bodies and souls flying through Time. But not me! cried Annie, without sound. I learned my lesson— you taught me! Just because you *can* go through Time doesn't mean you *should*.

Time let go.

She was just a panting girl in a cold room.

"Wow," said her brother, folding the carton tips together before handing over the orange juice, as if this were a germ protection device. "That was so weird, Annie."

"What was?" She did not know how she could talk. Oxygen had been ripped from her lungs.

"Your hair," he said nervously. "It curled by itself."

For a moment their eyes met, his full of questions and hers full of secrets. "Do you like my hat?" she said, because hair curled by Time was a tough subject.

"Yeah. Makes you look like a deranged fashion model."

Deranged. What if Tod was right? What if she was on some grim and teetery edge, and she was going to fall off her own sanity? What if she landed, not in another century like the last time, but in some other, hideously confused, mind?

Annie ran back upstairs, to get away from the collapse of Time and the sharp eyes of her brother. To get closer to Strat.

The image of Strat had faded over the months. When she thought of him now, it was loosely, like silver bracelets sliding on her arms.

Sometimes she went to Stratton Point, alone with the wind, but even Strat's mansion was only memory. Torn down. Nothing now but a scar on a hill. Annie would make sure there was no living person around—no footprints in the snow—no ski tracks—no cars parked below with the windows rolled down—and she'd shout out loud, "Strat! Strat! I love you!"

But of course nobody answered, and Time did not

open. There was just a teenage girl shrieking for a non-existent teenage boy.

This morning, in her bedroom, there was nothing wrong, nothing out of place. No clues to Time or any other secret. Piles of clothing, paperbacks, and CDs were right where she had left them, her drawers half open and her closet doors half shut. But today must be the day! thought Annie. That falling was Time's warning.

"Hi, Strat," she whispered to the mirror, as if he and his century were right behind the glass, and the opening of Time was ready.

The Strattons, she thought suddenly, had a Manhattan town house. I've been going to their beach mansion —their Connecticut summer place. But what if the passage back through Time is in New York City?

Old New York rose as vividly in her mind as if she really had visited there: romantic and dark, full of velvet gowns and stamping horses and fine carriages.

She stared at herself in her full-length mirror. If Time takes me, I'll be ready. I'll be elegant and ladylike.

Of course, not in front of her history class. They must not ask questions. She stuffed the hat into her old L.L. Bean bookbag.

It was midwinter. February, to be exact, and the snowiest winter on record. Annie could wear her best boots (best in fashion, not in staying dry), which were high black leather with chevrons of velvet. She dashed into Mom's room to filch Mom's black kid gloves and her winter coat pin: a snowflake of silver, intricate as lace. Mom had ordered it from a museum catalog,

5

which triggered such a flow of catalogs they threatened to snap the mailbox. (Tod loved this; he was always hoping for another, more explicit, *Victoria's Secret.*)

Annie had other secrets in mind. The secrets that the Strattons had carried through Time.

How many hours had Annie spent in the library since she and Strat parted forever? Combing yellow newspapers stacked in crumbling towers in the basement? Studying church records and town ledgers, hungry for a syllable about the Strattons?

Old newspapers covered Society, and the Strattons had been Society a hundred years ago. "Mr. Hiram Stratton, Jr., will soon begin his first year at Yale." "Miss Devonny Stratton will be voyaging to Paris." "Miss Harriett Ranleigh is again visiting her dear friends, the Strattons." "Mr. Walker Walkley has accepted the invitation of the Strattons to sail for several days on the family yacht."

This was proof that the Strattons were real: that Annie Lockwood really and truly had lived and loved among them.

And then, they ceased to be real. The Strattons vanished from the printed record. There was nothing written about them again. *Not ever.*

No marriage. No birth. No death. No property sold. No visitors mentioned.

The Strattons stepped off Time, leaving no tombstones, no letters and no clues.

Had Annie done that? Had she destroyed the Strattons by coming through Time and changing their lives?

What had happened to them? Where had they gone? Who had married whom?

She would never know—unless she fell through Time again and caught up.

Downstairs in the front hall, she took her mother's long formal black wool coat from its hanger. She pinned the silver snowflake on the narrow lapel. Carefully, using the violet-trimmed paper Mom kept by the hall phone, Annie wrote a note to the history teacher.

Everything in the note was a lie.

∽⧉∾

Tod was putting on his ice hockey jacket, which he never zipped no matter how cold it was. Tod tapped his sister's silver snowflake. "You think it's Halloween, maybe? You're going as a grown-up?"

"Do I look weird?" she asked anxiously. No matter what century you were in, nothing was worse than being a fashion jerk.

"You look great," said her brother gravely. Tod—who never gave compliments; it was one of the principles he lived by. "But it's a pretty dressy outfit," said Tod, very casually, "for a school field trip."

This was the tricky part for Annie. Tod would still be here and would still have to face reality. Annie was sick of reality. Especially Lockwood family reality. "Tod," she said, even more casually, "if I don't come home tonight . . . don't tell Dad."

Annie was suddenly deeply terrified. What if I get trapped in Time? she thought. What if Time takes me someplace else, instead of to Strat? What if he and Harriett are already married? What if they aren't?

Tod zipped his hockey jacket, which astonished her. The sound of the zipper closing was ominous, as if she were being closed out of her brother's life. "I just wonder, Annie, if you know what you're doing."

I have no idea what I am doing. Time will do it to me.

"I don't want to be a one-person family," said her brother.

"We're still a family," she said quickly. "Just scattered."

Last year, Dad had decided he had better things to do than maintain a family. He had become involved with Miss Bartten. When Mom fell apart over this, Dad said grumpily, "I'm not going to marry her. I'm not even asking for a divorce. I just want a different lifestyle."

Mom had not taken this well, especially when Dad thought he could have a different lifestyle but still bring Mom his laundry. Talk about la-la land. Dad was actually surprised when Mom destroyed his wardrobe. "By the way," Mom had said, talking over a sea of buttons no longer attached to shirts, "my brokerage firm is opening an office in Tokyo."

"Neat," Dad had said, clearly wondering if his credit cards were maxed out or if he could afford all new clothes. Sleeves were now being ripped off to join the buttons.

"They've asked me to go Japan for a month to set things up."

"Congratulations," Dad had said. There was no point

8

in hoping Miss Bartten would mend those torn clothes. The Miss Barttens of this world are not domestic.

Mom raised her voice, trying to tap into Dad's consciousness. "So you need to move back into this house full time for the month of February and take care of Annie and Tod while I'm in Tokyo."

"Sure," Dad said, and escaped from the house with his body intact, if not his clothing.

Annie and Tod knew their father had not been listening. He hadn't heard the word *Tokyo* or the word *Japan* and he definitely had not heard the sentence requiring him to live at home again for a month. Brother and sister had looked at each other with perfect understanding: they were about to be on their own for four weeks.

So Annie didn't want to think about Tod left all alone here. Not that he wasn't mature enough. He had his driver's license, and all, but still—he would be alone. And neither parent realized it.

I should confess, thought Annie, so that if something does happen, Tod will know. He deserves answers. *If something does happen* . . . like what? What do I think will go wrong? If Time takes me again, I'll be going to Strat. Won't I? He loved me so! Doesn't love conquer all? Or have I been lying about what really happened in 1895? I lie to everybody else. Am I lying to myself now too?

She turned to tell her brother some of the truth, but he was not there. Tod had gone on to school. She was alone in the house. There was nothing there but the hum of the refrigerator and the click of a clock.

Annie shivered.

Could people come and go from real life without her noticing them? Was she too busy noticing unreal people?

She almost tore up the note she had written to her teacher. It was too foolish.

But instead she tucked the note in her palm, and slid her hand into her glove, and there the note lay waiting, papery and warm and full of the future. *Or the past.*

Shackles work.

Strat stared at the chains on his wrists. He was young and strong—and chained.

He was willing to admit to anything they wanted now. He would make any promise if they'd just let him loose. "What year is it?" he asked the doctor.

Patient does not know year, the doctor wrote in Strat's casebook.

"I'm fine," Strat said to the doctor. "This is a mistake."

"Really? Your father chose this, you recall."

"I disobeyed my father. I was wrong. I won't do it again. I'm not insane. I agree that my father knows everything."

"Do you?"

"Please let me out."

The doctor shook his head. "You are a danger to yourself and others, Mr. Stratton."

Strat said, "Would you permit me more than one

hour a day of exercise? Please? I promise to be good. I promise not to try to scale the walls."

"You are fortunate," said the doctor, "that your father is wealthy. He has paid for a private asylum, where you will get all the help you need. Right now you need restraint, not exercise."

Strat's body screamed for exercise. Every joint shrieked to be moved, every muscle cried out to be swung and changed. But arguing would go in the casebook, and the casebook decided everything. "Did I get any letters?" he said, struggling for courtesy, for a normal smile. He must look normal at all costs. "Did Harriett answer me yet?"

The doctor smiled.

The doctor and Ralph, the attendant, moved Strat back to the crib. He fought, but they who owned the key to the shackles were in charge, no matter how young and strong Strat was.

The crib was an adult-size bed with barred sides and a cleverly fastened canvas lid. Strat could not get out. He could not undo the canvas. He could not sit up. It was a torture chamber with a mattress. They removed the chains once he was inside. False freedom. He could do nothing with those hands, so he used the only other tool available to him.

Bites canvas, wrote the doctor, and then the doctor left.

"No!" screamed Strat. "No, don't go, please, please, please, you're a civilized man, please . . ."

The door closed behind the doctor.

The building had been constructed as a lunatic asylum. Its walls were very thick and its doors very solid.

Ralph the attendant smiled. The wider Ralph smiled, the more danger the patient was in.

"Please, Ralph," said Strat, "please let me write another letter. This will be to my sister, Devonny. I'll give you all the money I have."

Ralph laughed. "I already have all the money you have."

Strat had no pride left. "Devonny will give you money. Just please let me have a pencil and paper."

Ralph walked slowly to the doctor's desk. The other four patients in the room watched to see if Ralph would actually bring a piece of paper, a pencil, a stamp, and an envelope. If there was hope for Strat, perhaps there was hope for them too.

Strat's heart was pounding. If he could get Devonny to come . . . or Harriett . . . or his mother . . .

But Ralph came back with Strat's casebook. Ralph couldn't read, of course; a lunatic asylum did not hire the sort of person who had conquered reading, but Ralph could recognize. Ralph held up the brown leather journal in which the doctor's spidery handwriting made daily entries. Ralph turned the pages midair, so not just Strat, but also the other patients, could see each page.

Every letter Strat had written begging for help was pasted into the notebook.

Not one had ever been mailed.

Sean picked Annie up in his latest vehicle. Sean was working at an auto repair shop now. He was in his glory. He no longer had to struggle to purchase cars; he could just slap on a dealer plate and drive off the lot with his prize.

They hadn't dated since Annie met Strat. (Not that Sean had the slightest idea who Strat was.) But Sean went right on adoring Annie, accepting the fact that he had no purpose in her life other than to give her rides in bad weather.

Sometimes Annie was ashamed of this, but not today. She wanted her boots dry and the hem of her long dress out of the snow. "Hi, Sean."

"Hi, Annie. Wow. Some outfit."

"This is how people dress to go into New York," said Annie defensively. She was worried about how the other girls would dress. She didn't want to stand out or get teased. But these clothes would move across Time with her.

"Hear from your mom?" said Sean. "She like Tokyo?"

"Yes," said Annie, though her last conversation with Mom had been at the airport, saying good-bye.

("Get us good presents, Mom," Tod had teased, hugging his mother gently. Mom was very teary, unable to leave her children. "We'll slaughter Miss Bartten for you," Tod offered. "Think of the alibi you'll have. Continents and oceans." Mom had managed to smile. "Make it painful," she told Tod. They shook on it.)

13

What if I'm gone for a long time? thought Annie. What if Tod has to tell Mom, and she's in Japan, and finds out I'm missing, and—

"We're here," said Sean. He smiled at Annie. Sean was a very good-looking young man. It was too bad he had no personality to go with it. Annie patted Sean's knee and Sean sighed. "How come I get pats, and never kisses?"

"I guess I'm not feeling very romantic these days," said Annie, which was one of her larger lies. She had thought of nothing but romance since meeting Strat. She worried about the extent and number of her lies. Was this a sign of insanity? Would she wake up one day, gently tranquilized, her scattered family gathered around her bed in a psychiatric unit?

"See you tonight," said Sean, and Annie was horrified. Had she promised Sean a date or something? But she needed tonight! If Time came . . .

"Don't look as if I threw up on you," said Sean irritably. "I'm just picking you up at the 6:03 train."

"I might not be on it," said Annie quickly. "I might stay at Mom's New York apartment."

Sean's jaw dropped. "I didn't know your mother kept an apartment in New York."

"Ever since Dad moved out," Annie lied. She would get caught on this one. Or maybe not. It was amazing, the number of lies you could tell without being noticed. The whole thing was in carrying it off.

She got on the train, lifting her skirts above the slush. The rest of the class had boarded and she was last. There was an uneven number of kids, and Annie sat alone. She would have minded terribly last year; she would have been crushed and humiliated and ready to die. Now she was delighted. She could think of Time and the Strattons.

The train lurched noisily toward Grand Central Station.

They stopped at Greenwich and Rye and Mamaroneck. At Larchmont and New Rochelle and Mount Vernon.

Don't do this, Annie said to herself. You're just going because you're selfish and curious. Don't pretend it's love. You know perfectly well Strat had to marry Harriett. She needed him most. You knew it then, you know it now. Don't you go back there and wreck that. And think of your own family. Things aren't bad enough already?

Annie felt much better after accusing herself of terrible things.

Besides, Time gave her no choice, did it? It would grab her by the ankles and throw her through the century.

And then I'll know, thought Annie. I'll have the answers. And that's what everybody wants from Life. The Answers.

From her chair on the glassed-in porch, Harriett looked at winter. Absolutely nothing happened in the Adirondack Mountains except weather. Frigid, twenty-below weather.

Indoors, the coal stove was red hot and the windows

15

had steamed up. The stove was a tall potbelly with peculiar side ridges. Moss, the nurse, had explained that it was a laundry stove, and the ledges would hold two dozen flatirons. The heating stove had exploded, Moss said, and this was the substitute. Harriett was not comforted by the thought of a stove exploding.

But Harriett was kept outdoors, so that clear, clean, cold air would climb into her lungs and scour out the consumption. She was wrapped in blankets and furs, a hot soapstone tucked beneath her feet. She would rather be inside with an exploding stove. They could call it a cure porch if they wanted, but Harriett, personally, called it torture.

Harriett had had a cough the previous winter and spring, but most people did, so she thought little of it. Even though she felt feverish every afternoon, she said nothing. She loved the pink in her cheeks. So romantic. And she was in love, wearing the sapphire ring Strat had given her, and was thinking of nothing but marriage.

The loss of weight, too, was delightful. Being slender and willowy was so much better than being solid. A child-woman is far more attractive than a womanly woman. It was relief to be frail, as a woman should be. All went well until one day the coughing was so severe that Harriett hemorrhaged, drenching handkerchiefs with blood.

This was consumption. Lungs that ate the body instead of air.

Naturally, one lied. Admit that a member of the family had consumption? Not likely. It would be the end of party invitations.

Still, only the very best people got consumption, and of course they had to have the very best treatment. Clear Pond featured a terribly expensive and exclusive cure.

There were "up" cottages, where patients could get out of bed, but Harriett was "on trays." Meals were carried to her because she had to be motionless. Her lungs must never struggle. Up patients could have activities: picnics in summer and sleigh rides in winter. Poor Harriett could only obey the cure and hope to stay alive.

Hope was strong in the heart of Harriett Ranleigh. She had plans! A life—a wonderful man—their perfect future together. Surely a cough would not end that forever.

She was not even permitted to use a pencil, since mental exercise was known to be as tiring as physical exercise. But Harriett composed a diary in her mind, as carefully and grammatically as if somebody really would read it.

I am afraid, she wrote in her mind. Why won't Strat answer my letters? How could he read those sentences I dictated to Moss, and not come to me? How could he be so hard of heart?

I am afraid of the weather too. How the wind screams. How the cold mountains stare. If I die, they will put me in that ground, and I will be cold forever. Is this your design, God? Have you chosen death for me?

God, don't you understand? I have a design too! I want to marry Strat and have babies and keep a home!

But only the wind replied, shrieking around the icicles.

They all had pet icicles; Harriett's was three feet long, but Beanie's was nearly four. An infinitely superior icicle, Beanie like to say smugly, as I am an infinitely superior person.

Harriett yearned for the day's visits. Charlie and Beanie could go skylarking and they would tell her about their activities. Charlie's cure was going well; he was actually permitted a ten-minute walk. Charlie was so slender as to be nonexistent, but in his bright-hued winter woolens, he looked puffy and plump.

Beanie and Charlie joined her on the glass porch, exhausted from the brief walk across the snow. Moss, the nurse, quickly tucked them into waiting furs and brought cups of hot tea to wrap cold fingers around.

Charlie rolled himself a cigarette and promptly set fire to his own sheets. Everybody was used to this and he was thrown a snowball with which to put it out.

Harriett whispered, "I still haven't heard from Strat."

They looked at her gently. Everybody knew that her fiancé had not once written or visited. Even Harriett's enormous fortune was not bringing Strat to her side. He was handsome. The finely framed photograph of him that she kept by her bed would have made any girl's heart pound. Probably had. Strat, it would seem, was busy with other hearts.

18

The students were packed tight in a hallway in the United Nations building listening (or pretending to listen) to a woman discuss the Middle East situation. I'd better not go through Time right now, thought Annie. We don't need an Annie Lockwood situation.

But nothing happened.

They wrapped up the United Nations, they bought roasted chestnuts or cappuccino or hotdogs at sidewalk stands, they took a bus to South Street Seaport, they steeped themselves in maritime history, and nothing happened.

Annie had been so sure Time was coming for her. The little note she had written to explain her absence was stupid and futile.

Annie looked at the twenty kids who thought they knew her. What would they say if they found out she was trying to step across a century? What would they say if they found out she really and truly believed she could do it?

They would lock me up, she thought. I'd be in a straitjacket.

She glared at New York, which was doing its best for everybody except her.

I know what! I have to get in position. I have to be on the right street, so all Time has to do is shift me through the century, not to another place.

She knew the Manhattan address; she had found it in a society report.

Okay, so I lied when I said I was going to let Time

19

handle it, thought Annie. So I'm going to help Time out a little. I'll dump my bookbag, too twentieth century, put on my squishy blue hat, all ladies wore hats in the nineteenth century, and find the corner of Fifty-second Street and Fifth Avenue.

She slid into a McDonald's line next to Heather. Once they had been inseparable—the kind of junior-high girlfriends who cannot get through the evening without an hour on the phone. Now Heather was just Heather, a nice girl Annie had once known. "Heather," whispered Annie, "would you give this note to the teacher after I'm out of here?"

Heather overreacted. "What are you talking about? Annie, it's one thing to wander off back home. This is New York City. It isn't safe. Get a grip."

"I'll be fine, I'm staying at Mom's apartment."

"Your mother has an apartment in New York? I didn't know that! Oooh, Annie, I want to stay too! Let's do something really cool."

Annie had not thought of this problem. "Next time," she said quickly. "This time I need you to cover for me."

Heather took the note dubiously. "Okay, but—"

"Thanks!" Annie took a quick look to be sure the rest of the class was thinking of french fries, and not her, and they were, so she slipped out of McDonald's, and also, she hoped, out of the twentieth century.

Devonny Aurelia Victoria Stratton felt like kicking a dog.

Nothing was going right.

Every plan had failed, every person she loved was in trouble, and every hope cut down.

Devonny held Miss Lockwood responsible. Oh! If she could get her hands around Miss Lockwood's throat! Strangling was too good for her.

For Anna Sophia Lockwood had existed: everybody admitted it. Even Father admitted it. He had, after all, danced with Miss Lockwood. But only Strat had insisted that Miss Lockwood had traveled through Time to be with them.

I hate you, Anna Sophia Lockwood! thought Devonny. But I need you. "It's now or never," she said fiercely to Time. "You send her right now! Right this very minute! Do you hear me!"

There was a knock at the door and Devonny nearly fainted. Did she have such power? "Yes?" she whispered.

The door opened.

It was not Time. It was the most dangerous person she knew.

"Were you talking to someone?" he said, looking around the empty room.

Talking to Time and Miss Lockwood had put Strat in an insane asylum. Devonny must be far more careful. She managed a sweet smile, because sweetness and smiles were the only weapons a girl had in 1898. "I was practicing flirting with you," she said. She tucked her slender, silk-gloved hand into Walker Walkley's crooked arm, and prepared herself to lie and connive and do anything it took to save her brother.

21

CHAPTER 2

Annie paced Fifth Avenue, trying this side and then the other, going up the near side of Fifty-second Street, and crossing over to the far side.

The city was relentlessly modern. Its cars and store windows, skyscrapers and fashions were maddeningly twentieth century. Ugly, pimpled steel and glass rose up to snow clouds so low that the buildings didn't scrape the sky; they vanished into it.

Chemical Bank, Citibank, and Japan Air. She was in her Time, all right, complete with parking meters to count car minutes.

The pout on her mouth and the frown on her forehead made her look like a street crazy with whom sane people did not make eye contact. Had Annie said to the people so carefully avoiding her that she was looking for the previous century, their worst suspicions would have been confirmed. But she was hunting, not talking.

Tod was right: in her fine black coat and her silly squashed hat, she looked like a runway model in the midst of losing her mind.

She stepped into a lobby with green marble floors and bored uniformed men and women guarding the elevators. She read the list of companies that could be found on floors two through forty. The name Stratton was not there.

I can't find the Strattons in the pages of their own society gossip and I can't find the Strattons in property records and church ledgers, but still I expect to find their name chiseled in modern buildings? I am crazy. This is proof.

She went back out. The weather had changed in only those few seconds. The wind howled down the corridors of Manhattan and icy sidewalks sucked the heat out of Annie's boots. The day had passed into night without stopping for dusk, and snow-swirled blackness strangled her.

Hunched, scurrying people jostled her, and bumped into her, and bruised her, and none of them noticed when she slipped in the slush and fell. Her skirts were soaked and her boots were ruined and her hat had vanished into the windy blast.

It took her three tries to get to her feet again, and nobody helped, or even saw.

I've lost my purse! she thought, horrified.

No purse. No money. No train ticket. No way home.

Perhaps the jostling people had been thieves, laughing at her, a pathetic suburban girl trying to find her way.

23

Slush filled her boots. Her mother's lovely coat was soaked and soiled. Annie Lockwood wanted nothing except to find her class and catch her train and go home. But without her purse? If I could get to Grand Central, she thought, it would be warm in there, and I'd use my phone card and . . .

And call whom? Mom was in Japan, Dad was at Miss Bartten's, Tod couldn't help. And even if she found her class, could she admit the string of lies? What excuse could she give? They'd laugh at her, or worse, take her seriously, and be kind to her little demented mind, and get the school psychiatrist in on it, and bring Mom home from Japan.

No. Whatever she did to get out of this, she had to do without confession.

She plodded street after street, legs stiff as icicles. There was no purpose to her journey anymore, but she could not find a place to stop. Her feet went on like some dreadful enchantment.

New York City splintered, and fell off itself, like pieces of a glacier. All the world except Annie moved fast, while Annie's slow feet seemed to freeze to the ground.

I have to get out of this wind, Annie thought. I am literally freezing to death. The cold could stop my heart. Leave me frozen on the stones like an abandoned kitten.

Halfway down a narrow side street was a row of large, elegant trees. Through the snow they seemed only half there, and half people seemed to move from half a house. The tree trunks were encircled by gold-tipped spears of black iron, part of an elaborate fence.

The half people moved toward her and, half frozen, Annie Lockwood half understood.

In the lunatic asylum, the patients were being fed. "Besides, Mr. Stratton," said Ralph when he brought supper, "you write to girls. What can a female do, huh? Females is of lower intelligence than men." To prove his point, Ralph hurt Katie a little: Ralph enjoyed slapping.

Katie's family didn't want to have a deformed child around the house and had sent her to the asylum, explaining to the neighbors that their daughter had died. She might as well have.

Supper was a large bowl of lukewarm oatmeal with milk and brown sugar. For Strat, there was a spoon, but Ralph was not in the mood to give Douglass and Katie spoons. They had to put their faces in the bowl and slurp it out, like animals.

Douglass had very little brain, and his family didn't want him because he had never acquired speech. He could make noises, and after being cooped up with Douglass for so long, Strat understood the fear sound and the hope sound and the happy sound. Douglass, amazingly, was often happy. When Katie read aloud, or massaged his neck, or combed his hair, Douglass would beam at her and make his happy sound.

Really ugly people and really dumb people and really crazy people were kept in the same place.

It was important not to let Society know that one of the family was below standard. How would the attractive members of the family get married if such news got out? It might be in the blood, and who wanted blood that failed?

Strat's blood had failed.

His father had sentenced him to a private lunatic asylum. There were only sixty patients, so it wasn't as bad as Utica, the state asylum, with thousands. But it was just as impossible to get out of.

Katie was allowed to read, though of course the only books were the Bible or collections of sermons. Luckily the Bible had many wonderful stories, and luckily Katie liked to read aloud, so they knew by heart everything about Daniel and the lion's den and Joseph's coat of many colors.

"It's 1898, Strat," said Katie gently, finally answering his question to the long-departed doctor. "You knew that. You know you've been here nearly six months. You know we had Christmas and New Year's."

Except during the precious hour of exercise, weather was gone from their world. The inmates had no windows. No sky. No sun. Strat missed the outdoors as much as he missed the rest of the world: friends, talk, college, sailing, tennis, good food.

Where did time go, when you lost it?

He thought of the last time he had seen Anna Sophia Lockwood. She had wavered, becoming a reflection of herself. She literally slipped between his fingers. He was holding her gown and then he wasn't. He'd had a strand of her hair, and then he didn't. Nothing of her was present. Just Strat and the soft beach air. When he stopped shouting, he tried whispering, as if her vanishing were a secret and he could pull her out.

She had not wanted him to address her as Miss Lockwood, but Strat could not manage anything as familiar as Annie. So he had called her Anna Sophia, singing her two names opera style: Anna Sophia; Sophia Anna.

But the situation had been resolved, and his engagement to Harriett made public, and there had been dances and fetes and dinners, and Strat knew that if he could not have Anna Sophia—and he couldn't—he wanted Harriett. She was the history of his own life, his companion since they were children; possibly his best friend.

The subject closed to them had been Anna Sophia. Harriett had met her, of course, been nearly ruined by her, and knew Strat's theory of century changing. But Strat's heart—lost to Anna Sophia—they did not discuss. It hurt each of them far too much.

Time. Where was Harriett all this time? His sister? His mother?

"I have lost half a year," he whispered. "How many more will I lose?"

"All of them," said Katie.

At the cure cottage, Beanie and Charlie were visiting Harriett.

Charlie, who had been an army officer, didn't want to lose any of his skills. He sat up on his cure chair with his rifle and shot apart glass bottles that his man put up on stones at the edge of the frozen pond. Come summer, nobody was going to do any barefoot wading along that part of the shore.

"In only three months," said Charlie proudly, "I have gone from being allowed ten minutes sitting up to being allowed a ten-minute sleigh ride. No doubt I shall soon be tobogganing every morning at forty below." This was a complete lie. He was getting worse. But he did not want Harriett to know.

If his dreams can come true, thought Harriett, perhaps mine will too. She allowed herself a delicious picture of life: a lovely house, a warm fire, laughing children, her beloved husband, Strat, smoking a pipe.

A fourth patient joined them. Phipps was not Harriett's favorite person, but in a society so isolated, any person was more desirable than no person.

"Hullo, Phipps," said Charlie, not very willingly.

"Hullo, Phipps," said Beanie, throwing a snowball at him. Phipps ducked and frowned at Beanie. As always, Phipps had some unpleasant subject to bring up. "I've spoken to Doctor. Supposedly our disease is caused by a little bacillus. I don't believe it. He says you can look at it through a microscope. I don't believe that either. We got sick because we offended God." This seemed to make him rather proud, as if he had accomplished something that mattered.

"How comforting," said Beanie. "In what way did I

offend God? I will have you know that I have led a blameless life."

"Nobody," said Phipps sharply, "has led a blameless life."

"Speak for yourself, you bacillus," said Beanie.

"Let's get along, please," said Moss the nurse. "Arguing isn't good for the cure. It's a strain on the lungs."

They stopped immediately. Nobody wanted a strain on the lungs. Harriett went to sleep every night now with a sandbag on her chest, to keep the ribs from moving.

When Charlie, Phipps and Beanie left, Moss gave Harriett a sponge bath, strong rubdowns with coarse towels, to improve her circulation. Then came a wonderful dinner, hot and filling. Except for the fact that she had been banished, because people were afraid of her breath, life here was good.

Moss read aloud a psalm, because Moss was a great believer.

Harriett went back and forth. There were times when she had great faith and knew God would save her, and if He didn't, heaven would nevertheless be wonderful. There were times, however, when she felt that religion was crap.

"Yea, though I walk through the valley of the shadow of death, I will fear no evil: for thou art with me," said Moss.

I, thought Harriett, do not want to walk through death until I am eighty! Do you hear me, Lord?

And then the coughing broke through.

It ripped her lungs open and blood spilled out. Moss

held her, keeping her tight, coaxing her to hang on through the agony, choke the cough down. Win. Stay alive.

When the cough ended, Moss and her helper Mario changed the sheets and blankets, again tucking Harriett in—clean, soft, white.

But would anything make her lungs clean and soft again?

This was most unusual. Dr. Wilmott himself, director of the asylum, had come to look them over.

Even more unusual, Strat was not confined, but permitted to walk about the room. It soothed him to count. He had stalked the twelve-foot-square room two hundred ninety-six times so far this afternoon. He had stepped over Melancholia and Conspiracy (two patients who really were lunatics, and whose shrieks and sobs and mutterings gave Strat headaches day and night) two hundred ninety-six times and they hadn't noticed him once. This is my life, he thought, and for the millionth time, not the two hundred ninety-sixth, he could not believe it.

"Dr. Wilmott, would you please give permission for me to exercise again today?" he said. "Sir," he added.

Dr. Wilmott shook his head. "You are a danger to yourself and others, Mr. Stratton."

If only that were true! He would love to be a danger to somebody. He would start with his father.

Strat's very own father had instructed Strat's very own Yale professor—for whom he had written the incriminating essay—to arrange the kidnapping. His professor had introduced two burly men with him as friends involved in a joke. Strat loved a good joke, as all college boys do, and willingly agreed to have his hands strapped together. Once those strapped hands were strapped to the interior of a very strangely outfitted carriage, the professor explained that Strat's beliefs in God were so incorrect that extreme measures had to be taken.

And then his father—appearing out of nowhere—glanced briefly into the conveyance. "Good," Hiram Stratton, Sr., had said. "Take him to the asylum."

Strat still thought it must be a joke, and did not fight back until it was far too late, and that, too, was counted against him—a normal person would have fought back. It was like being accused of witchery in old Massachusetts—they held you under water and if you died, then you were a normal person who needed air.

"Father," he had said, not yet scared, "what is this nonsense?"

"You need enclosure and treatment," his father had thundered. "Writing essays about *century changers* and *time crossing* and *girls who don't exist?*"

So it was about Miss Lockwood. Beautiful, funny, wonderful Anna Sophia. Even then, Strat was still in love with her—three years after she came and went, one year after his engagement to Harriett. His heart still filled with joy and loss whenever he thought of Miss Lockwood.

"You," said his very own, very angry father, "are an instrument of Satan."

31

"I'm your son!" Strat had shouted, but his father had not replied, and Strat was taken by force 275 miles north to the sort of place he had not dreamed existed.

Now, Dr. Wilmott said sternly to Katie, "Have you been studying your books of moral works?"

"Yes, sir."

Katie's face was so ugly, so misshapen, that the doctor did not look at her, but into the stale air above her. "You do understand," said Doctor, "that God has punished you, and there is nothing that I can do for you."

"I do understand, Dr. Wilmott, that you are a wicked, hideous, evil creation and God would never dream of working through you," said Katie calmly.

Strat froze. She must never talk to the staff like that! They would hurt her. They would punish her terribly. You had to beg from them, compliment them, you had to—

"You ugly deformed reject of society! You dare to address me like that!" hissed Dr. Wilmott. He raised his hand and Strat the athlete recognized the strength and rage in that moving arm.

But it was not Hiram Stratton, Jr., who moved to protect Katie.

It was Douglass.

Douglass stepped between the doctor and Katie and took the blow without a quiver, and took the next blow, too, and the next.

Stop it, said Strat, but to his shame no words came out.

"Stop it," said Katie to Dr. Wilmott. "You know Douglass has done no wrong."

Dr. Wilmott and Ralph strapped both Katie and Douglass to restraint chairs. Strat let it happen, and when they were done he said to Doctor, "I have been good, sir. May I be allowed some exercise outside?"

And Doctor smiled, and said yes.

"Well!" said Miss Bartten, beaming at Tod.

They were in a nice restaurant. Starched white tablecloths and linen napkins big enough to make beds with, and crystal glasses and scented candles.

"Your father and I are going to Mexico!" cried Miss Bartten. "Won't it be fun!"

Tod said to his father, "Maybe homicidal guerrillas will kidnap you. Maybe fire ants will eat off the soles off your feet. Or killer bees—"

"Stop it," said his father.

"Oh, I'm so sorry!" said Tod, hitting his forehead in remorse. "Miss Bartten, forgive me! I was being rude to you when all you did was ruin my parents' marriage. Gosh, what was I thinking of!"

"Tod," said his father through gritted teeth, "we are in public."

"Young people today have no standards," said Tod confidingly to Miss Bartten. "I mean, they actually think when a man promises to be faithful to his wife, he should do it! Can you believe that, Miss Bartten?" Tod laughed.

"*Stop it,*" said his father.

"Yes, I think we should stop," said Tod Lockwood.

"And the first thing we should stop doing is pretending that this is going to work."

Tod left the restaurant.

The point here was to upset Dad and Miss Bartten (whom he refused to call Peggy; Peggy was too friendly a name and he, Tod, was not going to be friendly; forget it) but the point also was not to let Dad notice that Annie was not here. Or if he did notice, he should be darned glad, because Annie had even more of a viper tongue than Tod.

He knew his father was saying to Miss Bartten, "Tod'll be back, he's ten miles from home, and there's no such thing as a taxi in this town."

Tod grinned into the falling snow. He had picked Dad's pocket. He had the car keys. It would be Miss Bartten who had to walk.

Hiram Stratton, Jr., age twenty-one, had not known that anything could be worse than being locked in a small room with a Melancholia, a Deformity, a Conspiracy, and an Idiot.

But now it was he, Strat, who was the deformity.

He had let them attack Katie. Let them take it out on Douglass. He had groveled, reminding them that he was a good little boy, and could go out into the sunshine. And sure enough, here he was, in a special, iron-fenced garden he had never seen before, and sure enough the setting sun glittered on the deep white snow, the first thing of beauty he had seen in six months.

All the tiny offenses of his life were nothing to this. He breathed in the fine clear air for which he had sacrificed his soul.

It was not worth it.

Whether God forgave him or God did not, the forgiveness he needed now was Katie's, was Douglass's.

Strat no longer needed to worry how he, the victim, the patient, had gotten here; he needed to worry how he could stay a man in spite of being here.

There was Katie, whom God had seen fit to deliver into this world twisted and wrongly shaped, and people punished her for it.

There was Douglass, whom God had seen fit to deliver into this world without intelligence, and people punished him for it.

Poor Melancholia, who ached with depression, was punished for his grief. As for Conspiracy, she believed her family had locked her up to get her money. Strat would have believed her, because look what *his* family had done to *him*, except that her stories were never the same; were not stories even, but mad ravings.

Oh, Anna Sophia! thought Strat. You thought I possessed every virtue. You told me you would never meet a finer man. How wrong you were. I have never been a worse one.

In the beautiful snow garden, under the lengthening blue shadows, Strat, too, was in pain. *What have I done? I have not helped Katie or Douglass. I am a person to be ashamed of.*

"May I go back to my room now?" he said quietly to Ralph.

35

Devonny Aurelia Victoria Stratton and Walker Walkley moved slowly toward Fifth Avenue. Each elegant house —French mansard, Italianate, Gothic Revival—had bulbous stairs leading steeply up to a high first floor, and from each, the snow was constantly swept, lest a lady or gentleman slip.

The party was not far: one of the Vanderbilt houses on Fifth Avenue. It was a good-bye party for Devonny herself, because she would leave for California in the morning, and her father had not told her when she would return to New York. Father and her stepmother, Florinda, had gone to California on a whim, and found it surprisingly warm and gracious. (This was Florinda's word—her father would not know what gracious was if he lived another fifty years.)

Walker Walkley was tall and dramatic in his beaver coat and top hat. Walk saluted another gentleman with his cane. "Good evening," they said back and forth, bowing and nodding.

Devonny was grateful for her hooded cape of sea otter, lined with wine-red velvet. She needed it against the terrible cold.

Pinkerton detectives hired by the Vanderbilts scattered the homeless and the beggars, which was good, because their presence ruined a party. And one never knew, there might be criminals or anarchists among them. Gangs were trying to take over the streets of New York.

And then, beyond Walker Walkley, Devonny saw something that even Pinkerton detectives would not know what to do about.

Miss Lockwood.

Lurching through the snow, peering, staring . . . lost.

Her clothes were ridiculous, frozen into pathetic shapes. Of course she had no hat, and her hair hung like an immigrant's from Ellis Island. *I expect her to rescue us?* thought Devonny.

And now the foolish girl was about to ask Walker himself for directions! Walker would recognize her! That must never, never happen, Walker was too dangerous. Any hope would be ruined.

Devonny stood tiptoe, making herself as tall as she could, hoping her cheeks were pink and romantic from the cold. She brought those cheeks very close to Walk's. "Walk, I have been hard of heart because of Strat." She managed to let her hood slip, so that her hair was fetchingly free in the romantic snow. "But I have had many long talks with the minister's wife and she has helped me understand how very, very kind you were to intervene in a desperate situation."

Walk looked startled, as well he might. Devonny never went to church if she could avoid it, and certainly never discussed anything with the minister's wife, who was a fool and a shrew. But this was the best Devonny could manage under pressure. Devonny withdrew one hand from her muff and gently stroked Walk's cheek. The intimacy of this gesture shocked him; shocked Devonny too. She felt as if she were stroking the devil.

"After all," said Devonny sadly and loudly, "when a young man loses his mind, and cannot speak intelligibly, and cannot think clearly, it is the duty of his closest friend to act swiftly. I see now that it was quite wonderful of you to find Evergreen Asylum and help Father bring Strat there for treatment."

Walk recovered quickly. It was one of his best skills. He smiled. "All is forgiven, Devonny my dear. Of course we cherished Strat, but lunacy must be taken off the streets and away from loved ones. I am confident the doctors will find a way to bring Strat back from his insanity."

You're hoping he dies first, thought Devonny. She tucked herself against Walk's heavy coat. Luckily beaver was so thick she could feel nothing of the man himself. Otherwise she would have become quite faint. "It will be a great relief to me to leave in the morning. The train trip to the West Coast will restore me. You were so clever to convince Father that what I need is to be in California with him and Florinda and not here in New York, sitting alone and worried at Number Forty-four, fretting about my poor unfortunate brother. Thank you, Walker."

Well, she just hoped Miss Lockwood was listening. This was for her benefit and if Anna Sophia Lockwood was not paying attention, they were both in trouble, because Devonny could hardly run through her instructions again.

Devonny dared not look up from her position. She

38

just had to pray that the pedestrian who swept behind them was Anna Sophia Lockwood.

"Your brother . . . ," said Walker Walkley.

If she had to listen to Walker talk about Strat, Devonny might just seize Walk's cane and ram it down his throat in revenge. "Flossie and I went to the Museum this afternoon, Walk," she said. "How I wish you had been with us. I do adore mummies. I want to go to Egypt shortly. I've shopped in Paris and seen theater in London and that's enough of that. I think a cruise on the Nile would be just right. I want to dig among the pyramids. I feel I am destined to find an important mummy of my own."

Actually Devonny would have liked to embalm Walker, and turn him into a mummy.

While her tongue rambled, her mind got sharp. Like her father, Devonny had always been able to think of several things at once. When she was little, Father had taken her often to his office. She had run around filling the inkwells, while people beamed at her. Little girls are so amusing when they play Office. But young ladies are not. Young ladies must be kept at home and taught to play Wife.

Devonny intended to be an excellent wife but she felt she could also run an excellent office. Right now she was going to run a superior rescue.

Somehow she would whip Miss Lockwood into shape. It did not look, from her brief glimpse in the dark, as if there were much to work with, but Anna Sophia Lockwood was all Devonny had. She would send Miss Lockwood to the insane aylum. This would prove that Strat had not made the girl up. Strat would then be released.

Devonny worried for a moment that the Asylum might keep Miss Lockwood instead, because what sane person would behave as she had? But Evergreen was a private asylum and cost a great deal of money, and her father was unlikely to pay the bill for Miss Lockwood. So that was fine, then, and soon Strat would be out and of course would rush to Harriett's side, and Harriett would be restored by love and get completely well, and everybody would live happily ever after.

It was a fine plan.

Devonny swept into the Vanderbilt Mansion as if it were her own. She was stunning in her peach brocade gown, with its intricate layers of lace and its careful stitching to show off her tiny waist. Naturally Devonny had eaten a cracker beforehand, so she would not feel hunger. Having food tonight was out of the question. Chewing was not pretty.

"Gussie!" she cried, kissing a friend. "Mildred! Alice!" Devonny kissed busily in circles, even people she disliked or had hoped would move to Philadelphia. Quickly she had lots of space between herself and Walker Walkley.

Her mind flew.

Miss Lockwood would need money. This was difficult. Devonny did not often have access to cash. Miss Lockwood would need a wardrobe. This was difficult too. Devonny's things were packed for the great journey, some already shipped, much else in trunks and valises and hatboxes. Miss Lockwood would need directions. Devonny did not precisely know where Evergreen was. Miss Lockwood would have to be resourceful.

The real looming problem was that Miss Lockwood's century was an ill-mannered place where ladies behaved improperly and wore horrifying pieces of cloth instead of fashion.

Devonny hoped that Anna Sophia would be an eager learner when it came to dress. Surely she would want to cast off those street-urchin rags.

Walker Walkley cut through the press of ladies, and there was no doubt from his stride that he meant to repossess Devonny.

Walker Walkley actually living in *her* town house! Disgusting! How dare Father treat Walk like a son? How dare Father take Walk's word for things instead of Strat's?

Devonny felt herself turning into her father, a ferocious human being, who, if the whiskey or claret did not suit him, would stomp his huge boot on the floor until the servants came running and improved themselves. Her features turned hard as a railroad baron's as she thought what she would like to do right now.

But Walk must suspect nothing. His whole mind must be consumed with rapture for Devonny.

She let her strong shoulders sag. She opened her rosebud mouth to soften her lips, lowered her long lashes and fluttered her wrists. She trembled so he would see his dominance.

It was a dance of sorts. He danced with strength. She danced with weakness.

But I will win, thought Devonny Aurelia Victoria Stratton. In the end, Walker Walkley, I will make an Egyptian mummy out of you.

CHAPTER 3

Strat stumbled after Ralph, his feet bumbling around as if he didn't ordinarily walk. And of course, for several months, he hadn't ordinarily walked. Ralph, too, was bumbling along. He was smiling, because Strat, whipped and beaten, had asked to be jailed once more. But he was not looking. What was there to look at?

Every fiber of Strat awoke.

Every molecule of energy raced to the surface. His apathetic soul leaped toward the most important thing: *escape*.

Evergreen was no remodeled mansion where difficult people had bedrooms. It had been constructed to store the insane. Its walls were thick stone, its windows high and narrow. Its doors were heavy with keyed locks, and the keys hung from brass circles which attendants like Ralph strapped through their belts.

Beyond the buildings were very high, iron grille

fences, and twenty yards beyond those, walls of mortared stone in which glass shards were imbedded.

Every guard carried something to hit with: flat sticks, circular bats, linked steel balls. Ralph was armed with a club.

When they passed from the snow garden into the building, Ralph actually held the door for Strat. Strat slammed the door into the attendant's face and knocked him out in a shower of blood. Strat stepped quickly back outside and surveyed the obstacles between himself and freedom.

Snow was in his favor.

Shoveled by trusted inmates against the iron fences, it was packed high enough for a three- or four-foot boost. Strat could easily grasp the top horizontal bar and swing himself over onto the white expanse. Then the only problem would be the glass-studded wall.

So he would cut himself. What were cuts in the hand compared to freedom?

Even as he ran, even as he found to his joy that the snow *would* hold him and his hands *did* have strength and he *could* vault over the eight-foot fence, he was planning his future.

He would never go home. What was there for him? A mother who had not come, a fiancée who had not written, a sister who had not visited, and a father who had chosen this.

No. He was going into the wilderness. He would vanish forever and build a new life, a manly life.

Not in America. It had no more wilderness, it was boring, there was no more Wild West. Alaska was a possibility, and of course Africa. The source of the Nile had been discovered, but surely there was something left for Strat to do.

Thinking of the Nile, of crocodiles and pyramids, Strat slogged through white drifts. It was slow going. The narrow windows of Evergreen had advantages. Even those who were allowed to look out rarely did.

He reached the stone wall. His bare fingers scrabbled against the jutting rocks, gripping a one-inch protrusion here and a half-inch ledge there. The cold he did not notice. When he hoisted himself up, supporting himself by shoving his toes in cracks supplied by the stonemason, he discovered that the glass was in a neat, straight line, and he could avoid it without the slightest difficulty.

Laughing, Strat tipped himself over, landing in a snowdrift, not getting a single bruise.

He had escaped.

Number Forty-four, thought Annie, and saw the immense building right away.

The town house looked as if several architects had owned their own quarries and each man had thrown his own stone at the walls and steps. Brownstone, limestone, granite and marble. Above that, stained glass and wrought iron.

Annie had known the Strattons were well-to-do, but she had not realized that their beach mansion was a simple summer cottage. A throwaway. Here was the real wealth and the real Mansion.

Devonny and Walker Walkley disappeared into the snow. Oh, Strat! thought Annie. I'm doing this for you, *and you're not here!*

She tried to cling to the memory of Strat, but there was nothing to cling to here, nothing at all.

High frightening steps climbed steeply to an immense front door. There was no comfy porch. Either the doorman admitted a caller promptly, or there was a risk of falling backward onto the distant sidewalk.

Annie knocked on Number Forty-four.

The door opened. Electric light from cute little pointy bulbs illuminated a huge hall. Hideous wallpaper shrieked at her. Immense oil portraits of frightening ancestors, a stag's head with sprawling antlers, and an enormous glass display stuffed with dead pheasants crowded the walls.

Annie dripped onto the carpet.

Two people regarded her with suspicion. The man wore a tailcoat, a high starched white collar and a fat black bow tie; the woman had on a floor-length black gown with a shiny black overdress. They looked like people on their way to a fashionable evening funeral, but she was pretty sure they were just servants, and the shiny overdress was actually an apron.

Frozen, slush-covered and torn, Annie tried to think of a way to make these people keep her. Or at least warm her up. "Good evening," said Annie. Her mind was time-sloshed. Strat, suffering loss of mind and thought? Strat, in an insane asylum? "I am Miss Anna Sophia Lockwood," she managed at last. "I am a very dear friend of Miss Devonny's from Connecticut. A dreadful thing has occurred. I most desperately require your aid."

The man was already taking her black coat, shaking off the snow and brushing it down with his gloved hand. "What is that, Miss Lockwood?" he said sympathetically.

What is that? wondered Annie. "I was robbed!" she improvised. "Some dreadful individual, some wicked man!"

"Oh, miss, how awful!" cried the maid, accepting her story right away. "The streets is full of such these days. No matter what the hour, criminals and gangs wander those sidewalks."

They escorted her into an immense, amazing room. The ceilings soared so high Annie felt as if she were in Grand Central Station again. Indigo-blue skies were painted with gold-leaf stars and crescent moons and suns with trembling rays. Layers of rugs covered the floors, and collections—Chinese bronze here, Tiffany glass there—were distributed as casually as schoolbooks.

Every piece of furniture was rounded: drawers on magnificent desks bowed outward and sides of enormous arm chairs puffed and heaved. Everything that could have gold on it did. Gold mirror frames, gold umbrella stands, gold feet on fern stands and gold statues and gold braid festooned on gold-threaded curtains.

"Are you all right, miss?" asked the butler anxiously. "Did he hurt you?"

"No," said Annie quickly, lest they send the police

looking for her fictional attacker. "But he took my reticule. I have no money and no ticket for the train
home." Annie was rather pleased with the word *reticule*,
but the maid looked confused. Perhaps Annie was
wrong about what they called a purse. Oh, well. Moving right along, she thought. "I'm soaked," she said. "I
must have a hot bath." She counted on being beautiful
to carry her through. Beauty was useful in life. People
thought it said things about you, and now she wanted
these two servants to think it said, *You want me for a
houseguest. I am the sort of houseguest you usually have.*
"Miss Devonny will be delighted to let me stay the
night," she assured them, "and now I am simply too
weary to go on. You must get me dry clothing. Hers
will fit me; we often exchange gowns when Miss
Devonny visits me in Connecticut."

The servants were used to obeying and believing.
Annie was whisked up the front stairs into a charming
guest room while a bath was quickly drawn. Tall radia-
tors against the walls clacked and bonged as hot water
boiled through them. The bedroom was stifling. It had
to be eighty degrees, the air stale with old perfume.

"What's your name?" she asked the maid.

"Schmidt."

Annie made her first error of the century by requesting Schmidt to open the windows. "It's so stuffy,
Schmidt."

It was not windows but Schmidt's mouth that
opened, in amazement. "We don't open windows, miss.
You mustn't let in night air. Surely you don't open your
windows out there in the country! Why, you have

48

swamps and marshes and all manner of unhealthy air out there." The horror of night air upset Schmidt so much that she unloosened vast, heavy draperies and yanked them shut over the offending sight of windows.

Schmidt undressed her for the bath, appalled at the lack of decent undergarments. No corset, no chemise, no long drawers, no woolen stockings. Annie's lovely blue knit dress Schmidt treated as an appalling rag, and held it with her fingertips. "It's ruined!" cried Annie. "That dreadful man ripped off all the ribbons and all the lace and all the—I can't talk about it."

Schmidt felt much better about the gown now that she knew the good parts had been torn off.

"I'll just rest in the hot water for a while," said Annie, hoping Schmidt would leave. But Schmidt sat on a three-legged stool next to the tub as if she were going to play the piano. It was difficult to have a witness. It made for a short, efficient bath. Annie was tucked into a bed so occupied by pillows there was hardly room to lie down.

A knock on the door was supper on a footed tray. The tray was beautiful. A tiny brass railing kept crystal glasses from slipping off. A frail bone-china cup held tea. There was a bowl of thick creamy soup and a funny little white pudding decorated with colored sugar fruit that Annie associated with inedible Christmas cakes. Annie sipped the dark red liquid in the smallest glass and nearly gagged. It was thick as syrup and absolutely disgusting. Was it medicine?

"The best claret, miss, good for chills."

"Lovely," said Annie. "Thank you so much." She

took no more risks, and sipped tea. It tasted as if it had been brewing since it left India. "I was so fond of young Mr. Stratton, Schmidt. I know the dreadful course of action that was taken. Please tell me how he is doing now. Is he all right?"

"Oh, miss, it's such a shame. His poor mother has tried to visit, but Mr. Stratton's instructions are no visitors. Poor lady sold her jewelry to get the train ticket, went all the way up north, and was not permitted in. But she said the Evergreen place was beautiful, and they reassured her that he is receiving the very best of treatment." Schmidt tended to the pillows, fluffing and rearranging.

Annie could not eat. She could only cry.

"Now, miss," said the maid comfortingly, "he's in the best of care. These asylums as they have for gentlemen, they're not like the state asylums."

Asylum. It conjured up cold gray stones and thin lumpy mattresses: crazy people screaming through the night.

She felt stalled, ruined. How was she supposed to cope with insanity? She hadn't brought tranquilizers. She had never counseled anybody in her life, just gossiped with her girlfriends.

Did I do it? she thought. Did falling in love with a girl who fell through Time send him over an edge of his own? Oh, Time. Did you bring me back to make me look at what a vicious thing I did, interrupting their lives? "And Miss Harriett?" asked Annie, sick with worry.

50

The maid drooped. "Bleeding of the lungs. Of course she couldn't stay here and make everybody else sick. They looked in the Blue Ridge Mountains for better air, but the towns there don't take lungsick. It ruins a town's looks, you know, to have all those thin, dying people around. Up in the Adirondacks, though, it used to be just for hunting and fishing and men who like that kind of thing, getting wet in their canoes and making campfires, but now of course it's for cure cottages, and I understand the mountain air cleans out the lungs." Schmidt took away the tray. "Sometimes, anyway," she added, striving to be precise. "Mostly they die."

Time, you monster! Why didn't you tell me to bring medicine? You brought me here to see the end of Strat and Harriett both?

I'm a lunatic myself, Annie realized. Look at me, addressing Time as if he exists and he's the bad guy.

Annie told the maid to let her sleep. "When Miss Devonny and Mr. Walk come in, Schmidt, please don't tell Mr. Walkley I'm here." How to keep him out of the picture? Walker Walkley had been rotten then and no doubt he was rotten now, or Devonny would not have kept his eyes cupped in her hands to prevent him from seeing Annie.

Possibly a half-truth would do. The sort they used in this century. "Once Mr. Walkley was forward with me," she murmured, "and I am uncomfortable in his company."

"I'll be ever so careful, miss, don't you worry."

Don't worry? thought Annie Lockwood. I changed Time to find Strat, and he's hundreds of miles away, locked in an asylum, and Devonny is dating Walk, who put him there?

On the bedside table was a lovely little calendar, painted by hand with cherubs and roses. February, it said. 1898, it said.

"1898?" she cried.

Schmidt stared at her.

"I mean, I'm really so tired, Schmidt," said Annie, who felt herself unraveling like an old towel, "you are so good to me, thank you so much." Only nine months passed in my century. How could three years have passed here? What is Time doing?

"Shall I sit with you until you are asleep, miss?" asked Schmidt, and Annie thought of her mother, who sat with Annie or Tod whenever they didn't feel well so they'd have company for falling asleep.

What is it about sleep that makes us afraid to fall alone? Where have I fallen . . . alone?

In the shanties north of Central Park, immigrants shuddered with cold and postponed as long as possible a trip to the outhouse.

But at the Vanderbilts', guests dined among real grape arbors, brought at great expense from southern greenhouses. At each place, tucked among fresh flowers rushed north by train, were gifts. The men received engraved silver boxes, whose round lids hinged up to take wooden matchsticks for lighting cigars; the ladies were given crystal perfume bottles, their stoppers encrusted with diamonds.

The soups were duck and turtle, the dinner was roast mountain sheep with puree of chestnuts, and wines of superior vintage accompanied the meal. An opera singer and her orchestra entertained.

Walker Walkley regarded opera as a series of Indian war whoops, and he would have preferred the Indians.

During the boring recital, he looked with approval at Devonny's friend Flossie. How refined she was! So thin that she literally could not support herself, but must lean upon her escort. Naturally Flossie hardly looked up and hardly spoke, and it was so beautiful, such weakness. This was how women should be.

Devonny, whose behavior could be quite unbecoming, went horseback riding every day when the weather was good and ice skating when it was not. After their marriage, he would put a stop to it. Walk would keep her in the house for a year, no exercise and no sun, because the girl was practically *brown* from being outdoors, and because restraint would calm her down.

When Devonny smiled at him, the usual surge of desire swept over Walk. He—he alone—was going to have that Stratton money. And if he could engineer it, he would also have Harriett Ranleigh's money.

Walk liked the finer things in life. He did not have enough of them. Soon that would change.

He smiled back at Devonny, but of course did not cease his conversation with Mr. Astor. Whatever it was that Devonny wanted to say would keep. (Anything any woman wanted to say would keep.)

Walk was content, thinking of putting Devonny where she belonged.

All day Harriett had been beautiful. Fever brushed her pink, accented her pallor and made her lovely.

The same fever had delivered night sweats so bad the entire bed was soaked and had to be changed in the dark. How could there be any liquid left in her? She was going to dry out and die a crisp little wafer.

"Now, dear," said Moss, "let's have a smile on that beautiful face, and then a glass of milk."

Six glasses of milk had to be swallowed every day. Harriett hated anything to do with cows now. "When I am well, I will go to the South Seas and eat mangos," she said to Moss.

Moss's assistant, Mario, a skinny boy who carried, emptied and lifted, changed her again. Consumption was a filthy disease. Nobody talked about that. It was important not to refer to the actual squalor of the sickroom. It was important to maintain the fiction that one died gently, setting an example, and going will-ingly to God.

But coughing hurt so much. Her whole body hurt. For the first time, Harriett was willing to give up her body. It was too hard to live in it.

I am so afraid, thought Harriett. And so cold.

Devonny had soaked her pillows many nights with her tears and fears. She had wept for her dearest friend, Harriett, whose decline had turned out to be consumption, and for her beloved brother, Strat, when Father turned against him. Now she soaked the pillows in her bedroom with tears of rage and frustration.

One of the problems here was that just because Father was in California did not mean that Father was out of reach.

In this dreadful new world, people were never out of reach. There were telephones and telegraphs. It was hideous. You could have Father on the opposite coast of America—*with thousands of miles in between*—and still, bad people like Walker Walkley could get in touch with him *that very day*.

Walker Walkley came into everything.

Suddenly Devonny realized that it was Walk who had taken the mail to the post each morning. The footman had always done it, but Walker insisted that he needed the exercise.

He didn't mail our letters, thought Devonny. Strat does not know we've been writing. Maybe even Harriett does not know we've been writing. Maybe they are both alone, without knowing they are loved and missed. All my letters of encouragement . . . they were never mailed.

Forget mummies. Devonny wanted Walker Walkley to kneel down with Marie Antoinette. A guillotine would improve him.

Exhausted from the party and the constant need to be helpless and clinging, Devonny was now far too close to sleep. Sleep would be a grave error. Devonny got out of bed and paced the hot room to keep herself awake.

Walk simply would not go to bed. What was the matter with that man? He was down there in Father's smoking room, striding back and forth as if he owned it.

Walker Walkley, you toad. It's good I'm going to California. I will find somebody to marry. Anybody. Anybody at all. As long as he's tall and handsome, of course, and speaks beautifully and is educated and well traveled. I'll marry him quickly and that will serve Walker Walkley right.

Her vision of California was wonderfully sunny, full of orange and palm groves, and rows of flawless men to whom she would be introduced.

Meantime, there was work to be done.

She ran her mind over the battalion of servants in the house. Naturally one didn't know them personally, and after the Lockwood problem at the summer cottage, Father had dismissed everybody and replaced them with strangers.

Devonny was going to have to entrust one or more of these strangers with the safety of Anna Sophia.

It would have to be Schmidt. Devonny was not fond of Schmidt, who talked steadily and boringly, but the woman had already let Miss Lockwood in and given her a bath, and unless Miss Lockwood had improved, Schmidt had probably already learned secrets a servant should not possess.

It was two in the morning.

Schmidt had gone to bed.

Devonny was annoyed. Servants had minds of their own these days. Father was right. A person had to be strict with them.

She buzzed Schmidt.

Katie had known, of course, that the truly insane at Evergreen were the attendants: men and women who loved to hit. Violence was constant. They would kick a person over any excuse or none. With those heavy key rings they liked to hit patients in the face. They told Katie they didn't hit her in the face because she was so ugly the scars wouldn't show. They struck her hands instead.

Poor Strat.

If he had been poor all his life, perhaps he could have completed his escape. But he had behaved like a rich man, expecting to be welcomed at an inn in the village and given a room with a hot bath. The innkeeper simply summoned the staff from the asylum.

Strat had fought, and now had no chance whatever of getting out of Evergreen. He truly was dangerous. He had broken a man's arm and knocked a tooth from another man's jaw, and as for Ralph, Ralph's head still rang from the collision of that door against his nose and eye sockets, and Ralph was not a forgiving person.

They put Strat in the straitjacket: a canvas shirt whose arms were mittened at the tips, with straps that tied Strat's arms to his chest. Then he was given treatment. The treatment consisted of reducing him to a mass of bruises.

From the only kind attendant at Evergreen, Katie obtained a cup of warm water and a relatively clean cloth. She bathed Strat's wounds when Ralph finally quit, and talked to Strat constantly, to keep him calm. When he swore or talked back, they simply hit him again. It was a very long night. Actually, it could have been day by now; Katie had no window and no sun by which to gauge.

"Katie," said Strat, through swollen painful lips, "why? Why doesn't even my mother come?"

Katie began working the knots out of his hair. She felt that Strat could not go on if he believed his mother did not love him, so she said, "Your dear mother loves you, but has never been told where you are. I expect your dear sister loves you, but has also been kept unaware. Or else they truly believe you are in some pleasant place receiving kind treatment."

Katie, who had never received kindness, knew how to give it.

"If they'd just let me out!" cried Strat.

Since they were not going to let him out, Katie continued to say nothing on that subject. She felt terribly sorry for him. It was easier for her, because she had not known much else.

"Katie, if you could get out," asked Strat, "where would you go?"

Katie did not laugh bitterly. She simply heard his question. "I have nowhere to go. I am deformed. I will always be deformed. No one would want me."

Douglass snuffled, making his "read to me" sound. Katie picked up her Bible and read.

"They'd have put Jesus in an insane asylum," said Strat.

"No, said Katie, "because he was beautiful. And so were his disciples. To be ugly is the worst thing. Nobody forgives you for that."

"We have very little time," said Devonny, giving the sleeping Miss Lockwood a rough shake, "and we must accomplish a thousand things before Walk appears in the morning. Noon, actually. He's never up before noon."

Annie struggled to wake up. She had centuries to cross and bad dreams to throw off.

"First of all," said Devonny Stratton to Annie Lockwood, "I want you to admit that this is All. Your. Fault."

❦ CHAPTER 4 ❦

Annie wished she were a hundred years later, safe in her own time, when people let you use any excuse at all. You never had to be responsible for what you did, because it could always be somebody else's fault.

"Listen to me, Miss Lockwood," said Devonny Stratton sharply. She did not look forgiving. "Because he wept for you—because he wrote an essay at Yale describing your century—because he wandered around the mansion grounds calling for you and looking behind trees for you—my brother looked insane."

How could such a perfect love have such a horrible result?

Oh, no, thought Annie, please no! It was true love, not insanity.

"Walker Walkley," said Devonny, as harsh as winter,

"found out about that essay and weaseled himself back into our lives, telling lies and more lies and greater lies to Father. Father believed him, and the ministers at Yale thought that Strat was godless and . . . well, it's all your fault, Miss Lockwood. My brother is not insane. But knowing you made him appear insane."

If only the lights were not on. In soft, cozy dark this would not sound so horrible. If she were under the covers it would sound like a scary bedtime story, not a death sentence.

"Everything *is* my fault," said Annie. Her heart wrenched apart, separated chambers beating against each other. It hurt terribly.

Such a beautiful room for such a confrontation. And even in the middle of the night, all three women were beautifully clothed: voluminous white gowns, with lace and ruffles and embroidered flowers. In contrast to daytime, they wore their hair down: Devonny's actually reached her waist, and Schmidt's reached below hers. Schmidt's was streaked with gray and Devonny's with gold. Even their hair said who they were in life, and what they owned.

Annie's hair, which once Strat had threaded through his fingers and made into horsetails, lay straight and dark on her shoulders. "I'm sorry," she whispered. "I didn't go through Time on purpose. I didn't choose your family. Time chose you."

Schmidt was gaping at them. High and broad in her heavy nightgown, she looked like an overweight Statue of Liberty.

"However, Anna Sophia . . . ," said Devonny. Her voice cracked. She was only a teenager herself, no older than Annie. (Annie was so completely her name: Anna Sophia felt like somebody else.)

Devonny soldiered on. "In spite of the terrible things you did to us, Anna Sophia, we loved you."

They loved me, she thought. And I loved them. But I loved Strat the most. Strat, what have I done to you? How can I make up for it?

"Even Harriett loved you," said Devonny, "and you were such a threat to her future."

Does Harriett even have a future now? thought Annie. Surely they can't blame me that she got sick.

"But now," said Devonny, "now you must prove your worth, Miss Lockwood."

Prove her worth?

Right.

Annie wasn't worth anything even to her own father.

How glad she was to be lying among soft pillows. You could count on pillows to comfort you, even when everybody in your life turned against you. Annie hugged a pillow.

"Repack the trunks, Schmidt," said Devonny, stabbing a finger toward the proper clothing. "Silently. Nobody must hear a sound from this room. Miss Lockwood is heading north. Find warm things for her. She must be stylish. Fashion will be important. She must impress people in order to get my brother out of Evergreen."

Oh, good, thought Annie. I get to live.

Schmidt chose a trunk so large you could carry a

bodyguard in it, or enough clothing to last a generation.

"Schmidt will order a cab to take you to the Hudson Nightline Pier, whence you will take a steamboat to Albany. From thence, the Delaware and Hudson train, disembarking at Evergreen, New York. This is the site of the asylum to which my brother has been confined. I do not know the exact address, but I presume the natives keep track of their lunatic asylums and will guide you."

Annie was stunned. Devonny was sending her out into some wilderness to a lunatic asylum? "But Devonny, how can I possibly do that?"

"You'll behave yourself like a proper lady. You won't talk to people," explained Devonny. "It isn't ladylike to address strangers. But you'll use feminine wiles, of course."

"No, Devonny, you have to go with me!"

"I cannot. Walker Walkley reports to Father. Walk will put me on the train to California tomorrow and I must take it. If I don't, he will know something is happening and he will stop it. You must be very careful of Walker Walkley, Miss Lockwood. He will stop at nothing. There is so much money at stake."

"What do you mean, he will stop at nothing?" said Annie. "Do you mean he's a murderer or a kidnapper?"

"He's a kidnapper anyway. How do you think they got Strat to an asylum? They tricked him and kidnapped him."

Annie flopped back on the pillows as if she were Raggedy Ann.

Schmidt filled a hat box: towering impossible hats, with built-in neck scarves and posturing feathers and hanging beads.

Fashion is supposed to get me in there? Annie wondered about this theory. I'm supposed to use a hat to break down locks?

"You must address the situation there," said Devonny, kneeling on the bed. "I do not know what Father has set up." Devonny bounced angrily. "Your job is to make it clear to the authorities that my brother is *not* a lunatic! You must substantiate that *you exist.*"

Schmidt, folding gowns, paused.

"This is not your affair, Schmidt," said Devonny severely.

"Yes, miss," said Schmidt.

It seemed to Annie that Schmidt was packing an excess of nightgowns and not enough morning, afternoon, and evening gowns, but if she were overhearing this conversation, her packing skills might be off too. "What if they don't believe me, Devonny? I'm a good liar, and I've had lots of practice lately, but what if I don't pull it off?"

"Then you will have to take Strat with you into your own Time. I have given this a great deal of thought, Anna Sophia. What matters is my brother."

Take Strat back into her own Time.

What an astonishing thought. Whisk him over the decades, holding his hand as they fell up a century. There he would be—handsome, funny, sweet strong Strat.

And then what? Annie couldn't manage a father and mother, or friends, or school trips, or even a purse. She was too dizzy to move Strat to the twentieth century. And yet . . . how lovely it would be.

"Devonny, wait a minute. You expect me to take on lunatic asylums and buy train tickets and carry my own trunk? Look at the size of that thing. I'd need a squad just to carry it."

"That's what porters are for," said Devonny irritably. "You pay people to carry your trunk." Devonny grabbed her shoulders. "Listen. You started this and you have to finish it. I have not been able to leave the house without Walker Walkley escorting me! I have not been able to mail my own letters. Our mother, because Father divorced her, of course has no standing and can accomplish nothing. She had to sell a brooch in order to get money to travel to Evergreen, and then they would not break Father's instructions just for a woman! They never let her see her son."

"I'm a woman too," said Annie feebly. Where were the gala balls and fine gowns? She did not want responsibility! There was enough of that in other centuries. In this century, a woman was supposed to be sheltered and entertained.

"I have been sent for," said Devonny harshly. "Father is requiring me to come to California. I can make no choices. But *you* are different. You told us so. You said in your century you make the choices. We're counting on you."

Annie hated being quoted at awkward times. I'll

choose to go home after all, she thought. This won't be a romantic adventure. Strat isn't even here! In every way, this will be dark and icy and slippery.

"You said women can do anything," Devonny told her.

Annie flushed. She probably had said that. She had probably even believed it. But surely, when you changed centuries, you got to change burdens. Is that why I came? she thought. So it would be easier?

Schmidt, who was not supposed to be listening, said, "I came from Germany, miss. I did not speak English. I learned how to get here and how to get a job. So you can learn how to get up the Hudson River."

Immigrants were always boasting about how hard they had struggled. In her own time, men rowed in leaky rafts across shark-infested waters in order to leave Haiti and find jobs in America and take better care of their families—and she, Annie Lockwood, wouldn't even take a cab across Manhattan?

"Thank you, Schmidt," said Devonny when she saw that Annie was conquered. "You shall be rewarded." This was as much attention as she gave a maid, however. "You'll need money, Anna Sophia. I have taken everything I can find. Actually the only person with cash is Walker, so I have appropriated his. He owes it to me, anyway."

Devonny had appropriated Walk's cash? What did that mean? Had she lifted his wallet? Emptied his checking account? Or wherever people kept their dollars in 1898? But that was stealing. Annie was supposed to spend those stolen dollars? Belonging to a man who had already kidnapped and Devonny thought would murder too?

Annie said anxiously, "What if he has some household servant arrested for it? What if he suspects"— Annie tried not to look at Schmidt—"one of your maids or something?"

"These things happen," said Devonny, who, indeed, was very like her father. "Now, for Harriett. She has consumption. I know that she can be cured by true love. I absolutely know this. So once you get Strat out, you must journey onward to Clear Pond."

"Is that in the Adirondacks too?"

"Everything is. Mountain air is of use both to the insane and to the consumptive. Questions?"

Annie would like to have taken Devonny back to the twentieth century with her and have Devonny straighten Miss Bartten out. But the words that came from Annie's mouth were nineteenth-century words. "I shall not let you down," she said firmly. The words resounded in the Victorian bedroom, and Annie was proud.

"Good," said Devonny. "Schmidt, it is practically dawn. Let's get her dressed."

It was morning in the Adirondacks too.

Harriett was awestruck by the beauty of new-fallen snow. Everything was a choir robe, a child in a Christmas play. All dark branches of all dark trees bowed down with snow in their arms.

And indeed, the sounds of children could be heard.

In this silent isolation, a family had come to visit! They had come by sleigh, the snow and the sable furs all part of a great adventure.

I would find it a great adventure, too, thought Harriett, if it had what all adventure requires—going home again.

Children dashed through the snow, whooping and hollering.

How wonderful their voices sounded to Harriett.

When I die, she thought, will I hear the voices of children again? It takes such courage to stay here. It is so awful, so dull, so cold, so alone. We try to bolster each other, but it is hard. We patients want two things.

To be well.

To be home.

And I . . . I want a third.

Strat.

∽

Tod Lockwood knocked on his sister's bedroom door.

Nobody answered.

It had that complete dusty silence of when nobody is there.

Slowly, Tod opened Annie's door.

Nobody was there.

He didn't want to think about it. The other times— those two terrifying, maddening times when she had gone off by herself—the community and the police searching for her—Mom and Dad nuts with worry— himself realizing that he actually loved his sister . . .

Well, she had done it again.

And Tod Lockwood did not love her for it.

"Fine," he said to the silent room. "Be rotten. See if I care."

He slammed the door and stomped out of the house to school.

He wouldn't cover her tracks for her because he had no idea where her tracks were. She had covered them pretty darn well the other times.

But he wouldn't tell on her either.

He wouldn't let Mom in Japan worry and he wouldn't allow Dad back into the family he'd deserted.

So there.

"How intriguing!" cried Beanie.

The peddler beamed from beneath his mustache.

"You're not going to buy one, are you, Beanie?" said Harriett disapprovingly.

"Harriett, darling, I'll try anything." Beanie fitted the glass helmet over her head. It didn't go. She had to take off her earmuffs and scarf. Now it fit. Harriett giggled, looking at her.

"What on earth?" demanded Moss the nurse. "Take that monstrosity away from your face immediately, Miss Beatrice."

"It's a re-breather, Moss," said Beanie. From behind the glass bowl, her voice was muffled. Her breath fogged the glass and it was so cold on the porch Harriett expected the glass to frost.

"I beg your pardon," said Moss, more frostily than the weather. "The point of the cure is to breathe fresh mountain air."

"Ah ha!" cried the peddler. "Except if it's not working. And then the newest thing is to rebreathe your own used breath. Those special gases have healing properties."

"You are responsible for following all rules of the cure, Miss Beatrice!" said Moss. "I'm sure I cannot be responsible for what happens if you neglect the procedure."

Beanie rebreathed lustily.

Fundamental to cure were the rules. The slightest break might lead down the path of death instead of the path of life. Beanie's rebreather might remove the fragile barrier between herself and her Maker.

Charlie, having just left the billiards room, came slowly up the path, smoking his pipe, assisted by his man and two canes. Of course he wanted to try on the rebreathing apparatus.

Harriett distracted Moss. "Did you go to school, Moss?" asked Harriett.

"I finished eighth grade, Miss Harriett. Then I nursed my mother, who died of consumption, my father, who died of it, and then my aunt, and then I decided to be a nurse here."

"You're a wonderful nurse," said Harriett.

"Thank you," said Moss happily. "I have climbed quite a ladder."

Harriett thought it a very short ladder. But the ladders of women usually were. "How is Lucy Leora?"

Harriett asked. Lucy Leora had the cottage behind the fir trees and Moss often helped Lucy Leora's nurse.

"She died in the night, Miss Harriett," said Moss calmly.

Beanie and Charlie were not listening. They were giggling and wasting lung energy over the glass helmet. They did not know that Death had come in the night.

Moss bustled around, replacing Harriet's cooled-off foot warmer with a hot soapstone just off the stove. "Lucy Leora had a good easy death. In her sleep. You may thank God."

Harriett did not thank God. He was too mean. Lucy Leora had been sixteen.

Dear Lord, prayed Harriett (because even if He was mean and took sixteen-year-olds, He was all Harriett had), I am still betrothed to Strat. It still counts, I know it does. I still wear his ring, and if he has not written to tell me he loves me, at least he has not written to tell me he loves another! *I must get well*, and we *will* have children, and live happily ever after, I know we will!

The traveling hat, which tied under her chin with broad wool streamers, had a wide black velvet brim and five garnet-red ostrich plumes. It gave Annie grace and dignity, explained Devonny. A swollen roll of veiling collected around the hat rim, waiting to be unwrapped. Annie had no intention of veiling her face. There was such a thing as going too far.

Her dress was a pale-gray velvet, difficult swollen

buttons streaming down the back, fastened not into holes but into silk loops. The lower twelve inches of the dress was skirted with moiré, which could be detached and cleaned if the street soiled the hemline. The dress ribbons were garnet to match the hat plumes.

Beneath the dress of course was a corset laced tight enough to break ribs, a chemise to cover her limbs, and wool stockings held up above her knees with killer elastic bands.

Her ankle-length coat was sleek dark mink. Her black gloves reached her elbows, and her mitt was mink inside and out. Annie figured the costume was a quick way to gain fifty pounds.

Schmidt did not even smuggle Annie out of the town house. "Mr. Walker's still in bed, miss," explained Schmidt. "He's fond of his brandy. It takes him time in the morning to open his eyes and he needs even more brandy to do that." Servants carried Devonny's trunk—now Annie's—down the stairs.

"But what if he comes out and sees me?" she hissed at Schmidt. "What will you say?"

"I'll say 'Good morning, sir.'"

I have to be that calm, thought Annie. I have to hold my chin high and my plumes high and my muff high, and say things like "Good morning, sir," and swirl away in a haughty ladylike fashion.

The butler ordered a taxi. To Annie, this meant a Yellow Cab. But of course, it was a horse-drawn taxi—without wheels.

"A sleigh!" cried Annie, laughing. *Bells on bobtail ring,*

72

making spirits bright, what fun it is to ride and sing a
sleighing song tonight. Oh jingle bells, jingle bells . . . !

And they did jingle.

The two horses were adorned with leather straps
hung with jingle bells bigger than anything on a door
wreath: fat silvery bells, a hundred to chorus and jan-
gle.

Devonny had not come down to see her off.
Devonny in fact had gone back to bed, and according
to Schmidt was sleeping soundly. Annie did not think
this was fair.

The driver and his two horses seemed interested in
suicide. They trotted between horse-drawn omnibuses
and wired trolleys. They whipped under elevated railroads and sped between the convergence of tracks lying
on the street. They aimed at pedestrians. People swore
at them in various languages and shook their fists and
once threw something.

Annie could have used a seat belt. What with one
hand steadying her plume tower and one hand gripping the sleigh rim, she was exhausted.

The stench of New York was amazing. Annie bet that
a hundred thousand horses had plopped dung into the
streets. The sleigh hit all of it.

There were homeless people. Annie could not look
at them now any more than she could bear looking at
them a hundred years later.

The buildings were magnificent, and yet there was a
gaunt, spare coldness to the city that frightened her.
She could not tell, because they flew so fast over the

packed snow, whether it was the newness of the buildings that was frightening or her own newness. She was as weak and vulnerable as the greenest immigrant to step off the boat.

When they arrived at the pier, the steamboat was much larger than she had expected. Open and squat like an enormous ferry, it had two huge, factory-size smokestacks. Smoke billowed, thick with ash and soot. Real sparks flew. She could hear the steam engines, hear the boilers smacking with the metallic sounds of gears and grinding. What a fire trap, she thought. I'm getting on that?

The driver stopped.

She was ashamed of the trunk. It was so huge. And the hatbox and the valise—she could hardly manage that paper hatbox, what with staying erect under the weight of all this clothing.

But it was immediately clear that people did not travel light in 1898.

Mountains of luggage were piled at the gangplanks. One single family ahead of her had as much baggage as a 747 carries to Europe. Annie's trunk and bag looked paltry and forlorn. She began to fret that she would not have enough to wear after all.

Porters were everywhere, which was a good thing, considering how much work they had ahead of them. They wore fine uniforms, like Marine officers on parade.

Every woman was veiled, and they were smarter than Annie. The soot and filth of the coal engines were coating her like paint. She tugged the veil down after all, and tucked it into her coat the way the other women did.

She didn't have to figure out how to buy a ticket; her driver and the porter accomplished this. She did buy a Coke, which cost a nickel. It made her happy to buy a Coke in a glass bottle and pay five cents for it. But that was the only happy thing.

Don't speak to strangers, Devonny had said sharply. It isn't becoming behavior for a lady.

But they were all strangers. How was she to manage without a single person in the world on her team? She could not possibly do this without Devonny.

At least she had a great hat.

It had taken Walker Walkley two whole years to convince Mr. Stratton senior that young Strat was crazy.

Solid intense labor. Paper proof. Stealing Strat's English essays at Yale. Seizing Strat's diary from his locked room. He'd had to add a few sentences here and there, incriminating sentences in careful Strat-style handwriting.

But Walk had won.

Mr. Stratton could not allow the Stratton fortune to go to somebody whose mind was not intact. The man had fought and slashed his way to the top—he would never give that hard-won money to somebody at the bottom. Somebody to be ashamed of.

Strat, in other words.

So Strat would have none, Devonny would have it all, and Walker Walkley would marry Devonny.

The plan was taking longer than Walk had thought, and Devonny had been more difficult, but he was close.

He awoke slowly to his hangover. It was past noon before he could actually open his swollen eyelids. Following Mr. Stratton's example, Walk banged hard on the wall to summon his manservant Gordon and blame the whole headache on him.

Gordon was annoying, as were all servants, but he had been the one who actually subdued Strat. Hulking and iron-muscled, Gordon had literally sat on Strat to prevent the young man from causing difficulties on the long route to Evergreen. Nevertheless, Walk would get rid of Gordon as soon as he had the Stratton money. There were just too many people around who had been involved in delicate procedures.

Delicate. How Walker Walkley liked that word. Last night, Devonny had been perfect in her delicacy. He had won there too.

Walk smiled to himself. Women must be shaped into what men required of them. Once the shape was complete, they could be discarded. He would buy a house to keep Devonny in, or perhaps confine her to the beach cottage, so that he could live in freedom and not be nagged by a wife.

"Mr. Walkley, sir," said Gordon.

The man was just too large. He took up too much space, towering like that; he made Walk feel small. "What are you wearing?" snapped Walk. "How dare you attend me in those clothes? What do you think you are doing, buying fish?"

"Miss Devonny had a visitor last night. I thought you would like to know. The visitor departed early this morning. I followed."

Walker Walkley paled. Could Gordon mean *a male visitor*?

"A beautiful woman," said the servant. "A Miss Lockwood."

The wind over the Adirondack Mountains had risen. It carved channels into the lake snow. Like fluted quilt patterns, the surface glittered silver and gold and diamond.

Mario brought in yet another load of fresh laundry so that Moss could remake the stained bed. "Miss Harriett," he said gently, "how pretty you look today." He meant that the fever was back, rouge on her cheeks.

He had such a New York City accent. "How did you end up in the mountains?" Harriett asked.

"I was a Fresh Air Child."

"You were! How lovely. I always wanted to sponsor a child." Her guardian, Mr. Stratton senior, had forbidden it. Fresh Air children were certain to be unclean, and carry lice, and use foul language. Plus they probably stole from you.

The boy smiled at her. "Last year, fifteen thousand of us were sent to the country. The *Herald Tribune* does it. It's wonderful."

"And they let you stay in the mountains?"

Mario shook his head. "My parents died after I got

back to the city. I wrote Moss, who had had me for the week, and she said to get on the train and come up to work for her."

"Moss," said Harriett respectfully, "you work all week long nursing consumptives and yet you had time to sponsor a Fresh Air Child?"

"Children deserve a summer," said Moss. "Mario went fishing and wading and canoeing."

Children deserve a summer, thought Harriett, and young women deserve a life. Well, I cannot do anything about my life, because it's over, but I can see that children have a summer.

"Moss," she said, "send for an attorney. I must write a new will."

CHAPTER 5

Moss penned a note.

Moss loved handwriting, especially her own. Hers was elegant and gracious, from years of penmanship in grammar school.

There were not many things you could count on in this wicked world, but the postal system was one. Her letter would arrive in New York City in two days. She loved the idea of news traveling so fast. If only it could be good news.

Moss never thought of the telephone.

There were occasions when a person might use that apparatus, but such an occasion had never arisen in Moss's situation.

Dear Mr. Walker,

Following your instructions to keep you informed of all that occurs, so that you may be of immediate

In the insane asylum, Katie was crocheting. It was one of the few activities she was allowed, and she loved it. From that slim silver hook and a ball of plain string would flow circular lace, with arches and whorls, pineapples and crescents. Strat watched it pour off her hook. In the background, the Melancholia wept and begged and the Conspiracy muttered and gnashed.

Strat thought of Anna Sophia. Harriett had loaned her a ballgown that wondrous night. He remembered Miss Lockwood in lace, her hair piled in dark glory. He remembered even the gloves she had worn, the thinnest, most fragile lace, the patterns pressed up against his own palm. There had been nothing fragile about Miss Lockwood except the borrowed clothing. He wrenched his mind from Anna Sophia. "What happens to the lace after you're done, Katie?" he asked.

She shrugged and went on crocheting.

"I mean, really," he protested.

"The laces are taken from me. I expect they are sold."

80

Katie's hair was thin and crinkly. Anna Sophia's hair had made Strat crazy. There was not the slightest curl to Annie's hair; it might have been ironed. Touching it was like threading silk ribbons through his fingers.

I'm thinking of her as if she is here, thought Strat. I'm thinking Annie, instead of Miss Lockwood, as if we are close again, and can touch again, and maybe even laugh again.

He focused on Katie's crochet hook. What uses might that slender tool have? Could he pick a lock with it?

Katie laughed. "You're going to get out of here eventually, Strat. I can feel it. Someday you'll see the hole in their strategy and you'll slip out and be gone." There was a tear on her cheek, which was unusual. Katie was so strong.

Strat felt strangely at peace with himself because he no longer noticed her misshapen body, just sweet Katie herself.

Then as usual, he *became* selfish: Okay, God, I'm a better person, so ease up and let me out of here.

God, as was usually the case, did not seem to be listening that carefully. So Strat talked in his heart to Annie, who always listened.

He remembered dancing with Annie. She had been so light on her feet. She and Strat had spun across the dance floor like autumn leaves falling from trees: at one with the melody and the wind. He remembered their few kisses. It was not decent to be forward with a lady, and all his gentlemanly self-control had been required, lest he go beyond the bounds of good behavior. He remembered best the kiss he had laid on her soft cheek, with which he had sealed his intent toward her.

I love you, she had said when she left him. *Be good to Harriett,* she had said when she left him.

The thought of Miss Lockwood and every other loss he had endured brought a single tear to Strat's face too, and then, to his fury, Dr. Wilmott was standing there, taking notes.

Patient weeps, the doctor entered in Strat's casebook. "You know, Mr. Stratton, normal young men do not cry. It is a serious indication of your delusions."

"If we were to talk about my delusions in your office, sir, we could solve them better than if we talk here, while I am strapped down."

For once Dr. Wilmott did not just smile and exit. From the safety of the door, he said sharply, "You are an insult to your family and to God. You attacked an innocent man trying to assist you. You will remain restrained. Be thankful that you are fed and housed."

Walker Walkley thrashed around, half caught in the sheets and blankets. He scrubbed the stubble on his chin with his palm. He wet his lips. The name *Miss Lockwood* upset him badly. His eyes flew around his bedroom. All too well he remembered the ghastly sight of that girl materializing out of nothing.

"Don't just stand there! Tell me about her!" shouted Walk.

His servant said, "The cab took her to the docks. I

asked the maid who was sweeping off the steps when Miss Devonny's friend was leaving. She said Miss Lockwood was going to Albany."

Albany.

"She will have taken the overnight boat," said Walker Walkley. He felt excitement beginning to rise. What a chase it would be! And what a fine ending. *His* ending. The way he dictated things! That's how it would end. "The night boat is slow. People take it because it is spacious and elegant. It is a treat as well as a journey. I must reach Albany before the boat. Before that evil girl. So I will catch a train."

His manservant looked puzzled. No doubt the fellow did not know where Albany was. He certainly did not know what happened at Albany. Albany was where you changed transportation. From Albany you went north . . . to the Adirondacks . . . to Strat.

Mr. Walkley pointed to his wallet on the dresser. His man fetched it.

The wallet was empty.

So was the sock in the second drawer, and so was the silk-bound keepsake book where Walk kept cash between pages instead of theater tickets or autographs.

Miss Lockwood took my money, he thought. *How could she have known it was here? How could she . . .*

But Walk was one of the few who had seen Anna Sophia Lockwood come through Time. He had watched a ghost emerge in the road, and seen flesh come to her, seen her hair grow and her smile appear. He had seen the wicked clothing she had worn out of her own time—short little white pants and half a shirt.

83

He knew that she could do anything she chose. Now it appeared that she could scent out the locations of paper and silver money.

Walk sucked in his breath. "Call Miss Devonny's maid to me. Schmidt. Bring her here."

"What was her name?" said Katie.

"Whose name?"

"The girl for whom you are here," said Katie. "I know all about Harriett and Devonny and Florinda, but I know nothing of *her*."

Strat shook his head. "I cannot talk about her. Not even to you." Then he was ashamed. Katie deserved the story. And what else did he have to give Katie? It was his turn. "Katie, if I tell you about her, you will also believe that I am crazy and deserve to be here."

"Start with her name," said Katie.

But it had not started with a name. First he had seen her: a ghost becoming flesh. Then he had walked a lonely beach with her, and laughed in the sun, and built a sand castle. "Anna Sophia Lockwood," said Strat, as if repeating sacred words. "She wanted me to call her Annie."

"Oooh," said Katie happily. "Let me guess. She was Roman Catholic and you agreed to convert and your father has you here instead of shooting you."

"No."

"You had a storehouse of gold, and you gave it to Anna Sophia's poodle."

Strat laughed. "No."

84

"I give up. I can't think of anything else involving a girl that would make your father put you here."

"She said she was from another century." Strat whispered in case Ralph was in earshot. "She believed she came through a hundred years of Time. She said they had orange juice every day, and didn't use horses, and could fly in machinery like birds, and not only used telephones but their telephones printed books for them."

Katie really laughed. "And they locked *you* up?"

He loved Katie then. He loved her for her good cheer and her good company. "Katie, I never told you that I'm sorry."

"Sorry for what?"

"For not getting between you and Ralph when you talked back. For letting Douglass be the one to save you, so they beat him too. For taking advantage of it so I could go outside. For running away to help myself instead of staying to help you."

Katie's smile was no longer hideous to his eyes, but warm and affectionate. "Douglass is full of love," she said quietly.

And what am I full of? wondered Strat.

For she had not accepted his apology.

Steam was up!

Vapor rose thicker than clouds—more like blankets. Great gray swirls of cottony heat. Bells rang and people shouted and pipes clanked and water churned. At last, the steamboat pulled away from the dock and headed up the Hudson River. You would have thought they were departing for Paris, there was so much fanfare.

The Hudson River did not impress Annie. It was dirty-looking and it had dirty-looking ice on it too. The ice sort of hung around, as if there had been a party and it was left over. The steamboat paid no attention to it, but churned through the slush with an ugly whiffling sound, as if mashing innocent things in the water.

The day was grim and dark.

The steamboat was not romantic, but thick and ponderous and noisy. To her safety-conscious, next-century eyes, it looked ready to blow up. It smelled like mothballs and rotted flowers and sweat. People were jammed everywhere. The people terrified her. No woman wore makeup, and they uniformly seemed sallow and desperate.

Even the snowy banks of the Hudson River were pocked and gray. It was not a pretty snow. It hid no sins. It marked them out instead.

She was the object of considerable scrutiny from the men on board. The women were full of contempt for her too: she traveled alone. Of what worth was a woman without a man? Did no one wish to marry her? Did no father or brother care what happened to her? Could she not even find a clergyman or a cousin to escort her?

Her clothing was beautiful, and fashionable, and not the wear of a fallen woman. But alone? It was unthinkable.

The wind and the people were so cold.

The half-enclosed deck was like a vault where they

kept bodies until spring so they could bury them in the hard, hard ground.

"Miss!" said a sparkly bright uniform: red and gold, like a child's toy soldier in the midst of this gray nightmare. "You're on the wrong deck, miss. Come with me."

And the right deck, where the first-class cabins were, was as charming as an immense parlor. Individual scarlet upholstered chairs with matching ottomans were comfortably set around gleaming walnut tables, mostly occupied by stout men smoking cigars and sipping port. Port, said the attendant, was not suitable for ladies. What would she have? Coke, said Annie.

And when she tasted a familiar drink, how much less scary the world was, and how much less frightening her task.

Time changes go better with Coke, she told herself, and she grinned behind her heavy veil and her hat plumes.

❦

"Inform Miss Devonny," said Walker Walkley, "that she will have breakfast with me. Now."

Schmidt was solid and thick. Her heavy black dress and its heavier black apron turned her into furniture. Nothing to notice. Simply a servant. No employer ever thought of a servant as having a personality or a soul.

"Miss Devonny is indisposed," said Schmidt. She wondered when Mr. Walkley would discover that he was missing a great deal of cash. She wondered who would be blamed.

"Then fix trays. I shall have my coffee in her room with her."

Schmidt had not considered this reply. But she had a better one. "Female problems, Mr. Walkley," said Schmidt.

Walker Walkley nearly threw up. He could not believe Schmidt had said such a thing in his presence! Men should never have to consider the distasteful biology of women. He rallied. "Did Miss Devonny have an overnight visitor, Schmidt?"

"I cannot imagine what you are implying, sir," said Schmidt. "I am shocked. Miss Devonny's morals are above reproach."

"A Miss Lockwood," said Walker Walkley.

"I have heard that old Lockwood story," said Schmidt, "from the staff in the country. Before they were dismissed." She allowed herself a little smile at Mr. Walkley's expense. "The time traveler? The one who supposedly came out of thin air at the seaside? I cannot credit, sir, that you, too, believe in time travel."

Walker Walkley snorted. "She was rea—" He broke off, suddenly aware of the danger.

"Real, sir?" Schmidt finished the word for him. "You thought Miss Lockwood was real, sir? Did not young Mr. Stratton find himself in a lunatic asylum when he said that? Was this not your very own choice, sir, to lock up a man who believed in time travelers?"

The woman spoke excellent English. Hardly an accent. Really, there was no time in which immigrants were not infuriating. Either they spoke no English or too much. He said stiffly, "Will Miss Devonny be able to take the California train this afternoon as planned?"

"I shall inquire, sir."

"Get out," said Walker Walkley.

"David," said Peggy Bartten, "let's set a date for the wedding."

The father of Tod and Annie Lockwood nearly crushed his popcorn box. "Peggy, we're just seeing a movie. We're not getting married."

"I want to be married," said Peggy Bartten.

"I've been married," he explained. "It's not what I want anymore."

"David, either we get married or it's over."

"Nonsense," said Mr. Lockwood, patting her knee. "Shh. The movie is starting." He munched popcorn. He loved the fake butter they poured over it. He didn't care whether it was healthy.

"David," she whispered, right during the first shoot-out on the screen, "I'm serious."

He patted her again. He was many things, and serious was not one of them. Women always dragged up this subject, and you had to make it clear where you stood.

"Oh, Schmidt, you are brilliant!" said Devonny. "Female problems! I shall lean on your arm. Swathe me in extra layers. Since men never have the slightest idea what a female problem is, Walk won't be able to argue."

Schmidt hoped this would mean another tip. Devonny's tip at dawn had been a blessing. Schmidt earned so little, and had so many people to support. Paying for heat was difficult, and this winter was severe. Her mother was always cold. Schmidt's one goal was to keep her mother warm.

"Schmidt," said Devonny, "you will come to California with me. I need somebody to manage things. You are a wonderful manager." Devonny smiled happily at this decision.

"But miss!" said Schmidt, horrified. "You already have a maid attending you. And my family depends on me. I cannot—"

"Schmidt!" Devonny frowned. "I've made my decision. Now pack your belongings swiftly because Mr. Walkley will be calling for the carriage in a few hours." Devonny swept into her private sitting room, her silvery traveling gown whispering as it followed her around on the carpets.

Schmidt stood stunned. She had a brother who had never recovered from the war in which he'd fought, a sister who was tubercular, another sister who had been let go from her position, and a mother so arthritic and bent she could not get out of a chair by herself. Schmidt was the only one who could shop and run and go for them. The only one actually earning anything! How . . .

But Miss Devonny did not care how. It was not her problem. Therefore it was not a problem.

California, thought Schmidt.

So far away. She would be so completely, totally

gone. And yet if she did not obey, who would earn the money to keep her family?

California, she thought, dazed. She rushed up the servants' stair to her chilly cubicle and packed what she had: uniforms and heavy shoes and a coat not thick enough. But California is warm, she thought. The sun always shines.

Why, she was going to have an adventure—a great train—a vast journey. California!

She could not telephone her family to let them know. They had no telephone and did not know anybody who did. She would have to post a letter. Tomorrow, when she was in some other state, they would discover that they did not have her anymore.

I can't do that, thought Schmidt, her brief hot dream of California vanishing. If only I had money. If only . . .

But there was money. Schmidt knew of one more place where hard cold cash was kept. Cash Miss Devonny had not taken for Miss Lockwood. Cash that perhaps even Miss Devonny did not know about.

If I took it . . . thought Schmidt.

And money glowed as warm and sunny as California in her mind.

CHAPTER 6

"Why, Schmidt," said Walker Walkley very softly.

She snapped toward the far wall. She didn't have a heart attack, but her knees folded. Her sight became blurry and her hands, full of somebody else's money, turned both sweaty and icy.

Walker Walkley smiled. "Schmidt, do you need money?" The man always smiled. There was something evil about the constancy of that smile. Nobody normal could have a smile endlessly tacked to the sides of his mouth.

Schmidt tried to stuff the money back. Wiped her hands on her skirt, as if she had not been stealing, he could not prove it, could not jail her, ruin her, destroy her and her family.

"No, no, no," said Walker Walkley. His smile never changed. "Take the money, Schmidt. I'm so glad to be able to assist you. Tell me, Schmidt. Do you have family in New York? Do you have people who will be cold, who might even die, if they don't have a warm place to live this winter? It's snowing out again, you know."

Schmidt could not speak.

"You keep the money," whispered Walker Walkley.

The whisper was more terrifying than speech. Schmidt was trembling now, her solid frame quivering like gelatin.

"Don't be afraid," said Walker Walkley. "Just tell me about Miss Lockwood. All the plans Miss Devonny made. Everything, Schmidt."

"Yes, sir," said Schmidt.

"There will be only nine courses for dinner, miss," the porter said apologetically. "I will come for you when your table is seated."

Nine courses! Annie tried to imagine staying interested in food that long. She tipped him two dollars for squeezing the huge trunk, valise and hatbox into her stateroom.

His jaw opened so far that his huge mustache fell into his mouth. He studied the two single bills as if nobody had ever tipped him so much. In 1898, for all she knew, that was a week's pay. Had she made a major mistake, marking herself out as a woman who didn't even know how to count money? Or had she made a close friend?

The porter assured her that anything she wanted, anything at all, she was just to raise a finger and she would have it.

She summoned appropriate speech for a lady. "I shall ring if I require assistance." That sounded more 1898 than "Hey, great, okay." She shut the door on him and then let herself sag with the relief of being alone and safe.

How sturdy, and how lovely, the lock was. The polished brass was inscribed with the steamship's initials, a flaring ornate plaque with curlicued handles. Everything was sumptuous. The cab driver had certainly obeyed Devonny's instructions to do this first class. First class in America a hundred years later was not half so first class.

Dinner, therefore, was a shock.

Ladies traveling alone were segregated.

In a back corner of the two-hundred-foot salon was a table whose flowers were wilted and whose cloth was stained. The women who were unescorted by men were served last, and the food was cold. Nobody complained.

Annie's mother was ferocious in restaurants. If she didn't get good service, Mrs. Lockwood whipped her waiter verbally, explaining that she was paying serious money for this meal, and they'd better provide seriously good service along with seriously good food, got it? (People got it.)

The women around Annie were ashamed of themselves, and did not attempt conversation, because what value could any other single woman have? Most were in black; black was as fashionable now as it was for her mother, a hundred years later.

Annie tried to get comfortable, but her clothing was

94

not intended for relaxation. The corset Schmidt had pulled so tight was intended to keep Annie's spine vertical and her waist thin and her kidneys shoved up against her lungs. She had so much sleeve she could hardly manage her fork over the plate. Of course, that kept down the amount of food she could eat and made her waist even thinner.

"What a shame," said Annie brightly, "that the weather is so ugly. I would love to stand on deck and see New York State go by."

They looked at her expressionlessly.

"You'd be disappointed. There's nothing to see," said a woman wearing a ruby-red gown, a wine-red shawl and a rusty orange scarf. Perhaps she was unescorted because she was dangerously color-blind.

"Where are you all headed?" Annie asked.

The women busied themselves with their unappetizing plates.

"I'm going to a place called Evergreen," Annie added.

Their eyebrows rose in concert. A row of thin noses swiveled toward her, and a woman in black shifted her plates and glasses over, creating space, as if Annie carried a fatal illness. "And who," said the woman, "is in Evergreen? Surely no one related to you."

Annie had no cover story prepared.

Their pale faces, free of makeup and compassion, were like old cloth dolls. Their cheeks sagged and their hair was limp. They were nothing; nobody treated them as anything; and yet Annie was afraid of them. If she needed help, it would not come from people who knew what kind of patient went to Evergreen.

"My brother," she said nervously. That might work, she thought. I could pretend to be Devonny. Yes! I'm Miss Stratton, not Miss Lockwood. Surely I can wheedle my way in as Strat's dear sister.

"Your brother is in Evergreen, miss?" said Ruby-wine-orange.

This was good practice for whatever happened at Evergreen. "I love him deeply," she said. "My family has disowned him. He is in despair and disgrace. I, his sister, Devonny Stratton, am going to him anyway." She lowered her voice. With all the drama she could muster, she added, *"Without my father's permission. For I love my brother. And he needs me."*

How they softened. On their hard and hard-used faces was kindness, and Ruby-wine-orange said gently, "You will have to be strong, Miss Stratton. You are facing many difficulties. Will your family disown you, too, once they learn what you have done?"

Annie decided on the lowering of eyelashes to answer this question. Let sorrow be her speech.

It worked.

Ruby-wine-orange, introducing herself as Miss Rosette, took Annie's bare hand and squeezed it gently.

A band struck up.

Annie loved music. This music had lots of rhythm, lots of brass, and demanded that feet snap across hard floors. Her heels tapped and her waist swayed. And, indeed, it was a dance! Several couples got up. "Oooh," said Annie happily.

"You must not dance!" said Ruby-wine-orange, horrified. "There are *bachelors* here."

Harriett's doctor listened to what Moss had to say. "I am afraid" he told her, "that given Miss Ranleigh's condition, I do not think we should wait for the post."

Moss did not understand.

"You must use the telephone," said the doctor.

Moss could not do that. She did not know how. It was too much to ask. But the doctor turned away, for he had important things to do, and she, Moss, must attack this herself.

Stiffening her resolve, she went to the main building, where the billiard and smoking and guest rooms were. There, too, high on the wall, was the large wooden and metal apparatus. She wiped nervous hands on her apron.

Luckily the telephone company did most of the talking for her. Eventually the connection took place. Very mysterious it was, the way the voice came through the wire. She was getting used to electricity, although of course only for other people, not herself. She would stick with kerosene lamps, thank you, and not little glowing bulbs of bursting glass.

The gentleman was most interested that Miss Harriett wished to change her will. "I will come myself," he said, with such courtesy and understanding that it warmed Moss's heart. What fine people Miss Harriett came from!

"Thank you, Mr. Walkley, sir," said Moss, and she curtsied, never thinking that on the telephone they couldn't see you.

Walker Walkley's rage grew through his bones like a fever. So Harriett Ranleigh wanted to leave her money to a scrubwoman or an Adirondacker! The fool!

No doubt this Moss woman had infected Harriett's mind, not that it would take much. Women who received education were always at risk. Thinking damaged them.

Walk's brain was exploding. How could Devonny and Harriett—*girls!*—have accomplished anything?

He loathed Harriett. It would be no loss to the world when Harriett left it. Should he rush to Clear Pond? But if Harriett was in the process of dying, better Walk should let her die with the old will in place.

But what if Harriett called a local attorney and got this new will written anyway? Walk could probably overturn it; women were incompetent to decide these things. But it was messy, and he wished to avoid mess, just collect money.

And what about Miss Lockwood, on her way to Strat?

Walk must not do anything too quickly. Thank God he lived in an age of instant communication. A telephone call to the asylum was in order, but first he must think carefully through all possible problems.

There was danger here, and it must be other people who suffered, not Walker Walkley.

Walker Walkley ordered two carriages to bring the traveling party to the railroad station. He did not want to be in the same carriage with Devonny. He did not want to imagine her smug look, hidden by her layers of veiling. He did not want her to see his own smug look, since he knew all her plans.

The private Stratton rail car was hooked on the back of the California-bound train, and behind it, another private car—the Colts of Colt Guns—had been fastened. The Stratton car was trapped. But that did not mean Devonny was trapped.

Walker almost wanted to smash her between cars, never mind send her to California. But he had to have her as his wife. She would pay. He liked thinking about how Devonny would pay.

Walk tipped Stephens, the officer in charge of the car, explaining that Miss Devonny was upset about her brother and might actually try to get off the train and visit young Mr. Stratton on her own. Stephens was to be understanding, but he was not to permit it. Stephens, who loved Miss Devonny, and had loved Strat, was very sad and agreed that Miss Devonny could not be permitted to have lunacy touch her.

Walk could hardly conduct the conversation. He could not gather his composure enough to bid Devonny good-bye. She waved to him through the window, and he saluted her with his hat and was maintaining his bow as the train left Grand Central.

Schmidt had been brought up in the Lutheran church, which was fond of guilt. Schmidt could feel guilty when she did not perfectly iron a sheet.

The guilt she felt over her betrayal of Miss Devonny

and Miss Lockwood was enough for Schmidt to hurl herself beneath the wheels of the train. And the money had not been Mr. Walkley's to give her, of course. It was young Strat's own money, tucked under his mattress, found by a maid months ago. The staff had discussed whether to send it to him, and decided that people who worked for asylums were probably thieves and would keep it for themselves, and it was better to tuck the money back for Mr. Strat, hoping there would be a healthy return.

So I've stolen young Mr. Strat's money, thought Schmidt, and I've betrayed Miss Devonny and betrayed Miss Lockwood and betrayed my entire upbringing and all my beliefs.

The train had a wonderful, almost soothing rhythm to it, its hundreds of wheels clattering over hundreds of track connections. There was a sort of safety in the repetition of wheel noise.

Miss Devonny was full of demands for this, that and the next thing. At least Schmidt did not have to go far to fulfill these demands. In fact, Schmidt did not have to go at all: the rail car had its own staff. Schmidt, to her astonishment and joy, had her own teeny little room. It was a sort of pocket in the wall, from which a bed folded down, and a sink poked out and a window looked upon the rushing world.

Never in her life had Schmidt had a room to herself.

She thought of the postal service, which whisked a letter in a single day to the proper address. She thought of the post box in Grand Central, beneath that fabulous dome of painted sky, where she had dropped the letter to her brother. A letter containing *one hundred dollars* telling him to spend it on heat and fuel and warm clothing.

Miss Devonny said, "What are your thoughts, Schmidt? You look so strange. Are you ill? Do you have motion sickness?"

"I'm thinking of California, Miss Devonny."

"California is a strange thought," agreed Miss Devonny, and then she required tea and hot sweet pastries and soft butter and also a map so she could see where they were heading.

Schmidt found the map, wondering if she herself were headed for Hell.

Since her porch had south, east, and west windows, Harriett had become a sunrise and sunset collector. She gathered colors in her heart: magenta and grape one evening, surpassed by sparkly gold or fluffy pink the next. Would there be color in Heaven? Would she hear the laughter of children there?

"Come now," said Moss robustly. "You will go into remission, Miss Harriett, I know it. A good patient gets another ten years, or even twenty. You will be one of those, because you are such a good obedient patient. An attorney is coming, but you must not think about wills and dying. Think about life and living!"

Charlie came to visit. A book of poems by John Greenleaf Whittier was lying open on Harriett's bed. "Harriett, you're not supposed to read," said Charlie. "It taxes you too much. Shall I read aloud to you?

Poems are best out loud anyway. And here's *Snow-Bound*. Nobody is more snowbound than we are."

But she did not want to hear Whittier. "You talk to me, Charlie."

"You would have loved last night's lecture," Charlie said. He held her hands gently between both of his and mourned that she was so cold, so limp.

"A naturalist from the Park Service talked. He was so proud, Harriett. It was quite touching. The Adirondacks are the largest park in America. A million acres. Just three years ago, 1895, the great State of New York voted to keep the land *forever wild*. Otherwise logging would destroy its beauty."

I will die where the world is forever wild, thought Harriett. I will be part of something that doesn't die. This world, when I die in 1898, will be the same world it was in 1398, and the same that it will be in 1998. "Keep talking, Charlie," she whispered. "It comforts me."

Stephanie Rosette admired herself in the looking glass. She loved her outfit. She loved the hot intense look of the reds and oranges against each other. She loved how people cringed when they looked at her clothing.

Stephanie Rosette had lost her job in the shirt factory and was going to be a nurse in one of those huge cheap tuberculosis asylums. The kind with many cots in each ward. The kind where people go to die, not get well.

Stephanie Rosette was strong and tough, and she could nurse, and she supposed she would get used to the wilderness of the Adirondacks, not that she wanted to. Stephanie preferred civilization. Her last precious week in New York, she had spent the last of her pitiful savings. She had gone to the zoo and the aquarium, the symphony and the library with the lions in front and the Natural History Museum, saying good-bye to all the things she loved about New York. She window-shopped in the great stores: Tiffany's and Abraham & Straus.

Then she accepted her fate, and got on the steamship to go to a job that would last twelve hours a day, six days a week. Forever.

This short overnight voyage would be her final joy in life.

The beautiful girl who had shared the dinner table had been most interesting. Miss Stratton had slipped once and called herself Miss Lockwood. Most odd. A lady, definitely, but without a lady's manners. Sweet and courteous, but off-key.

She was startled by a knock on her door. "Yes?"

"Porter, ma'am. Miss Stratton, ma'am, wonders if you would be kind enough to assist her in her state-room."

Stephanie Rosette was puzzled but willing. Flipping the long ends of her orange scarf to help herself think, she followed the porter. She was big and bulky and her colors were loud and unforgiving. He was a little afraid of her, which Stephanie enjoyed.

Miss Stratton let her in quickly. "I'm so embarrassed," she said. "Please forgive me for asking you to do this."

One look at Miss Stratton's gown and Stephanie knew that the girl could not undress herself. She was buttoned and laced and strapped and tied. Stephanie shook her head. Ladies. Really, there were times when Stephanie was grateful not to be one. "You usually travel with a maid, don't you?" she said, trying not to be annoyed. "Here. I will get you into your night-clothes." Practiced fingers whipped down a row of forty tiny tight buttons in little silken loops. She unknotted the stays and released the corset. Stephanie unlocked the huge trunk and pawed through it to find night-clothes.

Oh, the beautiful stuff that lay so gently folded between lengths of tissue! Satins and laces, fur trims and velvets. Ruffles and pleats and eyelets and silk. The sheer loveliness of Miss Stratton's fashions brought tears to Stephanie's eyes. Just once in her life, how she would love a gown like one of these.

"Miss Stratton," breathed Stephanie, fingering the beautiful stuff. "How lovely you must look in these!" She thought ruefully that Miss Stratton's waist was about one third of her own. "Sleep tight. I will come to your room early in the morning to help you dress for the day. Do not open the door to anybody but me." Ladies had little sense. They believed the world was peopled by gentlemen, when in fact it was peopled by fools and rowdies.

There was something so forlorn and lost about this young girl. How old was she? Sixteen? And going on a quest that could not possibly succeed. She would only be terribly punished by her family. And yet Stephanie admired her. To save a beloved brother. Had not women since Antigone sacrificed for their brothers?

Sleep tight. No bad dreams, no lost blankets, no cold feet, no scary noises. If Miss Stratton's brother were trapped in an asylum for the insane, he had not once slept tight.

Stephanie prayed gently for the sleep of both.

Late in the evening, the same gentle attendant who had brought water and rags before brought Katie a piece of candy. A long stick. A peppermint-colored candy, whose sweet drippy scent filled the entire room. Strat actually forgot Anna Sophia at the sight of that candy. Six months of oatmeal, bread, baked beans, beets, and more baked beans had made Strat crave sweetness.

Katie gave it to Douglass. All of it. The entire stick. She could have broken it in five, and each of them, even Conspiracy and Melancholia, could have had a bite.

But Katie said everybody else had more than Douglass and that Douglass needed it most. Douglass was completely happy with his candy, as if he were not in an asylum, as if people really were kind and good things really did happen.

Strat thought about desserts. Fudge. Taffy. Chocolate. If somebody gave him a sweet, he'd gobble it down so fast he'd never even taste it, never mind share. How would Strat ever be nice enough to raise Katie's opinion of him?

He was thinking less. Using less of his mind. Around

him the weeping and swearing of Melancholia and Conspiracy seemed quite reasonable. He listened to it as if listening to a dance band. It occurred to Strat that the technique of Evergreen was working well: he was becoming less sane. As time went on, he would fit the diagnosis they had chosen for him.

He wanted to laugh, but his emotions seemed to have departed. He was just there, and Douglass had the candy.

Walker Walkley did not care for the Adirondacks.

He disliked uncivilized places.

He did not care about maple trees that turned red in the fall and spruces that went black in winter. He did not care about lakes and streams. He did not care about dead ducks or live ducks. He did not wish to wear red plaid, red flannel, or snowshoes. He did not wish to eat venison or trout, and he certainly did not want to snare it himself and get soiled and wet in the process.

The only place to be was New York City. Those upper regions of acreage should be called something else entirely, as it cast a pall over the great name of New York to include that pointless wilderness and those endless dull farms.

One might receive postcards from idiots who did go there, but one should not be forced to go oneself.

He had been forced. Devonny and Anna Sophia Lockwood had backed him into a corner.

Albany. And to think that the state capital was there, up where nobody lived or mattered.

Luckily Miss Lockwood had taken the boat. He, Walk, would take a night express train. It would be less comfortable. In fact, it would not be comfortable at all. It would be hideous and filled with the lower classes.

But it would be fast.

He would arrive in Albany before her.

And then there would be *two* patients in the lunatic asylum, put there by Walker Walkley.

He would see just how far through time or space the beautiful Miss Lockwood could travel once she was in a straitjacket.

~~ CHAPTER 7 ~~

How Stephanie enjoyed dressing Miss Stratton in the morning. She had put the thick straight hair up into an elaborate twist, and fastened it with a dozen long U-shaped pins. She chose a dress of deep green, layers of watered silk and velvet and taffeta. How Miss Stratton rustled when she moved! How her skirt filled the entire hallway. And for her coat, black, and also layered, with two capes, one short, one long. But no hood. Instead, from the hatbox, a delirious hat: a hat gone crazy with itself, a hat of velvet and ribbons and veiling and green wreathing plumes like ferns, and silk roses jauntily perched on one side.

Miss Stratton looked like a million dollars. And Miss Stratton had actually given Stephanie the mink coat. Its cut was so huge it actually fit Stephanie. Stephanie had protested, but not much. She wore the coat now, thrilled by its warmth.

The steamboat had arrived in Albany three hours behind schedule, slowed by the slushy river. It was remarkable that they had gotten upriver. Usually, ice closed off the Hudson. But although the winter had been the snowiest in memory, it had not been the coldest. At Albany, the water was still open.

Miss Stratton and Stephanie stood in a glassed-in parlor to watch the docking maneuvers. Railroads were not far, and all manner of horses and carriages and wagons awaited passengers and cargo. The activity was delightful: other people's labor was always so much more interesting than one's own.

How prettily the snow fell. Stephanie loved snow as long as she did not have to be out in it.

The dock was complete chaos. People were slipping on snow. Baggage was sliding on ice. The clanking of the great steam engines melded with shouts of porters and cries for taxis and yelling of drivers and swearing of teamsters. Hundreds of travelers were crossing narrow spaces cluttered with their hundreds of trunks and bags and boxes and cartons.

A few intrepid people had come to greet loved ones as they left the ship. A most handsome young gentleman in a thick fur coat and splendid hat strode back and forth, peering this way and that.

"Oh, no," said Miss Stratton. She stepped away from the window and put her hands up to block her face.

"What's wrong?" said Stephanie Rosette.

"That man on the dock."

"What about him?"

"He's— Oh, Miss Rosette, what shall I do? He would — I can't— He mustn't—"

Ladies, thought Stephanie Rosette. They are so helpless. She doesn't have a prayer of retrieving her brother. She can't even get down the gangplank.

"Will you help me?" whispered the girl. "Please. I am desperate. He is dangerous. We must run back to my stateroom before they take my trunk off the ship. You will take the trunk because I cannot be burdened with it. Yes, you are to have the trunk and everything in it. Will you lie for me? Please, Miss Rosette?"

Stephanie Rosette was actually rather fond of lying. It gave excitement to an otherwise dull life. "I," she said proudly, "am an accomplished liar."

Charlie kissed the pale cold cheek of the sleeping Harriett.

Moss said, "I want you to go back to your cottage in a wheelchair, sir."

Charlie shook his head. He was not going down that way. He would walk till death took him.

Snow had fallen again. In the Adirondacks, it often seemed to snow without thinking about it, the air full, as if snow just lived there, defying gravity.

Out on Clear Pond, where ice had been harvested all day long, snow covered the gaping hole in the ice. The hole had been marked out with sweet little treetops. It looked like rows of petite Christmas trees waiting for candles and ribbons and sparkling glass orbs. Neither

Harriett nor I, thought Charlie, will have another Christmas.

And Charlie hated Strat for letting Harriett slide toward her death without his love.

Walk examined every departing passenger. He would know Miss Lockwood even if she dressed as a cabin boy, but she had no reason to be looking out for Walk. She would be the lady Devonny had dressed her to be.

A woman in a splendid mink coat approached him. Walk bowed, respecting the sum of money it had taken to acquire such a coat. "Madam," he said.

"Could you be Mr. Walkley, sir? A most strange thing has occurred on board, and if you are Mr. Walkley, I believe that none except you can handle this situation."

He was suspicious. "How do you know my name?"

"A young lady on board has had a fit of confusion. A most disturbing episode. Fortunately *I* was present."

"A fit of confusion?" repeated Walk. It had a ring of Miss Lockwood. Or rather, how people felt when they were around her.

"I really did *not* understand what happened," said the woman. "She is a *very* confused young girl, Mr. Walkley, and I consider it *most* fortunate that you are here to take *control.*"

"What is the young lady's name?" breathed Walk.

The woman turned and walked back toward the ship. "We are not altogether sure. She gave us several choices. Stratton was one. Lockwood was another. It was necessary," she explained, "to lock the young lady in her cabin." She glanced briefly back at Walk, looking him up and down to be sure he was useful. "It will require strength to subdue her," she added.

Walk was smiling again. Gloating changed his face. His cheeks turned into heavy jowls. He followed the mink coat.

"I do not know what can have happened to the young lady's mind," said the woman severely. "I do hope, sir, that she will be kept confined in the future."

Walker Walkley was delighted to reassure the good woman that the young lady would be confined in the future.

❧

The instant Walk disappeared into the cabinway, Annie floated out. She might have only seconds of safety. "Just the valise and hatbox going with you, then, miss?" said Annie's porter.

"Please." The huge trunk required too much of her. Stephanie Rosette could sell the gowns or remake them. Annie could not be managing that vast container and the porters it required. Not in the middle of this nightmare. Walker Walkley! Here! Right upon her! It was too much.

The porter and carriage driver lifted her into a carriage without doors, designed to allow the huge fashions of ladies enough room, and her valise and hatbox were laid on the carriage floor by her feet. Annie wondered what was in them, and whether she needed it.

112

Off they went. The station, and the train north, were barely a street away.

She was stunning in her travel outfit: fabulous dress, sumptuous hat, veil, caped coat, boots, mitts, brooches. Nobody could miss her. Walker Walkley could so easily find her again. Yet Devonny had insisted that Annie needed to be dressed like this to impress the staff at the asylum.

It was a regular local passenger train. No private cars here, no staterooms, no sleeping cars, no dining car. Just transportation.

He will be only one train behind me, she thought. Please, Stephanie, hold him long enough that he doesn't make this one.

With the help of two conductors, she climbed the high steps into the gleaming, snow-trimmed passenger car.

It took Annie several minutes to adjust her yards of fabric: her skirts and capes and coats and bindings. She slithered on her own satin, but finally established herself in a seat meant for two. She took up all of it and could have used more.

With a cloud of steam-borne cinders, they were off for the mountains.

For some time, Annie simply sat, exhausted and safe.

When she tried to plan or think, her mind did not cooperate. Like the rhythmic wheels drumming on the tracks, her mind simply ran over and over the same fact.

Walk was upon her.

Walk recognized Devonny's clothing immediately. The beautiful gown strewn across the unmade bed was the same one Devonny had worn to the Vanderbilts' good-bye party. It enraged him that Devonny had given that to Miss Lockwood. He wanted to rip it up or strangle Miss Lockwood with it.

He was barely in the stateroom, however, when he registered the fact that no Miss Lockwood was within. No girl was bound to a bedstead, awaiting Walk's decision about her future.

He wasted precious seconds, thinking that Miss Lockwood had gotten out of her bonds by slipping through Time, hating her for having power that he did not. Nobody should have anything that Walker did not have more of.

The woman in mink was smiling. He recognized that smile as if it were his own in a mirror. It was danger. He tried to react, but he was too late.

Her scarf—a hideous, orange, unladylike color—was upon his face. He knew nothing except pressure and cloth and drugs.

Chloroform.

He tried not to breathe, but hungry lungs obey nobody, not even Walker Walkley, and he shuddered and went limp and then he was simply flesh on the floor.

It was good to be a nurse, and be equipped for such occasions.

A man who had accused that lovely girl's brother of being insane? A man who had kidnapped the helpless boy? Used lies and ruses so he could marry the beautiful thing and have her fortune to himself?

Such a man deserved a long-term delay.

Stephanie Rosette dusted her hands. She hung the DO NOT DISTURB sign on the outside of the cabin door. She followed her new trunk out onto the dock, summoned a carriage, and had the trunk placed within.

She hoped that the poor young lady's choices were wise ones. Most of all, she hoped that the young lady understood that she had hours of safety now—but not days.

And she, Stephanie Rosette, must make speed also. The man would be dangerous when he awoke.

Stephanie Rosette felt the wonderful sleek warmth of her new mink coat and thought of the money she could get when she sold the fabulous clothing in the vast trunk, and she prayed for the safety of a young lady who had no idea what she was about to face.

It seemed to Annie Lockwood that her train had gone so far north, she should be seeing reindeer.

Thick forests and logged forests.

Rocks piled in great slabs. Pencil-thin birches and the stunted tips of young spruce poking through the snow.

It was not beautiful so much as cruel.

Annie's heart and hopes seemed to have traveled to some cold and dread place also. She had no plans, only velocity. She was rushing forward as if she actually knew what she was doing.

Strat seemed like a myth. She was afraid of all that snow and ice. She was afraid of getting off the train. She was afraid of Walker Walkley behind her, and the asylum before her.

"Evergreen, miss," said the conductor.

The train stopped.

It was a genuine whistle-stop. The train stopped because somebody on board yanked the whistle.

The railroad station at Evergreen was a charming, tall cottage with scalloped shingles and a dragon's back roof. These were iced with snow, like a gingerbread castle.

Only Annie disembarked. The two conductors deposited her beneath a porch roof, set her valise and hatbox at the hem of her coat, accepted her tips, and the train left.

"I don't care," said Peggy Bartten, actually stomping her foot. Mr. Lockwood had never really seen a person stomp a foot in fury. It was not attractive. "You file for divorce now, David."

"Peggy, the thing is, I don't want a divorce."

"Then what are you having this affair for?" she yelled.

He was perplexed. He was having it for fun, of course. Why must she get all serious about it?

This time she put her hands on her hips. "Then get out," she said. "It's over. I want a husband. If it's not going to be you, then I have to start looking elsewhere."

He tried to laugh. All of a sudden he realized that she was going to rip up the only clothing he had left: everything that his wife had missed. Quickly he stuffed his possessions into a suitcase. "What about tonight?" he said nervously. "We have tickets for that new play at—"

"Here's the play," said his gym-teacher girlfriend very seriously. "Either you file for divorce, or you're not on my team. Got it?"

He got it.

He went to his car with his suitcase and wondered what to do next. Vaguely he recalled his wife saying he ought to be staying with the children while she was away. Was that now or later? What sort of risk would he run stopping off at the house? Perhaps he would call Annie and Tod from a pay phone first, to make sure that his wife was gone.

"Yup," said his son, Tod.

"Yup what?" said Mr. Lockwood, feeling testy. What had given his children the right to get rude?

"Yup, Mom's gone."

Mr. Lockwood brightened. He had a place to stay. He didn't want to do this motel stuff: too lonely. Maybe he could get Tod or Annie to go to the play instead. The

117

tickets had been expensive; he didn't want to waste them.

Devonny stared out the train window. She had expected this to be an adventure and it wasn't. Instead of great cities, they passed through slums and warehouses. Instead of spacious farmland, recently logged stretches that were harsh stubs under dirty snow. Instead of pretty villages, worn and tired houses whose laundry had frozen on the line.

And she, too, was frozen on the line.

She seemed to have forgotten so many details. And what if she had not given Anna Sophia enough money? What if Miss Lockwood failed? Or lost her courage?

As the miles clicked by, Devonny realized that crossing the continent was the worst choice. She literally could never reach her brother now. She should have disobeyed Father and gone by herself to Evergreen. But Mother had done that. And they had not let a woman in.

"Oh, Schmidt," Devonny said sadly, "I'm worried about Miss Lockwood."

Schmidt burst into tears.

Her confession was short and terrible.

Devonny had truly forgotten something. She had forgotten what a skunk Walker Walkley was, and how his stink rested on anyone around him.

The train hurtled westward.

"At the next station," said Schmidt desperately, "I could get off and send a telegraph."

"To whom?" said Devonny. "I do not know where Miss Lockwood is. I have no way to warn her."

"We could notify the asylum," said Schmidt.

"They would just keep her from seeing my brother. Perhaps they would lock her up too. Certainly they would telegraph my father."

"Notify Miss Harriett?" asked Schmidt.

But a dying woman could not do anything.

And Devonny's friends in New York and Connecticut were also women and could do nothing without the permission of a father, brother or husband.

I don't want to travel through Time, thought Devonny. But oh! if I could travel through space! If only there were some way to fly off this train and fly to Evergreen and fly my brother away!

But time and miles were not on Devonny's side. Even if Stephens would let her off the train, she would be days behind.

"Schmidt," said Devonny, for the first time in her life using a handkerchief to wipe away the tears of a servant, "I do not hold you responsible. Walker Walkley makes people do terrible things."

Schmidt shook her head. "If I were a good person, I would have stood up to him, no matter how terrible he is."

They were nothing then but two women who had failed. "Because Walk is a man," said Devonny, "I agreed that he must be in charge of me. I must stop such behavior. From now on, I must say, I am a *woman*, therefore *I* am in charge."

It was too ridiculous. They both laughed out loud.

And the train continued west, and they continued to be women, and helpless.

I am here just before machines, thought Annie. No chainsaws, no snowmobiles, no cars.

But there were lights. Not electric lights, but soft yellow gaslights in a strip of buildings across the snowy road. She walked to the hotel, grateful for its big painted sign.

How warm it was inside. How softly lit. She went to the desk to check in. She would have a hot dinner and a hot bath and think things through. She was perilously close to tears, and that must never happen.

"Yes, miss?" said a clerk most courteously. "Your booking?"

"I don't have a reservation. I would like a single room, please."

The clerk stared. "You are not expected by anyone?"

She started to shake her head, but this was difficult with the vast hat. A motionless profile was the only way to go while wearing a tower. "I am not," she said.

"You are traveling—alone?" said the clerk, enunciating his syllables as if to be sure of each and every one. He sported a thin waxed mustache. It really did curve in circles, like a cartoon of old-time barbers. "You cannot stay here, miss."

She stared at him. "You're full?"

"No." He pointed toward the door. She looked at the door for an explanation, saw none, felt very confused, and said once more, "I'd like a room for the night, please."

This time his finger stabbed more sharply, and Annie saw the sign.

WE DO NOT ACCEPT LOGGERS, JEWS
OR UNACCOMPANIED FEMALES.

"There are always rooms for people suited to our ideals," the clerk said grandly. "But doubtful or deficient characters need not ask." He sneered beneath his circular mustache.

When she did not move, he came out from behind his desk, lifting a flat section of the surface to pass through. There was a smile on his face, like the smile of Walker Walkley.

She backed away and he advanced on her, until she had backed out the door and was standing again in the snow.

The Adirondack Mountains blocked the sun. Blue shadows turned little Evergreen into a dark cavern. Huge spruce trees blackened the last of the sky.

It was like being in a terrible cathedral of night and snow and cold.

She was afraid.

And she was alone.

Only cruel winter was at her side.

❦ CHAPTER 8 ❦

By the clock over the railroad station, it was ten past four.

It was still the same day.

I won't cry, she said to herself. I won't stand out here in the snow and cry. If I don't get a room for the night, I won't worry about a room for the night. I'll go to the asylum now and see my brother, Strat.

She went inside the railroad station. It must still be the 1890s, because a clerk was on duty. In the 1990s the station would have been turned into a boutique open on alternate weekends.

The clerk in the station looked exactly like the clerk in the hotel. It was the beard-mustache thing, and the black-suit-with-vest-and-pocket-watch thing. She approached him.

"Where is the Asylum, may I ask?"

"Two miles north of town, miss." He stepped away

from her, finding things to do deep within his office, among his green-shaded lamps and tickets on rolls.

What would my mother do now? thought Annie.

Immediately she knew that both her mother and Devonny would make a triumphal entry. She had forgotten the towering plumes and the ermine muff. Instead of relishing the corset, which kept her upright, proud and snobbish, she was sagging onto it, as if it were a wall on which to lean.

Annie straightened. She sharpened her features. She tilted her nose, the better to look down it. "Summon a conveyance," she said to the clerk, as snippily as she knew how. "The day grows late," she said severely, "while you are fiddling about accomplishing nothing."

"Certainly, miss," said the station clerk. "I'm sorry, miss," and he hopped to it. In so tiny a village, the "conveyance" department was not far. A beautiful, bell-ringing, horse-stomping sleigh crossed the street from the stable.

"That will never do!" said Annie imperiously. "An *open* sleigh? I am frail. I require a closed carriage. Kindly return that unsuitable conveyance at once."

I love this, thought Annie. Perhaps I shall become an actress, specializing in out-of-date stage plays.

The men tipped their hats to her, which she had read about, but never seen. They didn't actually move their hats, but touched their fingers to the rims, as if saluting. Annie was fond of this response, too, and thought that perhaps prior to becoming a famous actress, she would be an army officer, inspect recruits, and force them to salute her often.

"That," she said to the clerk, "is more reasonable." She tipped him two dollars, and he beamed and wished her a safe, warm journey.

The driver sat outside on a high bench, while she was within the carriage. It was not cozy. It was a small dark round refrigerator. The clerk brought a foot warmer: an odd little container of shiny metal, in which something hot rested. It felt wonderful beneath her frozen boots. It did nothing for the rest of her body.

There were so many advantages to the 1990s. Instant warmth alone was a perfectly good reason to move up a century.

The winter sun had not seemed to rise at all that day, and as afternoon turned toward evening, it did not seem to set. Gloom, the shape and color of crushed hopes, froze in the sky.

They turned away from the village, and passed through an evergreen forest that was not green but black. A forest in which children had rightly feared wolves. A forest in which wolves really did eat grand-mothers.

Beyond the forest were meadows, wide and bleak.

The forest trimmed the meadows in an oddly circular fashion, as if cut by kindergartners learning curves. Trees rushed down to the meadow edge, and there, roots clutching rocks, the trees tilted dangerously, swept out over the snow like sails.

"Where are we?" said Annie through the little front opening.

"Evergreen Pond," said the driver. He flicked the

reins. "Bad accident here last week, miss," he said, gossiping over his shoulder like any taxi driver. "That's not a field, of course, but a lake, and it never froze up right. See, we had snowfall before the ice got solid, and then the snow turned into a blanket, see, kept the water from ever freezing. City people, here for a ski holiday, they didn't know any better. Rode their sleighs out on it."

He stopped talking.

"What happened?" said Annie.

He seemed surprised that she required more explanation. "They went through, miss."

"And were they saved?" she asked, horrified.

He was more surprised. "No, miss," he said. "The lake is deep, and the sleighs and the horses were heavy."

Annie gulped.

So the snow, which looked so pure and clean, had secrets too. Secrets the snow kept close to itself, the better to kill by.

Annie trembled, and threw the thoughts out of her mind.

The carriage stopped. Without the sleighbells ringing, without the horses pounding on the snow, she could hear again.

What she heard was a horrible chorus, as if some ghastly birds were gathering for migration. Croaking and screaming and wailing.

The driver hopped down and came around to open her carriage door. We're here? she thought. I don't want to do this. A lunatic asylum? I think I'm checking out. "What is that sound?" she whispered.

His face grew sympathetic. "Those are the lunatics. They scream all the time. That's why their asylum is so far out of town."

❧

Walker Walkley awoke to a vicious hangover. His head throbbed agonizingly. His mouth ached. Even his teeth ached, as if somebody had slugged him in the jaw.

"Somebody did," said the local doctor. "You had a real Mickey Finn there. Who doesn't like you?"

"I did not have a Mickey Finn," said Walk angrily. "Nobody slipped a narcotic into a drink. Some female held a scarf over my face and knocked me out with it. The same anesthetic dentists use. I believe it was chloroform."

The police laughed at this. "A man your size got knocked out by a woman and a scarf?"

Walker Walkley was surrounded by people laughing at him. He hated them. He hated all of northern New York. He would get that woman in mink, he would . . .

But the woman was nothing; she was a sideline. The important person was Miss Lockwood. He would kill her. No one humiliated Walker Walkley. Certainly not a female.

Rage percolated through him. It felt good. It felt hot and purposeful and certain.

He would kill her.

These pathetic little pretend detectives and this sad so-called doctor—that was what happened when you left the city; you got shabby excuses instead of competent people—would never find Miss Lockwood. Luckily, he knew where she had gone.

Evergreen.

He was many hours behind her.

But telephones, those blessed inventions of his time, were behind nothing.

All right, Annie Lockwood said to herself. I'm breaking into an insane asylum. Who should I use as a role model?

The driver offered his arm, lest she slip on the ice, and slowly, like a processional, they left the horses, passed between magnificent stone pillars, circled a snow-covered shrub garden, went up five broad and slippery steps, and approached the entrance to the Evergreen Asylum for the Deranged.

Deranged, thought Annie. De-ranged. Patients are cattle taken from their range: locked in stalls to be fed now and then.

I must not be afraid. In a moment, the driver will let go of me and I will have to do this on my own. *Who am I?*

Devonny? 1890s and proud?

Harriett? 1890s and brilliant and nervous and plain?

Florinda? 1890s and a flibberty-gibberty stepmother in need of constant assistance?

127

Or am I my mother? Tough as nails on the outside, ferocious in restaurants? Cut to pieces and floundering on the inside?

No! I'm Miss Bartten! I'm a woman who can get a man to do anything. I appeal to his superior strength, his manly personality, the pleasure of his wonderful company.

Annie added a sensual twist to her snobbish demeanor. She made her lips pouty. She filled her actress's mind with thoughts of adoration.

Whoever you are, you pathetic little superintendent of asylums, you are mine now.

Annie wore a veil over her face. It did not hide her features: its delicate black threads were woven in triangles, and yet it had the effect of sunglasses. She was truly behind it and others were distant on the far side of the lens. Or veil. It was *just* like sunglasses—sexy and dark.

Dr. Wilmott was tall, and the elongated suit made him taller, for the sleeves hung low, the jacket tails hung low, and heavy boot soles raised him up. His beard was ornate, carved around his ears, cheeks and chin. His mustache swooped, its waxed ends poking out into the air like Q-tips. He was very proud of this hair display, and continually stroked his tips and brushes.

Annie wasted no time. "Oh, Doctor," she said, for the nurse and the secretary to whom she had spoken both called him Doctor, reverently, as if he were God. "I am so relieved at your strong presence. I know how painful a reunion with my dear sick brother will be. I'm going to need your support." She thought beautiful thoughts. She tilted in a needy sort of way.

Doctor swiftly came from behind his huge, intimidating sprawl of a desk. The man actually knelt by her chair and took her hand. Annie allowed him to do this, but of course did not respond. That would have been forward. Plus, he was nauseating.

"Oh, Doctor," she said, admiring the disgusting waxwork of his facial hair, "please tell me about your achievements here. All through the terrifying journey on the train—oh, Doctor, that was so difficult—I have never traveled without my father before and I have learned such a lesson! I shall never take such risks again!—but all through that journey, I thought only of how you must be helping my brother."

Dr. Wilmott ushered her to a tiny hard sofa, so they could sit next to each other. She perched on the rim and kept her eyes lowered. How long would she have to simper over things Doctor had probably not done for Strat in order to be permitted to see Strat?

"We use the moral method, of course," said Doctor. He definitely never abbreviated his status. This was a man who every moment of his life and yours expected to be honored, because *he* was *Doctor*. "We treat many sad nervous systems, such as insanity, idiocy and epilepsy. Also, of course, cases of deformity."

Annie almost said, "What kind of jerk are you? How do you treat cases of deformity by telling them to have higher morals?" But instead she cried, "Oh, Doctor! I am sure that by your example alone, many have recovered."

Did he throw up?

Did he say, "Stop playing games with me, kid, and tell me why you're here?"

Did he say, "How would you know what kind of example I set, lady? You've known me five minutes."

No. He practically swooned.

She could tell just by the beard that Doctor liked himself better than anything else around. How much he must need to hear garbage like this. After all, he was stuck out here in the woods with a bunch of shrieking maniacs. Who was there to remind him of his superior brain and ability?

Only me, thought Annie. And luckily I have looks as well as brains and ability. I don't care what century you're in; beauty convinces people every time.

Slowly, as if in a ballet, Annie removed her veil. It was a surprisingly sexy act. She actually blushed as she revealed her face. Naturally she could not meet Doctor's eyes, but murmured, "Doctor, please reassure me that during this hour of trial, you will be with me, and help me face whatever condition my poor dear brother is in."

Doctor felt he could do this. He explained that the visit would have to be in his office. She must remember how severely deranged so many of his guests were. It would be too difficult for a lady of Miss Devonny Stratton's position to be assaulted by the sounds and sights of the other patients.

"Oh, thank you! You are so thoughtful. Doctor, you won't leave me alone with Strat, will you?" she said anxiously. "I shall be able to count on your presence,

shan't I?" She had never said *shan't* out loud before. She
wondered if she sounded as abnormal as his patients. "I
have heard such frightening stories of guards in institu-
tions like these. I won't have to lay eyes on such a
creature, will I?" She fanned herself to show how appalling that would be.

Especially appalling once Walker Walkley found a
next train. I'd better get this show on the road, she
thought. Move it, Doc.

"I shall not leave your side" said Doctor, patting her
arm too. He smiled reassuringly. A couple of decades of
nicotine and little toothbrushing coated his teeth. Annie had to close her eyes, but luckily this was how
ladies behaved.

Strat could not believe what was happening to him.

They were giving him a bath. *In hot water.* They were
shaving him and combing his hair. *Gently.*

Strat was weak from so little activity, weak from the
rage that had consumed him, and then eaten itself up,
and left him sagging inside the restraints. His brain was
flat, as if the asylum had ironed his ability to think.
Maybe I am insane, he thought. Nothing is going
through my head the way it ought to.

He could not help hoping they were also going to
give him a real meal. Grown-up food, like roast beef
and fried potatoes and gravy and . . .

Whatever happens next, I must not let myself think
about gravy. I must think of escape.

He was too tired. He could not think of escape.

He could only hope that this lasted and lasted and lasted.

Soft warm socks. (They had not given him shoes.) Clean soft wool pants. (They had given him neither belt nor suspenders, so he was holding them up with one hand.)

He walked obediently between two escorts, too busy with texture and warmth and cleanliness to know much else. There was a change in scent as they went through a heavy set of bolted doors and turned down a different hall. No longer the stench of bad toilet closets and unwashed patients, but a smell both Christmasy and leathery. A sort of library-in-winter smell. He could sniff out cinnamon, too, and coffee.

And light!

A real window on one side of him with real glass, through which he could see a real world of snow-covered trees, and a statue, and a lamppost.

It overwhelmed him. Strat might have been a prisoner of war after months of suffering and isolation. He had little control.

In front of him were apparitions.

There was Dr. Wilmott who ran the asylum. Smiling and nodding, bowing and blushing. Yes. Blushing.

This could not be translated by a mind as dulled as Strat's.

There was a fine long walnut desk, a glass paperweight with dancing colors, and a lamp with a heavy brass bottom. There were books and the scent of books, chairs in dark green leather and a Persian carpet as fine as any back in Manhattan.

And a lady.

She wore a magnificent gown, as if about to leave for some gala affair. Jewels sparkled on her pale throat, and gloved hands were folded in her lap.

My mother? thought Strat dimly. His heart went crazy with hope. Harriett? Devonny? Had one of them come to rescue him?

She turned, and Strat saw her face.

Anna Sophia.

ᔋᔆᕊ CHAPTER 9 ᔋᔆᕊ

Annie had known that seeing Strat again would be wonderful, but she had not known it would be this wonderful.

She jumped up from the hard little sofa, caring nothing for the vast hat that required such perfect posture. She flung her arms around him. "Oh, Strat!" she cried, hugging and kissing. He was as handsome and fine as before. Thinner, paler—but perfect.

She had not one sisterly thought. All her thoughts were romantic. Plumes and ribbons and velvets were now halfway down her back. She wanted to feel every inch of him. She wanted to hold his cheeks in her two hands and kiss him for days.

She was out of breath with excitement. It had worked! Being a lady, being a flirt, being a liar—these things worked!

She wanted to dance like football players after a goal.

But Annie Lockwood had a goal of her own. Getting Strat out.

Strat, reasonably enough, was speechless. After all, depending on your viewpoint, he had not seen her in a hundred years.

Don't talk yet, she thought, let me handle this. "Oh, Doctor!" she cried. "You are so wonderful, Doctor. It is such a privilege to have met such a great man. What a cure you have wrought! How wonderful my brother looks! How deeply in your debt I am! Oh, kind Doctor! Your brilliance has no equal."

They really did talk like that in the 1890s. And Doctor responded as doctors did in Victorian times: he bowed in receipt of her praise.

Annie couldn't watch a man being so foolish. Anyway, she had somebody immensely better to look at. "Strat, darling," she said, "wake up, dear brother. It's your sister, Devonny."

"Devonny," he repeated. He nodded, as if tucking this away for future reference.

And now Annie Lockwood had a problem. She had Doctor where she wanted him and Strat where she wanted him. But Strat wore no shoes and no coat. His clothing was all too obviously the clothing of a well-cared-for patient, not a gentleman. The sleigh was waiting for her; the carriage was covered and would hide Strat. But it could not hide Strat from the driver, who might not cooperate with escape plans. The driver, after all, was afraid of lunatics.

She had not planned any further. She did not know how to get Strat and herself out. She did not know if

Strat was sufficiently with the program to pick up his feet and run. She did not know if Doctor had armed and dangerous backup. For all she knew, he had a buzzer beneath his desk to summon . . .

No, he doesn't! she thought. There were no utility poles leading out of Evergreen. And that lamp. It has no plug. It's kerosene. So there is neither phone nor electricity,. But it is winter out there, and Strat has neither coat nor shoes, no hotel will take us, and Walker Walkley must be on my heels. Now what? *Now what?*

"Doctor," she whispered. "Doctor, I am overcome with emotion. You must help me deal with this perilous situation."

Only women got the vapors.

Even here in the asylum, no matter how badly Strat was treated, nobody ever accused him of hysteria. A man was superior to a woman. No man suffered from silliness. That was for females. Even Doctor had acknowledged that Strat was not hysterical, but possessed.

In the deepest recesses of his mind, Strat had worried that what possessed him might be something *womanly*. What if his father were *right*—there was no Anna Sophia Lockwood?

But here she was.

His Anna Sophia Lockwood. His century changer.

He was not just starved for food. Strat was starved for reassurance. When her arms encircled him, when her soft cheek pressed his own, sanity returned to his body. His flaccid limbs, his tired brain, his fading eyes came to attention.

He swayed among dreams come true. Hesitantly, he touched her cheek, as she was touching his. Yes. She existed. Anna Sophia—his Annie—his Miss Lockwood —was actually here.

She was even lovelier than he had remembered. Her laughing bright eyes were real.

And the jewels that glittered in layers below her throat were Devonny's. She was calling herself Devonny. Saying that she was his sister. Strat had not one brotherly emotion. He wanted to dance with her— encircle her slender waist with his two hands and sweep her in joyful . . .

His mind stopped spinning. It was no longer a whirling wind of nonsense and failure. It was capable once more of thought. And possibly, also, capable of action.

What was her plan? How had she arrived? How was Devonny involved? What of his family? What should be done next? A hundred thoughts lined up in Strat's mind, and the first was sports: *I won.* Inning after inning, they beat me.

But I'm going to win now.

Weeping was over. He wanted to laugh and shout— and escape.

"My dear," said Doctor, swiftly coming to the beauteous Miss Devonny's side, his hand reaching her waist.

He, too, was trembling. One of the loveliest young ladies he had ever seen was literally within his grasp. This must continue. She already worshiped him for what he had accomplished with her brother. Who knew how much more might be accomplished with her?

A fortune was within his reach. What sane man wanted to spend his career among the insane? Doctor wanted to spend his life spending. And nobody had more to spend than the Strattons.

If he had known there was a sister so brave, so loving, so beautiful, *so rich* . . .

The door opened.

His secretary said, "Telegraph boy, sir."

The boy (who was Doctor's age) saluted like a private to a general. "Telegram, sir. A Mr. Walker Walkley in Albany."

Charlie, who had shot a thousand glass bottles into glass shatters at the river's edge, looked at Harriett as she slept on her deck chair, wrapped in her furs and woolens.

He had fallen in love with Harriett early on. But no gentleman could say such a thing to a lady who had a fiancé. Even if Hiram Stratton, Jr., had never written and never come, Charlie could say no word against the man, for Harriett loved him.

Charlie despised Strat for hurting Harriett. He could not understand a man who would abandon a lady. Charlie understood not coming to visit: consumption could leap from person to person. Refusal to visit the sick girl was sane.

But not to write?

Not to send tiny gifts from the heart—the book of poems, the box of candy—that made a hard day easier?

Every time he was with Harriett, Charlie yearned to speak his mind. Sentences lay in his heart like a stack of letters to be mailed.

I love you, Harriett.

I will take care of you, Harriett.

I will not desert you, Harriett. You are beautiful, Harriett. I love your mind and soul.

Harriett was dying.

Over and over again, Charlie wrestled with duty. Was it his duty to speak the truth? To tell this girl so desperately in need of love that she was loved? Or was it his duty to go on pretending that Strat, whom she adored, had an excuse for this?

What would God expect of Charlie? What would Harriett want?

From Harriett's porch, in the last spare light of day, Charlie shot bottle after bottle, all indigo-blue glass, broken pieces flying into the air, and thought how much he would like to do that to Hiram Stratton, Jr.

"I cannot believe," said Annie, in the hoity-toity-est voice she could manage, "that this secretary would interrupt so private and emotional an occasion!" Please let Doctor not recognize the name Walker Walkley.

Please let him not realize this telegram has anything to do with me.

She rested a gloved hand on Doctor's forearm. Her hair was falling out of its twists. Was she unladylike, or romantic and appealing?

The secretary said warningly, "Doctor, I believe it is essential to read this telegram now."

Doctor said, "Certainly not. Where is your sense of propriety? Leave the telegram, boy." He shut the door on them and apologized to Miss Stratton for the coarse behavior of his clerk.

"Oh, Doctor," she said, unable to believe how far she was going with this absurd language of theirs, "you were masterful."

He smiled. He believed her. Annie slid across the century for a moment, and wondered what kind of things Miss Bartten had been saying to her father that had been so delicious to believe.

"Where is your sister?" said Mr. Lockwood grumpily. The worst thing was laundry. You should not have to do your own laundry. Certainly Tod wasn't doing *his* laundry. It was a mountain in the hallway in front of the bathroom, since Tod liked to strip en route to the shower.

They were going to run out of clothing. It was a crisis. They needed a woman.

"I don't know where Annie is," said Tod.

"Well, you must know what friend she's staying with."

"I don't think I said that she's staying with a friend."

"Well, where is she?" demanded Tod's father.

"I don't know."

Mr. Lockwood disliked his son rather intensely at that moment. What made teenage boys so obstructive? At least Tod knew that men don't do laundry and he was just leaving it there.

"What did Annie say when you saw her last?" said Mr. Lockwood.

"She said not to worry."

Mr. Lockwood was going to have to wash a load of underwear. There was no other option. Furiously, he kicked the dirty clothing in piles, not wanting to touch anything with his hands. It wasn't his job. "When did Annie say that?"

"I don't remember," said Tod. "I haven't seen her in days." Tod, personally, did not mind wearing the same clothing day after day. He could outlast his father on the washing-machine problem.

"Very efficient," said Annie.

"I knew this moment would come eventually," said Strat. He set the heavy brass lamp back on the polished desk.

Doctor lay messily on the floor.

"You didn't hurt him badly, did you?" she asked.

Strat truly did not care how badly Doctor was hurt, but on the other hand, a murder accusation would be even messier than Doctor on the floor.

"Oh, Miss Lockwood! I thought of you so often! I

could not discover whether I made you up or you really existed."

"I exist," she said softly. And then, in that rather fierce way he so well remembered, she gave him orders. "And don't call me Miss Lockwood. It's too formal. Whatever happens now, you and I are in it together."

Together, thought Strat. Is there a lovelier word? "Anna Sophia, you do not know how much I have needed somebody with whom to do things together."

Strat had touched Anna Sophia so gently, so carefully, during the other visits across Time. Now he hugged her fiercely. He needed to prove that his arms moved and he could still clasp, and tighten, and accomplish. He needed to prove that she really did exist, and could be felt and kissed and loved. No vapor, no dream, but a girl.

He kissed her in a manner he had not permitted himself the last time she visited his century, as it would have compromised her virtue. How wonderful were kisses that strong! With each touch of lips, she was more his.

A joyful thing happened. He found strength to pull away, and kiss no more. That was the definition of love: not touching a lady until marriage.

They took Doctor's pulse. He had one.

"Take his boots, Strat," said Annie. "His coat's hanging on that repulsive twisted wood thing in the corner. Wear the hat too. Add that scarf." She kissed his hair before the hat landed, and his throat before the scarf closed in, and they both laughed.

Strat undid Doctor's belt and yanked it out of the loops. A heavy ring of keys fell with a muffled clank onto the Persian carpet. Strat stared at them for a moment, thinking of the doors it had kept him behind. Before he threaded the belt to hold his own pants up, he slid the key ring on it.

"Good idea," said Annie. "Pretend to be a doctor yourself. That will please the sleigh driver."

"Why on earth would we want to please a driver?" he said, buttoning up the vast coat of Doctor's. It was far too big for him, which worried Annie. They must not look like escapees. But this was the Strat Annie remembered: somebody who did not notice servants. "We want the driver to take us away," she explained. "Very important part of the strategy."

Strat laughed.

She had always adored his laugh. She tossed him Doctor's gloves. "You'll be Doctor— Doctor— think of a great name, Strat."

"Dr. Lovesick," said Strat. "Dr. Timecross."

"Don't be a jerk. Dr. Lockwood. We won't forget that one. I know what we'll say. You're taking me for dinner in the village, where you will assuage my worries about my brother."

"Dinner is such a good idea," said Strat. "I haven't had a real dinner since they brought me here."

"I believe you," she said, pinching his ribs before she closed the last button on the huge beaver coat.

They dared not go out the door. Secretary would know he was no doctor. Secretary had read the telegram, which no doubt required a response. And no doubt the telegraph boy was standing right there in the reception room, waiting for Dr. Wilmott to emerge.

They went out the window. Here in Doctor's office, where sane people—people who gave him money—people who mattered—must sit, the windows must not be terrifying. No bars, no locks.

Strat lifted the sash. He went out first with his immense coat flapping and his beaver hat falling into the snow. He didn't look half so ridiculous as Annie, with her vast yardage to be squashed through, and her hat in her hands.

Dark had fallen. They need not worry about being seen. No exterior lights illuminated the grounds. After all, what visitor would come here in the night?

Deep snow soaked the hems of Annie's clothing and would give them away if anybody looked. But who would look, or could, in the dark? They hastened around the corner of the building. Strat's feet swam in the boots of Dr. Wilmott.

The driver was pacing back and forth, slapping his arms against his chest to keep his blood moving, stomping his feet to keep them from freezing. He had lit lamps on the four corners of the carriage, small yellow orbs which made the sleigh gay and cheery.

"The journey was so difficult!" Annie said to Strat. She handed the driver a five-dollar bill and prayed it was not so much that the driver would wonder, and think, and see the truth.

On the other hand, a girl who had just helped bop the asylum's superintendent over the head with a lamp and engineer the escape of a violent patient is not going to have a low profile whether she gives out pennies or gold bars. "Dr. Lockwood," she said, for the benefit of the driver, "I had to travel *alone*. It was so distressing. I am in such need of comfort. I cannot bear more travail."

Strat, being of his generation and not hers, took her literally. "My poor lady!" he cried. He meant it. "Alone! It is unthinkable. What a sacrifice."

"I love my brother," she said.

The driver was awed by the five-dollar bill. He earned seventy-five cents a day. With five dollars, he could buy two acres of land. "Where are we headed?" he said in the tone of voice that said Chicago would be fine.

Neither Strat nor Annie had made plans for this. Where *were* they headed? She could hardly say, "The farther the better. Just go."

She said, "We are famished, my dear man. Won't you recommend a fine dining place to us?"

"There ain't such a fine one in Evergreen, madam. But we could go to Saranac. It's not but four miles. A easy ride, what with snow. Smooth like. Take about a hour. First we head back to Evergreen, then west to Saranac."

"You are so clever, sir. Saranac it is."

She and Strat climbed in.

They had a wonderful time adjusting each other's clothing. The simple acts of pinning Annie's hair back up, of stationing her tower hat once more—these took half a hundred kisses to accomplish. And Strat's too-big coat—it had to be unbuttoned, so that Annie could snuggle next to his warm body instead of the fur of beavers.

It was so romantic—a sleigh in the night! How the horses stamped on the crispy packed snow! How the silver bells rang! A slender moon and a thousand stars decorated the black sky, and the white snow smiled up from the cold, cold ground.

Before long the little windows of the carriage frosted up from the hot breath of two excited occupants.

"Oh, Strat!" said Annie, suddenly in tears. "It's been so long!"

He kissed each tear. That a girl would weep for joy at seeing him! It was too wonderful.

He held her against him, knowing that in this strange moment, he really did need, along with Annie, a sister, and a mother, and a friend. It was not so much romance for which he was desperate as comfort. For he was not changing Time, like Annie, but changing worlds. He was leaving Hell behind.

"Oh, Annie!" he said, his own thoughts too complex for him.

They wept together, and in some way Annie knew that she was weeping for herself, too, and her own damaged family, and she said, "Oh, Strat!" and then they giggled helplessly, because they had only a two-word vocabulary between them.

In the village of Evergreen, the driver paused for traffic. A train had just come in (from the opposite direction of Albany, Annie saw with great relief) and sleds were taking away baggage and crates.

The little train station was lit by lovely romantic gaslights, and some of the carriages had torches. A trainman carried a lantern which swung by his side.

The passengers were silhouettes cut from dark paper: trailing gowns, flowing capes, tall hats, pipes. Cuddled against Strat, Annie laughed with joy. This was what she had come for: the complete and total romance of the nineteenth century.

Harriett dreamed

Once, years ago, they had all spent the summer at Walker Walkley's old hunting lodge, only a dozen miles as the crow flew from her cure cottage.

If it were summer, thought Harriett, if I were well . . . ladies in silks would rustle past, their ribbons fluttering, their laughter bubbling. Young bloods wearing corduroys and many-pocketed jackets would be returning with trophies of deer and woodcock. Fishermen would be flaunting their trout. Taxidermists would stop to collect these, and prepare them for walls. Stages laden with trunks and hampers and hatboxes, with folding tents and folding chairs and folding stools, and with rifle cases and cases of champagne, would be leaving the train station. Remember how we brought bales of china and huge rolled rugs, a dozen extra mattresses, chests of tea and coffee, and boxes of books and games?

Oh, Strat! Let me at least give you my last breath.

Annie and the boy she loved forgot the Time of watches and telegrams, the Time of telephones and police response.

They forgot the rage of a man who does not get his way. There is no rage equal to the rage of a man who has been made a fool of by a lady.

Walker Walkley would see her dead before he let her have Strat or Harriett or any of their money.

As for Dr. Wilmott, he was more sophisticated. He knew that Death is not the worst punishment. His own asylum would hurt her more.

And so from two ends of the Adirondacks came telegrams and telephone calls. From Walker Walkley and from Dr. Wilmott came promises to pay well.

And swiftly came men whose job it was to round up the dangerous and the insane.

The police.

❧ CHAPTER 10 ❧

Through the coziness and the clinging, Annie and Strat heard shouts. Their sleigh began to slow down.

"Hey! Whoa there! Ho!" came bellowing voices.

The driver was pulling back the horses' reins. The horses could not simply halt because the sleigh, on a downhill, continued to move. But the pace slowed.

Strat and Annie let go of each other, bolts of fear instead of love coursing through them.

"Ethan!" A deep man's voice. "Your passenger escaped from the Asylum!"

A wildly excited tenor voice. "He's violent!"

"Tried to kill Dr. Wilmott!" A third voice.

There was an actual posse after them.

Strat jerked open the glass panel between the passengers and driver. "Keep going, Ethan. Please. We have money."

Annie handed him her final wad of bills and Strat tried to give it to the driver.

But there are some things money will not buy, and driving into the night with lunatics is one.

The sleigh reached the bottom of the slope, and stopped.

For a moment, Annie and Strat were paralyzed by horror. "We can't get through the forests without a sleigh," whispered Strat. "We would die of the cold in minutes."

"Then we have only one hope. We must stay a lady and a gentleman. Bluff our way out." Annie forced open the half-frozen side window.

The police were already there. "Has he taken you a hostage, ma'am?" they asked anxiously, and to Strat, "Do not hurt this lady. You are surrounded and cannot get away. Now step out of the carriage quietly so we are not forced to hurt you."

Annie prayed. No flirting this time. She must be cool and tough and strong. She must be her mother on Wall Street.

"Gentlemen, you have been duped," she said. "As always in my experience, a man who pretends to be a doctor is believed. I understand you think Wilmott is actually a doctor. However, he is not."

Strat squeezed her hand. In a calm sturdy voice, he said, "This lady is a representative of the Lunacy Law Reform and Anti-Kidnapping League."

"Is that so?" said one of the men. "Well, why don't you get out of the sleigh and talk it over with us."

They had no choice. Annie got out first. She held out

150

a gloved hand for assistance. She required them to help with her skirts. She wished for more light, so that they could see her face, but she would have to make do with her voice. "I certainly thank you for your prompt response," she said as warmly but as haughtily as she could put together. "It is so good to know the police are so quick. However, your information is incorrect."

"We've known Dr. Wilmott many years," said the policeman.

"And have you not dealt with our representatives during that time?" said Annie, arching her eyebrows even though this was invisible behind the slope of her hat. An actress must follow through on detail.

"Well, yes," said one of them reluctantly.

For heaven's sake! There really was an Anti-Kidnapping League. "Mr. Hiram Stratton, Jr., is possessed of a vast fortune," said Annie. "If you were notified by a cad named Walker Walkley, this is the fiend responsible for kidnapping Mr. Stratton."

From the way the police looked at each other, it was clear that Walker Walkley had indeed notified them.

They shifted a little on the snow.

Three police and a driver were ranged against a girl swamped by her own clothing and a boy weak from imprisonment.

Annie said, "We are bound for Saranac, where—"

"I think not, ma'am," said the policeman. "No matter what League you say you're from, Dr. Wilmott was hurt. We are taking you back to Evergreen."

Walker Walkley hardly thought of Strat or of Harriett.

He hardly even thought of the money.

His mind whirled at Anna Sophia Lockwood.

He paced at the station in Albany.

No train till dawn. That was what happened in the north woods. Godforsaken nightmare up here.

Dr. Wilmott wanted to hit his secretary. How dare she posture and prance just because she had known the girl was a fake and he had not? It was necessary to hit somebody.

He chose Katie and Douglass.

It made him feel so much better.

And soon—yes, in this very cell—he would put the girl. Whoever she was. Who cared who she was? It was her suffering that mattered, and Dr. Wilmott knew how to make a person suffer.

He smiled, and Ralph the attendant smiled, and again he slapped Katie.

Strat bowed slightly to the opposition. Annie could not think what he meant by it. Was it surrender? They must not give in! They must fight, somehow. They could not allow themselves to be taken back to Evergreen.

"Dear friend," Strat said to her, his voice formal, "allow me to help you back in the carriage where you will be warm."

She resisted, glaring at him from under her hat brim

152

and the rolled-up veil, which was now unrolling and making it harder to see and think and believe. "Trust me," he breathed. She did trust him. But those four were stronger. If there were a fight, he was going to need Annie. However, in a fight, she would be doomed by these ridiculous clothes. She couldn't even bend down to take off her own boot and hit somebody with the heel, because a woman in a tightly laced corset could not bend.

His hand on her elbow moved her toward the door of the carriage and Annie heard herself sob. She lifted the skirts she now hated, the miles of satin and velvet, and managed to find the first high step with the sole of her boot.

Strat shoved her hard with his hand, throwing her into the carriage like a suitcase. She felt the sleigh rock dangerously and heard Strat shout to the horses.

The men shouted, too, but one slipped in the snow, one was holding the reins of his own horses, one was on the wrong side of the carriage, and the driver Ethan was thrown to the snowbank by the force of Strat's driving shoulder.

They were off!

Annie grabbed the edges of the door and hauled herself into the carriage. Easier said than done in a Victorian gown. Seams ripped under her knees and the wind threw her hat by the side of the road. Oh, well, she had the hatbox here. She'd wear the other one.

Annie yanked the flapping side door closed, got on

her knees to yank the little front window open and shouted to Strat's backside, "Way to go, Strat!"

He was laughing.

Annie loved a guy who could laugh under these circumstances.

"I haven't forgotten how!" yelled Strat, turning the horses expertly. He was having a wonderful time. He was nothing but one more teenage boy, taking the corners as fast and hard as he could.

The wind through the open slot was sharp as a weapon.

Annie wrapped herself like a cocoon in the furs. In her day, furs were not politically correct. But what the furs really were, was really warm.

A sleigh race.

Horses in the night.

Moon and stars keeping watch.

Strat shouted and whipped and threw his body weight left and right to help at the curves.

Pines screened the moonlight, like black lace.

A fox barked.

And behind them, four men, presumably four angry and possibly hurt men, followed.

Strat took a corner too fast, too hard, and the sleigh overturned.

Strat leaped clear of the falling vehicle. The horses staggered, but did not get tangled in each other or in the complex tack. He was relieved by that—he could never have left the horses to break each other's legs. He

154

would have had to clear them, and that would give their pursuers time to catch up.

He climbed onto the carriage side and opened the door awkwardly. Annie was shaken but unhurt. She could barely climb out in her skirts, but to take them off would mean freezing to death. She got out, and they slid to the ground.

Their pursuers' shouts and pounding horses were right above them.

"Into the woods," said Strat, and they ran, thigh deep in wet snow that clung and tugged and slowed and caught. Their feet stumbled on rocks and fallen branches at the bottom of the snow, and twice they fell together and crusty cruel snow tore at their faces.

Like crippled rabbits, they tried to hop over tangles and under branches. Tried to find a safe hole in which to crouch till danger flew by.

"Come back!" cried the tenor voice.

"You'll freeze to death in a hour!" shouted the bass.

"Don't go with the maniac, miss!" shouted Ethan, her driver. "The woods is terrible. There's bears and wolves. There's half-frozen ice and cliffs that break off from the weight of the snow! It's not a pretty way to die!"

They were deep among black and dreadful spruces, invisible to the road and to the four men and the huffing, stomping horses.

They had probably gone a hundred yards.

Nothing. No safety zone at all.

A horse stamped. Sleigh bells trembled softly.

They were all cold, and nobody had any source of

heat, but Annie and Strat were also wet, and wet was the greatest disaster.

The four men could simply return to their homes for a good night's sleep. When they returned at dawn, they would find the frozen corpses of Annie and Strat.

Devonny had told Annie to prove her worth. Well, she had failed. Annie did not know which pain was greater: the pain of failure or the pain of this terrible, vicious cold.

Nobody moved.

"Miss," said Ethan sadly, "the lunatic is not worth it."

But Strat was worth it. He had always been worth it. She loved him. Oh, Daddy! she thought, caught between centuries and sadnesses. Daddy, Mom is worth it too. Come back to her!

"Come back with us," cried the men. "Leave him there to die."

Strat wrapped the beaver coat tightly around Annie and pressed her to his body to give her warmth. It's my heart, she thought, my heart needs warmth.

"Does he have you prisoner, miss?" shouted Ethan.

Annie grit her teeth against the chattering of her jaws and after a long, long time, the two teams left. There were advantages to sleigh bells. Sound informed them what was happening. They knew, too, that both teams had gone back toward Evergreen.

"Come on," said Strat, "we have to use the road. These woods are too terrible to cut through."

"What if one of them is waiting for us?"

"One of them we could handle. We know at least two

are gone, since both teams left. And I cannot imagine that reasonable men would stand alone in the winter in the wilderness risking death. They'll come for us at dawn. But we won't be here."

They slogged back, falling and sliding. Her toes were so cold they hurt, her ankle was twisted and her face cut by the slapping of hemlock branches.

They reached the road. Moonlight gave it a faint glow. There was nothing in sight. They turned and ran toward Saranac. In twenty steps, they were out of strength. They walked. Tottered, Annie thought, would be a better word. "Too bad we don't have an all-terrain vehicle, or at least a Ski-Doo."

Strat looked at her nervously. It was this kind of vocabulary, vocabulary that didn't exist, that had caused some of the trouble in his famous essay.

"See," said Annie, "in my day it doesn't matter what the surface of the earth is. Roads don't count."

"Roads don't count?" repeated Strat. He could not comprehend her description of a snowmobile, for which barriers were nothing and to which no field or wood was closed.

They held each other up.

They could actually see the village of Saranac, a few lights in the night across a lake. Annie did not dare cross a lake after the story Ethan had told. What if they fell through where there was no ice, only a treacherous layer of snow?

But they would not live long enough to circle the lake. No human without the proper clothing could survive this. The police would come in the morning and scrape up the bodies like roadkill.

"We're not going to make it," she said. His lips were blue. Hers felt dead.

"Let me tell you about a friend of mine," said Strat. "Her name is Katie. If she can get up and keep going every day, so can we. We are going to make it. We're going to tell stories, and the rhythm of our words will match our feet, and we will make it to a building that is warm."

Annie tried to believe it.

"I'll start," he said. "We used to come hunting here, years ago, when life was good and my family was close. Autumn is the best season, of course. The sunlight is gold, the falling leaves are gold, and the hope that you will shoot a great buck is gold." He laughed at his poetry. "Tell me, Annie," he coaxed, making her participate, keeping her alive, "is it still forever wild?"

He meant a hundred years later. Had the stewards of this land, the people of New York, kept their bargain? She nearly said, "Strat, there is nothing wild left in my America. Only pockets of pretend wild." But this was storytelling, and he needed a story, and she said, "The wolves and the bears and forests of green are still there."

"Forever wild," said Strat happily.

"I, personally," said Annie, who thought that a nice Ford with a great heater would be a very good idea right now, "prefer forever civilized. Tell me about Katie."

He told her about Katie.

The story truly kept Annie going. "Why, Strat," she interrupted him, "it sounds like a cleft palate and harelip. That's nothing. Plastic surgery takes care of that when the baby's born. My brother Tod had that, and he hardly has a scar. He's handsome."

But Strat, of course, had never heard of plastic surgery, and it had never occurred to him or anyone else that they might simply sew up the deformity and be rid of it.

Walker Walkley wanted to rip the telephone out of the wall. "Where can they go?" he demanded. Every moment he had to stay in Albany made him more and more angry.

"Heaven or Hell," said the officer in Evergreen simply. "They won't be alive."

"You don't know that girl. I swear she has the devil on her side. Could they get to Saranac? Could they get anyplace else?"

"I couldn't. Three miles in that cold, wet clear through, and the cloth frozen to their skin? They're dead already, Mr. Walkley."

"Nevertheless, you warn those officials in Saranac, do you hear me?" Walk was shouting into the phone. He never quite trusted that wire. He said, "I can't believe you lost them to start with! Small towns! I would have thought you could manage a few weaklings like that without trouble."

"And did you manage the woman on the boat without any trouble?" said the small-town officer. "It was a woman, wasn't it, who—"

"Just you notify Saranac!" yelled Walk, slamming the phone down.

The Evergreen official put his phone down more gently. There was no need to notify anybody. Except the funeral parlor.

⊷⊷

They knocked on the door of the first farmhouse they came to. "Please," cried Annie as the door fell open. "Please help us."

Country people would not dream of failing to help. The frozen strangers were rushed in, their wet clothing stripped off without regard to modesty. They were put before a fire so hot it hurt. A stout, friendly woman in layers of skirts and aprons rubbed Annie's skin down, and put her bare feet in a basin of warm water. A thin, gnarled man with a gray spiky beard spooned hot soup into Strat's mouth. When Strat whispered that he would pay for a real meal—for beef and potatoes—the man grinned, and heated up a vast pot of stew: beef and turnips and squash and onions and gravy and potatoes. And Strat ate and ate and ate.

"Thank you," said Annie over and over again. "Thank you so much. Thank you so much."

"Whatever happened?" asked the woman. She was not suspicious. She was just comforting. Annie even had some stew. Normally Annie considered stew a sort of school-cafeteria idea: the kind of thing you steered around rather than ate. But this was delicious. She, too, ate and ate and ate.

"We went for a romantic sleigh ride in the night," said Strat, "and I lost control. We tipped over and the horses ran on. It was entirely my fault. If I had killed us both by us freezing in the night, I would have none to blame but myself."

"Well, now," said the woman comfortably, "didn't happen, did it? Now, we got no extra beds, but you'll curl up on the rug by the stove and be warm for the night. Whoever's worrying about you, they'll just have to worry till morning."

And they were wrapped in rugs, and left to sleep the night in peace. Annie was asleep in a moment, but Strat required no sleep. He had had a lot of sleeping in the last year.

He stared at Annie, asleep in the firelight.

How undefended she was in her sleep.

How young.

She had saved him, and in return he had nearly gotten her killed. It was so difficult to believe in himself as a person of worth. But Anna Sophia believed in him. She had crossed a century to come to him.

In the shadows, his hand a dark quiver by the light of the fading fire, he touched a strand of her hair. It was hot from lying near the embers. He wove it between his fingers, and thought of love, and Annie, and Harriett, and Katie. And he—supposedly a gentleman—what was he to do now? There must be a wise course to follow. But what was it?

By dawn's early light, police from both Saranac and

Evergreen would converge on the place where they had abandoned the sleigh. If they bothered to call the Anti-Kidnapping League on Fourteenth Street, they would know that Annie had not been employed by them. She was no innocent to be rescued from the maniac. Annie was in as much trouble as he was. Much as Doctor deserved death, Strat hoped that he had survived—if Strat and Annie had killed the man, hordes of police would descend upon them.

Strat and Annie must be gone and leave no tracks. How? In such snow, with so many witnesses? What must they do, and in what order? Where could they flee to?

At four in the morning, Strat got up and dressed. Annie's clothing was dry now, draped on a wooden clotheshorse by the kitchen coal stove. She slept in a ball, a mass of long dark hair hanging out of the furs and spread across the braided rug. He touched her hot cheek.

She woke instantly, throwing off the fur like a stranger.

She was wearing a huge white nightdress their hostess had brought. It buttoned right up to the throat, had long sleeves that tightly clasped her wrists, and reached to her toes.

Strat averted his eyes. It was a trespass, that he should see her in her nightclothes.

Annie herself woke up fast. She remembered all of it instantly: their whole success and their whole failure.

When Strat turned from the sight of her in her

nightie, she grinned. I love these 1890s guys. They're so cute. Well, one of them anyway.

She tucked herself up against him, snuggling until she found a really good hug spot, and they whispered. Travel could not occur until daylight and Strat was bursting with need. He told Annie about Walk and the essay and his professor and the accusations and his own father's betrayal.

Annie kissed his hand. Even his fingers were thin. "Oh, Strat! They were so terrible to you."

"Nobody ever even wrote to me!" Strat cried out, his whisper emotional and hurt. "Nobody ever came. Not my mother, not my sister, not even Harriett, who I thought would come to me over hell or high water."

"Your mother came," Annie told him. "She sold jewels to buy her ticket. Dr. Wilmott wouldn't let her in. He said it would disturb your treatment. As for Devonny, your sister wrote you all the time. But she has been almost a prisoner of Walker Walkley, and Walk interfered with the mail. None of Devonny's letters ever left the house."

"Walk handled the mail? But where are Father and Florinda?"

"Florinda and your father went out to California several months ago. Your father has decided there is more money to be made on the West Coast than on the East."

"How ridiculous," said Strat. "There's nothing out there but orange trees."

"Trust me, Strat, he's right on this one," said Annie. "Anyway, your father pretty much left everything in

163

Walker Walkley's hands. And you know those are sick and greedy hands."

"And Harriett?" he whispered. He knew how hard this question would be, for both Annie and Harriett had loved him: loved him at the same time, with the same hope.

How Annie wanted to skip the topic of Harriett. Strat's fiancée. In his own Time, Strat was a gentleman. In her Time, Annie was not acquainted with many boys to whom manners mattered. But being a gentleman also involved honor. And Strat, a man of honor, would want to do the right thing by the ladies in his world. She, Annie, must also do the right thing by the people in this life.

Annie set out the facts harshly and fast. "Harriett has consumption. She is at a cure cottage at Clear Pond, recovering her strength. Devonny instructed me to take you to her if at all possible. Harriett doesn't know you were locked in Evergreen. She was already at Clear Pond. In fact, I'm guessing that Walker Walkley coordinated things so neither of you would know the truth about the other. Your father and Walker Walkley felt that being told about your insanity would be another burden for her bad health. They said she could not bear the news that you had become insane."

Strat sat, as far removed from Annie as Time, caught in the world he had had once and did not have now. "Anna Sophia, I have some very ugly people in my life."

Truly, thought Annie. I'm luckier. Nobody in my life is so ugly. Not even Miss Bartten, or Dad. They're people who want everything their own way, even if it hurts the rest of us. But they aren't vicious.

Or are they? What would Mom say?

"Annie," said Strat finally, close enough to her in his heart to use the precious nickname, "does my poor Harriett think I have abandoned her?"

"I don't know. Devonny didn't know. I bet Walk stole Harriett's letters to Devonny too."

"We will go to Harriett then," said Strat. He was relieved, actually. It gave them a destination, and a very important one. He wasn't running away if he went to Harriett. He was her knight, her soldier, her fiancé.

"But Strat," protested Annie, "Walk will guess that that's where you'd go. Won't the police just follow us? Or be waiting for us? I think we should head for some city where we can vanish, and go see Harriett later."

For a few moments, he simply held on to her, fingering her silky hair, wondering what it could be like to live in a Time where disease was conquered. "There might not be a later for Harriett," he said tiredly. *Oh Dear God*, he prayed, for suddenly God was dear, and so was life, and so were Harriett and Annie; *Dear God, let me reach Harriett in time.*

The mantel clock chimed five.

Annie felt ambushed by Time and by facts. I am taking the man I love to the woman who loves him, she realized. They are engaged. People do not take that lightly whatever century they occupy. I don't want Harriett to have Strat now. Not after all this.

But what would I do with Strat after I have him?

Take him home with me to my century, like a prize at the bottom of the cereal box? Or would I stay with him in his century? Flee to Canada or California?

Strat, I love you so! But where is the right way for us? There must be one, or Time would not have brought me here. But what is it? How can both Harriett and I have you?

"Get dressed," instructed Strat. "These people probably have a cutter and a horse. We'll leave money, as much as we can, so they cannot accuse us of stealing. Write a note. Explain that we cannot wait for them to get up."

Annie was still doubtful. "I think it would be better if—"

Strat kissed her. It was not affection. It was a kiss to close her lips. "I know best, Anna Sophia. Don't worry your little head anymore. You have done very well to get so far, and I'll handle it from now on."

She had the brief thought that being a gentleman in Strat's Time was also being a very pushy chauvinist, but she set the thought aside, as many a woman had done, and let him handle it as he saw fit.

Annie's dress had dried in a million wrinkles. It was torn in several places and stained everywhere. The coat had survived no better. One of the two capes was hanging from threads, so she ripped it away, and then the coat looked positively deformed. She appropriated Doctor's plaid scarf, tying it around her head to protect her ears. Immediately she ceased to be a lady of wealth and station, and became an immigrant in pitiful hand-me-downs.

I'll whip Strat into shape, she decided. He believes men are destined to be in charge and ladies exist to say Yes and Thank You. I'm glad so much has changed in a hundred years.

In thinking of her own mother, however, Annie was hard-pressed to be sure that anything had changed.

At any rate, when she went outdoors, not only was the cutter ready and the horse harnessed but Strat was paying the husband, and this arrangement seemed to be just fine with everybody, and even reasonable.

The man kindly gave them road directions for Clear Pond, including a way to bypass Saranac Village, and they were off, minutes before first light. The cutter skimmed over packed snow. The dawning sun exploded. A fireball of crimson. The sky matched the finest jewels from Tiffany's.

In a few hours, they came to a village, where shops had begun to open. "We must bring Harriett a present," Strat insisted, so they stopped at stores and finally settled on a candy box: fifty sticks in colors and flavors Annie hardly knew: black paregoric, yellow molasses, brown horehound, birch, sassafras, and vanilla cream.

They had luncheon at an inn by the side of a lake which had been plowed clear of snow. Big clumsy ice-boats and skaters in bright red were slipping and sliding everywhere. Children were laughing, and bonfires on the shore were surrounded by people warming their hands. Sellers of hot chocolate were making the rounds. Annie loved the little kids' skates: funny little two-knifed shoes. These kids stared in envy at the few who wore white lace-up boot skates. A few men were skating actually *backward*, and everybody was awestruck.

They were not at Olympic levels here. But they were happy.

Strat and Annie sat in a wonderful dining room—huge peeled logs wrapping an immense two-story fieldstone fireplace in which a fire as tall as Annie burned. They held hands and talked and watched the laughing children come and go.

"I'm so glad to see happy, normal people," said Strat. "It's been so long for me—happiness or normalcy."

Happiness or normalcy, thought Annie Lockwood, with a little shiver. Shouldn't they go together? Shouldn't it be happiness *and* normalcy? Are we going to have to choose one or the other?

And Harriett—is she the one who will make Strat happy? Or am I?

And what do I want?

CHAPTER 11

The sun turned the snow to ribbons of gold, and the shadows of balsam and birch belonged on Christmas cards. The sky was shot with glitter and the frozen waterfalls were museum pieces.

Clear Pond was quite literally around the next bend. It was the most beautiful mile of all the beautiful miles they had come. It had its own entry lane: a swooping white road cut into white snow walls. It had its own lake, of course, an unplowed expanse of snow with funny little tiny trees peeking out here and there, way out in the middle of the pond. The sanitarium buildings were constructed from rough-hewn vertical logs trimmed in wooden lace.

It was exceptionally quiet, as if a president had died. All over the grounds, young men were leaning on their male nurses and having cigarettes or cigars or pipes.

"They're dying of lung disease and they still *smoke*?" said Annie.

Strat looked startled, as if there were no connection between smoke and lungs.

Annie and Strat found the main building and entered the office, where they were greeted by a woman dressed far better than Annie was.

"I am Hiram Stratton, Jr.," said Strat. "I am engaged to Miss Harriett Ranleigh."

The woman turned hard and disapproving. "And I," she said, "am Mrs. Havers. Miss Harriett has written you over and over, Mr. Stratton, begging for your presence. You come now, when she is in the arms of death?"

Arms of death? How horrible! thought Annie. Does Death have arms? A long reach and thin fingers and sharp nails?

"No," said Strat, too softly, as if his heart were lying with that syllable. It wasn't really *No*. It was *Yes, but I hoped I was wrong*. "She can't be. I can't have come too late."

He loves her! thought Annie, and her heart, too, lay crushed within that syllable.

"You have. What is your excuse for such vile behavior?" asked Mrs. Havers flatly.

If only we accused each other of vile behavior in my day, thought Annie. We're too busy being politically correct to admit that some people are just vile. And Strat knows so many of them.

"I have been imprisoned," said Strat, "in an asylum. Relatives wanted my money. They created lies about me and kidnapped me. No letter I wrote Harriett was ever mailed."

He had forgotten Anna Sophia. He was entreating Mrs. Havers as if she were an angel of judgment. "I beg you to believe me." He had never looked more appealing. His shaggy hair fell forward. His formal clothing hung around him with a sort of strength, as if he would fill it any moment. "I am perfectly safe, madam," he said. "I love Harriett. I must be with her."

The woman softened. "Yes," she said. "You must." For a moment, they were both angels: people doing their very best in a terrible situation.

Then, briskly, Mrs. Havers surveyed Annie and the wrinkled badly matched outfit. "Good. Another servant. Your name?"

Annie was so startled she told the truth. "Annie Lockwood." I don't think I want to be a servant, she thought. She expected Strat to deny this unwanted status. But he didn't. As they left the office, Mrs. Havers said over her shoulder, "Lockwood! Carry those bags."

What was with these people? On the one hand, they didn't want you to lift an ungloved finger. On the other hand, if you were a servant, you'd better lift, and lift fast. No backtalk. Annie struggled to hoist a large assembly of cartons without hurting her back.

"Lockwood! Don't dillydally."

Annie grunted.

"She has no manners," said the woman to Strat.

Strat apologized for Annie's failure to say "Yes, ma'am."

Being a lady was tons of fun, plus you got great hats.

Being a servant had already worn thin. Annie wasn't going to last long as a combination nurse and grocery cart. She wasn't ready to say "Yes ma'am." She was ready to tell Strat where to go, and how much to carry while he went there.

Walker Walkley could not believe how swiftly the tide had turned. The so-called police in Evergreen had found no frozen corpses. The so-called police in Saranac had found no trace of Strat and Miss Lockwood.

The only possibility now was Clear Pond, and Harriett Ranleigh. Miss Lockwood had retrieved Strat like a duck from a pond, and even now Strat was probably controlling Harriett. What if Harriett were swept to health by the mere presence of Strat? Where would her money go then? To Strat! Not Walk!

Devonny had engineered this. A vixen with no intention of marrying Walk, just a lying conniving female.

I will have that money, Walk thought over and over. The money glistened in his mind. It was the color of the ice under the sun. The color of silver and gold.

But at last, in Evergreen of all unlikely places, he had an ally.

Dr. Wilmott said, "I beg of you, Mr. Walkley. Permit me to go with you to Clear Pond. I, too, have scores to settle, and an inmate to return to his cell."

"Perhaps, Wilmott," said Walk, who considered doctors merely educated servants, "you will have room for another inmate."

"I am sure we could accommodate Miss Lockwood,"

said Dr. Wilmott. "Of course, there is the matter of payment."

"Bill me," said Walker Walkley.

Annie was shocked.

No gentle pallor, no rosy cheeks, no sweet fading girl.

How could this be Harriett? The Harriett of Annie's other trip through Time had danced and played croquet and raced upstairs and strolled on the beach.

Harriett's face was hollow and gaunt. Her limbs had become sticks from which muscles had melted off, leaving only skin. Each joint was a knot on a twig. Her fingers were bone, covered with white parchment. Harriett was gasping, her lungs too compromised to fill. The room was harsh with the sucking struggle for air.

So this was why they called it consumption. It had eaten Harriett.

Harriett stared at the man before her, throwing his greatcoat and hat and gloves to the invisible servant—Annie. "Strat," Harriett breathed. "Oh, Strat. Oh, thank you. Oh, dear sweet God, thank you." Harriett was addressing them both at once: God and Strat. She had no more voice than she had flesh: there was only a whisper of her left to the world.

Strat sat on the edge of her bed and wrapped her and her blankets in his arms. Rocking her back and forth, he murmured, "Harriett, Harriett. I cannot believe this happened to either of us. Harriett, I loved you all along.

I truly did." He kissed her lips, which no healthy person must ever do with a consumptive.

But Annie was glad. Yes, this was right. It would be like Sleeping Beauty. Strat was Prince Charming. He would kiss away death and sorrow.

She loved it: a fairy-tale ending, and everybody living happily ever after.

Except me, she thought. What am I supposed to do?

Strat kissed Harriett's thin, dry hair and the hands so weak they could not press back against his. Gently and briefly, he told her what had happened to him, the dreadful reasons he had not been at her side before.

"Oh, Strat," said Harriett, her thready voice thicker from relief. "You have been suffering too. I didn't know. I thought you had found another to love."

I'm the other, thought Annie. Harriett thought that I . . . *and I would have.* I love Strat. I want to be his other. But there is no way to divide a man. No matter which century.

Annie pressed against the wall. Harriett had not thought to glance at her. In this clothing, she was merely a person to change the linen, fill the hot water bottle, and stoke the stove.

"You will get well now, darling Harriett," said Strat.

In every motion of their embrace was their history together: for Strat and Harriett had known each other from childhood, and when she was orphaned, Harriett had become Mr. Stratton's ward, and Harriett and Devonny had been best friends, and it had always been expected that Strat and Harriett would wed.

Only the appearance of Anna Sophia Lockwood in 1895 had interrupted the flow of events.

But I've put it back together, thought Annie. All the king's horses and all the king's men—who needs them? Just call me.

"I will take you away, Harriett," said Strat. "I know doctors approve of ice-cold air for the lungs, but I have been cold this winter and I have come to believe in warmth. I will take you to Mexico. Think of heat, Harriett, and golden sun. Think of love, and our children, and the home we will make for them."

Annie's soul leaped a hundred years. Was Daddy saying this to Miss Bartten? Were they planning a vacation in Mexico, thinking up baby names for a new family? But what about *our* family? cried Annie. The people who come first should stay first!

"I have thought of nothing else for so long," said Harriett. She found the strength to touch his cheek. In her terrible wasted condition, she became somehow beautiful: love did transform her.

And it was not her own love, because she had loved Strat all along; it was Strat's love, confirming that Harriett mattered, that he adored her.

"Would you leave us?" said Strat to the nurse and to Annie. The nurse, whose nametag said MOSS, took Annie's arm and led her out of the sickroom. Annie did not mind. She hurt all over, for love was too complex and went in too many directions and involved too many people.

I want true love to save Harriett, she thought.

But I want true love for myself.

Strat's true love.

In the asylum at Evergreen, Katie did not cry. The loss of Strat was too great and awful for mere tears. Strat's company had held her together against the assault of the asylum.

God forgive me this sin, she thought. Strat has escaped and instead of rejoicing for him, I want him caught and brought back.

How did he get out? she wondered. Is he all right? Is he warm? Has winter hurt him? Is he having the dinner of roast beef and gravy that he wanted so much? Is he among decent people who use courtesy and kindness?

What is kindness? Shall I ever know it again, now that Strat is gone?

The door opened.

For a terrible moment—the worst her soul had had —she wanted it to be Strat.

But it was a woman, thin and gray and angry, shrieking, "You cannot do this to me! I have done nothing to merit this! Let go of me!"

Of course Ralph and Dr. Wilmott paid no attention but enclosed her in the crib.

Katie turned her head. This is my life, she thought. One lunatic after another, their screams no different from the last set of screams.

Douglass made his lonely sounds and scruffled toward her and Katie tried to sing a song of comfort, but they were both beyond that now.

Moss fixed a pot of tea. She did not take a tray to Harriett and Strat. Annie was not fond of tea, which in her opinion was discolored water, but she enjoyed the heat of the pretty little cup and the act of holding its tiny curly handle as she lifted it in a ladylike way to her lips.

An hour went by.

Annie thought of Mexico, and warmth, and Harriett getting well.

"Moss," called Strat wearily from the sickroom. "Annie."

Harriett Ranleigh was dead.

She had managed to hang on for the only really important thing: the presence of the boy she loved. And when she had that, it was enough.

Death was not supposed to win!

Annie wanted to beat her fists against Death's chest, and kick Death in the shins, and shriek obscenities at Death. But Death had so obviously come for Harriett. There was something so completely missing from Harriett now. Not just breathing, not just heartbeats.

The beautiful soul of Harriett Ranleigh was gone forever.

Annie had never seen death. In her century, death was kept neatly in the hospital. You didn't actually ever get near it.

In 1898, death was casual. The nurse did not flinch.

Other patients, a man named Charlie and a girl named Beanie, were not surprised. Even Strat, who wept, was not shaken. The girl-like thing in his arms was no longer dear Harriett. He held her—it—for some time, and then gently lowered what had once been Harriett back into the pillows and kissed the forehead and did not let go of the limp hands.

Then he faced Annie. He did not wipe away his tears. They lay motionless on his face, defying gravity, a memorial to Harriett. "She gave you her love, Annie," said Strat. "She asked that I name my first daughter Harriett," he said, "and I gave her my word."

Annie could not look at them anymore. She stared out the window. White birches with black twigs gathered along a path. How feminine the birches were. Young girl trees. Harriett would not see spring. No color green. No sunlight on meadows, no birds singing, no warmth of summer.

If I had known, she thought, if Time had told me, I would have brought antibiotics and medications and cures. How cruel and vicious Time is, to let one generation get well, but not another.

Strat's eyes were shiny with grief. "Annie, without you, I would not have had this great gift. You gave me this. We made peace, Harriett and I, and I held her. She did not cross the bar alone. I was with her."

"You must let go now, sir," said Moss calmly. "I will prepare the body. Lockwood, I will need your assistance. Mr. Stratton, here is Miss Harriett's dear friend, Charlie, who will sit with you in your sorrow."

Florinda fanned herself. California was astonishing. Every single day it was warm. It never once rained and the sky didn't turn gray. Florinda felt that California had possibilities. Of course, they had no Society, and people here were vulgar. But each day you woke up with the sense that all would be well, whereas in New York you often woke up convinced that nothing could ever go well.

She could hardly wait for her stepdaughter, Devonny, to arrive. Florinda had met all sorts of adorable young men. They were all poor, and all needed Devonny's fortune, but that was to be expected. The important thing was, they were not Walker Walkley.

She pondered the mysterious telegram.

FLORINDA TELL DEVONNY HER MONEY WAS WELL SPENT STOP FIRST GOAL REACHED STOP MUCH LOVE ANNA SOPHIA.

Well, of course, Florinda remembered every single detail of the beautiful Miss Lockwood, and the scandal and the excitement and the chase! And most of all, the delicious hour in which *she*, Florinda, saved them all from evil.

Anna Sophia is back! thought Florinda. Her mind could not compass such an incredible thing.

Any message insisting that money had a good use and that people loved each other was a good message.

Still, Florinda wished she knew what the first goal was, and what the second would be.

"Florinda!" bellowed her husband.

She tucked the telegram safely away and hastened to his side. Hiram Stratton, Sr., had a very large side. He was consuming even more food and wine here in California than he had in New York. It was quite astonishing.

He just wanted to gaze upon her. Florinda did her very best to look lovely and pale. Staying pale was not an easy undertaking in southern California.

"I have just received a telegram!" he thundered.

Florinda quailed.

"My son has escaped from the asylum!" he shouted.

Florinda just managed not to smile in triumph. Undoubtedly, money well spent. "Ah, sir," she said to her husband, "it comes from your side of the family. That courage in adversity! That determination! That physical strength. That relentless quality."

He looked at her.

"No doubt," said Florinda serenely, "Strat has recovered. I am so proud of him. Are you not proud, Hiram? How lovely it will be to have your son back among us."

"He hurt Dr. Wilmott quite badly."

Florinda shook her head. "Doctor should have known better than to interfere with a Stratton." She kissed her husband's cheek. It was huge, and rolled down into more than one chin. She said, "We are blessed, aren't we, Hiram?"

Florinda felt the heat of the beautiful telegram in her pocket. She would spend the next few days saying fine,

fine things about her stepson, Strat. Then it would be time to begin saying bad, bad things about Walk. She beamed at Hiram. "How clever you were to come to California, my dear. The people here are quite dim. You have completely conquered them."

He glared, waving his telegram. "Did you have something to do with this?"

"Hiram, really. I'm only a woman. It takes a man to defeat walls and locks and chains and guards."

"This is true," said Hiram Stratton, recognizing the manhood in his son.

"Hi, Mom," said Tod. "How's Tokyo?"

Apparently Tokyo was wonderful. Work was wonderful. Everything was very exciting. And how was Tod?

"I'm fine."

And was his father there in the house, as he was supposed to be? Mom didn't want to talk to Dad, or anything like that, she just wanted confirmation.

"Dad's here," said Tod cheerfully. "He's doing laundry right now."

"Your father is doing laundry? I find that hard to believe."

"Me too," said Tod. The person who found it hardest to believe was of course Dad himself.

"Let me talk to Annie," said Mom.

"She isn't around, Mom. I'll give her the message, though. She'll be sorry she didn't get your call." Big lie. The days were piling up and he didn't have the slightest idea where old Annie was. Tod hated her for it. But he wasn't going to have Mom out there on the other side of the world having kittens over it.

"Everything's cool, Mom." He told her about school, and his job at Burger King, and how the ice hockey team was doing.

"It doesn't sound as if you miss me at all," she said, too casually.

"I miss you a lot, Mom. Especially in the morning when I get up and it's cold and the house is empty."

"Empty?" she said. "But—"

"Of you, I mean. You know. No coffee perking and stuff." He was going to be almost as good at lying as his sister by the time his parents wrapped this up.

No.

Nobody could ever lie as much nor as well as Annie Lockwood.

Charlie listened to the description of the insane asylum. He was not sorry for young Stratton. Charlie didn't care how many excuses were produced; the fellow should have been at Harriett's side all along.

Charlie was full of grief.

He had seen so much death. And now Harriett was lost. Already the world seemed colder and thinner. Less worth the fight. One more good soul was gone.

Charlie was very, very tired.

For the first time, he admitted to himself that he was not going to make it either. He, too, would lie here forever, in the cold, cold ground, under the shadow of the mountains.

The Stratton boy stroked a brass ring four inches in diameter, thick as a thumb, hung with heavy, almost architectural keys. The doors they opened were probably just as thick and brutal as the keys.

Lockwood, the servant, came striding right up to them. When had this girl gotten off the boat? She was remarkably rude. Charlie could not imagine keeping a servant who spoke like that. "Listen, Strat," the girl said, "enough already. This is not my kind of thing, helping Moss with that. You get me out of this." Charlie could just barely follow her dialect. He had no idea what part of the country spoke like that.

Strat nodded and took her hand. "Come. The grounds are lovely. Let's wander. I have things to tell you."

Charlie was glad Harriett could not see how those two held hands. It was shocking, a man of Strat's station with a lower-class woman like that. On the other hand, she certainly was lovely, and Charlie had once had enough energy to be impressed by things like that.

Now he just missed Harriett. He wanted to howl like a wolf on the horizon, and let the entire heavens know that he opposed the death of Harriett.

Off the huge main building was a great covered porch, its screens stored for the winter. It would have a lovely view of the lake during the summer. Now it looked out only on snow, snow, and more snow.

Strat brushed snow from a bench, and they sat together in the heat of the sun, and were strangely warm in spite of the cold.

"Annie," he said.

It was bad news. She knew from his voice, quiet and determined, and from his face, held away from her. She had his profile, and not his eyes, and the profile was beautiful and the eyes full of secrets and pain.

She waited. His hands curled around hers as if he had never held hands before. "I love you. I love you completely," said Strat, and his eyes filled but did not overflow. "I love you forever."

There was a *but*. She already knew what it was. She had known since she stepped through Time. She shrank from it; she still thought there must be a way to defeat it. She wanted to be a daughter of the twentieth century and get what was hers. But she was here; a daughter of the nineteenth century; she must, instead, do what was right.

"But you must go home, Annie," he said. He had no air beneath his words, and the speech lay as faint as the cold mist before their faces.

"I love you too, Strat," she whispered. "Completely and forever." I want us to be *us*, she prayed. Please, please, let there be a way for us to be together.

He waited a beat before he went on, and it was the pause of gathering strength. It hurt him. "I must stay in my century, Annie. I have things I have to do."

"I could do them with you." Her voice was pleading, putting more burdens upon him, trying to force things to go her way.

"Yes. And that would be wonderful. Nobody would be better company than you." Strat was trying to smile, but it wasn't working; his face was falling apart in grief. "But you have your family to go to, and I have mine."

He was separating from her because of his family? These people who had hurt him so? "You're going to California?"

"No, no, not that family. I cannot make peace with a father who had me locked up rather than listen to my side of the story."

Annie cried, "But what about Devonny? What about your sister who *sent* me here? She loves you. She needs you, Strat."

Strat gave her the sweetest, saddest smile. "Devonny doesn't need me as much as she once did. You taught her something, Annie. You taught it to Florinda too. You taught them to be strong. They thought only men could be strong."

I was strong, thought Annie. Like my mother. In the end, the woman I admired most was the strongest. "And your mother?" she said softly.

"That hurts," he said. "But I cannot see her now. They would just find me. She will have to wait. The day will come."

It sounded like prophecy, like something already written, his mother waiting, and the day would come. Poor Strat's mother!

"I no longer believe that my father's money is worth having, and I will make no attempt to be his heir or his son," said Strat. "I know now what has worth."

"Love has worth," she said desperately, "and we love each other."

"Oh, yes," said Strat, and this time his full voice was there, declaring love. "Oh yes, we do love each other." He kissed her, and it was a wonderful kiss, but she was in too much anxiety to kiss back; it was his kiss, but not hers.

"I have debts, Annie," he whispered, "and I must pay them. My greatest debt is to you, for saving me. For bringing me to Harriett in time. I can never repay that. I can't even try. But there is one debt I can repay."

He was not going to tell her what the debt was. She knew from the farness in his eyes that the debt was his secret; and he would carry it through Time and history, and she would never know.

Please don't be a gentleman, Strat. Forget honor and valor and virtue. Forget debts. Stay with me!

But she said none of it aloud, for she would have to carry this secret through Time with her too: that she was not as nice as Strat; that she wanted herself and her plans to come first, not last.

"I want my previous life," said Strat, his voice breaking on the syllables, "to be history."

"History," repeated Annie. Why didn't people cooperate with her plans? Why must they always be themselves, instead of extensions of her?

"That's what I am to you, anyway, Annie. You told

186

me yourself. You looked me up in archives. Ancient dusty places where the records of dead people lie."

"You're not there," she said quietly. She had, after all, another parting gift for him. "You disappeared from the written record. I couldn't find you there. You are *not* in the archives, Strat. You are *not* in history."

"Really?" Strat was stunned and relieved. "No trial for attacking a doctor? No jail record?"

"Nothing they wrote about in the newspaper, anyway." He won't tell me his secrets, thought Annie, but I'll tell him mine. "My father damaged my mother so much, Strat. He damaged all of our lives. And I had to find out if I damaged the person I loved too. I had to find out if I'm just like my father—throwing away the things that count. I was so worried about you, Strat. I longed to see you, but I really came in order to see if it was my fault."

He had taken off the thick gloves. His cold hands cupped her cold cheeks. Two colds made a warm. She could have sat forever with those big strong hands heating her face. But they were done with forever.

"You didn't throw me away, Annie," he said. "You stepped back into your own Time. It took such courage. Last time, you were the one brave enough to know. You told me that you loved me enough to give me back to Harriett. Now I, too, am brave enough. We must part once more."

She would never hear a man speak like this again. A speech of poetry and honor. She took his hands and kissed his palms and the back of his hands and the flat

187

of his thumbs and dried her tears against them. "What will you do?"

"I'm going to Egypt," he said, switching from poetry to adventure, and giving her the greatest grin on earth. "I'm going to excavate for mummies and kings. I'm going to find great tombs and the entrances to pyramids."

How could she agree never to see that grin again?

"I'll bet," said Strat, "if you look me up in books about Egypt, you will find me."

She swallowed. The swallow didn't happen. She was shut off from her heart and soul and hopes. She could only pat him and silently wish him well and weep for her own dreams.

"Do you still have money, Annie?" he asked anxiously.

She dug in her pocket. She had a hundred dollars. It was a fortune in this time.

"That'll be fine," said Strat. "I have money too. Harriett gave me all she possessed."

She did, too, thought Annie. Harriett died for him. She waited till he came, and she gave him her last breath, and her last love, and she took with her a promise: *name your daughter after me.* Whose daughter will that be? Not mine. He's sending me away.

"I wish I had something of you, Annie. I have memory and your stories. And I will hold you in my heart, but I would like a piece of you. But the clothing and the jewelry you are wearing are Devonny's, it is nothing of you."

She felt his waist. On the stolen brass key ring was a

pocket knife. For a moment she stared at the blade she switched out, the gleaming fearsome sharpness of it. Then she cut a lock of her long dark hair, wound it in circles, and put it in his hand. With both her hands, she closed his fingers over it.

When he opened his hand, the hair straightened itself, and hung, a black ribbon. "The color of mourning," he said. "I will mourn for you. For us."

There. He had said it. *Us.* The word she wanted more than anything else on earth. Two letters, she thought, and they matter so much.

"You will travel safely back, won't you?" he said, still anxious. "You did the other times. You'll just step through, won't you?"

She nodded. If Harriett, after all, could cross the bar to death for her journey, could not Annie cross the bar of Time for hers? How could Annie pretend to be afraid, when it was only Time she faced?

But she was afraid. If only she were with Devonny and Florinda, warm and sunny. If only . . . if only . . .

"I must go now," said Strat. "Walk and Doctor can't catch up to you, but they can certainly catch up to me. They will be here by nightfall, I am sure of it."

Once again, she had had only moments with him. Why did she always have to be strong? Why couldn't she be the one for whom it worked out, and was just right, and went on to happily ever after?

Being strong was tiring. You couldn't go on forever, being strong.

But I don't have to be strong forever, she thought

189

sadly. I just have to be strong till he's out of sight. Out of Time.

"You can step through easily?" he said once more. "You're sure?"

"I'm sure."

They stood together, in that awful moment of goodbye, when there is nothing left but one person leaving and the other person staying. "I love you," she said. The words seemed alive in the air, like the coming of snow. *I love you.*

"Safe journey," said Strat quietly. "I thank you for saving me and giving me that hour with Harriett."

She hugged him, and he hugged back, so tightly, and for a long time. There was a strange finality to that touch. As complete as doors shutting, or seasons ending.

It was forever.

"I love you, too, Annie," he said, "and I always will." It was the last thing he ever said to her, and then he drove away in the cutter, he and his dark horses vanishing into the trees.

The father of Tod and Annie parked his car in the only shoveled parking area at the former Stratton estate.

The town had owned the place for many years. It had beaches, tennis courts and marinas, holly gardens and meadows for picnics.

In February it had the sad abandoned look of all New England halfway through winter. It looked, in fact, like his family. Strange and cold and separated.

There was something frightening about the picnic tables stacked behind the barns, tilted on their sides like huge wooden playing cards. The drinking fountains were wrapped in canvas. The snow-covered foundations of the old Stratton mansion were nothing but knobs under dirty snow. The little pond, where once Hiram Stratton had docked a yacht, was too salty to ice over, but it had the dingy crust of winter by the sea, rolled-up tissues of slush.

He was afraid to tell anybody that he was such a lousy parent, he didn't even know when his daughter had disappeared.

The fact that she had done this twice last year would work in his favor. They would say that Annie was bad: a runaway, incorrigible, worthless—a typical teenager.

He tried to decide what kind of parent he was. Bad? Incorrigible? Worthless? Typical?

He had come to Stratton Point as if he could find a clue in the spot where his daughter disappeared before. He found nothing but cold.

What'll I do? thought Mr. Lockwood. Call the police?

He wanted his wife. It had been a long time since he had felt that way.

Well, he was too little, too late. If he called her in Tokyo and said, Guess what? I have no idea where our daughter is and no idea when she left . . . No, this did not have the sound of apologies that put marriages back together.

"No, Mr. Walkley," said the village attorney calmly. "Miss Harriett Ranleigh did not leave her fortune to some ragged logger or some foul nurse. She willed her fortune to the Fresh Air Fund."

"What!" shouted Walk. "That liberal idiocy? City people who cannot be bothered to raise their own children properly? Immigrants and guttersnipes who expect their neighbors to do it for them? Disgusting little urchins with bad teeth and no morals?"

Both Dr. Wilmott and Walker Walkley were beside themselves. Money belonged to people who had money; it must never belong to people who did not. Walk smacked his palm with the side of his beaver hat. Doctor pounded his fist on the top of a high leather chair.

The attorney, some hack from the North, some small-town person who could not possibly know his job, failed to be impressed by the presence of Walk or Doctor. "I will ensure that Miss Ranleigh's wishes are carried out," said the attorney calmly. "Now if you will excuse me, gentlemen, I am busy."

They did not excuse him. They blocked the attorney's exit from Harriett's former sickroom. Already, the room had been scoured. Its next occupant would arrive on tomorrow's train.

"Who is this Moss woman?" shouted Walk. "I demand to see the viper who turned Harriett Ranleigh to this insanity."

Two servants cowered by the stove. Their exit, too, was blocked by Doctor and Walk. One was fat, the other thin. One was properly clad in starched white, the other by her bowed head and pitiful rags was probably a washerwoman.

"You may not lay a hand upon Moss," said the attorney.

But the fat servant turned out to be Moss herself. "Miss Harriett was proud to give her money to the Fresh Air Fund. She said that way she would have the laughter of children every summer."

Moss and the attorney looked at each other gladly, but Doctor and Walk looked at the woman in fury. Walk's skin grew red, his body literally flaming with lost hopes.

However, Doctor and Mr. Walkley were nothing now except blockades to getting the room ready. Moss was sick of them. "Lockwood," said Moss, "show Mr. Walkley to a guest room in the main building."

"Lockwood?" repeated Walker Walkley.

"Lockwood?" repeated Dr. Wilmott.

How they smiled.

It was very late at night, almost dawn once again, but in the asylum, it was difficult to tell.

Katie did not look up when the door opened. Hope had dried like a leaf in autumn.

She could hardly remember autumn now. She had not seen one since she was little, and the stories she told Douglass about autumn sounded unlikely. Could trees really turn bright colors?

When hands circled her, Katie did not fight back nor question. She was accustomed to pain without explanation.

The hands stood her up, and a finger was laid on her lips, and now she looked.

She did not believe what she saw.

"It's me," whispered Strat. "Don't say a word."

In the cacophony of screaming, sobbing, chattering, mindless patients, this was a ridiculous instruction.

They both giggled. Their laughter blended into the laughter of hysterics.

"We're going to Egypt," whispered Strat.

This did not sound any more impossible than trees turning color. "All right," said Katie.

"You hold Douglass's hand. Otherwise he'll be difficult."

Katie held Douglass's hand. He was not difficult. He made his Strat noises and Katie promised to tell him a story soon. Although it was Strat's story that would be interesting.

Strat had simply unlocked the doors, knowing exactly where the attendants would be sleeping, for none stayed awake through the night. A patient who needed help in the middle of the night waited till morning. Or waited for days, depending on the mood of the helpers.

Strat quietly relocked each door behind them. Then they were outdoors.

Outdoors! Out of the asylum! Beyond the gates!

Katie felt winter wind, and bitter cold, and icy snow, and it was beautiful.

Two horses were tied behind black trees, and a sleigh with a cover, so she and Douglass would be toasty and warm and out of the wind. She stared. The black mane blowing in the wind. The scent of horse. The crescent of moon in the sky. The pattern of stars and the crackle of ice.

Strat boosted her into the carriage. "Clothing," he said, pointing to a small leather trunk. "I want you to look lovely."

I hardly even met the wind, she thought, as he shut

her out of the weather. What other adventures will I have? What else will I meet that I have never met before? "Strat, I may go to Egypt," said Katie, "but I will never be lovely."

"Harriett said your personality would make you lovely," said Strat. "She said to wear a heavy veil to keep away the gaze of strangers. You will be my sister, Katie, and Douglass, my brother."

Harriett's gowns for Katie, and Charlie's clothes for Strat and Douglass. He had packed swiftly, and with only Harriett for witness, and then Charlie. Not even Annie knew where he was now.

"But Strat," whispered Katie, "people will think ill of you, having a defective brother and sister."

"But I will be proud of myself," said Strat, "and Harriett will be proud of me, and we'll settle for that." And Annie? he thought. Annie, whom I could not tell? How will she feel, in her other century, with her other life? Will she honor me? Will she look in her archives? Will she remember my name and wonder about my fate?

"And a bath?" whispered Katie. "With hot water?"

"A bath," promised Strat. "With hot water."

"And roast beef?" said Katie. She did not actually remember roast beef, but Strat had talked about it a lot.

"Yes, and pie and ice cream."

Strat shut the door, and Katie held Douglass so he would not be afraid. The horses moved, and Katie and Douglass felt wonderful new things: rhythm and speed and bumps. They laughed, and together they touched every new surface and felt every new texture.

Never had Katie been wanted. Never had she hoped

to be all these at once: warm, clean, fed, clothed, and among friends.

"Thank you, Harriett," she whispered. "I will honor your name forever."

Outside, she thought she heard the howl of a wolf, and she was both thrilled and terrified.

But it was no wolf, raising its muzzle to the dark sky; it was Strat, like Charlie, without words for his grief. He had lost Harriett to death, and Annie to Time.

And he had loved her so, but it was his own words that had sent her away forever.

I had to save Katie, he told Annie, the tears he could not seem to prevent freezing to icicles on his cheeks in the mountain wind. You will be all right wherever you are, but she would not be.

And I owed her.

The world owed her, but it was my responsibility.

But Time did not come for Annie Lockwood.

She screamed and fought. She broke free of Doctor's iron grip. She kicked Walk brutally in the shins. She smashed the teacups and even grabbed the boiling pot from the stove to pour on them.

But she did not get free of them, and Time did not come.

The attorney and Moss and Mrs. Havers were very distressed. Charlie, outdoors on a chair, his man still putting glass bottles on the stone wall, listened to the commotion.

Strat, Strat, thought Charlie. You keep doing what

you think is best, but behind you, when you've shut the door, life chooses its own way. Its own terrible cruel way.

"You see," said Dr. Wilmott, "that she truly is insane."

"I do see," said Havers. "What a shame."

Annie faced the sky, screaming, "Time! Time! Let me through. Come for me!"

The sky, of course, remained sky. It did not speak, nor whirl forward in a tornado to whisk her away. They would have laughed at her had it not been so hideous. A lost mind was quite dreadful to witness.

Mrs. Havers said, "To think I would have hired her to work for me."

They all shook their heads sadly at the ways in which this girl had deceived them.

"Notify police at railroad stations," said Doctor, "that young Mr. Stratton will be attempting to travel. He is alone, out of money, and wearing clothing far too large for him." Doctor smiled at Miss Lockwood. "He won't get far," he assured her. Doctor said to Walker Walkley, "I shall capture young Stratton. It will be a great pleasure to me. I still nurse a wound and a headache. You must deliver Miss Lockwood to my institution."

How they smiled.

"Indeed," said Walker Walkley, "it will be even more of a pleasure to me."

Doctor sped away after Strat, whipping horses as cruelly as he had ever slapped a patient.

And Walker Walkley turned to Annie Lockwood.

They strapped her in a terrifying garment: a sort of bag, as if meant for a corpse. Her arms and legs were trapped within, and all the screaming in the world had no effect upon the harsh canvas.

Is this what Strat endured? she thought. But what Anti-Kidnapping League will come for me? I have no allies. My only ally is Strat, and he has left.

And Time, Time has left, too.

She tried praying to Time, like a god; and she tried threatening Time, like a bad boy; and she tried bribing Time, as if she had something Time needed.

Time ignored her.

Only the presence of Mrs. Havers and Moss and the attorney kept Walk from hurting her. But soon they would be out of sight of Clear Pond, and then Walker Walkley could do whatever he chose.

Each time she tried to change centuries, she merely convinced strangers that she was insane.

Moss, however, remained kind. She brought furs. "These were Miss Harriett's own," she said. "She would want to protect this sad creature from the cold. It is twenty below. Mr. Walkley, do take care of the poor thing. Do not let her escape. Death would be swift, in this cold."

"And we do not want death to come swiftly, do we?" whispered Walker into Annie's ear. "We want you to linger, don't we? We want you to suffer, don't we?"

Walk tied her canvas bag to the seat of the cutter and

carelessly threw a fur over her. "Think, Miss Lock-wood," he said, "of all the years you will spend in that asylum. And think, too, about Strat, whom you adore. He will join you soon. You will watch each other in Hell."

He set off.

How dare the bells still jingle and the horses still toss their beribboned manes? Annie was being turned into a lunatic, to be treated like an animal, and still there was music and beauty.

On Clear Pond, soft ice beckoned. If I could get Walk out on it! thought Annie. "Going over the pond would be a shortcut," she said, but she was too obvious, and Walk burst out laughing.

"Do you think I cannot tell that they have been cutting ice?" He shook his head at her dumbness.

The sleigh curved toward the steep hill that would take them away from cure cottages and toward Evergreen. The slope was covered with hay to slow the vehicle so it would not catch up to the horses and break their ankles from behind. Annie thought of what Walk and Doctor would do to her. Would they break her ankles from behind?

I am a twentieth-century toughie. I am not Harriett in a decline. I can escape.

Oh yeah? How?

She tried to think herself through Time, to hurl her body out of its bonds and across the decades, but nothing happened. She lurched against the bonds, but nothing happened. She screamed one more time, but nothing happened.

Walk flicked the reins and laughed.

She was his property.

She stared again at the wide, wide ice. Suppose she got free and ran across the pond. Would it hold her weight? Could she get to some sort of safety? And what if she fell through the ice? Would she freeze as she sank, becoming an ice coffin of herself? Or could she make herself fall through Time, instead?

Everything was so real. Too real.

The rough canvas.

The bitter wind.

She thought of the horrors in the lunatic asylum that Strat had described to her. *No. Not me.* She had not realized that she had mouthed the words until Walk laughed again, and shouted, "Yes! You!" He yanked the fur rug away from her, leaving her with nothing but canvas, at twenty below zero.

Then he half stood, adjusting Harriett's fur around himself instead of around Annie. It was a trophy. And she, she, too, was a trophy: proof that if he had lost fortunes, he had at least captured a victim.

Charlie said to his man, "I really am an excellent shot." He took the rifle and turned slightly in his chair.

He said to dead Harriett, whose heart and goodness he still cherished, "I would have preferred to shoot Strat, my dear. But he did have an excuse. I had to accept his excuse, Harriett. Certainly you accepted his excuse. And I cannot let your Miss Lockwood suffer simply because Walker Walkley's greed was not satisfied."

Charlie pulled the trigger.

He really was an excellent shot.

He said to his man, "Go after the sleigh. Dump Mr. Walkley's body through the soft ice and free Miss Lockwood."

Charlie's man said, "Sir?" He was very nervous. Very pale. Understandable. He had never before been employed by a murderer.

"Yes?" said Charlie. He desperately needed to lie down. His lungs would not accept this sort of activity. He was going to follow Harriett very soon. If only he could be assured that he would find her there, wherever death lay.

"Miss Lockwood is gone."

"What do you mean?" said Charlie.

"I don't know, sir," said his servant. "I released her from the restraints, and she gave me—sir, I did nothing to encourage it—she gave me a kiss and a hug. And then, sir, she was there . . . and then she wasn't."

Charlie was too tired to answer. Too tired to stay awake. So Harriett was right about that too. The Lockwood girl could travel through Time.

He wondered if death could be that easy. A shift through Time.

If so, Harriett, he said to her in his heart, I'm coming.

The fall was terrible, terrible.

The spinning was deeper and more horrific. There were faces in it with her: hideous, unknown, screaming faces of others being wrenched through Time.

I am not the only changer of centuries. And they are all as terrified and powerless as I.

Her mind was blown across like the rest of her. *Strat!* she screamed, but it was soundless. The race of Time did not allow speech, Her tears were raked from her face as if by the tines of forks.

It ended.

The falling had completed itself.

She was standing. Not even dizzy.

The fear of opening her eyes, and finding herself in the wrong place, or the wrong Time, kept her frozen, as if she had been thrown through ice, like Walk, instead of Time.

Strat, she thought, and the image of him was already distant: framed, like an old photograph on a grandmother's wall. Oh, Strat, you are the Past. Not the Present.

"Annie?" said a familiar voice.

She opened her eyes.

On the snow pack in front of Annie Lockwood was no cure cottage, no Clear Pond, no Walker Walkley, no horse and no sleigh.

Her own father stood before her, snow falling on his down jacket, the cute vibrant one he got to go skiing with his cute vibrant girlfriend.

Annie and her father stared at each other. She had no idea what story to make up, or what emotion to display. She had no idea what story she had just left, or what emotions she had been carrying.

It was just gone.

Strat and Devonny, Harriett and Moss—they were history now. And would she find Strat in archives? Would Egypt have his name?

He has my lock of hair, she thought, but I have nothing of him. Why didn't I take something of Strat? What will I have for the rest of my life?

Only memory.

"Annie?" whispered her father. He seemed afraid of her. His expression was exactly that of Charlie's manservant.

She was pretty sure that Dad was not going to want details on where she had been, or how she had gotten there and back.

Strat. In that syllable lay a hundred years of pain and loss. But love, too. She still loved him. Love had crossed Time with her.

But the part of Annie that had become a daughter of the nineteenth century vanished. In the twentieth century, you looked at things a little more harshly. Love is better, thought Annie, when there's a person to share it with.

A terrible, twentieth-century anger seized her: anger that she had not gotten her way.

From across Time came a vision of other people who had not gotten their way either: Harriett, Strat, Katie, Devonny, Florinda.

"We could have a snowball fight, Dad," said Annie at last. "Or fall backward and make snow angels. Which do you want?"

Her father swallowed. He swallowed a second time. He said, "It's probably my only chance to qualify for angel." He went first, trusting the snow to pillow him. In the thick white blanket, he waved his arms until the wings of angels appeared at his sides.

So Annie fell backward too. Their wings overlapped. She thought of the lives she had invaded on the other side of Time. And for what?

So that others would have love.

For just the shortest moment in Time, but one she could hold, and remember, Annie knew that she really had been an angel: she had brought peace and safety and release.

She tried to reconcile her twentieth-century anger with her nineteenth-century courage. *I want love. I want love of my own! Here, in my Time. But it's Strat I want and he will be always, forever, in his Time.*

"I'm pretty confused, Dad," she said, after they had made a whole row of angels.

He said he was pretty confused too.

"But you're here, Daddy," she said, and suddenly she knew that that was a wonderful, wonderful thing: just to be here. She even loved him, which was a nice change from last year.

They got up from the snow.

How had Time done that: taken her from the Adirondacks to a New England beach to drop her down in front of her own father?

They linked arms and walked slowly back to the car, and she thought of the heater that would be in that car, and the cold, cold sleigh in which Strat had disappeared, and she put her arms around her father and sobbed.

"It's okay, honey," he said desperately. "Everything's going to be okay. Whatever went wrong, it'll be okay, I'm sure of it."

Annie was touched, that anybody could be sure that everything would be okay. Let it be okay with Strat, she prayed. Let it be okay for us too.

"Show me the telegram," demanded Devonny. She could not get over the amount of sunshine they had here in California! It was delicious. You could almost taste it. It was unbearable to be swathed in New York layers when sand and palms and orange groves beckoned.

Florinda showed her the telegram.

"They made it," whispered Devonny. "Do you think we shall ever hear from them again?"

"Of course we shall. Your brother won't ignore his inheritance."

Devonny wondered.

"Anyway, there are other things to think of, Devonny." Florinda gave a little happy bounce. "I want to introduce you to a darling young man who was actually *born* here! In California!"

"One doesn't think of people as starting here," agreed Devonny.

"He's very civilized," said Florinda in a tone of surprise. "Eats with a fork and everything."

"Well!" said Devonny, laughing. "We'd better ask him over."

❧

"But what is that?" whispered Katie. She was getting used to the wonderful clothing now. The hat didn't fall off every time she moved, and the scarf didn't tug away, and she had finally trained Douglass to hang all over Strat instead of all over her. She was becoming quite judgmental of fashions. Hers were better than anybody's.

Katie loved the veil. Behind it, she could think clearly, with no interruptions from friend or foe who thought she was hideous. Inside the veil was safety.

"That," said Strat, "is our steamship."

Katie was awestruck by the size of it. A man-made transport that large? Surely Noah's Ark had not been so immense!

They had even seen Doctor at the train station. But he had not seen them, for Strat was a gentleman tilting a beaver hat to keep the sleet from his face, and Katie was a lady with a veil, and Douglass was a stumbling adolescent being a pain. Strat had bought a private room and from the safety of their very own room, they had watched Doctor pace the platform.

They left him there, looking for a lone young man in clothes that were too big.

How Douglass and Katie had loved the train! You

207

each had your own red velvet chair, and your view of an astounding world, and meals that came on trays. Hot, delicious, exciting, impossible meals. Wonderful new things like Coca-Cola and candy bars. And wonderfully, it was Strat who told the stories during their train ride. Stories to be locked up by, in Katie's opinion. Vehicles that flew in the sky, vehicles that needed no horses, vehicles that used no wheels, vehicles that did not even need roads!

Every night, instead of prayers, Katie thanked two girls she would never meet, for one was dead and one was Out of Time. Dear Harriett: I thank you for everything. Dear Annie: I thank you most of all, for courage, for Strat, for a chance.

"That ship will take us to Spain," said Strat.

"*Spain?*" It wasn't very close to Egypt. There were maps in Katie's Bible—she knew where these places were. There was the whole Mediterranean Ocean still to cross beyond Spain.

"That's all the ticket I could afford for three of us," said Strat, grinning and shrugging. "So in Spain we get off the boat—and, hey, who knows?" He was laughing now. "I'll have my sister and brother to support and I'll think of something." He stared at the Atlantic Ocean, and he was twenty-one years old and saw nothing but waves of adventure and challenge.

She looked at Strat, who had come back. Who had saved her. Who was kind, and believed in kindness.

And Katie knew that she was afraid of nothing.

Spain, Egypt, who cared? There was not a hole in the world that could compare to the hole over which she and Douglass and Strat had triumphed.

The ship's whistle blew long and strong.

Time to board.

Time, thought Katie, stunned by the beauty of good times. *My time.*

Strat saw Katie and Douglass safely into their stateroom. Then he returned to the deck, and from a flower vendor rushing from dock to deck, he bought roses. Lovely soft pink roses. It was silly. He had no money to waste.

But it was not a waste.

The boat pulled away from America. From his history. From every footprint on the land where he and Annie had walked together. One by one, he threw the roses into the leaping winter waves. Good-bye, Annie, he said in his heart. Please love me anyway. I will always love you.

It was summer before Annie Lockwood looked in the library again. The old room was hot and dusty, the scent of Time gone by.

The Egyptian collection was large. Everybody loves tombs and King Tut and mummies and the Nile. She checked every index of every book, and every reference in every article. No Hiram Stratton, Jr., ever appeared.

But Hiram Stratton, Sr., did. The century had changed, and in the year 1915, Hiram Stratton, Sr., died.

Annie finally stumbled on his obituary in the yellowing old newspaper pages: the long detailed column of his long cruel life. A successful life, for he had triumphed in money and land, invention and investment.

He was survived by his beloved daughter. There was no mention of a son.

So Strat had accomplished it, whatever that secret goal of his had been. He had stepped out of his own Time, as well as hers.

Annie Lockwood shut the last volume of newsprint, her final hope of seeing Strat's name in print once more.

Time kept all its secrets.

Except one.

The secret that she had loved him, each Time, enough to give him up.